NICANDER

THE POEMS
AND
POETICAL FRAGMENTS

CODEX PARISINUS SUPPL. 247 (Π), fol. 5 recto (1 × 1)

Theriaca 87–97. Below, γεωργὸς τρίβων βοτάνας—μολόχη—ῥόδον—κάμπη—σίλφιον

NICANDER

THE POEMS
AND
POETICAL FRAGMENTS

Edited with Introduction,
Translation and Notes by
A.S.F. Gow & A.F. Scholfield

Bristol Classical Press

G.W.L.
VETERIS PIGNVS AMICITIAE
D.D.
EDITORES

First published by the Syndics of the Cambridge University Press, 1953

This edition published, with permission, in 1997 by
Bristol Classical Press
an imprint of
Gerald Duckworth & Co. Ltd
61 Frith Street
London W1D 3JL
e-mail: inquiries@duckworth-publishers.co.uk
Website: www.ducknet.co.uk

This impression 2002

A catalogue record for this book is available
from the British Library

ISBN 1-85399-528-2

Printed in Great Britain by
Antony Rowe Ltd., Eastbourne

CONTENTS

PREFACE

Nicander has some claims upon the attention of students both of ancient literature and of ancient science. Medicine, zoology, botany, and mineralogy are the themes of his two extant poems; whatever his exact date he belongs to a period from which little Greek literature of any kind has survived; and among later writers Virgil and Ovid were in his debt. Yet for all that he has been little read either by scientists or by Classical scholars, nor is the reason far to seek. His contorted style and fantastic vocabulary put him beyond the reach of scientists unless they are also Greek scholars, and Greek scholars competent to face these considerable difficulties are commonly deterred by lack of interest in his subject-matter. Moreover even those who wish to read him are at present faced with a serious obstacle, for the only tolerable text, that of Otto Schneider, was published nearly a century ago and has long been hard to come by.

The aim of the present edition is very modest. It is to provide would-be readers with a text, and with first-aid in reading it; but we do not claim to provide more than first-aid. Apart from passages in which the text is certainly or probably corrupt, there may well be places in which the version here facing it is demonstrably incorrect; there are others in which our translation is only tentative; others where alternative interpretations will present themselves to the next reader, as they have often done to ourselves; others again in which an otherwise plausible rendering of the Greek will be rejected by scientists competent in the theme under discussion. Still, at the worst, we hope that the version will save even Greek scholars a good deal of recourse to lexicons and other works of reference, from which, incidentally, they would often extract extremely dusty answers.

Our title-page mentions the poems and poetical fragments since we have printed the text of the poetical fragments only. There will however be found in the notes a brief account of each fragment omitted by us but printed in Schneider's collection, including those from works certainly or possibly in prose; and since his collection is standard we have preserved his enumeration throughout. Our exegetical notes are usually brief and do not constitute a continuous commentary. They represent such results of our own often incomplete inquiries as seemed likely to be useful to others, and we would emphasise again that the book makes no pretence to be a definitive edition. If that is ever to be written it will involve, besides much work on the vocabulary and style of the poet, the collaboration of a number of scientists with somewhat unusual qualifications.

The book has been supervised by both editors, and in particular the translation, the first draft of which was complete before this edition was contemplated, has been much altered and revised. The primary responsibilities however are as follows. The text, the introduction except for the section on botany, and Appendix I are by A.S.F.G.; that section, the translation basically, Appendixes II and III, and the Indexes are by A.F.S. Among the notes, those on the text, on the lost works of Nicander, on the fragments not here printed, and most of those on zoology, are by A.S.F.G.; those on botany nearly all by A.F.S., who has taken charge of this subject throughout. The remainder, which deal chiefly with geography and mythology, may be by either, but are often conflations of what the editors had jotted down independently in the course of their work.

It remains to express our thanks to scholars in various fields who have helped us. Our heaviest debt is to Professor D. L. Page and to Mr F. H. Sandbach, who very kindly found time to read our proofs. Both have saved us from numerous slips and oversights, and text and translation alike have been much improved by Professor Page's acute suggestions. Many other scholars have answered our inquiries on particular points, and we are glad to express here our thanks to Professor D. G. Catcheside, Dr K. C. Dixon, Dr U. R. Evans, Mr P. Fraser, Mr H. Gilbert-Carter, Mr J. S. L. Gilmour, Professor James Gray, Mr A. F. Huxley, Dr R Keydell, Mr E. Lobel, Dr P. Maas, Dr W. Morel, Dr C. F. A. Pantin, Mr H. W. Parker, Professor R. Pfeiffer, Dr M. G. M. Pryor, Mr J. E. Raven, and Dr W. H. Thorpe. Our Frontispiece is from H. Omont *Fac-similés des plus anciens MSS grecs de la Bibliothèque Nationale* Pl. LXV, which proved more suitable for reproduction than the photograph kindly supplied by the authorities of the Library.

We are grateful to the Syndics of the University Press for undertaking the publication of the book, and to the staff of the Press for the care they have expended on its production.

CAMBRIDGE
April 1952

A.S.F.G.
A.F.S.

INTRODUCTION

I. THE LIFE OF NICANDER

A. *Vita Nicandri in* Σ *Th.*: Νίκανδρον τὸν ποιητὴν Διονύσιος ὁ Φασηλίτης ἐν τῷ περὶ τῆς ᾿Αντιμάχου ποιήσεως Αἰτωλὸν εἶναί φησι τὸ γένος· ἐν δὲ τῷ περὶ ποιητῶν ἱερέα φησὶν αὐτὸν τοῦ Κλαρίου ᾿Απόλλωνος ἐκ προγόνων τὴν ἱερωσύνην δεξάμενον. καὶ αὐτὸς δὲ ὑπὲρ αὑτοῦ ἐν τῷ τέλει τῆς βίβλου φησί (*Th.* 958)

τὸν ἔθρεψε Κλάρου νιφόεσσα πολίχνη.

Κλάρος δὲ τόπος ἐστὶν ᾿Απόλλωνος ἱερός. υἱὸν δέ φησιν αὐτὸν Δαμαίου οὕτω λέγων (*fr.* 110)·

αἰνήσεις υἷα πολυμνήστοιο Δαμαίου.

χρόνῳ δὲ ἐγένετο κατὰ ῎Ατταλον τὸν τελευταῖον ἄρξαντα Περγάμου ὃς κατελύθη ὑπὸ ῾Ρωμαίων, ᾧ προσφωνεῖ λέγων οὕτως (*fr.* 104)·

Τευθρανίδης ὦ κλῆρον ἀεὶ πατρώιον ἴσχων,
κέκλυθι μηδ᾿ ἄμνηστον ἀπ᾿ οὔατος ὕμνον ἐρύξῃς,
῎Ατταλ᾿, ἐπεί σεο ῥίζαν ἐπέκλυον ῾Ηρακλῆος
ἐξέτι Λυσιδίκης τε περίφρονος, ἣν Πελοπηίς
῾Ιπποδάμη ἐφύτευσεν ὅτ᾿ ᾿Απίδος ἤρατο τιμήν.

διέτριψε δ᾿ ἐν Αἰτωλίᾳ τοὺς πλέονας χρόνους, ὡς φανερὸν ἐκ τῶν περὶ Αἰτωλίας συγγραμμάτων καὶ τῆς ἄλλης ποιήσεως ποταμῶν τε τῶν περὶ Αἰτωλίαν καὶ τόπων τῶν ἐκεῖσέ τε καὶ ἄλλων διαφόρων διηγήσεως, ἔτι δὲ καὶ φυτῶν ἰδιότητος.

B. Suidas: Νίκανδρος, Ξενοφάνους, Κολοφώνιος, κατὰ δέ τινας Αἰτωλός· ἅμα γραμματικός τε καὶ ποιητὴς καὶ ἰατρός, γεγονὼς κατὰ τὸν νέον ῎Ατταλον, ἤγουν τὸν τελευταῖον, τὸν Γαλατονίκην, ὃν ῾Ρωμαῖοι κατέλυσαν. ἔγραψε Θηριακά, ᾿Αλεξιφάρμακα, Γεωργικά, ῾Ετεροιουμένων βιβλία ε᾿, ᾿Ιάσεων συναγωγήν, Προγνωστικὰ δι᾿ ἐπῶν· μεταπέφρασται δὲ ἐκ τῶν ῾Ιπποκράτους Προγνωστικῶν· περὶ χρηστηρίων πάντων βιβλία τρία· καὶ ἄλλα πλεῖστα ἐπικῶς.

C. (i) Γένος Θεοκρίτου (p. 2 Wendel): ἰστέον ὅτι ὁ Θεόκριτος ἐγένετο ἰσόχρονος τοῦ τε ᾿Αράτου καὶ τοῦ Καλλιμάχου καὶ τοῦ Νικάνδρου· ἐγένετο δὲ ἐπὶ τῶν χρόνων Πτολεμαίου τοῦ Φιλαδέλφου.

(ii) Γένος ᾿Αράτου (p. 325 Maass): ἦν δὲ ᾿Αντίγονος υἱὸς Δημητρίου τοῦ Πολιορκητοῦ, καὶ παρέλαβε τὴν ἀρχὴν περὶ

ἑκατοστὴν¹ καὶ πέμπτην ὀλυμπιάδα, καθ' ἣν Πτολεμαῖος ὁ Φιλά-
δελφος Αἰγύπτου ἐβασίλευσεν. ὥστε καὶ θρυλούμενόν ἐστιν ὑπό
τινων ὡς ἦν [sc. Ἄρατος] κατὰ τὸν αὐτὸν χρόνον Νικάνδρῳ τῷ
Κολοφωνίῳ τῷ τὰ Θηριακὰ γράψαντι.

(iii) Γένος Λυκόφρονος (p. 4 Scheer): εἷς δὲ ἦν τῶν ἑπτὰ ποιητῶν
οἵτινες διὰ τὸ εἶναι ἑπτὰ τῆς Πλειάδος ἐλέγοντο· ὧν τὰ ὀνόματα
Θεόκριτος ὁ τὰ βουκολικὰ γράψας, Ἄρατος ὁ τὰ Φαινόμενα γράψας
καὶ ἕτερα, Νίκανδρος Αἰαντίδης ἢ Ἀπολλώνιος ὁ τὰ Ἀργοναυτικά,
Φίλικος, Ὅμηρος ὁ νέος τραγικός...ὁ Ἀνδρομάχου Βυζάντιος ὃς
δράματα ἐποίησεν νζ', καὶ οὗτος ὁ Λυκόφρων, κἂν ἕτεροι μὴ εἰδότες
ἄλλους φασὶν εἶναι τῆς Πλειάδος. ἦσαν δὲ οὗτοι ἐν χρόνοις Πτολεμαίου τοῦ Φιλαδέλφου καὶ Βερενίκης.

(iv) Γένος Ἀράτου (p. 326 Maass): λέγονταί τε προτεῖναι ἀλλήλοις
ὁ μὲν Νικάνδρῳ σκέψασθαι τὰ Φαινόμενα, ὁ δὲ Ἀράτῳ τὰ Θηριακά.
τοῦτο δὲ καταφανῶς ἐστι ψεῦδος· ὁ γὰρ Νίκανδρος δώδεκα ὅλαις
ὀλυμπιάσι νεώτερος φαίνεται.

(v) ib. (p. 78): οἱ δὲ λέγοντες Νίκανδρον τὸν Κολοφώνιον μετὰ
Ἀράτου Ἀντιγόνῳ συγκεχρονικέναι καὶ Ἄρατον μὴ εἶναι ἐπιστήμονα
τῶν οὐρανίων μήτε Νίκανδρον τῶν ἰατρικῶν (λέγουσι γὰρ ὡς ἄρα
ὁ Ἀντίγονος Ἀράτῳ μὲν ὄντι ἰατρῷ ἐπέταξε τὰ Φαινόμενα γράψαι,
Νικάνδρῳ δὲ ἀστρολόγῳ ὑπάρχοντι τὰ Θηριακὰ καὶ τὰ Ἀλεξι-
φάρμακα, ὅθεν καὶ ἑκάτερον αὐτῶν ἐσφάλθαι κατολισθαίνοντα ἐπὶ
τὰ ἴδια τῆς τέχνης) ψεύδονται· ἀγνοοῦσι γὰρ ὡς οὐ συνήκμασε τῷ
Ἀράτῳ Νίκανδρος, ἀλλ' ἔστιν αὐτοῦ πολὺ νεώτερος· Ἀντίγονος
γάρ, ᾧ συνεγένετο Ἄρατος, κατὰ τὸν πρῶτον καὶ δεύτερον γέγονε
Πτολεμαῖον, Νίκανδρος δὲ κατὰ τὸν πέμπτον.

D. Dittenberger Syll. Inscr. Gr.³ 452 (Delphi): ἀγαθᾷ τύχᾳ.
Δελφοὶ ἔδωκαν Νικάνδρῳ Ἀναξαγόρου Κολοφωνίῳ ἐπέων ποιητᾷ
αὐτῷ καὶ ἐγγόνοις προξενίαν, προμαντείαν, ἀσυλίαν, προδικίαν,
ἀτέλειαν πάντων, προεδρίαν ἐν πάντεσσι τοῖς ἀγώνοις οἷς ἁ πόλις
τίθητι, καὶ τἆλλα ὅσα καὶ τοῖς ἄλλοις προξένοις καὶ εὐεργέταις τᾶς
πόλιος τῶν Δελφῶν. ἄρχοντος Νικοδάμου, βουλευόντων Ἀρίστωνος,
Νικοδάμου, Πλείστωνος, Ξένωνος, Ἐπιχαρίδα.

From Nicander himself we learn, in the fragment cited in A, that
his father was named Damaeus, and from other passages² that Clarus

---

¹ Presumably καὶ εἰκοστήν has here dropped out. Ol. 105 is 360–357 B.C.;
Ol. 125, 280–277. Demetrius in fact died in 283 B.C.
² Th. 958, Al. 9: cf. fr. 31.

4

was his home. Clarus was the seat of an immemorial cult of Apollo, and of an oracle, of which we know something since Germanicus's visit to it is described by Tacitus.[1] It is close to Colophon, and was perhaps little more than a temple-precinct with attached houses for those connected with the cult,[2] and Nicander's common designation, ὁ Κολοφώνιος, involves no contradiction.[3] He was not the only poet of Colophon, which laid claim to Homer and could boast without dispute of Mimnermus and Xenophanes, Antimachus, Hermesianax, and Phoenix.[4] The statement of Dionysius of Phaselis cited in A and echoed in B that Nicander was Aetolian by origin is probably an addition to his family history rather than a rival theory of his birth, for Dionysius can hardly have been unaware of Nicander's references to Clarus, and in fact himself asserts that the poet held a hereditary priesthood at that shrine, perhaps an inference, though not an unplausible one, from *Al.* 11.[5] The statement, whether true or not, that he spent much time in Aetolia is also plausible, for the works ascribed to him show a marked interest in that country, nor need his duties at the temple, if he had any, have prevented him from absenting himself from Clarus—as may be seen from the epitaph of a certain Gorgus, who is described as Κλαρίου τριπόδων Λητοΐδεω θέραπα but was nevertheless buried in Athens.[6]

The remaining statements contained in the passages set out above involve us in immediate difficulties. B calls Nicander's father not Damaeus but Xenophanes, and marked disagreement is shown as to the poet's date. C i–iii[7] disclose a belief that he was a contemporary of the first generation of Hellenistic poets, i.e. that he lived in the

---

[1] *Ann.* 2.54.　[2] For excavations on the site see *Jahresh.* 15.41, *B.C.H.* 39.33.
[3] Antimachus of Colophon is similarly called *Clarius poeta* in Ov. *Tr.* 1.6.1.
[4] Also of an unknown Cleander, described as ἐπῶν ποιητής, who received a decree of προξενία at Delphi in the 2nd century B.C. (*B.C.H.* 18.269).
[5] It is more plausible if the less well-attested reading ἐ3όμενος is accepted.
[6] *Ath. Mitt.* 11.427, Wilamowitz *Hell. Dicht.* 1.106. Gorgus was apparently the compiler of a poetical anthology. In the cult of Clarus, at any rate at a later date, the priest who received the responses of the god was *ignarus plerumque litterarum et carminum* (Tac. *Ann.* 2.54) though the oracles were issued in verse. Hymns also played a large part in the ritual (*Rev. Phil.* 22.269; cf. *Jahresh.* 15.46, inscr. no. 2, 3, 5, 8–12, 18, 25, 27–9). Possibly Nicander and Gorgus, when at home, assisted in these poetical exercises. Nicander's style would be a godsend to any oracle.
[7] iii may be discounted. Lists of the Pleiad vary, but nobody else names Nicander, and in this aberrant list he is only one of three competitors for a place to which Aeantides has a better-supported claim. See generally Susemihl *Gr. Lit. d. Alexandrinerzeit* 1.269.

first half of the third century; C iv and v combat this belief and are roughly in agreement, the first dating him half a century later than Aratus, the second assigning him to the reign of Ptolemy V Epiphanes (205–181 B.C.), but A asserts confidently that a poem there cited was addressed to Attalus III Philometor (138–133 B.C.), and B seems, though confusedly[1], to assign him to that date. The language of the fragment would suit Attalus II Philadelphus (159–138 B.C.), who succeeded his brother on the throne, equally well, and perhaps even Attalus I (241–197 B.C.), for though he succeeded not his father but a cousin, πατρώιον might in this context mean Τεύθραντος. We have therefore as approximate dates 270 (C i–iii), 200 (C iv, v) and 135 (A, B) B.C. The dates are flexible, and it would have been possible for a friend of Aratus to survive into the reign of Ptolemy Epiphanes; possible also for one born in that reign to celebrate Attalus III. But neither contingency offers a plausible solution of the inconsistencies, and we are left with the one certainty that *fr.* 104 addressed to an Attalus must have been written between 241 and 133 B.C.

Further uncertainty is imported by D, a Delphian decree conferring προξενία on Nicander, an epic poet of Colophon whose father was named Anaxagoras. The dating of this inscription on the evidence so far available is a highly complex problem, and the principal authorities on Delphian chronology are not in agreement. It must suffice to say here that G. Daux (*Chron. Delph.* 38: G 24) favours 254/3 B.C., and that R. Flacelière (*B.C.H.* 59.22, *Les Aitoliens à Delphes* 458: 44) a date about 220 B.C. It is thus plain that if it was the third Attalus whom the author of the *Theriaca* addressed, the inscription must refer to an earlier namesake and compatriot. If however he was a contemporary of Aratus an inscription of 254 B.C. might, so far as the chronology is concerned, refer to him; and again if he was a contemporary of Ptolemy Epiphanes, so might an inscription of 220 B.C. His father's name however presents an obstacle, for he calls himself son of Damaeus, whereas the poet of the inscription is described as son of Anaxagoras. This difficulty is best met by those who accept the identification with the supposition that Damaeus was his father by adoption.[2]

[1] It was the first Attalus who defeated the Gauls, the third who bequeathed his kingdom to Rome, and τὸν Γαλατονίκην seems to be a mistaken addition.

[2] Damaeus, not Anaxagoras, since Delphian inscriptions add the words καθ' υἱοθεσίαν in such cases (Dittenberger *ad loc.*). Susemihl (*Gr. Lit. d. Alexandrinerzeit* 1.891) said that Damaeus must be corrupt, whereupon E. Maass (*Aratea* 311) proposed to write Ἀνάξου. It is unlikely that he will have many followers.

As between the three dates for the didactic poet, that which makes him a contemporary of Aratus is, apart from any question of style, hard to credit. The anecdote in C iv and v is plainly fictitious, and the authors who give it the lie do so with a confidence which suggests some positive and adverse information. That dating would also oblige us to suppose that the Attalus addressed in *fr.* 104 was the first of the name, whereas the third, or possibly the second, seems much more probable. And, finally, Nicander appears to borrow from Numenius, who was a pupil of the physician Dieuces and cannot well have written before the middle of the third century; and from Euphorion, of whom much the same may be said since, according to Suidas, he was born in Ol. 126 (276–3 B.C.)—roughly a generation later than Aratus and his contemporaries.[1]

If the early date is mistaken, there are reasons which might account for or contribute to the mistake. In the first place the *Theriaca* is addressed to one Hermesianax,[2] and it appears that some took him for the poet of that name, though this view is combated by the scholia, which say that Nicander elsewhere refers to the poet as older than himself (*fr.* 12); in the second, C iv, after refuting the view that Nicander the poet was Aratus's contemporary, goes on to mention a Nicander of Colophon, a μαθηματικός, who really was so; and this Nicander may have been mistaken for the poet. And if the Delphian decree belongs to 254 B.C., there was a poet of Colophon named Nicander and in fact contemporary with Aratus to encourage confusion.

If on the other hand the decree belongs to the last quarter of the century it is similarly evidence for a Nicander of Colophon at that date, who, if he was not the author of the *Theriaca*, might have been taken for him and have led to the dating given in C iv and v, to which the address to Attalus, if believed to refer to the first king of that name, might possibly contribute. The case against this date is however less strong than against the earlier, and it may be that the

---

[1] For these borrowings see *Th.* 237, 256, 406, *Al.* 433 nn.; cf. *Al.* 13, 161 nn. Our notes record also apparent debts to Aratus (*Th.* 456; cf. 10, 469, 620), Callimachus (*Th.* 109, 457, *Al.* 62, 99, 463, 618), Theocritus (*Al.* 185, *fr.* 74.24; cf. *Th.* 697), and possibly to Apollonius (*Al.* 13). Minuter scrutiny would no doubt disclose more, but neither they nor the bizarre vocabulary which Nicander shares with Lycophron (e.g. σπληδός, τράμπις) seem to throw light on Nicander's date.

[2] The name is quite common (see *Stud. It.* 20.74), but Nicander's friend was presumably a connexion of the poet.

extant poems were in fact written at the end of the third century. Those who take this view would then, if they accept 220 B.C. as an approximate date for the inscription, be free to suppose that it refers to their author. They would not however be compelled to do so and might hesitate over the discrepancy in the father's name.

The problem hardly admits of final solution, but on the whole the statements in the *Life* and in Suidas seem to deserve more credence than the others, and we incline to the view that the Attalus addressed was the third, and that this poet flourished, not in the third, but in the mid-second century or somewhat later, and was thus roughly a contemporary of Moschus. If so, he must, whichever date we choose for the inscription, be distinguished from an earlier namesake, who is likely to have been either his grandfather or his uncle. Nicander is indeed a common name, but poets in more than one generation of a Greek family are also common, and the very rare name Damaeus of the second Nicander's father occurs more than once at Delphi but apparently nowhere else.[1]

Of the elder poet there are no certified fragments, but since he also was of Colophon it is obvious that some may be mistakenly credited to the younger. Of the poetical works of which appreciable fragments remain all seem likely to belong to the younger man, unless indeed the combination of a repulsive style with considerable metrical accomplishment which links them to the *Theriaca* and *Alexipharmaca* was hereditary in the family. There are other recorded works however of which we know next to nothing, and it is possible that some of these were by the Nicander of the inscription. The *Aetolica*, and perhaps the *Europia* and *Ophiaca*, might be so ascribed,[2] but though there is nothing against such an ascription there is no evidence in its favour.

A picture of Nicander conversing with a snake appears with those of other ancient physicians on f. 3 v. of the Vienna Dioscorides. No other representation of him exists.

---

[1] *Stud. It.* 20.65. The third name, Xenophanes (in B), may be a figment, but one may wonder whether Anaxagoras, the philosophically-named father of the elder poet, is not in some way connected with it.

[2] Cf. *Stud. It.* 20.107, Wilamowitz *Hell. Dicht.* 1.35.

II. THE TEXT

It is needless to trace editions of Nicander beyond the year 1856 for O. Schneider's *Nicandrea* of that date at once superseded its two predecessors—those of J. G. Schneider (*Alexipharmaca* 1792, *Theriaca* 1816) and F. S. Lehrs (1843, printed in the Didot *Poetae Bucolici et Didactici* of 1851 and reprinted in 1862). O. Schneider's was the first respectable text of the poems. It is also the last, for they have not been edited since 1856.

O. Schneider's principal service was to bring into use the ms which he called Π, to which attention had already been drawn by Bussemaker in his edition of the scholia, for Π presents a text noticeably different from, and in general much superior to, that of all other mss at present known. Schneider also obtained collations of some other fresh mss, though these are not of the first importance, made many corrections in the text himself, and equipped it with an elaborate *apparatus criticus*, which, if not always a model of tidiness, contains all the information as to variants which a reader can require. Nicander's chief need at present is another ms of the same family as Π but without Π's extensive lacunae.

The mss used by Schneider were the following:

Π Parisinus Suppl. 247, s. x vel xi.

This remarkable ms, acquired by the Abbey of St Germain des Prés in 1748, was dated by K. Weitzmann (*Byz. Buchmalerei* 33) from the style of the miniatures in the mid-tenth century, by H. Bordier (*Descr. des Peintures...dans les mss grecs de la Bibl. Nat.* 175) and by H. Omont (*Inv. Somm. des mss du Suppl. gr.*, 1883, 31) in the eleventh. Its leaves number 48 and measure up to 148 × 118 mm., and when devoted solely to text usually contain 22 lines to the page. On many pages however the text is curtailed or ousted by miniatures[1] depicting creatures, plants, or scenes suggested by the poet. Their style is peculiar, and they would seem to echo, if somewhat distantly, illustrations of much earlier date.[2]

[1] Or from *Al.* 249–549 with blank spaces for miniatures unexecuted.
[2] Tertullian (*Scorp.* 1), writing of scorpions, says *Nicander scribit et pingit*, and may be supposed to have possessed or seen an illustrated ms. Wellmann (*Herm.* 43.379) supposed the works of Apollodorus, Nicander's main source (see p. 18), to have been illustrated.

9

The ms is unfortunately defective and lacks *Th.* 57–75, 204–30, 389–540, 564–624, 715–66, 833–47, 885–958, *Al.* 1–33, 74–106, 157–248, 335–46, 483–94, 611–30.[1]

Ten of the most important miniatures were reproduced in colour by F. Lenormant and E. de Chanot in *Gaz. Arch.* 1. Pll. 18, 32, and 2. Pll. 11, 24. In black and white all appear in H. Omont *Miniatures des plus anc. mss grecs de la Bibl. Nat.* (1929)[2] Pll. 65–72; specimens in E. Bethe *Buch u. Bild* figs. 2, 42, C. Diehl *Manuel d'Art Byz.* 2. 605, P. Lemerle *Le Style Byz.* Pl. 39, *J.H.S.* 47.4, Weitzmann *op. cit.* fig. 228, Bordier *op. cit.* 176. The last work, and Omont *Miniatures etc.* p. 34, contain the most detailed accounts of the ms yet published. The frontispiece to this edition shows, together with some lines of text, one of the minor figure-scenes, and drawings of a caterpillar and three plants. We have discussed the plant-drawings in Appendix I and have given reasons for thinking them valueless to students of ancient botany.

In addition to Π Schneider made use of the following mss:

A. Monacensis 494, s. xv vel xvi. Contains among miscellaneous prose and verse *Th.* 1–178. Schneider used a collation by Hermann.

B. Leidensis 39, s. xv. Contains also scholia to Ap. Rhod. and Pindar. Collated for Schneider by E. Mehler.

G. Goettingensis, Philologus 29, s. xiii. Described in *Abh. Gött. Ges.* 38.3, where G. Wentzel discusses its scholia. Lacks *Th.* 176–185. Contains also Pindar: see A. Turyn *de cod. Pind.* 36. Collated by J. G. Schneider.

H. Vaticano-Palatinus 139, s. xv vel xvi. Contains much other Greek poetry. *Al.* and *Th.* 1–132 collated for Schneider by H. Keil.

K. Vaticanus 305, s. xiii. Contains *Th.* only. Collated for Schneider by H. Keil—badly according to S. P. Peppink *Observ. in Ath.* 9.

L. Lorrianus. An unidentified ms of which J. G. Schneider had a collation by a doctor in Paris named Lorry.[3] What he collated it with is unknown and the readings of the ms are constantly in doubt.

M. Laurentianus xxxii. 16, A.D. 1280. A large collection of Greek poetry. The portion of the ms containing Nicander is, according to C.

---

[1] *Al.* 537–49, reported missing by Omont, are 616–28 as transposed by J. G. Schneider.

[2] The earlier edition of his book, entitled *Fac-similés des miniatures etc.* (1902), reproduces, on Pll. 65–68, sixteen pages only.

[3] Possibly Anne-Charles Lorry (1726–83), a distinguished physician who attended Louis XV. The collation was sent to Schneider in 1775 by 'Liber Baro de Sancta Cruce', perhaps G. E. J. Guilhem de Clermont-Lodève, baron de Sainte-Croix (1746–1809), the author of works on ancient history and religion.

Gallavotti, in the hand of Planudes (see *Riv. Fil.* 62.361, *Stud. It.* n.s. 11.289). A collation made by A. Sarti for Bandini checked for Schneider by H. Keil. Lacks *Th.* 1–60, 194–259, *Al.* 245–75.

P. Parisinus Reg. 2728, s. xv. Contains also Apollonius and Aratus. Collated by J. G. Schneider.

R. Riccardianus 18 (now 56), s. xv. Collated for Bandini by A. Sarti.

V. Venetus Marcianus 480, s. xv. A collection of Greek poetry written by the Cretan J. Rhosos for Bessarion. Collated for Lehrs by F. R. Dietz.

p. Parisinus 2403, s. xiii. Contains *Th.* and *Al.* 1–28 with other miscellaneous prose and verse. Collated for Schneider by H. Keil.

v. Venetus Marcianus 477, s. xv. Collated for Lehrs by Dietz, and again in *Th.* and *Al.* 1–175 for Schneider by H. Keil. Lacks *Th.* 715–811.

In addition to these mss Schneider had, and reported, collations of a few lines of five other mss, Ambrosiani C 32, C 80, D 529, Laurentianus xci. 10, Urbinas 145; also some lections of a Moscow ms recorded by J. G. Schneider, lections from unidentified mss noted by Stephanus, Bentley, and d'Orville, and from the Aldine *editio princeps* of 1499. None of these seems important, and we have disregarded them.

That the twelve mss set out above had a common archetype with Π is plain from places in which all agree upon a corrupt text (e.g. *Th.* 46, 292, *Al.* 258, 500) or upon one inferior to that preserved elsewhere in a citation (cf. *Th.* 802, *Al.* 310). That they themselves all descend from a later archetype (or hyparchetype) is plain from the constant opposition of Π and ω (our symbol for these mss). That the ancestor of the common class contained variant readings is likely in itself, and suggested by the frequent mention of such in the scholia and by the sporadic agreements with Π found in individual members of the class. It is also to be noted that, though none of the mss of the common class is old enough to be out of reach of Byzantine interpolation, some at least of the readings which distinguish ω from Π are of great antiquity for some of them occur in *p. Ox.* 2221, which is assigned to the first century A.D. Nor is this the only evidence that the text was early exposed to change. At *Th.* 921 f. (where Π is absent) the mss have σικύην χαλκήρεα λοιγέι τύψει | προσμάξας ἰόν τε καὶ ἀθρόον αἷμα κενώσεις, but 921 is expressly cited by Athenaeus for the word σίνηπτυ in the form . . . χαλκήρεα ἠὲ σίνηπτυ.

Mustard is prescribed for snake-bite by later physicians,[1] and since 922, suitable for a cupping-glass, is less so for a mustard plaster, it is perhaps more likely that Athenaeus's line is due to someone who wished to incorporate this remedy in Nicander than that the mss present an alteration by someone who disapproved of it; but one text or other is plain evidence of deliberate interpolation, and, if the ms text is original, of interpolation at an early date. In general, though mss of the common class seem to us to preserve the truth against Π in more places than Schneider would allow, the text of ω is markedly inferior to that of Π, having undergone the kind of changes, accidental and deliberate, which might be expected from the bewildered scribes and readers of such an author. It will be well to remember that this process began early, and may, for anything we know, have made substantial headway before the archetype of Π and ω was written.

The relationships of the mss in the common class are complicated, and Schneider did little to elucidate them. He said that they had depraved their archetype in various degrees, *qua in re modestissimos gessisse se invenio eos qui exararunt codices G et M, impudentissimos qui scripserunt codd. ABHPV, reliquos autem, i.e. KLRpv, mox illorum modestiam, mox horum impudentiam esse imitatos*, and he claimed applause *quod, ubi* Π *defecerit, codd. G et M sequi voluerimus, rarius KLRpv solos, sed ABHPV solos nunquam*. In practice, even where Π is absent, an editor is not very often under the necessity of printing a lection presented by a solitary ms of this class, and it is not quite clear from Schneider's last words whether his second and third groups were regarded by him as two families of mss, or whether they were a classification by merit regardless of relationship. In either case they are misleading.

It might well prove difficult, and we do not here attempt, to relate the mss conclusively in a *stemma codicum*, but something may be said of their affinities. Of Schneider's least trustworthy class, BHP, together with A for the few lines which it contains, are in close agreement. All four, for instance, have ἐσθλοῦ for ἐν μέν θ' at *Th*. 92, and the three survivors omit *Al*. 497–502. B is a little better than the others, and for the present purpose two representatives of a family which contributes little of value seem sufficient; we have therefore discarded A, which is only a fragment, and H, which is unknown in most of *Th*. G and M, which Schneider rightly favoured, in several

---

[1] Plin. *N.H.* 20.236, [Diosc.] *Ther.* p. 77, Scribon. 174.

places agree with Π in a true reading lost in the other mss—G sometimes (e.g. *Th.* 641, *Al.* 525), M less often (e.g. *Al.* 45, 394: cf. 132), alone, but GM together frequently (e.g. *Al.* 449, 452, 530). R however sometimes accompanies them (e.g. *Th.* 344, *Al.* 437) and MR without G are common companions and are often alone in agreement with Π (e.g. *Th.* 127, 308, *Al.* 62, 64). V, though despised by Schneider, occasionally alone (e.g. *Th.* 47, 808) but more often in company with G, M, or R (e.g. *Th.* 142, 339, *Al.* 114), joins Π against the rest, and its kinship with MR may be clearly seen at *Th.* 791, *Al.* 469. The superiority of R and V to the company to which Schneider condemned them may be conveniently noted in the *apparatus* to *Th.* 323–44. L also, so far as can be seen, belongs to this group (e.g. *Al.* 79 καὶ, 115 σιτηβόρου, 287 ὄγμῳ), but it is a nuisance in an *apparatus* owing to the continual uncertainty as to its readings, and since a true reading is nowhere credited either to L or to ΠL alone we have discarded it.

There remain Kpv, which are found sometimes together but more often paired Kp (e.g. *Th.* 374 ἀμφιπρονένευκε, 655 τλίπλοον) or Kv (e.g. *Th.* 543 περιστέφει, 946 ἀφιαρῆς). These mss have little of importance to contribute, and as v and Kv when not alone keep better company than p and Kp we have dispensed with p, which lacks most of *Al.* and, like L, is nowhere alone or alone with Π in preserving a true reading. By the dismissal of AHLp the mss of the common class are reduced in the *Theriaca* to eight—BGKMPRVv—and in the *Alexipharmaca*, where K is absent, to seven. We use the symbol ω to denote their agreement or substantial agreement.

In reporting the mss we are somewhat more hospitable to the mistakes of Π than to those of other mss, but in general we disregard trifling variants and blunders, and we omit a certain number of plainly false readings presented by the inferior mss. The reader will not, for instance, find in our *apparatus* at *Th.* 84 ἐλίσφακον BKP ἐμελίσφακον M μελίσφακον R ἐαλίσφακον v, or at *Th.* 839 φαιὰ BP, or some blunders of Π decipherable in our frontispiece. By contrast we may be thought too punctilious in recording *variae lectiones* from the scholia and citations, though the truth is occasionally to be found in one or other place. We do not note accentuation, aspiration, or the presence or absence of iota subscript (or adscript), and very seldom words falsely divided.

Apart from Philumenus Περὶ ἰοβόλων ζῴων (see p. 20) and *Etymologicum Genuinum B* (E. Miller *Mélanges de Lit. Gr.*, 1868), from which we have added one or two variants, the only published evidence known to us but unknown to O. Schneider is *Oxyrhynchus Papyrus* 2221, mentioned above, which contains a fragmentary commentary on *Th.* 377–95 with substantial remains of those lines in the lemmata. An unpublished papyrus from Oxyrhynchus of the second or third century A.D., to which we refer by courtesy of the Egypt Exploration Society, contains some letters from the centre of the lines *Th.* 333–44. It has no novelties except for a lection in 338 which we cannot explain.

Bentley's adversaria on Nicander were made at the request of his friend Dr Richard Mead in the margins of a copy of J. Gorraeus's text (Paris 1557) which Mead had lent him. It was returned to its owner in August 1722, and is now in the British Museum (classmark C 19 c 15). The *Theriaca* was published from it in the *Museum Criticum* 1.370, 445. O. Schneider's knowledge of the *Alexipharmaca* was derived *ex apparatu Gronoviano*,[1] E. Mehler having sent him a transcript. The record is not quite complete, but what it omits is not very important.[2] In more modern times very few scholars have concerned themselves with the text of either poem. H. Klauser *De dicendi genere in Nic. Ther. et Alex.* (*Diss. Vindob.* 6.1) occasionally comments on the text; A. D. Knox put forward a few emendations in a paper entitled *Atacta Alexandrina* (*Proc. Camb. Phil. Soc.* 1915.17); and W. G. Headlam made a few notes in the margin of his copy of Schneider now in the library of King's College, Cambridge. We mention them here since their names occur in our apparatus, but our text is not much indebted to any of them. There will be found in the notes a good many references to a paper by A. S. F. G. in the *Classical Quarterly* (45³.95), which, though not composed for the purpose, may be regarded as preparatory to this book.

[1] It appears from J. Geel's catalogue of the Leiden mss (70, no. 280) that A. Gronovius was at some time contemplating an edition of Nicander.

[2] Many of Bentley's corrections in both poems anticipate readings now known from mss, and some merely correct misprints in the wretched text before him. In *Al.*, apart from these, Schneider reports him wrongly at 83 ὑποτρύζει, 308 χαρακτοῦ, 422 φαίνοντος vel φύοντος, 453 καὶ εἰ (not *conj.*, but *ex ms*). At 184 ἐπὶ ῥάγεσσι anticipates Dindorf, at 290 οἷοις vel ἦμος O. Schneider, at 410 the transposition (since found in Π) J. G. Schneider. Schneider, if he had had a complete record, would have added 32 ἔτ᾿ ἀφρ. (ex ms), 116 κεῖνα, 205 μελίζωρον, 297 ὑπ᾿ ἔκγονον, 400 (after lacuna) ἴχνεσι δὲ, 483 φοινήεντος, 507 ἐφημένη, 607 κόψαις.

[3] Wrongly numbered 44. It is 'N.S. vol. 1'.

II. THE TEXT

The bulk of Nicander's poetical fragments is preserved by Athenaeus, who has been edited since O. Schneider's *Nicandrea* of 1856 by A. Meineke (1858–66), G. Kaibel (1887–90), and C. B. Gulick (1927–41). We have consulted these texts, and occasionally also S. P. Peppink's text of the Epitome (1937–9).

Since the chief purpose of this book is to enable readers to acquaint themselves with the contents of the poems we have sometimes admitted to the text emendations which fall short of certainty but have seemed to us to further that end. The fragments, lacking the protection of scholia, have suffered worse than the two poems and contain a good deal of which we can make neither head nor tail.

III. SCHOLIA, COMMENTARIES, AND TRANSLATIONS

The scholia to the *Theriaca* were edited by H. Keil for O. Schneider and printed in his *Nicandrea*. Keil did not edit those to the *Alexipharmaca* but reprinted U. C. Bussemaker's text from the Didot *Scholia in Theocritum etc.* of 1849. They have since been edited, better but with what should have been unnecessary frequency, by E. Abel and R. Vári (Budapest, 1891), by G. Wentzel in *Abhandl. Gött. Ges.* 38 (1892),[1] and by H. Bianchi in *Stud. Ital.* 12 (1904) 321. We have used Bianchi's text. Besides the scholia, which contain together with much genuine learning from ancient commentators[2] a great deal of nonsense, there are paraphrases of the two poems by Eutecnius, a σοφιστής of unknown date who also paraphrased Oppian. This work is of surprisingly little use to an editor of Nicander but will be found in the Didot volume mentioned above, and, less conveniently, in J. G. Schneider's editions, where the paraphrase of the *Theriaca* is printed separately but that of the *Alexipharmaca* served out piecemeal in the notes.

O. Schneider's *apparatus* and preface contain a number of notes relating to his constitution of the text and occasionally to its interpretation, but the only extensive commentary[3] is that of J. G. Schneider, who was industrious in collecting relevant matter from Pliny and from ancient scientific and medical writers but gives little

---

[1] Wentzel printed only the scholia from G, which had been misunderstood and misused by Abel and Vári.

[2] The scholia cite Theon, Antigonus, and Demetrius Chlorus in terms which make it plain that they had written commentaries on Nicander. It is known from other sources that Diphilus of Laodicea (Ath. 7.314D), Pamphilus of Alexandria (Suid.), and Plutarch (Steph. Byz. 375.11) also did so. Diphilus and Plutarch wrote on the *Theriaca*, and the first three are cited only on that poem, though that may be an accident. On Pamphilus see p. 204; on the scholia, Wilamowitz *Herakl.* 1.188. It should be recorded that according to Reitzenstein (*Gesch. d. gr. Etym.* 210) the *Etymologicum Genuinum* (from which only excerpts have been printed) preserves Nicander-scholia in a form differing widely from that of the mss.

[3] There are notes in the editions of J. Lonicerus (1531) and J. Gorraeus (1557) and perhaps in other early editions and translations which we have not seen. We have not derived anything to our purpose from either book, though Gorraeus, who was himself a doctor, shows considerable familiarity with ancient medical writers.

help in construing his text, which is indeed very frequently uncon-struable. Since the brief notes in this book are not intended as a commentary we have not transferred to them the scientific matter provided by J. G. Schneider, and his editions should be consulted by anyone studying Nicander from that point of view. It will cost him some labour to identify Schneider's references, particularly those to Aëtius, and we may perhaps venture the opinion that until it has become clearer how far the medical writers copy from one another or draw from a common source, the compilation of parallel passages may be somewhat misleading.[1]

Nicander was translated into Latin several times in the sixteenth century and a version in hexameters by J. Gorraeus (see p. 14 above) was printed by Lehrs parallel with his text. Versions in Latin prose were appended by J. G. Schneider to his editions of the poems, but his text was such that his translation is seldom of much help in a difficulty. O. Schneider provided a reasonable text, but the only attempt to translate it has been that of Dr Max Brenning, incon-veniently printed as a feuilleton in the *Allgemeine Medicinische Central-Zeitung* 1904, pp. 112–14, 132–4, 327–30, 346–9, 368–71, 387–90. We have occasionally consulted Gorraeus's version, and regularly J. G. Schneider's and Brenning's. The last contains many brief footnotes proffering identifications of Nicander's creatures and plants.[2]

[1] M. Wellmann's editions of Dioscorides and Philumenus contain valuable collections of references to corresponding and similar passages in other authors.

[2] A Parisian doctor, J. Grévin, attached a translation in French verse to his *Deux Livres des Venins*, printed at Antwerp in 1568 and dedicated to Queen Elizabeth; another in Italian verse by A. M. Salvini appeared in Bandini's edition of 1764. We have not consulted either.

IV. THE SUBJECT-MATTER OF THE POEMS

The reader of Nicander who concerns himself with the subject-matter should bear in mind from the start that he is not, at any rate in the didactic poems, in contact with an original authority. According to Suidas (p. 3 above) Nicander's *Prognostics* was a paraphrase of Hippocrates; according to Cicero (p. 209) his *Georgics* showed no personal competence in their theme; and so with the *Theriaca* and *Alexipharmaca*. No doubt the mythological and other ornaments are his own, and it is likely enough that here and there he adds something from personal observation or hearsay, but the bulk of his matter is borrowed, as Aratus in the *Phaenomena* borrowed his from Eudoxus. The difference between the two poets is that whereas the uninstructed reader may learn a good deal of astronomy from Aratus, the victim of snake-bite or poison who turned to Nicander for first-aid would be in sorry plight.

As O. Schneider established,[1] Nicander's principal source in the *Theriaca* was a work Περὶ θηρίων (cited in the scholia to *Th.* 715, 858) by one Apollodorus, who seems to have lived at the beginning of the third century B.C. and to have been the prime source of later writers on venomous creatures. An Apollodorus is cited in the scholia to *Al.* 570 and by later writers in connexion with poisons, the similarity of design in Nicander's two poems suggests a common authority, and it is generally and plausibly supposed that the *Alexipharmaca* derives from a second work by the same author, though its title is nowhere recorded.[2]

Before we proceed to what little we have to say on Nicander's Zoology and Botany it may be worth while to enter a second caveat, applicable, like the first, to both. The naturalist who attempts to identify the creatures or plants mentioned by the poet must necessarily do so in terms of genera and species. He should however remember that these are modern concepts, and that the Greeks

---

[1] *Nicandrea* 181 ff., where the fragments of Apollodorus are collected.
[2] On Apollodorus see also *RE* 1.2895 (no. 69), Susemihl *Gr. Lit. d. Alexandrinerzeit* 1.784, Christ *Gr. Lit.*, ed. 6, 2.297.

classified rather by similarities of appearance or habit which a modern systematist might in many cases dismiss as superficial and irrelevant. A single name is likely to be used for resembling species and even for members of different genera which have some conspicuous quality in common; varieties may be taken for species and be given distinct names. Conversely, in Greek as in other languages, one species, as Nicander himself often reminds us,[1] may have more than one name. Zoologists as well as botanists will be well advised to read the paper by R. M. Dawkins mentioned on p. 25 and to take its cautions to heart.

A. ZOOLOGY

Nicander's mammals and birds are few in number and present few difficulties, but in some other orders, particularly snakes, scorpions, and spiders, the problems are numerous and often, we suppose, insoluble. For editors as ill-equipped as we are to deal with them the easy and perhaps the prudent course would have been to pass them by in silence. Since however Brenning's notes are virtually inaccessible, and since other literature and the relevant places in the *Real-Encyclopädie* are not always easy to discover, we have thought that it might be helpful to record in our notes some other passages in ancient authors dealing with the same creatures, and also such modern identifications as we have noticed. If any zoologist should read them he should not expect to find there all the information he needs; he might hope to find some which he would otherwise have missed, and clues to be followed in his inquiries. And if he does so we trust that he may be lenient to the scientific shortcomings which will be apparent here as elsewhere in this book. We add some notes on the difficulties and on the authorities.

(i) REPTILES

(a) *Snakes*

Prima facie the snakes mentioned by ancient authors should not be difficult to identify. Their names commonly provide information as to their appearance (ἀσπίς, κεγχρίνης, κεράστης, σκυτάλη, τυφλώψ), or habitat (δρυίνας, ὕδρος, χέρσυδρος), or habits (ἀκοντίας,

---

[1] *Th.* 522, 537, 554f., 627, *Al.* 36ff., 47.

ἀμφίσβαινα, μύαγρος), or the result of their bites (αἱμορροΐς, διψάς, σηπεδών, σήψ); and besides these Nicander mentions only βασιλίσκος and δράκων (which are partly at any rate fabulous), ἔχις and ἔχιδνα, and, cursorily, ἔλοψ, λίβυς, and μόλουρος. Except in the case of the last three he adds a good deal to the information implicit in the names, and more may be found in other sources, particularly in Philumenus Περὶ ἰοβόλων ζώων: yet a score of these snakes are identified uncertainly or not at all. No serious doubt arises about the two Africans, ἀσπίς and κεράστης: ἔχις and ἔχιδνα are of uncertain species, and probably of more than one, but are at any rate vipers; on the rest ophiologists either speculate or decline to do so.

Of the authorities known to us the most complete is the article *Schlange* by H. Gossen and A. Steier in *RE* 2 A 494, where the snake-names are arranged in alphabetical order; but confidence in its ophiological competence, which we cannot judge, is somewhat shaken by its other defects, which have been severely but not unjustly criticised by W. Morel in a paper in *Philologus* 83.345 to which we occasionally refer. At the point at which each snake is mentioned in the *Theriaca* our notes record Gossen-Steier's conclusions and also those which Brenning supplied in the footnotes to his translation. Brenning did not usually give the source of his information, and his identifications may often have been original,[1] but he sometimes mentions H. O. Lenz, *Zoologie d. alt. Griechen u. Römer* (Gotha, 1856) and we have added a few references to that book and to O. Keller, *Die ant. Tierwelt* (Leipzig, 1913). Comparatively few of Nicander's snakes however appear either in Lenz or in Keller. We have also summarized such descriptions of the snake as are provided by Philumenus, whose book was first printed by M. Wellmann in vol. 10 of the *Corpus Medicorum Graecorum* (Leipzig, 1908). Philumenus, a medical writer who seems to have been nearly contemporary with Galen, was himself a compiler, but was apparently directly or indirectly the principal source for matter of this nature in later medical writers, references to whom will be found in Wellmann's edition.[2] To these particulars we have occasionally added information from other ancient authors which may assist in identifying the snake. In one case, that of the αἱμορροΐς, we have pursued our inquiry

---

[1] He was the author of a work entitled *Vergiftungen durch Schlangen*.

[2] See also *Hermes* 43.373, *RE* 20.209.

beyond the printed authorities, and our note on *Th.* 282 may serve to illustrate the difficulty of such problems.

Scientific nomenclature presents pitfalls for the uninitiated. So far as we can discover from G. A. Boulenger's *Cat. of Brit. Mus. Snakes* the three names offered for κεράστης (*Th.* 258 n.) connote no difference of opinion, but we have detected no similar case.[1]

(b) Lizards

These are few in number even if Nicander classes some as snakes, and except for σήψ at *Th.* 817 raise no difficulties. Our note on that line refers to the article *Krokodile u. Eidechsen* (also by Gossen-Steier) in *RE* 11.1947.

(c) Tortoises and turtles

These are discussed, again by Gossen-Steier, in *RE* 2 A 427 *s.v. Schildkröte*, and in Keller *Ant. Tierwelt* 2.247, but Nicander's two specimens (*Al.* 560 and *Th.* 703, *Al.* 558) present no problem.

(ii) FROGS AND TOADS

M. Wellmann *s.v. Frosch* in *RE* 7.113, Keller *Ant. Tierwelt* 2.305. Nicander's references to frogs are casual and give no indication of species; those to toads are more problematic. See *Al.* 567, 575 nn.

(iii) FISH

We have relied entirely on D. W. Thompson, *Gloss. of Greek Fishes* (1947), which deals with shellfish as well as the vertebrate fishes and provides ample references to the ancient literature.

(iv) SCORPIONS AND SPIDERS

These are discussed by Steier *s.v. Spinnentiere* in *RE* 3 A 1786, and in Keller *Ant. Tierwelt* 2.461.

(a) Scorpions

It appears from Plin. *N.H.* 11.87 that Apollodorus mentioned nine varieties, which he distinguished mainly by their colour. Nicander in his section on this subject (*Th.* 769 ff.), no doubt following

---

[1] Brenning's *Vipera prester* (διψάς) seems to be the same as his *Pelias berus* (ἔχις, κεγχρίνης).

Apollodorus, also mentions nine varieties, and for seven gives a colour as the distinguishing characteristic. It is however a bad criterion, for scorpions do not differ very markedly in colour, and those described as white and harmless (*Th.* 771) are probably so not because they constitute a species but because they are newly born. Apollodorus would seem to have been weak on scorpions, for he had not even counted their segments correctly (*Th.* 781), one of his species is winged, and some (according to Pliny) had two stings. Steier attempts to name four of the nine varieties, but Keller is silent, and Brenning is probably right in thinking the descriptions insufficient to justify identifications. It may be noted that Philumenus (14), who here follows Archigenes, attempts no descriptions, saying merely that there are several varieties but that the stings of all produce the same symptoms.

(b) Spiders

Steier and Brenning refer to R. Kobert *Beiträge z. Kenntniss d. Giftspinnen*, the latter also to Sprengel (work not named). Nicander's spiders are discussed by O. Taschenberg in a paper entitled 'Bemerkungen z. Deutung gewisser Spinnentiere die in d. Schriften d. Altertums vorkommen' (*Zool. Annal.* 2.213), where some opinions are cited from Kobert, and also from A. A. H. Lichtenstein *Naturgesch. d. Solipuga*, and A. Menge *Preuss. Spinnen*. The views of Lichtenstein, Menge, and Sprengel we report only at second hand. It is possible that in this genus a diversity of scientific names sometimes conceals an agreement in identification, but enough disagreement is visible to make it doubtful whether the majority of these spiders are really identifiable.

According to Aristotle (*H.A.* 622 b 27) there are many kinds of ἀράχνια and φαλάγγια, two of the latter being δηκτικά. One is μικρὸν καὶ ποικίλον καὶ ὀξὺ καὶ πηδητικόν, resembles those called λύκοι, and is named ψύλλα (presumably because it jumps). The other is larger, black, with long front legs, sluggish, feeble, and not given to jumping. Of other spiders stocked by druggists some do not bite, the rest do so only feebly. Philumenus (15) says that of many varieties of φαλάγγια six are chiefly mentioned by θηριακοί. He names them ῥάγιον (no doubt = ῥώξ, *Th.* 716), λύκος (*Th.* 734, but not there considered dangerous), μυρμήκιον (*Th.* 747), κρανοκολάπτης (*Th.* 759), and two species not mentioned by Nicander, σκληροκέφαλον and σκωλήκιον. Pliny in *N.H.* 11.79 mainly follows Aristotle, in 29.84 Nicander or his source.

If we exclude λύκος, whose reputation is unblemished, but include, as Philumenus seems to do, the winged monster of *Th.* 759 ff., Nicander has seven species, of which all but one (ἀγρώστης, *Th.* 734) produce alarming symptoms by their bite. The bite of a spider, like any other wound or abrasion, may become septic from infection, but it seems that only two Old World spiders can be considered at all dangerous to human beings.[1] It is possible that some of Nicander's spiders are improperly so classed (see *Th.* 747 n.), but even so his list must owe something to superstitious terrors.

(v) INSECTS, ETC.

Nicander mentions moths (*Th.* 760) and some flies (*Th.* 417, 735 f.) casually, but except in so far as he may have included some insects among his spiders, and for two myriopods, ἴουλος and σκολόπενδρα, classed as insects by Aristotle (see *Th.* 811 n.), his references are otherwise confined to the bee and wasp family, and to beetles. From the first family, besides μέλισσα and σφήξ, he mentions βέμβιξ, πεμφρηδών, and τενθρήνη: of beetles βούπρηστις and κανθαρίδες.

Bees are discussed by Olck *s.v. Biene* in *RE* 3.431, which has not yet reached *Wespe*; bees, wasps, and hornets in Keller *Ant. Tierwelt* 2.421. Beetles by Gossen *s.v. Käfer* in *RE* 10.1478, and in Keller 2.406; myriopods in Keller 2.481.

B. BOTANY

The work of Apollodorus (p. 18 above) from which Nicander derived most of his botany seems to have been restricted to such plants as were medicinal or poisonous, and his descriptions included a wealth of synonyms. M. Wellmann[2] has established that Apollodorus in his turn, like Theophrastus and subsequent writers on pharmacology, owed much to Diocles of Carystus, the foremost representative of the Sicilian school of medicine early in the fourth century B.C. He was the first to describe plants and their effects upon

---

[1] *Lathrodectus* and in a less degree *Chiracanthium* (see J. Vellard *Le Venin des Araignées* 24); they do not seem to be Aristotle's pair. On the first, which arachnologists spell variously *Latro-* and *-dectes*, see *Th.* 716, 725, 752 nn.

[2] 'Das älteste Kräuterbuch der Griechen' (in *Festgabe für F. Susemihl*, Leipzig, 1898); *RE* 5.802.

the human body. The scholiast on *Th.* 647 cites his[1] Ῥιζοτομικόν, a work which held the field at least as late as the first century A.D.

The interpretations of ancient Greek plant-names put forward by those who have given much time and thought to the study differ widely; many are tentative and uncertain, while some plants have so far defied identification. It is plain moreover that, as was said above, in ancient as in modern Greek[2] the same name was often used for different plants, and that the same plant often had more than one name; and in Nicander the difficulties of identification, already formidable in themselves, are enhanced by the doubt whether the poet knew what he (or his authority) was talking about. True, he occasionally pauses to tell us that such-and-such a plant has a golden flower, or that its roots are shallow, or that it thrives on mountains, and the like, but even so his descriptions do not always tally with the known habits of the plant of which he is supposed to be speaking. For instance at *Th.* 630 ῥάμνος is said to resemble ὀλίγη μηκωνίς. If ῥάμνος is correctly rendered *buckthorn*, and ὀλίγη μηκωνίς *little wild lettuce*, the resemblance is one which no common eye can detect. Nor if ῥάμνος is equated with πολεμώνιον (*Hypericum olympicum*) are we any nearer to guessing what he had in mind. In Dioscorides ἑλξίνη bears two meanings, (i) *pellitory*, (ii) *convolvulus*; both, but especially the former, flourish in dry places. Yet Nicander asserts that ἑλξίνη delights in streams and water-meadows. Elsewhere he prescribes νῆρις (*savin*) as a remedy for snake-bite (*Th.* 531). It was indeed employed in certain feminine complaints, but nowhere else does it appear as an antidote to poisons. When therefore we find Dioscorides (4.81) proclaiming the medicinal virtues of νήριον (*oleander*) when applied to the bites of poisonous creatures, it is hard to resist the conclusion that the poet, whether deliberately or by accident, has written νῆρις for νήριον. And a like suspicion attaches to θάψος, *fustic* (*Th.* 529), which Wellmann and Brenning show no hesitation in regarding as the poet's substitute for the metrically intractable θαψία (*Thapsia garganica*: cf. *Th.* 529 n.). If θαψία is in fact what Nicander intended, then the victim of snake-bite who swallowed *fustic* in place of *thapsia* might fairly complain that he had been misled.[3]

---

[1] The name is disguised as Eteocles.   [2] Cf. *J.H.S.* 56.2.

[3] It is of course open to those more solicitous than we are to uphold Nicander's scientific competence to suppose that in some parts of the Greek-speaking world νήριον and θαψία were called νῆρις and θάψος.

In such circumstances the most competent botanist could feel no assurance that his translation had always interpreted the intentions of the poet aright, and for the layman the safest, indeed the only, course seems to be *unius iurare in verba magistri*. We have accordingly followed the interpretations offered by Sir William Thiselton-Dyer in the ninth edition of Liddell and Scott's *Greek Lexicon*, and have indicated in the notes our reasons for departing from them in the few places where we have done so. It is not to be expected that all our renderings, be their source what it may, will commend themselves to every reader; we can only hope that our positive errors in botanical matters are few.

The only modern scholar who has made a particular study of Nicander's plants is Brenning, and it seemed proper to record the divergences (happily not numerous) between his interpretations and those of Liddell and Scott: they will be found in the Index of Fauna, Flora, etc. marked with the letters 'Br.'. Two articles by the Greek botanist E. Emmanuel entitled 'Étude comparative sur les plantes dessinées dans le codex Constantinopolitanus de Dioscorides', which appeared in the *Schweizerische Wochenschrift für Chemie und Pharmacie*,[1] 61 (1912) 45–50, 64–72, offer a number of identifications differing from those of Brenning and of Liddell and Scott. These we have incorporated in the Index, marking them with the letters 'Em.'. Brenning pays tribute to the work of J. Berendes, *Des Pedanios Dioskurides...Arzneimittellehre...übersetzt und mit Erklärungen versehen* (Stuttgart 1902), and we have borrowed from it whatever suited our purpose.

The notes contain occasional references to Thiselton-Dyer's papers 'On some Ancient Plant-Names' in *J. Phil.* 33.195, 34.78, 290, and to R. M. Dawkins 'The Semantics of Greek Names for Plants' in *J.H.S.* 56.1. In the first of those papers Thiselton-Dyer wrote, 'Little has been done to explain the mass of plant-names in Nicander. Meanwhile they have drifted into lexicons merely with meanings which tell nothing'; and in the last Dawkins said of ancient botany generally, 'We must never press our identifications too far'. Readers of this book will do well to bear these sentences in mind.

[1] Also known as *Journal suisse de C. et P.*

SIGLA

| 𝔓1 | Pap. Oxyrhynchi 2221 | s. i p.C. |
| 𝔓2 | Pap. Oxyrhynchi ined. | s. ii. vel iii p.C. |

Π	Cod. Parisinus suppl. 247	s. x vel xi
B	Cod. Leidensis 39	s. xv
G	Cod. Goettingensis Philologus 29	s. xiii
K	Cod. Vaticanus 305	s. xiii
M	Cod. Laurentianus xxxii.16	s. xiii
P	Cod. Parisinus Regius 2728	s. xv
R	Cod. Riccardianus 56	s. xv
V	Cod. Ven. Marcianus 480	s. xv
v	Cod. Ven. Marcianus 477	s. xv
ω	Consensus codicum deteriorum	

Et in fragmentis ab Athenaeo conservatis

| A | Cod. Ven. Marcianus 447 | s. x |

---

codd.	Codices
cett.	Codices ceteri
Eutec.	Eutecnii Metaphrasis
Σ	Scholia
v.l.	Varia lectio

Virorum doctorum nomina in apparatu decurtata:

Bent(ley)	Mus(urus)	OSch(neider)
Cas(aubon)	Scal(iger)	Schweig(häuser)
Dind(orf)	JGSch(neider)	Wilam(owitz)
Mein(eke)		

TEXT AND TRANSLATION

ΝΙΚΑΝΔΡΟΥ ΘΗΡΙΑΚΑ

Ῥεῖά κέ τοι μορφάς τε σίνη τ᾽ ὀλοφώϊα θηρῶν
ἀπροϊδῆ τύψαντα λύσιν θ᾽ ἑτεραλκέα κήδευς,
φίλ᾽ Ἑρμησιάναξ, πολέων κυδίστατε παῶν,
ἔμπεδα φωνήσαιμι· σὲ δ᾽ ἂν πολύεργος ἀροτρεύς
5 βουκαῖός τ᾽ ἀλέγοι καὶ ὀροιτύπος, εὖτε καθ᾽ ὕλην
ἢ καὶ ἀροτρεύοντι βάλῃ ἔπι λοιγὸν ὀδόντα,
τοῖα περιφρασθέντος ἀλεξητήρια νούσων.
Ἀλλ᾽ ἤτοι κακοεργὰ φαλάγγια, σὺν καὶ ἀνιγροὺς
ἑρπηστὰς ἔχιάς τε καὶ ἄχθεα μυρία γαίης
10 Τιτήνων ἐνέπουσιν ἀφ᾽ αἵματος, εἰ ἐτεόν περ
Ἀσκραῖος μυχάτοιο Μελισσήεντος ἐπ᾽ ὄχθαις
Ἡσίοδος κατέλεξε παρ᾽ ὕδασι Περμησσοῖο.
τὸν δὲ χαλαζήεντα κόρη Τιτηνὶς ἀνῆκε
σκορπίον, ἐκ κέντροιο τεθηγμένον, ἦμος ἐπέχρα
15 Βοιωτῷ τεύχουσα κακὸν μόρον Ὠαρίωνι,
ἀχράντων ὅτε χερσὶ θεῆς ἐδράξατο πέπλων·
αὐτὰρ ὅγε στιβαροῖο κατὰ σφυρὸν ἤλασεν ἴχνευς
σκορπίος ἀπροϊδὴς ὀλίγῳ ὑπὸ λᾶϊ λοχήσας·
τοῦ δὲ τέρας περίσημον ὑπ᾽ ἀστέρας ἀπλανὲς αὔτως
20 οἷα κυνηλατέοντος ἀείδελον ἐστήρικται.
Ἀλλὰ σύ γε σταθμοῖο καὶ αὐλίου ἑρπετὰ φύγδην
ῥηιδίως ἐκ πάντα διώξεαι, ἢ ἀπ᾽ ἐρίπνης,
ἠὲ καὶ αὐτοπόνοιο χαμευνάδος, ἦμος ἂν᾽ ἀγροὺς
φεύγων αὐαλέου θέρεος πυρόεσσαν ἀϋτμήν
25 αἴθριος ἐν καλάμῃ στορέσας ἀκρέσπερος εὔδῃς,
ἢ καὶ ἀνυλήεντα παρὲκ λόφον, ἢ ἐνὶ βήσσης
ἐσχατιῇ ὅθι πλεῖστα κινώπετα βόσκεται ὕλην,

CODICES: Π ω = BGKMPRVv
PAPYRI: 𝔓1 (377–95), 𝔓2 (333–44)
Deest M.
3 κυδίστατε ΠBGPRV Eust. 215.12   κηδέστ-Κν   6 βάλοι BPVv¹ | ἐπίλοιγον Σ v.l.

THERIACA

Readily, dear Hermesianax, most honoured of my many kins-
men, and in due order will I expound the forms of savage
creatures and their deadly injuries which smite one unforeseen,
and the countering remedy for the harm. And the toiling
ploughman, the herdsman, and the woodcutter, whenever in
forest or at the plough one of them fastens its deadly fang upon
him, shall respect you for your learning in such means for
averting sickness.

Now I would have you know, men say that noxious SPIDERS,
together with the grievous reptiles and vipers and the earth's
countless burdens, are of the Titans' blood—if indeed he spoke 10
the truth, Ascraean Hesiod on the steeps of secluded Melisseeis
by the waters of Permessus. And it was the Titan's daughter who
sent forth the blighting Scorpion with sharpened sting, when
she compassed an evil end for Boeotian Orion, and attacked him
after he had laid violent hands upon the immaculate raiment of
the goddess. Thereupon the Scorpion, which had lurked un-
observed beneath a small stone, struck him in the ankle of his
strong foot. But Orion's wondrous sign is set conspicuous, fixed
there amid the constellations, as of one hunting, dazzling to behold. 20
You for your part will easily chase and dispel all creeping
things from farmstead and cottage, or from steep bank, or
from couch of natural herbage, in the hour when, to shun
parching summer's fiery breath, beneath the sky you make
your bed on straw at nightfall in the fields and sleep, or else
beside some unwooded hill or on the edge of a glen, where

9 ἔχθεα G v.l. Σ v.l.   11 ἐπ' Π ἐν ω   18 τυχήσας KRVvΣ v.l. δοκήσας Σ v.l.
19 ὑπ' ἀστέρας Π ἐν ἄστρασιν (-ροισιν, -ροις) ω   21 σταθμοῦ τε ω
24 αὐαλέου ΠΚVv -έος cett. | πνιγόεσσαν ΚΣ v.l.   26 ἀνυλήεντα Π v.l. ἀν'
ὑ- ω ἀν' ὑδρίεντα Π | ἐνὶ ΠG ἀνὰ cett.   27 ἐσχατιῆ OSch. -ιὴν codd.

29

[δρυμοὺς καὶ λασιῶνας ἀμορβαίους τε χαράδρας·]
καί τε παρὲκ λιστρωτὸν ἅλω δρόμον, ἠδ' ἵνα ποίη
30 πρῶτα κυΐσκομένη χνοάει σκιάοντας ἰάμνους,
τῆμος ὅτ' ἀζαλέων φολίδων ἀπεδύσατο γῆρας
μῶλυς ἐπιστείβων, ὅτε φωλεὸν εἴαρι φεύγων
ὄμμασιν ἀμβλώσσει, μαράθου δέ ἑ νήχυτος ὄρπηξ
βοσκηθεὶς ὠκύν τε καὶ αὐγήεντα τίθησι.
35 Θιβρὴν δ' ἐξελάσεις ὀφίων ἐπιλωβέα κῆρα
καπνείων ἐλάφοιο πολυγλώχινα κεραίην,
ἄλλοτε δ' ἀζαλέην δαίων ἐγγαγίδα πέτρην,
ἣν οὐδὲ κρατεροῖο πυρὸς περικαίνυται ὁρμή·
ἐν δὲ πολυσχιδέος βλήτρου πυρὶ βάλλεο χαίτην,
40 ἢ σύ γε καχρυόεσσαν ἑλὼν πυριθαλπέα ῥίζαν
καρδάμῳ ἀμμίγδην ἰσοελκέι· μίσγε δ' ἔνοδμον
ζορκὸς ἐνὶ πλάστιγγι νέον κέρας ἀσκελὲς ἱστάς,
καί τε μελανθείου βαρυαέος, ἄλλοτε θείου,
ἄλλοτε δ' ἀσφάλτοιο φέρων ἰσοαχθέα μοῖραν·
45 ἠὲ σύ γε Θρήισσαν ἐνιφλέξαις πυρὶ λᾶαν,
ἥ θ' ὕδατι βρεχθεῖσα σελάσσεται, ἔσβεσε δ' αὐγήν
τυτθὸν ὅτ' ὀδμήσαιτο ἐπιρρανθέντος ἐλαίου.
τὴν ἀπὸ Θρηικίου νομέες ποταμοῖο φέρονται
ὃν Πόντον καλέουσι, τόθι Θρήικες ἀμορβοί
50 κριοφάγοι μήλοισιν ἀεργηλοῖσιν ἕπονται.
ναὶ μὴν καὶ βαρύοδμος ἐπὶ φλογὶ ζωγρηθεῖσα
χαλβάνη ἄκνηστίς τε καὶ ἡ πριόνεσσι τομαίη
κέδρος, πουλυόδουσι καταψηχθεῖσα γενείοις,
ἐν φλογιῇ καπνηλὸν ἄγει καὶ φύξιον ὀδμήν.
55 τοῖς δὴ χηραμὰ κοῖλα καὶ ὑληώρεας εὐνάς
κεινώσεις, δαπέδῳ δὲ πεσὼν ὕπνοιο κορέσσῃ.

Deest M
28 (=489) in marg. habet Π damn. OSch.   29 παρὲκ Bent. -ὲξ codd.:
cf. 26   30 χνοάει σκιάοντας BP   σκιάει χλοάοντας cett.   31 αὐαλέων ω
32 ἐπιστείχων ω   35 θιβρὴν GKRVvHsch. θιμβ- ΠΒΡ: cf. Al. 555   37 δαίων
ΠG   καίων cett. | ἐγγαγίδα KVv -αγγί- cett.   40 πυριθαλπέα Π περι- ω

poisonous creatures feed in multitudes upon the forest, or beside
the levelled perimeter of the threshing-floor, and where the
grass at its first burgeoning brings bloom to the shady water- 30
meadows, at the time when the snake sloughs the withe :d
scales of age, moving feebly forward, when in spring he leaves
his den, and his sight is dim; but a meal of the fennel's sappy
shoots makes him swift and bright of eye.

You may expel the hot and harmful doom that snakes bring,
if you char the tined horn of a STAG, or else set fire to dry
LIGNITE, which not even the violence of a fierce flame consumes.
Cast also upon the fire the foliage of the MALE FERN with its
cloven fronds, or take the heated root of the FRANKINCENSE- 40
TREE mixed with an equal measure of GARDEN-CRESS; and
mingle the fresh, pungent horn of a ROE, putting an equal
weight of it in the balance. Burn also a portion no less heavy
of the strong-smelling BLACK CUMMIN, or else of SULPHUR,
or again of BITUMEN. Or you may ignite in the fire the THRACIAN
STONE, which when soaked in water glows, yet quenches its
brightness at the least smell of a drop of oil. Herdsmen gather
it for themselves from the river of Thrace which they call
Pontus, where the Thracian shepherds who eat ram's flesh 50
follow after their leisurely flocks. Again, the heavy-scented
JUICE OF ALL-HEAL stimulated over a fire, and the STINGING
NETTLE, and CEDAR cut with saws and ground to dust by their
many-toothed jaws, produce in burning a smoky and repellent
stench. With these means you may clear hollow clefts and
couches in the woods, and may sink upon the ground and take
your fill of sleep.

41 ἀμμίγδην Π ἀμμίξας ω   43 μελανθ(ε)ίου ω -είης Π   44 ἰσοελκέα ω
45 ἐνιφλέξαις Π Gal. 12.204 -ξας ω   46 ῥανθεῖσα V v.l. Gal. | αὐγήν Bernard
αὐτήν codd. Gal.   47 ὀδμήσαιτο ΠV -σηται cett. Gal. | ἐπιχρανθέντος Π
48 τήν δ' Π | φέρουσιν Gal.   49 ἀμολγοί Π   51 μοιρηθεῖσα ω   54 φύξιον
OSch. πύξιον Π φύξιμον ω   55 οἷς Π

Εἰ δὲ τὰ μὲν καμάτου ἐπιδεύεται, ἄγχι δέ τοι νύξ
αὖλιν ἄγει, κοίτου δὲ λιλαίεαι ἔργον ἀνύσσας,
τῆμος δὴ ποταμοῖο πολυρραγέος κατὰ δίνας
60 ὑδρηλὴν καλάμινθον ὀπάζεο χαιτήεσσαν·
πολλὴ γὰρ λιβάσιν παραέξεται ἀμφί τε χείλη
ἔρσεται ἀγλαύροισιν ἀγαλλομένη ποταμοῖσιν.
ἢ σύ γ' ὑποστορέσαιο λύγον πολυανθέα κόψας
ἢ πολιὸν βαρύοδμον, ὃ δὴ ῥίγιστον ὄδωδεν·
65 ὣς δ' αὔτως ἐχίειον, ὀριγανόεσσά τε χαίτη,
ναὶ μὴν ἀβροτόνοιο τό τ' ἄγριον οὔρεσι θάλλει
ἀργεννὴν ὑπὸ βῆσσαν, ἢ ἑρπύλλοιο νομαίου,
ὅς τε φιλόζωος νοτερὴν ἐπιβόσκεται αἶαν
ῥιζοβόλος, λασίοισιν ἀεὶ φύλλοισι κατήρης.
70 φράζεσθαι δ' ἐπέοικε χαμαιζήλοιο κονύζης
ἄγνου τε βρύα λευκὰ καὶ ἐμπρίοντ' ὀνόγυρον·
αὔτως δὲ τρήχοντα ταμὼν ἄπο κλήματα σίδης,
ἠὲ καὶ ἀσφοδέλοιο νέον πολυαυξέα μόσχον,
στρύχνον τε σκύρα τ' ἐχθρά, τά τ' εἴαρι σίνατο βούτην
75 ἦμος ὅταν σκυρόωσι βόες καυλεῖα φαγοῦσαι.
ναὶ μὴν πευκεδάνοιο βαρυπνόου, οὗ τε καὶ ὀδμή
θηρί' ἀποσσεύει τε καὶ ἀντιόωντα διώκει.
καὶ τὰ μὲν εἰκαίῃ παράθου ἀγραυλέι κοίτῃ,
ἄλλα δὲ φωλειοῖς· τὰ δὲ διπλάσσαιο χεείαις.
80   Εἴ γε μέν, ἐς τεῦχος κεραμήιον ἠὲ καὶ ὄλπην
κεδρίδας ἐνθρύπτων λιπάοις εὐήρεα γυῖα,
ἢ καὶ πευκεδάνοιο βαρυπνόου, ἄλλοτ' ὀρείου
αὖα καταψήχοιο λίπει ἐνὶ φύλλα κονύζης·
αὔτως δ' ἀλθήεντ' ἐλελίσφακον, ἐν δέ τε ῥίζαν
85 σιλφίου, ἣν κνηστῆρι κατατρίψειαν ὀδόντες—
πολλάκι καὶ βροτέην σιάλων ὑποέτρεσαν ὀδμήν.
εἰ δὲ σύ γε τρίψας ὀλίγῳ ἐν βάμματι κάμπην

Desunt M ad v. 61, Π a v. 57 ad v. 76
58 ἀνύσας P -σ(σ)αι cett.   59 πολυρραγέος G   60 καιτήεσσαν Σ v.l.
62 ἀγλαύροισιν G ἀγραύλ- cett.   67 ὑπὸ πέζαν G v.l. M   72 δὲ OSch.,
τε codd: cf. 84, 681   73 πολυαυχέα KvΣ v.l. -ανθέα Σ v.l.   74 τρύχνον

But if these things involve trouble, and night brings bed-time near, and you are longing for rest when your work is done, then gather to yourself among the eddies of some rushing river the water-loving, leafy MINT, for it grows in plenty by streams 6(and is fed with the moisture about their edges, as it delights in gleaming rivers. Or you should cut and strew beneath you the flowering WILLOW, or the strong-smelling HULWORT, which has a most offensive odour; so too have VIPER'S BUGLOSS and the leaves of MARJORAM, aye, or of WORMWOOD, which grows wild upon the hills in some chalky glen, or of TUFTED THYME from pasture-lands: tenacious of life it draws sustenance from a damp soil, deep-rooted, ever furnished with hairy leaves. And you 7(should mark the pale spikes of the low-growing FLEABANE and of the AGNUS CASTUS, and the pungent STINKING BEAN-TREFOIL. Likewise cut the rough twigs of the POMEGRANATE, or else young and flourishing shoots of the ASPHODEL, and DEADLY NIGHTSHADE, and the horrid HYPERICUM which injures the herdsman in the springtime when his cows are poisoned by eating the stalks; and further stems of the heavy-scented SULPHURWORT whose very odour scares snakes and chases them away should they approach you. So place some of these by you wherever you make a casual couch in the fields; others where snakes lurk, and a double quantity at their holes.

Now make in an earthen vessel or an oil-flask a paste of 8(JUNIPER BERRIES and anoint your supple limbs—or of the heavy-scented SULPHURWORT; or else pound thoroughly in Oil the dried leaves of FLEABANE from the hills, and likewise the healing SALVIA, adding the root of SILPHIUM, which the grater's teeth should grind small—many a time too have noxious creatures fled in terror from the scent of a man's spittle. But if you rub a CATERPILLAR from the garden in a little Vinegar, the dewy

OSch. coll. 878   78 καὶ ἀγρ. ω   79 φωλειοῖς OSch. -οῖσι codd. | διπλάσ-σαιο OSch. -σοιο Π ἐμφράξαιο ω | χεείαις Bent. χελεί- codd.   81 λιπάοις Π -όοις, -ώῃς ω   86 βροτέων ω   87 τρίψαις GMRV | ἐνὶ KMVv

33

κηπαίην δροσόεσσαν ἐπὶ χλωρηίδα νώτῳ,
ἠὲ καὶ ἀγριάδος μολόχης ἐγκύμονι κάρφει
90 γυῖα πέριξ λιπάσειας, ἀναίμακτός κεν ἰαύοις.
ψήχεο δ' ἐν στέρνῳ προβαλὼν μυλόεντι θυείης
ἐν μέν θ' ἀβροτόνοιο δύω κομόωντας ὀράμνους
καρδάμῳ ἀμμίγδην—ὀδελοῦ δέ οἱ αἴσιος ὁλκή—
ἐν δὲ χεροπληθῆ καρπὸν νεοθηλέα δαυχμοῦ
95 λειαίνειν τριπτῆρι· τὰ δὲ τροχοειδέα πλάσσων
τέρσαι ὑποσκιόεντι βαλὼν ἀνεμώδεϊ χώρῳ·
αὖα δ' ἐν ὅλπῃ θρύπτε, καὶ αὐτίκα γυῖα λιπαίνοις.
Εἴ γε μὲν ἐκ τριόδοιο μεμιγμένα κνώδαλα χύτρῳ
ζωὰ νέον θορνύντα καὶ ἐν θρόνα τοιάδε βάλλῃς,
100 δήεις οὐλομένῃσιν ἀλεξητήριον ἄταις·
ἐν μὲν γὰρ μυελοῖο νεοσφαγέος ἐλάφοιο
δραχμάων τρίφατον δεκάδος καταβάλλεο βρῖθος,
ἐν δὲ τρίτην ῥοδέου μοῖραν χοός, ἥν τε θυωροί
πρώτην μεσσατίην τε πολύτριπτόν τε κλέονται,
105 ἰσόμορον δ' ὠμοῖο χέειν ἀργῆτος ἐλαίου,
τετράμορον κηροῖο· τὰ δ' ἐν περιηγέι γάστρῃ
θάλπε κατασπέρχων ἔστ' ἂν περὶ σάρκες ἀκάνθης
μελδόμεναι θρύπτωνται· ἔπειτα δὲ λάζεο τυκτήν
εὐεργῆ λάκτιν, τὰ δὲ μυρία πάντα ταράσσειν
110 συμφύρδην ὀφίεσσιν· ἑκὰς δ' ἀπόερσον ἀκάνθας,
καὶ γὰρ ταῖς κακοεργὸς ὁμῶς ἐνιτέτροφεν ἰός·
γυῖα δὲ πάντα λίπαζε καὶ εἰς ὁδόν, ἢ ἐπὶ κοῖτον,
ἢ ὅταν αὐαλέου θέρεος μεθ' ἁλώια ἔργα
ζωσάμενος θρίναξι βαθὺν διακρίνεαι ἄντλον.
115 Εἰ δέ που ἐν δακέεσσιν ἀφαρμάκτῳ χροῒ κύρσῃς
ἄκμηνος σίτων, ὅτε δὴ κακὸν ἄνδρας ἰάπτει,
αἶψά κεν ἡμετέρῃσιν ἐρωήσειας ἐφετμαῖς.
τῶν ἤτοι θήλεια παλίγκοτος ἀντομένοισι

88 om. Π, fort. recte   89 μαλάχης (cf. Ath. 2.58D) ἐγκύμονα καρπόν ω
90 ἀνήμυκτός Bent.   92 ἐσθλοῦ ἀβρ. BP   93 καρδάμου Π | δ' ἔχοι Π
94 δαύκου ω -χου, γλυκύ Σ v.ll. -χνοῦ Bergk: cf. Al. 199   98 μεμαγμένα

Caterpillar with a green back, or if you anoint your limbs all about with the teeming fruit of the MARSH MALLOW, then you 90 will pass the night unscathed. Also cast in and rub down in the stony heart of a mortar two leafy sprays of WORMWOOD mixed with GARDEN-CRESS—an obol's weight is suitable—and with a pestle pound therein to smoothness a handful of fresh berries from the BAY; then mould into rounds and put to dry in a shady, wind-swept spot; when dry break them in pieces in an oil-flask, and you can anoint your limbs with it at once.

If however you can cast SNAKES coupled at a crossroads, alive and just mating, into a pot, and the following medicaments besides, you have a preventive against deadly disasters. Throw in 100 thirty drachms' weight of the marrow of a freshly killed STAG and one-third of a *chous* of ROSE-OIL,—essence which perfumers style 'prime' and 'medium' and 'well-ground'—and pour on an equal measure of raw, gleaming OIL and one-quarter of WAX. These you must quickly heat in a round, bellying pot until the fleshy portions are softened and come in pieces about the spine. Next take a shaped, well-made pestle and pound up these many ingredients in a mixture with the snakes; but cast aside the 110 vertebrae, for in them a venom no less deadly is engendered. Then anoint all your limbs, be it for a journey or for a sleep or when you gird yourself after work at the threshing-floor in summer's drouth and with pronged forks winnow the high pile of grain.

But if you should chance to come upon biting creatures when your skin is unmedicined and you are fasting—that is the time when disaster strikes a man—you may readily save yourself by our precepts. It is the Female Snake that attacks with its bite those who encounter it; besides, it is thicker right down to the

Bent.   99 βάλλοις ω   100 om. M   103 μοῖραν ῥοδέου ω   104 τε
κλέονται Gow: cf. *fr.* 71.5   καλέονται Π -έουσι ω

35

δάχματι, πλειοτέρη δὲ καὶ ὁλκαίην ἐπὶ σειρήν·
120 τοὔνεκα καὶ θανάτοιο θοώτερος ἵξεται αἶσα.
ἀλλ' ἤτοι θέρεος βλαβερὸν δάκος ἐξαλέασθαι
Πληιάδων φάσιας δεδοκημένος, αἵ θ' ὑπὸ Ταύρου
ἀλκαίην ψαίρουσαι ὀλίζωνες φορέονται·
ἢ ὅτε σὺν τέκνοισι θερειομένοισιν ἀβοσκής
125 φωλειοῦ λοχάδην ὑπὸ γωλεὰ διψὰς ἰαύῃ,
ἢ ὅτε λίπτῃσιν μεθ' ἑὸν νομόν, ἢ ἐπὶ κοῖτον
ἐκ νομοῦ ὑπνώουσα κίῃ κεκορημένη ὕλης.
μὴ σύ γ' ἐνὶ τριόδοισι τύχοις ὅτε δάχμα πεφυζώς
περκνὸς ἔχις θυίῃσι τυπῇ ψολόεντος ἐχίδνης,
130 ἡνίκα θορνυμένου ἔχιος θολερῷ κυνόδοντι
θουρὰς ἀμύξ ἐμφῦσα κάρην ἀπέκοψεν ὁμεύνου·
οἱ δὲ πατρὸς λώβην μετεκίαθον αὐτίκα τυτθοί
γεινόμενοι ἐχιῆες, ἐπεὶ διὰ μητρὸς ἀραιήν
γαστέρ' ἀναβρώσαντες ἀμήτορες ἐξεγένοντο·
135 οἵη γὰρ βαρύθει ὑπὸ κύματος, οἱ δὲ καθ' ὕλην
ᾠοτόκοι ὄφιες λεπυρὴν θάλπουσι γενέθλην.
μηδ' ὅτε ῥικνῆεν φολίδων περὶ γῆρας ἀμέρσας
ἂψ ἀναφοιτήσῃ νεαρῇ κεχαρημένος ἥβῃ,
ἢ ὁπότε σκαρθμοὺς ἐλάφων ὀχέῃσιν ἀλύξας
140 ἀνδράσ' ἐνισκίμψῃ χολόων γυιοφθόρον ἰόν·
ἔξοχα γὰρ δολιχοῖσι κινωπησταῖς κοτέουσι
νεβροτόκοι καὶ ζόρκες· ἀνιχνεύουσι δὲ πάντῃ
τρόχμαλά θ' αἱμασιάς τε καὶ ἰλυοὺς ἐρέθοντες,
σμερδαλέῃ μυκτῆρος ἐπισπέρχοντες ἀυτμῇ.
145 Ναὶ μὴν καὶ νιφόεσσα φέρει δυσπαίπαλος Ὄθρυς
φοινὰ δάκη, κοίλη τε φάραγξ καὶ τρηχέες ἀγμοί
καὶ λέπας ὑλῆεν, τόθι δίψιος ἐμβατέει σήψ.

119 δάχματι ΠG² δήχ- G¹M δάγ- cett. quae variatio alibi non notatur
121 δάκος ω κακὸν Π 123 ὁλκαίην ΩΣ v.l. Σ Arat. 172, 254 124, 5 om. M
127 ὑπνώουσα ΠMR -ώσ(σ)ουσα cett. 128 δάχμα OSch. δῆγμα codd.
129 θύῃσι ω | τυπῇ OSch. -ὴν codd. | χολόεσσαν Gal. 14.239 130 θαλερῷ
OSch. δολερῷ Bent. 131 ἀμύξ ΠΣ v.l. ὀδὰξ ω Gal. 134 ἀναρρήξαντες

trailing tail, and for that reason the doom of death will come 120
more swiftly. But chiefly in summer must you be on your guard
against harmful snakes, observing the rising of the Pleiads, those
smaller stars which graze the tail of the Bull in their course,
when the DIPSAS either sleeps unfed with the young it broods,
lurking in the recesses of its hole, or when it makes eagerly for
its feeding-ground, or when therefrom, sated with the forest, it
goes sleepily to its lair. Beware of meeting at the crossroads the
dusky MALE VIPER when he has escaped from her bite and is
maddened by the blow of the smoke-hued Female, in the 130
season when, as the Male covers her, the lustful Female fastens
upon him, tearing him with her foul fang, and cuts off the head
of her mate; but forthwith in the act of birth the young vipers
avenge their sire's destruction, since they gnaw through their
mother's thin flank and thereby are born motherless. For alone
of snakes the Female Viper is burdened with pregnancy, whereas
oviparous snakes of the forest warm a membrane-enclosed
brood. Beware too when the Viper, having doffed the wrinkled
scales of age, comes abroad again exulting in his new-found
youth; beware when, after escaping in his hole from the
trampling feet of Deer, he darts in fury his limb-corroding 140
venom at men; for Red Deer and Roe cherish a special anger
towards long reptiles and track them down, exploring on every
side stone-heaps, walls, and lurking-places, following hard after
them with the dreadful breath of their nostrils.

Furthermore the snow-capped crags of Othrys too bear
deadly serpents, and hollow gully and rough crags and woodland
scaur, where haunts the thirst-provoking SEPS. It has a varying

Gal. **135** κύματι τοὶ ω **136** om. BPV **137** περὶ Π ἀπὸ ω **140** ἀνδράσ'
JGSch. -ρὸς codd. | ἐνισκίμψῃ ΠG -σκήψῃ, -ει cett. | θυμοφθόρον ω **141** κινω-
πηστὰῖς ΠG -πιστᾶῖς cett. **142** πάντῃ ΠMV -τα cett. **143** ἰλυοὺς Π Et.M.
35.14 εἰλ- ω | ἐρέοντες ω **146** φάρυγξ Π **147** ἐμβροτέει Π

χροιὴν δ' ἀλλόφατόν τε καὶ οὐ μίαν οἶαδὸν ἴσχει,
αἰὲν ἐειδόμενος χώρῳ ἵνα χηραμὰ τεύξῃ.
150 τῶν οἱ μὲν λίθακάς τε καὶ ἔρμακας ἐνναίοντες
παυρότεροι, τρηχεῖς δὲ καὶ ἔκπυροι· οὔ κεν ἐκείνων
ἀνδράσι δάχμα πέλοι μεταμώνιον ἀλλὰ κάκηθες.
ἄλλος δ' αὖ κόχλοισι δομὴν ἰνδάλλεται αἴης,
ἄλλῳ δ' ἐγχλοάουσα λοπὶς περιμήκεα κύκλον
155 ποικίλον αἰόλλει· πολέες δ' ἀμάθοισι μιγέντες
σπείρῃ λεπρύνονται ἀλινδόμενοι ψαμάθοισι.
   Φράζεο δ' αὐαλέῃσιν ἐπιφρικτὴν φολίδεσσιν
ἀσπίδα φοινήεσσαν, ἀμυδρότατον δάκος ἄλλων,
[τῇ μὲν γάρ τε κέλευθος ὁμῶς κατ' ἐναντίον ἕρπει
160 ἀτραπὸν ὁλκαίην δολιχῷ μηρύγματι γαστρός.]
ἢ καὶ σμερδαλέον μὲν ἔχει δέμας, ἐν δὲ κελεύθῳ
νωχελὲς ἐξ ὁλκοῖο φέρει βάρος, ὑπναλέῳ δὲ
αἰὲν ἐπιλλίζουσα φαείνεται ἐνδυκὲς ὄσσῳ·
ἀλλ' ὅταν ἢ δοῦπον νέον οὔασιν ἠέ τιν' αὐγὴν
165 ἀθρήσῃ, νωθῆ μὲν ἀπὸ ῥέθεος βάλεν ὕπνον,
ὁλκῷ δὲ τροχόεσσαν ἄλων εἰλίξατο γαίῃ,
λευγαλέον δ' ἀνὰ μέσσα κάρη πεφρικὸς ἀείρει.
τῆς ἤτοι μῆκος μέν, ὃ κύντατον ἔτρεφεν αἶα,
ὀργυιῇ μετρητόν· ἀτὰρ περιφαίνεται εὖρος
170 ὅσσον τ' αἰγανέης δορατοξόος ἤνυσε τέκτων
εἰς ἐνοπὴν ταύρων τε βαρυφθόγγων τε λεόντων.
χροιὴ δ' ἄλλοτε μὲν ψαφαρὴ ἐπιδέδρομε νώτοις,
ἄλλοτε μηλινόεσσα καὶ αἰόλος, ἄλλοτε τεφρή,
πολλάκι δ' αἰθαλόεσσα μελαινομένη ὑπὸ βώλῳ
175 Αἰθιόπων, οἵην τε πολύστομος εἰς ἅλα Νεῖλος
πλησάμενος κατέχευεν ἄσιν προῦτυψε δὲ πόντῳ.

Deest G a v. 176
149 τεύχῃ, -χει ω   150 λιθάδας Π   151 δὲ Π   τε ω | ἔμπυροι ω: cf. [Arist.]
846b 16   152 πέλει ω   153 δ' ἐν Π   154 λοπὶς Π   λεπίς ω: cf. Al. 467
φολὶς Σ v.l.: cf. [Arist.] 846b 14   156 σπείρην Page | λεπραίνονται Π: cf. 262
157 αὐαλέῃσιν Bent. -έαις μὲν codd.   159f. om. Π, 160 om. M damn.
JGSch.: cf. 265   162,3 ὑπναλέοις...ὄσσοις ω   164 αὐδήν ω   165 νωθῆ Gow

hue and not one alone, ever taking the colour of the place wherein it has made its hole. Those that live in stony ground 150 and cairns are smaller but fierce and irascible: no bite of theirs can fail of effect on man, but is malignant. Another's body is like a land-snail; yet another has scales of greenish hue which variegate its huge coil; and many there are that frequent dusty places and make their coils rough by wriggling in the sand.

Consider now the murderous ASP, bristling with dry scales, the most sluggish of all snakes. Its form is terrifying, but when 161 in movement, it uncoils its weight slowly and ever seems to wear a fixed look in its drowsy eyes. Yet when it hears some strange noise or sees a bright light, it throws off from its body dull sleep and wreathes its coil in a circular ring upon the ground, and in the midst it rears its head, bristling in deadly fashion. Its length, horrible beyond that of any other of earth's creatures, measures a fathom, and its thickness is seen to be that which a spear-maker fashions for a hunting-spear for fighting 170 bulls and deep-voiced lions. Sometimes the colour spread over its back is dust-like, sometimes it is the yellow of a quince and sheeny, at other times an ashen hue, but often, when it grows dark with Aethiop soil, a smoky brown like the sludge which the many-mouthed Nile in flood pours into the sea, as it dashes against the waves. Above the brow over the eyes there appear,

-θρὴ Π -θρὸν ⲱ   167 σμερδαλέον ⲱ: cf. 161 | πεφευγὸς Π   169 περιβάλ-
λεται ⲱ   171 τινὲς ἀθετοῦσι τὸν στίχον τοῦτον, Σ | κάπρων τε MR
172 ψαφαρὴ JGSch. (et ut vid. Σ) -ροῖς codd.   173 ἄλλοτε μ. ⲱ ἢ περι μ. Π|
μηλινόεσσα ΠG μειλ- cett.   174 μελαινομένη ⲱ -νην OSch.   175 πολύστομος MVv Σ v.l. -στονος cett.

δοιοὶ δ' ἐν σκυνίοισιν ὑπερφαίνουσι μέτωπον
οἷα τύλοι, τὸ δ' ἔνερθεν ὑπαιφοινίσσεται ὄμμα
πολλὸν ὑπὲρ σπείρης, ψαφαρὸς δ' ἀναπίμπραται αὐχήν
180 ἄκριτα ποιφύσσοντος ὅτ' ἀντομένοισιν ὁδουροῖς
ἄϊδα προσμάξηται ἐπὶ ζαμενὲς κοτέουσα.
τῆς ἤτοι πίσυρες κοῖλοι ὑπένερθεν ὀδόντες
ἀγκύλοι ἐν γναθμοῖς δολιχήρεες ἐρρίζωνται
ἰοδόκοι, μύχατος δὲ χιτὼν ὑμένεσσι καλύπτει·
185 ἔνθεν ἀμείλικτον γυίοις ἐνερεύγεται ἰόν.
ἐχθρῶν που τέρα κεῖνα καρήασιν ἐμπελάσειε·
σαρκὶ γὰρ οὔτ' ἐπὶ δάχμα φαείνεται, οὔτε δυσαλθές
οἶδος ἐπιφλέγεται, καμάτου δ' ἄτερ ὄλλυται ἀνήρ,
ὑπνηλὸν δ' ἐπὶ νῶκαρ ἄγει βιότοιο τελευτήν.
190 Ἰχνεύμων δ' ἄρα μοῦνος ἀκήριος ἀσπίδος ὁρμήν,
ἠμὲν ὅτ' ἐς μόθον εἶσιν, ἀλεύεται, ἠδ' ὅτε λυγρά
θαλπούσης ὄφιος κηριτρόφου ὤεα γαίῃ
πάντα διεσκήνιψε, καὶ ἐξ ὑμένων ἐτίναξε
δαρδάπτων, ὀλοοῖς δὲ συνερραθάγησεν ὀδοῦσι.
195 μορφῇ δ' ἰχνευτᾶο κινωπέτου οἷον ἀμυδρῆς
ἴκτιδος ἤ τ' ὄρνισι κατοικιδίῃσιν ὄλεθρον
μαίεται, ἐξ ὕπνοιο συναρπάζουσα πετεύρων
ἔνθα λέχος τεύχονται ἐπίκριοι ἢ καὶ ἀφαυρά
τέκνα τιθαιβώσσουσιν ὑπὸ πλευρῇσι θέρουσαι.
200 ἀλλ' ὅταν Αἰγύπτοιο παρὰ θρυόεντας ἰάμνους
ἀσπίσι μῶλον ἔχωσιν ἀθέσφατον εἰλικοέσσαις,
αὐτίχ' ὁ μὲν ποταμόνδε καθήλατο, τύψε δὲ κώλοις
τάρταρον ἰλυόεσσαν, ἄφαρ δ' ἐφορύξατο γυῖα
πηλῷ, ἀλινδηθεὶς ὀλίγον δέμας εἰσόκε λάχνην
205 Σείριος ἀζήνῃ τεύξῃ δ' ἄγναπτον ὀδόντι.
τῆμος δ' ἠὲ κάρην λιχμήρεος ἑρπηστᾶο

Desunt G ad v. 186, M a v. 194, Π a v. 204
177 δ' ἐν ω δὲ Π | μετώπου, -πῳ ω   179 ὑπὲρ (vel ὑπὲκ) ut vid. Eutec. ὑπὸ
codd. | ἀναπίμπραται MV | -πλαται cett.   180 ὁδίταις ω Σ v.l.   187 οὔτε
τι δῆγμα ω   192 κηριτρόφου ΠGM κηροτ- cett.   197 καθαρπάζουσα ω |

as it were, two calluses, while its eye beneath them glows
bright red aloft over its coil and its dust-coloured neck swells
up as it hisses continuously, when in the violence of its wrath it 180
fastens death upon wayfarers who meet it. It has four fangs,
their underside hollow, hooked, and long, rooted in its jaws,
containing poison, and at their base a covering of membranes
hides them. Thence it belches forth poison unassuageable on
a body. Be they no friends of mine whose heads these monsters
assail. For no bite appears on the flesh, no deadly swelling with
inflammation, but the man dies without pain, and a slumberous
lethargy brings life's end.

Now the ICHNEUMON alone escapes unharmed the Asp's on- 190
set, both when it comes to fight and when it breaks on the
ground all the baneful eggs which the deadly serpent is brooding,
as it shakes them out from their membranes by biting them and
crushes them in its destroying teeth. The form of this snake-
tracking creature is that of the puny marten which seeks the
destruction of domestic fowls, snatching them from their
perches as they sleep, where they roost upon a beam or foster
their feeble chicks, keeping them warm beneath their breast.
But when amid Egypt's rush-grown water-meadows they join 200
with the wriggling Asps in a fearsome struggle, forthwith the
Ichneumon leaps into the river, strikes the slimy bottom with
its paws, and rolling its small body smears its limbs at once with
the mud, against the time when the Dog-Star's heat has dried
its fur and made it so that no fang may rend it. And then it
either springs upon the frightful head of the reptile with the

πετεύρων ΠG -αύρων cett.   198 ἐπ' ἴκριον, -ίῳ Ѡ   201 om. V | ἄγησιν Ѡ
203 εἰλυόεσσαν Π   205 ἄγναπτον P   ἄγναμπ- BGRV   ἄγραπ- Kv   206 κάρη
Rv: cf. 131, 249

THERIACA

σμερδαλέην ἔβρυξεν ἐπάλμενος ἠὲ καὶ οὐρῆς
ἁρπάξας βρυόεντος ἔσω ποταμοῖο κύλισεν.
Εὖ δ' ἂν ἐχιδνήεσσαν ἴδοις πολυδευκέα μορφήν,
210 ἄλλοτε μὲν δολιχήν, ὁτὲ παυράδα· τοιάδ' ἀέξει
Εὐρώπη τ' 'Ασίη τε· τὰ δ' οὐκ ἐπιείκελα δήεις.
ἤτοι ἀν' Εὐρώπην μὲν ὀλίζονα, καί θ' ὑπὲρ ἄκρους
ῥώθωνας κεραοί τε καὶ ἀργίλιπες τελέθουσιν,
αἱ μὲν ὑπὸ Σκείρωνος ὄρη Παμβώνιά τ' αἴπη,
215 'Ρυπαῖον, Κόρακός τε πάγον, πολιόν τ' 'Ασέληνον·
'Ασὶς δ' ὀργυιόεντα καὶ ἐς πλέον ἑρπετὰ βόσκει,
οἷα περὶ τρηχὺν Βουκάρτερον, ἢ καὶ ἐρυμνός
Αἰσαγέης πρηὼν καὶ Κέρκαφος ἐντὸς ἐέργει.
τῶν ἤτοι βρεχμοῖς μὲν ἐπὶ πλάτος, ἠδ' ὑπὲρ ἄκρον
220 ὁλκαῖον σπείρης κολοβὴν ἐπελίσσεται οὐρήν
ἀζαλέαις φρίσσουσαν ἐπητανὸν φολίδεσσι·
νωθεῖ δ' ἔνθα καὶ ἔνθα διὰ δρυμὰ νίσσεται ὁλκῷ.
πᾶς δέ τοι ὀξυκάρηνος ἰδεῖν ἔχις, ἄλλοτε μῆκος
μάσσων, ἄλλοτε παῦρος· ἀκιδνότερος δὲ κατ' εὖρος
225 νηδύος, ἡ δὲ μύουρος ὑπ' ἀλκαίῃ τετάνυσται,
ἴσως μὲν πεδανὴ δολιχοῦ ὑπὸ πείρασιν ὁλκοῦ,
ἴσως δ' ἐκ φολίδων τετρυμένη· αὐτὰρ ἐνωπῆς
γλήνεα φοινίσσει τεθοωμένος, ὀξὺ δὲ δικρῆ
γλώσσῃ λιχμάζων νέατον σκωλύπτεται οὐρήν·
230 Κωκυτὸν δ' ἐχιαῖον ἐπικλείουσιν ὁδῖται.
τοῦ μὲν ὑπὲρ κυνόδοντε δύω χροῖ τεκμαίρονται
ἰὸν ἐρευγόμενοι· πλέονες δέ τοι αἰὲν ἐχίδνης,
οὔλῳ γὰρ στομίῳ ἐμφύεται, ἀμφὶ δὲ σαρκί
ῥεῖά κεν εὐρυνθέντας ἐπιφράσσαιο χαλινούς.
235 τῆς καὶ ἀπὸ πληγῆς φέρεται λίπει εἴκελος ἰχώρ,

Desunt M, Π ad v. 231
207 σμερδαλέην Gow -έης codd. -έως Bent.   208 κύλισεν B -ισσεν cett.
209 πολυδευκέα K²Σ v.l. -δερκέα cett.   210 τοιάδ' OSch. τοῖα'' v τοῖ'' K
τοῖον cett.   214 αἱ OSch. οἱ codd.   216 ὀργυόεντα BPRV   217 οἷά
περ ἢ Bent.   219 βρεχμοῖς Gow -μοὶ codd.   221 ἀζαλέαις Bent. ἀργα-

42

flickering tongue and bites it, or seizing it by the tail, sends it
rolling into the weedy river.

You would do well to mark the various forms of the VIPER.
It may be long, it may be short; for so Europe and Asia breed **210**
them, but you will not find them alike. Thus, in Europe they are
smaller, and above the tip of their nostrils they are horned and
white, those, that is, beneath the mountains of Sciron and the
Pambonian steeps, Rhype, and the hill of Corax and hoary
Aselenus; whereas Asia breeds snakes a fathom long and even
more, such as are about rugged Bucarterus or are contained within the strong headland of Aesagea and in Cercaphus. The front
of their heads is flat, and at the trailing end of its coil the creature **220**
wriggles a stunted tail which is abundantly rough with dry
scales. And this way and that through the brakes it strays with
sluggish coil. But every Male Viper is seen to have a pointed
head. In length he is sometimes larger, sometimes short, and in
breadth of belly he is slimmer, while his tail stretches tapering
away, and may be flattened towards the end of its trailing length
or rubbed smooth of scales. But the eyes in his face turn blood-
red when he is angered, and as his forked tongue flickers rapidly,
he lashes the end of his tail. Wayfarers call him the snaky **230**
Cocytus. Two fangs in his upper jaw, as they spit poison, leave
their mark upon the skin, but of the Female always more than
two, for she lays hold with her whole mouth, and you can
easily observe that the jaws have opened wide about the flesh.
And from the wound she makes there oozes a discharge like oil

---

codd.: cf. 357   **225** ὑφ' G ἐφ' cett. | ἀλκαίη OSch. ὀλκ- codd.: cf. 123
227 τετρυμ(μ)ένη GKVv τετριμμ- cett.: cf. 287   **229** σκωλύπτεται, -ύνεται
Σ v.ll.   **230** ἀθετεῖται ὁ στίχος οὗτος ὡς ὑποβολιμαῖος, Σ | ἐχιαῖον OSch.
-ιναῖον codd. Et.M. 404.34   **235** ἀπὸ καὶ Π | εἴκελος ΠΚ ἰκ- cett.

ἄλλοτε δ᾽ αἱματόεις, τοτὲ δ᾽ ἄχροος· ἡ δ᾽ ἐπί οἱ σάρξ
πολλάκι μὲν χλοάουσα βαρεῖ ἀναδέδρομεν οἴδει,
ἄλλοτε φοινίσσουσα, τότ᾽ εἴδεται ἄντα πελιδνή·
ἄλλοτε δ᾽ ὑδατόεν κυέει βάρος, αἱ δὲ χαμηλαί
240 πομφόλυγες ὡς εἴ τε περὶ φλύκταιναι ἀραιαί
οἷα πυρικμήτοιο χροὸς πλαδόωσιν ὕπερθεν.
σηπεδόνες δέ οἱ ἀμφὶς ἐπίδρομοι, αἱ μὲν ἄτερθεν
αἱ δὲ κατὰ πληγὴν ἰοειδέα λοιγὸν ἱεῖσαι.
πᾶν δ᾽ ἐπί οἱ δριμεῖα δέμας καταβόσκεται ἄτη
245 ὀξέα πυρπολέουσα· κατ᾽ ἀσφάραγον δέ τε λυγμοί
κίονά τε ξυνιόντες ἐπασσύτεροι κλονέουσιν.
ἀμφὶ καὶ εἰλίγγοις δέμας ἄχθεται· αἶψα δὲ γυίοις
ἀδρανίη βαρύθουσα καὶ ἰξύι μέρμερος ἴζει,
ἐν δὲ κάρῃ σκοτόεν βάρος ἵσταται· αὐτὰρ ὁ κάμνων
250 ἄλλοτε μὲν δίψῃ φάρυγα ξηραίνεται αὔῃ,
πολλάκι δ᾽ ἐξ ὀνύχων ἴσχει κρύος, ἀμφὶ δὲ γυίοις
χειμερίη ζαλόωσα πέριξ βέβριθε χάλαζα.
πολλάκι δ᾽ αὖ χολόεντας ἀπήρυγε νηδύος ὄγκους
ὠχραίνων δέμας ἀμφίς· ὁ δὲ νοτέων περὶ γυίοις
255 ψυχρότερος νιφετοῖο βολῆς περιχεύεται ἱδρώς.
χροιὴν δ᾽ ἄλλοτε μὲν μολίβου ζοφοειδέος ἴσχει,
ἄλλοτε δ᾽ ἠερόεσσαν, ὅτ᾽ ἄνθεσιν εἴσατο χαλκοῦ.
    Εὖ δ᾽ ἂν καὶ δολόεντα μάθοις ἐπιόντα κεράστην
ἠΰτ᾽ ἔχιν· τῷ γάρ τε δομὴν ἰνδάλλεται ἴσην.
260 ἤτοι ὁ μὲν κόλος ἐστίν, ὁ δ᾽ αὖ κεράεσσι πεποιθώς,
ἄλλοτε μὲν πισύρεσσιν, ὅτ᾽ ἐν δοιοῖσι κεράστης,
χροιῇ δ᾽ ἐν ψαφαρῇ λεπρύνεται, ἐν δ᾽ ἀμάθοισιν
ἢ καὶ ἁματροχιῇσι κατὰ στίβον ἐνδυκὲς αὔει.
τῶν ἤτοι σπείρῃσιν ὁ μὲν θοὸς ἀντία θύνει
265 ἀτραπὸν ἰθεῖαν δολιχῷ μηρύγματι γαστρός·
αὐτὰρ ὅγε σκαιὸς μεσάτῳ ἐπαλίνδεται ὁλκῷ

Deest M ad v. 260
236 τοτὲ ΠΚVν   ποτὲ cett.   239 χαμηλαί ΠΣ v.l.   θαμιναί ΩΣ v.l.   240 τὼς
ω | πυρὶ ω   243 λ. ἐᾶσι Π   247 δὲ γόνος (?) Π   250 αὖον ω   253 δ᾽ η

or, it may be, bloody or colourless, while the skin around starts up into a painful lump, often greenish, now crimson, or again of livid aspect. At other times it engenders a mass of fluid, and about the wound small pimples like slight blisters 240 rise flabbily from the skin, which looks scorched. And all around spread ulcers, some at a distance, others by the wound, emitting a dark blue poison; and over the whole body the piercing bane eats its way with its acute inflammation; and in the throat and about the uvula retchings following fast upon one another convulse the victim. The body is oppressed also with failures of sense in every part, and forthwith in the limbs and loins is seated a burdening, dangerous weakness, and heavy darkness settles in the head. Meantime the sufferer at one moment has his throat parched with dry thirst, often too he 250 is seized with cold from the finger-tips, while all over his frame an eruption with wintry rage lies heavy upon him. And again a man often turns yellow all over his body and vomits up the bile that lies upon his stomach, while a moist sweat, colder than the falling snow, envelops his limbs. In some cases his colour is that of sombre lead, in others his hue is murky, or again it is like flowers of copper.

You would do well also to learn of the crafty CERASTES, who attacks like the Male Viper, which he resembles in equality of size. True, the Viper is hornless, whereas the Cerastes boasts 260 sometimes four horns sometimes two, and his dust-coloured skin is rough, and it is his habit to sleep in the sand or in the ruts down a road. The Viper writhing himself darts swiftly forward on a straight course with the long winding of his belly, whereas the Cerastes rolls on with clumsy movements of his middle,

χολόωντας ἐπήρυγε Π   257 ἠερόεσσαν BPRVv -εσσα ΠG -εντας K | ὅτ' ΠV
τότ' cett. | χάλκης Σ v.l.   260 post 261 colloc. BKP (?)   261 ὅτ' ἐν Π   τότ'
ἐν, τότε δ' ἐν Ω   263 κατὰ Et.M. 174.37   παρὰ codd.   265 γαστρῆς Π

οἶμον ὁδοιπλανέων σκολιὴν τετρηχότι νώτῳ,
τράμπιος ὁλκαίης ἀκάτῳ ἴσος ἤ τε δι' ἅλμης
πλευρὸν ὅλον βάπτουσα κακοσταθέοντος ἀήτεω
270 εἰς ἄνεμον βεβίηται ἀπόκρουστος λιβὸς οὔρῳ.
τοῦ μέν, ὅτ' ἐμβρύξῃσιν, ἀεικέλιον περὶ νύχμα
ἥλῳ ἐειδόμενον τυλόεν πέλει· αἱ δὲ πελιδναί
φλύκταιναι πέμφιξιν ἐειδόμεναι ὑετοῖο
δάχμα πέρι πλάζονται, ἀμυδρήεσσαι ἐς ὠπήν.
275 ἤτοι ἀφαυρότερον τελέει πόνον, ἐννέα δ' αὐγάς
ἠελίου μογέων ἐπιόσσεται, οἶσι κεράστης
οὐλόμενος κακοεργὸν ἐνιχραύσῃ κυνόδοντα.
διπλῷ δ' ἐν βουβῶνι καὶ ἰγνύσιν ἀσκελὲς αὔτως
μόχθος ἐνιτρέφεται, πελιὸς δέ οἱ ἐμφέρεται χρώς·
280 τῶν δέ τε καμνόντων ὀλίγος περὶ ἅψεα θυμός
λείπεται ἐκ καμάτοιο· μόλις γε μὲν ἔκφυγον αἶσαν.
Σῆμα δέ τοι δάκεος αἱμορρόου αὖτις ἐνίψω,
ὅς τε κατ' ἀμβαθμοὺς πετρώδεας ἐνδυκὲς αὔει,
τρηχὺν ὑπάρπεζον θαλάμην ὀλιγήρεα τεύχων
285 ἔνθ' εἰλυθμὸν ἔχεσκεν ἐπεί τ' ἐκορέσσατο φορβῆς.
μήκει μὲν ποδὸς ἴχνος ἰσάζεται, αὐτὰρ ἐπ' εὖρος
τέτρυται μύουρος ἀπὸ φλογέοιο καρήνου,
ἄλλοτε μὲν χροιῇ ψολόεις, ὁτὲ δ' ἔμπαλιν αἰθός.
δειρὴν δ' ἐσφήκωται ἅλις, πεδανὴ δέ οἱ οὐρή
290 ζαχρειὲς θλιφθεῖσα κατομφάλιος τετάνυσται.
τοῦ μὲν ὑπὸ νιφόεντα κεράατα δοιὰ μετώπῳ
ἔγκειται πάρνοψι φάη λογάδας τι προσεικῆ·
σμερδαλέον δ' ἐπί οἱ λαμυρὸν πέφρικε κάρηνον.
δοχμὰ δ' ἐπισκάζων ὀλίγον δέμας οἷα κεράστης
295 μέσσου ὅγ' ἐκ νώτου βαιὸν πλόον αἰὲν ὀκέλλει,

268 τράμβιδος Π τράμπιδος OSch. | καμάτῳ GMΣ v.l.   271 ὅταν βρύξῃσιν ω | νύχμα GM νύγ- cett., quae variatio alibi non notatur   274 πέρι PG πέριξ cett. | ἀμυδρήεσσαν ἐνωπήν Π   276 ᾧ κε Bent.   277 οὐλόμενον ω   278 διπλοῖς...βουβῶσι ω   281 μόγις GMVv πολεῖς Σ v.l.   282 αὖτις Π Et.M.245.38 αὐτίκ' ω | ἐνίψω Et.M. -ίσπω codd.   283 ἀμβαθμοὺς OSch.

46

meandering on a crooked path with his scaly back, like to the
dinghy of a merchantman dipping its whole side in the brine
when the wind is contrary, as it forces its way to windward 270
when driven back by the south-westerly gale. When the
Cerastes bites, the disfiguring wound turns callous all around
like a wart, and livid blisters like drops of rain move round
about the bite, dimly discernible to the eye. True, the man in
whom the deadly Cerastes strikes his mischief-working fang
goes through less acute pain, but nine suns of suffering does he
behold. And in either groin and the hams the trouble festers
persistent ever, while his skin has a livid appearance. And from 280
their suffering little strength is left in the joints of those afflicted,
and with difficulty do they escape death.

Next I will tell you what marks the BLOOD-LETTING snake,
which always sleeps in rocky ascents, making a small, rough lair
under a hedge. There it has its lurking-place when it has gorged
its fill. It equals a footprint in length, but as to breadth it
dwindles tapering from the fiery head down. At times it is of
a sooty hue, or again a reddish brown. It narrows moderately
at the neck, and its tail is sharply compressed and stretches 290
flattened from the middle onward. In its forehead beneath its
snow-white horns are planted two eyes, of which the irises are
somewhat like those of locusts, and on high rises terrible its
devouring head. And with an oblique and halting movement it
ever steers its little body on its brief journeys from the middle of

βαθμοὺς Π εἰλυθμοὺς ω Et.M. 299.47 | αἰὲν ἰαύει Et.M.: cf. 263   287 τέτρυ-
πται, τέθρ- ω   290 ζαχραὲς V -άης Π | παρομφάλιος Π   291 ὑπὸ OSch. ὑπὲρ
codd. | καρήατα Π   292 τι προσεικῆ OSch. τε προσεικής codd.   295 σκαιὸν
Bent.: cf. 266

γαίη ἐπιθλίβων νηδύν, φολίσιν δὲ καὶ ὁλκῷ
παῦρον ὑποψοφέων καλάμης χύσιν οἷα διέρπει.
νύχματι δ' ἀρχομένῳ μὲν ἐπιτρέχει ἄχροον οἶδος
κυάνεον, κραδίην δὲ κακὸν περιτέτροφεν ἄλγος·
300 γαστὴρ δ' ὑδατόεσσα διέσσυτο, νυκτὶ δὲ πρώτῃ
αἷμα διὲκ ῥινῶν τε καὶ αὐχένος ἠδὲ δι' ὤτων
πιδύεται χολόεντι νέον πεφορυγμένον ἰῷ,
οὖρα δὲ φοινίσσοντα παρέδραμεν· αἱ δ' ἐπὶ γυίοις
ὠτειλαὶ ῥήγνυνται ἐπειγόμεναι χροὸς ἄτῃ.
305 μήποτέ τοι θήλει' αἱμορροῖς ἰὸν ἐνείη·
τῆς γὰρ ὁδαξαμένης τὰ μὲν ἀθρόα πίμπραται οὖλα
ῥιζόθεν, ἐξ ὀνύχων δὲ κατείβεται ἀσταγὲς αἷμα,
οἱ δὲ φόνῳ μυδόεντες ἀναπλείουσιν ὀδόντες.
εἰ ἔτυμον, Τροίηθεν ἰοῦσ' ἐχαλέψατο φύλοις
310 Αἰνελένη, ὅτε νῆα πολύστροιβον παρὰ Νεῖλον
ἔστησαν βορέαο κακὴν προφυγόντες ὁμοκλήν,
ἦμος ἀποψύχοντα κυβερνητῆρα Κάνωβον
Θώνιος ἐν ψαμάθοις ἀθρήσατο· τύψε γὰρ εὐνῇ
αὐχέν' ἀποθλιφθεῖσα καὶ ἐν βαρὺν ἤρυγεν ἰόν
315 αἱμορροῖς θήλεια, κακὸν δέ οἱ ἔχραε κοῖτον.
τῷ δ' Ἑλένη μέσον ὁλκὸν ἐνέθλασε, θραῦσε δ' ἀκάνθης
δεσμὰ πέριξ νωταῖα, ῥάχις δ' ἐξέδραμε γυίων·
ἐξ ὅθεν αἱμορόοι σκολιοπλανέες τε κεράσται
οἷοι χωλεύουσι κακηπελίῃ βαρύθοντες.
320 Εὖ δ' ἂν σηπεδόνος γνοίης δέμας, ἄλλο μὲν εἴδει
αἱμορόῳ σύμμορφον, ἀτὰρ στίβον ἀντί' ὀκέλλει,
καὶ κεράων δ' ἔμπλην δέμας ἄμμορον, ἡ δέ νυ χροιή
οἵη περ τάπιδος λασίῳ ἐπιδέδρομε τέρφει·
κράατι δ' ἐμβαρύθει, ἐλάχεια δὲ φαίνεται οὐρή
325 ἐσσυμένῃ· σκολιὴν γὰρ ὁμῶς ἐπιτείνεται ἄκρην.

296 ἐπιθλίβων OSch. ex Ael. N.A. 15.13   ὑποθ- codd. | ὁλκῷ Σ v.l.   οἴμῳ codd.
299 κραδίη OSch.   301 δι' Π   καὶ ω   302 πηδύεται ΠΜ(?)R(?)V
303 κατέδραμεν ω | ὑπὸ ω   304 ἄζῃ ω   308 μυδόωντες ω | ἀναπλείουσιν
ΠΜR² -πρίουσιν cett.   309 εἰ γ' ω: cf. 826   312 ἀποψύχοντα Π Et.Gud.

the back like the Cerastes, scraping its belly over the earth, and with its scaly body it makes a slight rustling as though crawling through a heap of straw. But when first it bites, a swelling of dark, unhealthy hue rises, and a sore pain freezes the heart, and the stomach's content turned to water gushes out, while on 300 the first night after, blood wells from the nostrils and throat and ears, freshly infected with the bile-like venom; urine escapes all bloody; wounds on the limbs break open, hastened by the destruction of the skin. May no Female Blood-letter ever inject its venom into you! For when it has bitten, all together the gums swell from the very bottom, and from the finger-nails the blood drips unstaunchable, while the teeth, clammy with gore, become loose.

If the tale be true, Bane-Helen coming from Troy was angered with this species when her company beached their 310 vessel by the tumultuous Nile as they fled before the dread onset of the north wind, what time she beheld Canobus, the helmsman, swooning on the sands of Thonis; for as he slept a Female Blood-letter, on which he had pressed, struck him in the neck and belched forth its deadly poison into him, turning his rest to ruin. Therefore Helen crushed the middle of its trailing shape, breaking the ligatures of the back about the spine, so that the backbone started from its body. From that day forward the Blood-letter and the crooked-roving Cerastes alone of snakes move haltingly, oppressed by their injury.

You would do well to recognise the form of the SEPEDON, 320 which in other respects resembles the Blood-letter in appearance, but it steers a straightforward path; moreover it is almost without horns, and its colour, like that of a carpet, is spread over a rough surface. Its head is heavy, but its tail appears short as it moves, for it curls the end like the rest of its body. Truly

297.52 ἀνα- ω   313 εὐνῆ Π αὐτόν ω   316 τῷ OSch. τῶν codd. | ἐνέκλασε, ἀν- ω   320 ἄλλο Eutec. ἀλλ' ὁ codd.   321 σύμμορφος ω   323 δάπιδος ω | ἐπιδέδρομε ΠGMR περι- cett.   324 κῆρα ἂτ ηδ' ἐμβαρύθουσα λοχεῖα Π 325 ἐσσυμένης MR

τῆς δ᾽ ἤτοι ὀλοὸν καὶ ἐπώδυνον ἔπλετο ἕλκος
σηπεδόνος, νέμεται δὲ μέλας ὀλοφώιος ἰός
πᾶν δέμας, αὐαλέη δὲ περὶ χροῒ καρφομένη θρίξ
σκίδναται ὡς γήρεια καταψηχθέντος ἀκάνθης·
330 ἐκ μὲν γὰρ κεφαλῆς τε καὶ ὀφρύος ἀνδρὶ τυπέντι
ῥαίονται, βλεφάρων δὲ μέλαιν᾽ ἐξέφθιτο λάχνη·
ἄψεα δὲ τροχόεντες ἐπιστίζουσι μὲν ἀλφοί,
λεῦκαί τ᾽ ἀργινόεσσαν ἐπισσεύουσιν ἔφηλιν.

Ναὶ μὴν διψάδος εἶδος ὁμώσεται αἰὲν ἐχίδνῃ
335 παυροτέρη, θανάτου δὲ θοώτερος ἵξεται αἶσα
οἷσιν ἐνισκίμψῃ βλοσυρὸν δάκος· ἤτοι ἀραιή
αἰὲν ὑποζοφόεσσα μελαίνεται ἄκροθεν οὐρή·
δάχματι δ᾽ ἐμφλέγεται κραδίη πρόπαν, ἀμφὶ δὲ καύσῳ
χείλε᾽ ὑπ᾽ ἀζαλέης αὐαίνεται ἄβροχα δίψης·
340 αὐτὰρ ὅγ᾽, ἠύτε ταῦρος ὑπὲρ ποταμοῖο νενευκώς,
χανδὸν ἀμέτρητον δέχεται ποτὸν εἰσόκε νηδύς
ὀμφαλὸν †ἐξξέρρηξε† χέῃ δ᾽ ὑπεραχθέα φόρτον.
ὠγύγιος δ᾽ ἄρα μῦθος ἐν αἰζηοῖσι φορεῖται,
ὡς, ὁπότ᾽ οὐρανὸν ἔσχε Κρόνου πρεσβίστατον αἷμα,
345 Ν ειμάμενος κασίεσσιν ἑκὰς περικυδέας ἀρχάς
Ι δμοσύνῃ νεότητα γέρας πόρεν ἡμερίοισι
Κ υδαίνων· δὴ γάρ ῥα πυρὸς ληίστορ᾽ ἔνιπτον.
Α φρονες, οὐ μὲν τῆς γε κακοφραδίης ἀπόνηντο·
Ν ωθεῖς γὰρ κάμνοντες ἀμορβεύοντο λεπάργῳ
350 Δ ῶρα· πολύσκαρθμος δὲ κεκαυμένος αὐχένα δίψῃ
Ρ ὥετο, γωλειοῖσι δ᾽ ἰδὼν ὀλκήρεα θῆρα
Ο ὐλοὸν ἐλλιτάνευε κακῇ ἐπαλαλκέμεν ἄτῃ
Σ αίνων· αὐτὰρ ὁ βρῖθος ὃ δή ῥ᾽ ἀνεδέξατο νώτοις
ἤτεεν ἄφρονα δῶρον· ὁ δ᾽ οὐκ ἀπανήνατο χρειώ.

Aliquot litteras vv. 333–44 conservat 𝔓2
327 μέλας ΠΜR μέγας cett.   332 τροχόεντες ΠΜRV(?) -εντα cett.
333 ἐπισσεύουσιν OSch. ἐπεσ- Π]σευου[𝔓2 -σεύονται ω (ἐπισ- K)
336 ἐνισκίμψῃ ΠV -χρίμψῃ ΜΣ v.l. -σκήψῃ cett.   337 ὑποζοφόωσα ω
338 δὲ φλ. Π | κρα[.]αθο ωπροπα[(αθο m. altera) 𝔓2   339 χείλε᾽ P(?) -λη

the wound of the Sepedon is deadly and agonizing, and its black, destroying poison pervades the entire body: upon the parched skin everywhere the hair withers and is dispersed like the down of a thistle when it is rubbed. For from the head and 330 the brows of the man who has been bitten the hairs break off and from the eyelids the dark lashes perish, while round spots bespeckle his limbs and leprous eruptions swiftly spread a chalk-like rash.

Again, the form of the DIPSAS will always resemble that of a small Viper; yet death will come quicker to those whom this grim snake assails. Its thin tail, darkish throughout, grows blacker from the end forward. From its bite the heart is inflamed utterly, and in the fever the dry lips shrivel with parching thirst. Meanwhile the victim, bowed like a bull over 340 a stream, absorbs with gaping mouth drink past measuring, until his belly bursts his navel, spilling the too heavy load. Now there is a tale of ancient days current among men how, when the first-born seed of Cronos became lord of heaven, he apportioned to his brothers severally their illustrious realms, and in his wisdom bestowed upon mortals Youth, honouring them because they had denounced the Fire-Stealer. The fools, they got no good of their imprudence: for, being sluggards and growing weary, they entrusted the gift to an ass for carriage, and the 350 beast, his throat burning with thirst, ran off skittishly, and seeing in its hole the deadly, trailing brute, implored it with fawning speech to aid him in his sore plight. Whereat the snake asked of the foolish creature as a gift the load which he had taken on his back; and the ass refused not its request. Ever

cett. | αὐαλέης Π | αὐαίνεται 𝔅2 ΠGMV ἀϑαί- cett.   342 ἐκρήξειε ꙍ]. ε 𝔅2 fort. ἐκρήξῃ τε | χέῃ 𝔅2ΠMR² χέει cett. χέοι Bent.   344 πρεσβ Ύστατ[𝔅2 -βύστατος Kv | αἷμα ΠGMR υἱός cett.   348 οὐ γὰρ Π   349 νωθεῖ ꙍ Et. Gen. B 29   -θοὶ Et. M. 85.30 | ἀμορμεύοντο Et. M.   ἀμοργ- Et. Gen. B 351 φωλειοῖσι MR   354 χρειοῖ, -εῖ, -ῃ ꙍ

THERIACA

355 ἐξότε γηραλέον μὲν ἀεὶ φλόον ἑρπετὰ βάλλει
ὁλκήρη, θνητοὺς δὲ κακὸν περὶ γῆρας ὀπάζει·
νοῦσον δ' ἀζαλέην βρωμήτορος οὐλομένη θήρ
δέξατο, καί τε τυπῇσιν ἀμυδροτέρῃσιν ἰάπτει.
Νῦν δ' ἄγε χερσύδροιο καὶ ἀσπίδος εἴρεο μορφάς
360 ἰσαίας· πληγῇ δὲ κακήθεα σήμαθ' ὁμαρτεῖ·
πᾶσα γὰρ αὐαλέη ῥινὸς περὶ σάρκα μυσαχθής
νειόθι πιτναμένη μυδόεν τεκμήρατο νύχμα,
σηπεδόσι φλιδόωσα· τὰ δ' ἄλγεα φῶτα δαμάζει
μυρία πυρπολέοντα· θοαὶ δ' ἐπὶ γυῖα χέονται
365 πρηδόνες ἄλλοθεν ἄλλαι ἐπημοιβοὶ κλονέουσαι.
ὃς δ' ἤτοι τὸ πρὶν μὲν ὑπὸ βροχθώδεϊ λίμνῃ
ἄσπειστον βατράχοισι φέρει κότον· ἀλλ' ὅταν ὕδωρ
Σείριος αὐήνῃσι, τρύγη δ' ἐν πυθμένι λίμνης,
καὶ τόθ' ὅγ' ἐν χέρσῳ τελέθει ψαφαρός τε καὶ ἄχρους,
370 θάλπων ἡελίῳ βλοσυρὸν δέμας· ἐν δὲ κελεύθοις
γλώσσῃ ποιφύγδην νέμεται διψήρεας ὄγμους.
Τὸν δὲ μετ' ἀμφίσβαιναν ὀλίζωνα βραδύθουσαν
δήεις ἀμφικάρηνον, ἀεὶ γλήνῃσιν ἀμυδρήν·
ἀμβλὺ γὰρ ἀμφοτέρωθεν ἐπιπρονένευκε γένειον
375 νόσφιν ἀπ' ἀλλήλων· χροιή γε μὲν ἠΰτε γαίης,
ῥωγαλέον φορέουσα περιστιγὲς αἰόλον ἕρφος.
τὴν μὲν ὅθ' ἀδρύνηται, ὀροιτύποι, οἷα βατῆρα
κόψαντες ῥάδικα πολυστεφέος κοτίνοιο,
δέρματος ἐσκύλευσαν, ὅτε πρώτιστα πέφανται
380 πρόσθε βοῆς κόκκυγος ἑαρτέρου· ἡ δ' ὀνίνησι
ῥινῷ δυσπαθέοντας ὅτ' ἐν παλάμῃσιν ἀεργοί
μάλκαι ἐπιπροθέωσιν ὑπὸ κρυμοῖο δαμέντων
ἠδ' ὁπόταν νεύρων ξανάᾳ κεχαλασμένα δεσμά.
Δήεις καὶ σκυτάλην ἐναλίγκιον ἀμφισβαίνῃ

Fragmenta vv. 377–95 in scholiorum lemmatis conservat Φι
355 ἀεὶ Π ἀπὸ ω   356 γ. ἰάπτει Π: cf. 358   357 ἀργαλέην ω: cf. 221
360 θησαίας Π   361 ὑδαλέη OSch. | μυσαχθῆ Bent.   362 δῆγμα Σ v.l.
364 θοῶς ω   366 ἐπὶ βρ. ω   367 χόλον Et. Gen. B 48   368 ἀζήνῃσι
ω | ἐν ΠGM ἐνὶ cett. | fort. τρύγη (vel -ῃ)...λίμνη   371 ἀγμούς Σ v.l.

52

since then do trailing reptiles slough their skin in old age, but grievous eld attends mortals. The affliction of thirst did the deadly brute receive from the braying ass, and imparts it with its feeble blows.

Come now and learn that the forms of the CHERSYDRUS and of the Asp are alike in appearance. Signs of a malignant nature 360 follow on his bite: all the skin upon the flesh, dry, loathsome, and bloated with putrid sores, breaks out from below, disclosing a clammy wound, while innumerable and fiery are the pangs which overcome the man, and sudden swellings are raised upon his limbs, plaguing him by turns now in this quarter now in that. This is the snake that first beneath some shallow mere wreaks his truceless malice upon the frogs; but when the Dog-Star dries up the water and drouth is upon the floor of the lake, then upon dry land he becomes dust-like and shabby, as he 370 warms his grim body in the sunshine, and with hissing tongue he haunts the thirsting ruts along the highways.

After him you shall learn of the AMPHISBAENA, less in bulk and slow of gait, two-headed, ever dull of eye. From either end a blunt chin protrudes, the one far from the other. Its body is earth-coloured and wears a skin ragged, speckled, and sheeny. This snake, when it comes to full growth, do wood-cutters, as though they had cut for a walking-stick a stem of twisted wild-olive, strip of its skin as soon as it appears, before the note of 380 the cuckoo in spring. The Amphisbaena benefits those with afflicted skin when crippling chilblains break out upon the hands of men overcome with cold, also when the bonds of their sinews slacken and weary.

You shall learn too of the SCYTALE, like in appearance to the

372 ὀλίζωνα ΠΚ   -ζονα cett. | καὶ μινύθουσαν ω (om. καὶ Vv)   373 γλήνεσ-
σιν, -αισιν ω   376 περιστιβὲς ΠΣ v.l.   377 βατῆρες Et. Gen. B 259 βοτῆρα Μ
Σ v.l. -ρες ᵽι ut vid.   380 τέττιγος ω   381 ἀεργοί ᵽι ω -γοῖς Π
383 ἠδ' ᵽι ω ἢ Π   384 αμφισφα[ίνη ᵽι

385 εἶδος ἀτὰρ πάχετόν τε καὶ οὐτιδανὴν ἐπὶ σειρήν
μάσσον᾽, ἐπεὶ σκυτάλης μὲν ὅσον σμινύοιο τέτυκται
στειλειῆς πάχετος, τῆς δ᾽ ἕλμινθος πέλει ὄγκος
ἠὲ καὶ ἔντερα γῆς οἷα τρέφει ὄμβριος αἷα.
οὐδ᾽ ἄρ᾽, ὅταν χαράδρεια λίπῃ καὶ ῥωγάδα κοίλην
390 ἦρος ἀεξομένου ὁπόθ᾽ ἑρπετὰ γαῖα φαείνῃ,
ἀκρεμόνος μαράθοιο χυτὸν περιβόσκεται ἔρνος,
εὖτ᾽ ἂν ὑπ᾽ ἠελίοιο περὶ φλόον ἄψεα βάλλῃ,
ἀλλ᾽ ἤγ᾽ ἀρπέζαις τε καὶ ἐν νεμέεσσι πεσοῦσα
φωλεύει βαθύϋπνος, ἀπ᾽ εἰκαίης δὲ βοτεῖται
395 γαίης οὐδ᾽ ἀπὸ δίψος ἀλέξεται ἱεμένη περ.
Τεκμαίρευ δ᾽ ὀλίγον μὲν ἀτὰρ προφερέστατον ἄλλων
ἑρπηστῶν βασιλῆα· τὸ μὲν δέμας ὀξυκάρηνος,
ξανθός, ἐπὶ τρία δῶρα φέρων μῆκός τε καὶ ἰθύν.
οὐκ ἄρα δὴ κείνου σπειραχθέα κνώδαλα γαίης
400 ἰυγὴν μίμνουσιν ὅτ᾽ ἐς νομὸν ἠὲ καὶ ὕλην
ἠὲ καὶ ἀρδηθμοῖο μεσημβρινὸν ἀΐξαντες
μείρονται, φύζῃ δὲ παλιντροπέες φορέονται.
τύμματι δ᾽ ἐπρήσθη φωτὸς δέμας, αἱ δ᾽ ἀπὸ γυίων
σάρκες ἀπορρείουσι πελιδναί τε ζοφεραί τε·
405 οὐδέ τις οὐδ᾽ οἰωνὸς ὑπὲρ νέκυν ἴχνια τείνας,
αἰγυπιοὶ γῦπές τε κόραξ τ᾽ ὀμβρήρεα κρώζων,
οὐδὲ μὲν ὅσσα τε φῦλα νομάζεται οὔρεσι θηρῶν
δαίνυνται· τοῖόν περ ἀϋτμένα δεινὸν ἐφίει.
εἰ δ᾽ ὀλοὴ βούβρωστις ἀϊδρείηφι πελάσσῃ,
410 αὐτοῦ οἱ θάνατός τε καὶ ὠκέα μοῖρα τέτυκται.
Κῆρα δέ τοι δρυΐναο πιφαύσκεο, τόν τε χέλυδρον
ἐξέτεροι καλέουσιν· ὁ δ᾽ ἐν δρυσὶν οἰκία τεύξας
ἢ ὅγε που φηγοῖσιν ὀρεσκεύει περὶ βήσσας

Fragmenta vv. 377-95 in scholiorum lemmatis conservat 𝔓1. Deest Π a v. 389
385 πάχετόν τε JGSch. -το πε Π -τος τε 𝔓1 ω (γε BGv) | σειρήν 𝔓1 ω δειρήν Π
386 πάσσον᾽ ω   387 στειλειὸν Π | πλεει 𝔓1 | ὄγκος 𝔓1 ω ὀλκός Π
388 ὄμβριος 𝔓1Κ ὄ(μ)βριμος cett.   389 οὐδ᾽ ἄρ᾽ OSch. οὐ γὰρ codd. |
κοίλην 𝔓1 πέτρην codd.   390 ὁπόσ᾽ OSch. | φαείν]η 𝔓1 -νει, -νοι codd.

54

Amphisbaena, though thick, and bulkier down to its useless tail, for the Skytale is of the thickness that men make the haft of a mattock, while the Amphisbaena's bulk is that of a maw-worm or of such earth-worms as the earth breeds after a shower. Nor at spring's oncoming, after it has quitted gully and hollow 390 cleft in the season when earth brings reptiles to light, does it browse upon the waving shoots on the fennel's branch, when it clothes its limbs with their new skin beneath the sun; rather does it retire to hedges and glades and lurk deep in slumber and feed upon what the earth may chance to yield, nor does it stave off its thirst for all its desire.

Consider too the King of Snakes, small indeed yet far excelling all others: his head is pointed; he is golden-hued and three palms' width in outstretched length. Truly none of the heavy-coiled monsters of earth abide his hissing when to feeding- 400 ground or forest or in craving for a watering-place they dart forth at noontide, but they turn and flee. His bite swells a man's body, and from the limbs the flesh falls away livid and blacken-ing. Nor even will a bird pursuing its track above the corpse, be it eagle or vulture or raven that croaks of rain, nor yet any species of wild beast that pastures upon the hills, feed upon it; such the terrible stench that it sends forth. Yet if so be that fatal greed draws one of them near in ignorance, death and a swift 410 ending are wrought for it on the spot.

Learn now the doom inflicted by the DRYINAS, which others call *Chelydrus*. It makes its home in oaks or may be Valonia oaks and dwells in mountain glens. For after it has deserted the

391 ἀκρεμονας 𝔓1   392 ἄψεα codd   ερ[𝔓1   394 βορειται 𝔓1   φορεῖται Σ v.l.
395 ἀλεύεται Σ v.l.   401 ἀίξαντες Et. M. 137.45   -τος codd.   402 φύзῃ G
-ξῃ, -ξει cett. | δὲ om. BKVv   404 ἀπορρείουσι BP   -ραίουσι, -ρέουσι cett.
407 νομάзεται Bernard   ὀνομ- codd.   408 τοῖσί(ν) περ GKv | ἐφίει JGSch.
ἐφείη codd.   409 πελάσσῃ GV   -σσοι, -σ(σ)ει cett.

[ὕδρον μιν καλέουσι, μετεξέτεροι δὲ χέλυδρον] ·
415 ὅς τε βρύα προλιπὼν καὶ ἕλος καὶ ὀμήθεα λίμνην
ἀγρώσσων λειμῶσι μολουρίδας ἢ βατραχῖδας
σπέρχεται ἐκ μύωπος ἀήθεα δέγμενος ὁρμήν.
ἔνθα κατὰ πρέμνον κοίλης ὑπεδύσατο φηγοῦ
ὀξὺς ἀλείς, κοῖτον δὲ βαθεῖ ἐνεδείματο θάμνῳ.
420 αἰθαλόεις μὲν νῶτα, κάρη γε μὲν ἀρπεδὲς αὕτως
ὕδρῳ εἰσκόμενος · τὸ δ᾽ ἀπὸ χροὸς ἐχθρὸν ἄηται
οἷον ὅτε πλαδόωντα περὶ σκύλα καὶ δέρε᾽ ἵππων
γναπτόμενοι μυδόωσιν ὑπ᾽ ἀρβήλοισι λάθαργοι.
ἤτοι ὅταν κώληπας ἢ ἐν ποδὸς ἴχνεϊ τύψῃ,
425 χρωτὸς ἄπο πνιγόεσσα κεδαιομένη φέρετ᾽ ὀδμή ·
τοῦ δ᾽ ἤτοι περὶ τύμμα μέλαν κορθύεται οἶδος,
ἐν δὲ νόον πεδόωσιν ἀλυσθαίνοντος ἀνῖαι
ἐχθόμεναι, χροιὴ δὲ μόγῳ αὐαίνεται ἀνδρός.
ῥινοὶ δὲ πλαδόωσιν ἐπὶ χροΐ, τοῖά μιν ἰός
430 ὀξὺς ἀεὶ νεμέθων ἐπιβόσκεται · ἀμφὶ καὶ ἀχλύς
ὄσσε κατακρύπτουσα κακοσταθέοντα δαμάζει ·
οἱ δέ τε μηκάζουσι περιπνιγέες τε πέλονται,
οὖρα δ᾽ ἀπέστυπται · τοτὲ δ᾽ ἔμπαλιν ὑπνώοντες
ῥέγκουσιν, λυγμοῖσι βαρυνόμενοι θαμέεσσιν,
435 ἢ ἀπερευγόμενοι ἔμετον χολοειδέα δειρῆς,
ἄλλοτε δ᾽ αἱματόεντα · κακὴ δ᾽ ἐπιδίψιος ἄτη
ἐσχατίη μογέουσι τρόμον κατεχεύατο γυίοις.
    Φράζεο δὲ χλοάοντα δαεὶς κύανόν τε δράκοντα,
ὅν ποτε Παιήων λασίῃ ἐνεθρέψατο φηγῷ
440 Πηλίῳ ἐν νιφόεντι Πελεθρόνιον κατὰ βῆσσαν.
ἤτοι ὅγ᾽ ἄγλαυρος μὲν ἐείδεται, ἐν δὲ γενείῳ
τρίστοιχοι ἑκάτερθε περιστιχόωσιν ὀδόντες ·
πίονα δ᾽ ἐν σκυνίοισιν ὑπ᾽ ὄθματα, νέρθε δὲ πώγων

Deest Π
414 Damn. JGSch.: cf. 421 noverant Σ Lyc. 909, Σ Arat. 946   421 εἰσκόμενος
Bent. -νον codd.   422 δέρε᾽ OSch. -ρη codd. *Et. Gen. B* 200   423 γναπτόμενοι G γναμπ- cett. *Et. Gen. B*   424 ὅταν κώληπας OSch. ὅτ᾽ (ὅγ᾽ MR)

water-weeds, the marsh, and the congenial lake, and is hunting
molurides and small frogs in the meadows, it is sent speeding in
expectation of the Gadfly's distasteful onslaught; whereat slip-
ping swiftly into the stem of some hollow oak it coils itself
and builds its lair in the depths of the wood. Its back is of 420
a smoky hue, but in the flatness of its head it resembles the
Hydrus, and from its skin exhales a hateful air, as when about
the damp horse-skins and hides the scraps of leather ooze
beneath the paring of the tanner's knives. And truly, when it
strikes the hollows of the knee or on the sole of the foot,
a stifling smell is diffused from the flesh; also there rises up
a dark swelling about the victim's wound; moreover he is
distraught, hateful distress shackles his mind, and his body is
parched with suffering. His skin hangs loose about him, so
consuming is the fierce poison which feeds ever upon him, and 430
an encircling mist, veiling his eyes, overcomes him in his sore
affliction. Some men scream and choke, and their urine is
stopped; or again they fall asleep and snore, oppressed with
frequent retchings, or from their throat discharging a bilious or
sometimes a bloody vomit; and last of all a dreadful plague of
thirst sheds a trembling upon their afflicted limbs.

Learn and consider the green and dark-blue DRAGON, which
once on a time the God of Healing fostered in a leafy oak upon
snow-capped Pelion in the vale of Pelethronius. Radiant indeed 440
does he appear, but in his jaw above and below are arrayed
three rows of teeth; gleaming eyes are beneath his brows, and
lower down beneath his chin there is ever a beard of yellow

ἐν κώληπος codd. *Et. Gen.* B | ὅτ' ἐν π. *Et. Gen.* B   425 κεδαννυμένη Σ v.l.
432 μυκάζουσι BGKP: cf. *Al.* 214   433 τοὶ δ' BKP   437 ἐσχατίη JGSch.
-ίη codd.   440 δρυφόεντι M   441 ἄγραυλος BPV   442 τρίστοιχοι G
-στιχοι cett.

THERIACA

αἰὲν ὑπ' ἀνθερεῶνι χολοίβαφος. οὐ μὲν ὅγ' αὔτως
445 ἐγχρίμψας ἤλγυνε καὶ ἢν ἔκπαγλα χαλεφθῇ·
βληχρὸν γὰρ μυὸς οἷα μυληβόρου ἐν χροῒ νύχμα
εἴδεται αἱμαχθέντος ὑπὸ κραντῆρος ἀραιοῦ.
τῷ μέν τ' ἔκπαγλον κοτέων βασιλήιος ὄρνις
αἰετὸς ἐκ παλαχῆς ἐπαέξεται, ἀντία δ' ἐχθρήν
450 δῆριν ἄγει γενύεσσιν ὅταν βλώσκοντα καθ' ὕλην
δέρκηται· πάσας γὰρ ὅγ' ἠρήμωσε καλιάς,
αὔτως ὀρνίθων τε τόκον κτίλα τ' ὤεα βρύκων.
αὐτὰρ ὁ τοῦ καὶ ῥῆνα καὶ ἠνεμόεντα λαγωόν
ῥεῖα δράκων ἤμερσε νέον μάρψαντος ὄνυξι
455 θάμνου ὑπαΐξας· ὁ δ' ἀλεύεται· ἀμφὶ δὲ δαιτός
μάρνανθ'· ἱπτάμενον δὲ πέριξ ἀτέλεστα διώκει
σπειρηθεὶς καὶ λοξὸν ὑποδρὰξ ὄμμασι λεύσσων.
Εἴ γε μὲν Ἡφαίστοιο χαλαίποδος ἐν πτυχὶ νήσου
βήσεαι ἠὲ Σάμον δυσχείμερον, αἵ τ' ἐνὶ κόλπῳ
460 Θρηικίῳ βέβληνται ἑκάς, Ῥησκυνθίδος Ἥρης
Ἕβρος ἵνα Ζωναῖά τ' ὄρη χιόνεσσι φάληρα
καὶ δρύες Οἰαγρίδαο, τόθι Ζηρύνθιον ἄντρον,
δήεις κεγχρίνεω δολιχὸν τέρας, ὅν τε λέοντα
αἰόλον αὐδάξαντο, περίστικτον φολίδεσσι.
465 τοῦ ιτάχετος μῆκός τε πολύστροφον, αἶψα δὲ σαρκί
πυθεδόνας κατέχευε δυσαλθέας, αἱ δ' ἐπὶ γυίοις
ἰοβόροι βόσκονται· ἀεὶ δ' ὑπὸ νηδύσιν ὕδρωψ
ἄλγεσιν ἐμβαρύθουσα κατὰ μέσον ὀμφαλὸν ἴζει.
ἤτοι ὅτ' ἠελίοιο θερειτάτη ἵσταται ἀκτίς,
470 οὔρεα μαιμώσσων ἐπινίσσεται ὀκριόεντα
αἵματος ἰσχανόων καὶ ἐπὶ κτίλα μῆλα δοκεύων,
ἢ Σάου ἠὲ Μοσύχλου ὅτ' ἀμφ' ἐλάτῃσι μακεδναῖς
ἄγραυλοι ψύχωσι, λελοιπότες ἔργα νομήων.

Deest Π
444 ἔπλεθ' ὑπ' BP | ἀνθερεῶνα KPVv   445 χολωθῇ MR   446 μυληβόρου
Eust. 705.63 Σ Il. 8.178   μυχη- GM²Σ v.l. Et. Gen. B 66   νυχη- cett.   ἀμυλη-

stain. Yet when he fastens on a man he does not hurt as other snakes, even though his rage be violent, for the wound upon the skin of one whose blood is drawn by his slender fang seems slight as that of a meal-nibbling mouse. From his earliest days the King of Birds, the Eagle, grows up cherishing fierce wrath against him, and against him with his beak he wages a war of 450 hate whenever he espies him moving through the forest, for every nest he lays desolate, devouring alike the young and the cherished eggs of birds. Nevertheless when the Eagle has just snatched in his talons a lamb or a swift hare, the Dragon will easily rob him, springing up from a thicket. The Eagle avoids him: and then there is a battle for the feast. But as the Eagle hovers round, the writhing snake is after him without cease, watching him with sidelong glance and grim eyes.

Should you chance to walk in some valley of limping Hephaestus's isle or go to storm-beaten Samothrace—these lie far off in the Thracian Gulf, where are Hebrus, the river of 460 Hera of Rhescynthium, and the snow-crested mountains of Zone and the oaks of Oeagrus's son, where too is the cave of Zerynthus—you will find the long monster CENCHRINES, which men call the spangled lion, dappled with scales. His bulk and his length vary, but in a twinkling he sends upon the flesh a shower of putrid sores which will not heal, and these with their consuming poison feed upon the limbs; and ever deep in the belly the dropsy with its load of pain settles about the mid-navel. At the hour when the sun's rays are at their hottest this snake eagerly resorts to rugged mountains, athirst for blood and 470 on the watch for the gentle sheep, while beneath the tall pines of Saüs or Mosychlus the shepherds cool themselves, forsaking

OSch. | ἔπλετο δῆγμα Et. Gen. B   449 ἐξ αἴθρης Σ v.l.   458 χωλοίποδος, κυλλόποδος Σ v.ll.   459 Σάμου δυσχειμέρου Bent.   465 πολύτροπον Gesner 466 αἵ τ' BV   470 λαιμώσσων Σ v.l. | ὀκρυόεντα BPR

μὴ σύ γε θαρσαλέος περ ἐὼν θέλε βήμεναι ἄντην
475 μαινομένου, μὴ δή σε καταπλέξῃ καὶ ἀνάγχῃ
πάντοθι μαστίζων οὐρῇ δέμας, ἐν δὲ καὶ αἷμα
λαιφάξῃ κληῖδας ἀναρρήξας ἑκάτερθεν.
φεῦγε δ' ἀεὶ σκολιήν τε καὶ οὐ μίαν ἀτραπὸν ἴλλων,
δοχμὸς ἀνακρούων θηρὸς πάτον· ἦ γὰρ ὁ δεσμούς
480 βλάπτεται ἐν καμπῇσι πολυστρέπτοισιν ἀκάνθης,
ἰθεῖαν δ' ὤκιστος ἐπιδρομάδην στίβον ἕρπει.
τοῖος Θρηικίῃσιν ὄφις νήσοισι πολάζει.
Ἔνθα καὶ οὐτιδανοῦ περ ἀπεχθέα βρύγματ' ἔασιν
ἀσκαλάβου· τὸν μέν τε ῥέει φάτις οὕνεκ' Ἀχαιή
485 Δημήτηρ ἔβλαψεν ὅθ' ἄψεα σίνατο παιδός
Καλλίχορον παρὰ φρεῖαρ, ὅτ' ἐν Κελεοῖο θεράπναις
ἀρχαίη Μετάνειρα θεὴν δείδεκτο περίφρων.
Ἄλλα γε μὴν ἄβλαπτα κινώπετα βόσκεται ὕλην,
δρυμοὺς καὶ λασιῶνας ἀμορβαίους τε χαράδρας,
490 οὓς ἔλοπας λιβυάς τε πολυστεφέας τε μυάγρους
φράζονται, σὺν δ' ὅσσοι ἀκοντίαι ἠδὲ μόλουροι
ἠδ' ἔτι που τυφλῶπες ἀπήμαντοι φορέονται.
Τῶν μὲν ἐγὼ θρόνα πάντα καὶ ἀλθεστήρια νούσων
φύλλα τε ῥιζοτόμον τε διείσομαι ἀνδράσιν ὥρην,
495 πάντα διαμπερέως καὶ ἀπηλεγές, οἷσιν ἀρήγων
ἀλθήσῃ νούσοιο κατασπέρχουσαν ἀνίην.
τὰς μὲν ἔτι βλύοντι φόνῳ περιαλγέι ποίας
δρέψασθαι νεοκμῆτας—ὃ γὰρ προφερέστατον ἄλλων—
χώρῳ ἵνα κνῶπες θαλερὴν βόσκονται ἀν' ὕλην.
500 πρώτην μὲν Χείρωνος ἐπαλθέα ῥίζαν ἑλέσθαι,
Κενταύρου Κρονίδαο φερώνυμον, ἥν ποτε Χείρων
Πηλίου ἐν νιφόεντι κιχὼν ἐφράσσατο δειρῇ.
τῆς μὲν ἀμαρακόεσσα χυτὴ περιδέδρομε χαίτη,

Deest Π
475 καταπλέξῃ GM² -φλέξῃ cett. | ἀνάγκη GKPV   479 δεσμούς GVv -μοῖς,
-μός cett.   480 καμπῇσι M κα(μ)πτ- BG(?)PV γναμπτοῖσι KRv   482 πολάζει OSch. πελ- codd.   483 ἐπαχθέα Bent.   486 περὶ BPV   490 πολυστρεφέας

the tasks of herdsmen. Do you not dare, bold though you be, to face him in his fury, for fear he wind about and strangle you as he lashes your body all around with his tail, and gorge your blood after he has broken both your collar-bones. But in fleeing weave ever a crooked, manifold track, and baulk the beast's course by starting aside. For by the many turnings and **480** twistings of the spine he injures its ligaments; whereas he moves rapidly and at his swiftest when his path is straight. Such is the serpent which haunts the isles of Thrace.

There too are the bites of the GECKO, hateful, though he is of no account. Of him the tale is current how the Sorrowing Demeter did him injury when she marred the limbs of him as a boy by the well Callichorum, after wise Metaneira of old had received the goddess in the dwelling of Celeüs.

Harmless reptiles also there are however which feed in the forest, the brakes and thickets and gullies in the country; and men call these *Elopes, Libyans,* and curling *Mouse-hunters*; and **490** with them all the *Darters* and *Moluri* and *Blind-eyes* too which are reported innocuous.

Now all the simples and remedies for these ills, the herbs and the time to cut their roots, I will expound to mankind thoroughly and in straightforward fashion,—herbs by whose aid a man may heal the urgent pain of sickness. While the wound is still bleeding and painful, pluck your herbs freshly (this excels all other remedies) from some place where snakes.feed in the thick wood. Choose first the medicinal root of Chiron; it bears the **500** name of the Centaur son of Cronos, and Chiron once on a snow-covered col of Pelion found and took notice of it. Its waving leaves, like Sweet Marjoram, encompass it about, and

OSch. **491** δ' OSch. θ' codd. **492** ἢ ἔτι OSch.: cf. 845, *Al.* 88 **497** βλύοντι GMR -зουτι cett. **498** νεοκμῆτας ὁ OSch. -τα τὸ codd. -τι τὸ Bent. **502** Πηλίου G -ίῳ cett.

ἄνθεα δὲ χρύσεια φαείνεται· ἡ δ' ὑπὲρ αἴης
505 ῥίζα καὶ οὐ βυθόωσα Πελεθρόνιον νάπος ἴσχει.
ἣν σὺ καὶ αὐαλέην ὁτὲ δ' ἔγχλοον ὅλμῳ ἀράξας,
φυρσάμενος κοτύλῃ πιέειν μενοεικέος οἴνης·
παντὶ γὰρ ἄρκιός ἐστι· τό μιν πανάκειον ἔπουσιν.
Ἤτοι ἀριστολόχεια παλίσκιος ἐνδατέοιτο,
510 φύλλ' ἅτε κισσήεντα περικλυμένοιο φέρουσα·
ἄνθεα δ' ὑσγίνῳ ἐνερεύθεται, ἡ δέ οἱ ὀδμή
σκίδναται ἐμβαρύθουσα, μέσον δ' ὡς ἀχράδα καρπόν
μυρτάδος ἐξ ὄχνης ἐπιόψεαι ἢ σύ γε βάκχης·
ῥίζα δὲ θηλυτέρης μὲν ἐπιστρογγύλλεται ὄγκῳ,
515 ἄρσενι δ' αὖ δολιχή τε καὶ ἂμ πυγόνος βάθος ἴσχει,
πύξου δὲ χροιῇ προσαλίγκιος Ὠρικίοιο.
τὴν ἤτοι ἔχιός τε καὶ αἰνοπλῆγος ἐχίδνης
ἀγρεύσεις ὄφελος περιώσιον· ἔνθεν ἀπορρώξ
δραχμαίη μίσγοιτο ποτῷ ἔνι κιρράδος οἴνης.
520 ναὶ μὴν καὶ τρίσφυλλον ὀπάζεο κνωψὶν ἀρωγήν
ἠέ που ἐν τρήχοντι πάγῳ ἢ ἀποσφάγι βήσσῃ,
τὴν ἤτοι μινυανθές, ὁ δὲ τριπέτηλον ἐνίσποι,
χαίτην μὲν λωτῷ, ῥυτῇ γε μὲν εἴκελον ὀδμήν.
ἤτοι ὅτ' ἄνθεα πάντα καὶ ἐκ πτίλα ποικίλα χεύῃ
525 οἷόν τ' ἀσφάλτου ἀπερεύγεται· ἔνθα κολούσας
σπέρμαθ' ὅσον κύμβοιο τραπεζήεντος ἑλέσθαι
καρδόπῳ ἐντρίψας πιέειν ὀφίεσσιν ἀρωγήν.
Νῦν δ' ἄγε τοι ἐπίμικτα νόσων ἀλκτήρια λέξω.
Θρινακίην μὲν ῥίζαν ἕλευ γυιαλθέα θάψου
530 σμώξας, ἐν δὲ σπέρμα χυτὸν λευκανθέος ἄγνου,
νῆριν, πηγάνιόν τε περιβρυές, ἐν δέ τε θύμβρης
δρεψάμενος βλαστὸν χαμαιευνάδος ἥ τε καθ' ὕλην
οἷας θ' ἑρπύλλοιο περὶ ῥάδικας ἀέξει.

Deest Π
506 ἀζαλέην BP   507 κοτύλῃ Bent. -λην codd.   509 πολύσκιος M
510 ἅτε OSch. τε codd.   518 ἀγρήσεις Bent.   520 τρίσφυλλον Et. M. 279.11

its blossoms are golden to view; its root, at the surface and not deep-set, is native in the dell of Pelethronius. This when dry or while still green, after crushing in a mortar, mingle in a *cotyle* of pleasant Wine, and drink. It is of service in every case; th e-fore men call it *Panacea* (all-healing).

Assuredly let BIRTH-WORT which grows in the shade be commended; the leaves it bears are like those of the Woodbine 510 with its ivy-shaped leaves, but its flowers are red with scarlet, while the odour diffused from it is heavy, and the fruit in the midst you will see to be like the Wild Pear upon the Cordate Pear-tree or the common Pear. The root of the female shrub is rounded into a lump, but that of the male is lengthy and extends down as much as a cubit, and in colour it resembles the boxwood of Oricus. This you will search after as a surpassing aid against the dread blow of Male and Female Viper. From it let a portion of a drachm's weight be mixed in a draught of tawny Wine.

Furthermore take to yourself the TREACLE-CLOVER as a pro- 520 tection against snakes, be it on some stony hill or in some steep glen (some call it Brief-flower, others would call it Trefoil); its leaves are like the Melilot, but its scent is like Rue. When however it sheds all its blossoms and its mottled leaves, it exhales a smell of bitumen. Then cut off enough seeds to fill the sauce-boat on your table, pound them in a mortar, and take to drink as a remedy against snakes.

Attend now and I will rehearse some compound remedies against disease. Grind down and take the strength-giving Sicilian root of FUSTIC; add a heap of the seed of the bright- 530 flowered AGNUS CASTUS, SAVIN, and the luxuriant RUE, and pluck a shoot of the earth-pillowed SAVORY, which in the forest spreads abroad fronds like those of the Tufted Thyme. Again

τριόφ- codd.　**522** ἐνίστοι GMPR² -πει cett.　**524** ποι. τεύχει BP　**527** πιέειν δ' *An.Par.* 4.65.12　πείθειν δ' *Et. Gen. B* 177　**528** δείξω M　**533** ῥακίδας BP: cf. Hsch.

THERIACA

ἄγρει δ' ἀσφοδέλοιο διανθέος ἄλλοτε ῥίζαν,
535 ἄλλοτε καὶ καυλεῖον ὑπέρτερον ἀνθερίκοιο,
πολλάκι δ' ἐν καὶ σπέρμα τό τε λοβὸς ἀμφὶς ἀέξει,
ἠὲ καὶ ἑλξίνην, τήν τε κλύβατιν καλέουσιν,
ὕδασι τερπομένην καὶ ἀεὶ θάλλουσαν ἰάμνοις·
πῖνε δ' ἐνιτρίψας κοτυλήρυτον ὄξος ἀφύσσων
540 ἢ οἴνης· ῥέα δ' αὖτε καὶ ὕδατι κῆρας ἀλύξαις.
    Ἐσθλὴν δ' Ἀλκιβίου ἔχιος περιφράζεο ῥίζαν.
τῆς καὶ ἀκανθοβόλος μὲν ἀεὶ περιτέτροφε χαίτη,
λείρια δ' ὡς ἴα τοῖα περιτρέφει· ἡ δὲ βαθεῖα
καὶ ῥαδινὴ ὑπένερθεν ἀέξεται οὐδεῖ ῥίζα.
545 τὸν μὲν ἔχις βουβῶνος ὕπερ νεάτοιο χαράξας
ἄντλῳ ἐνυπνώοντα χυτῆς παρὰ τέλσον ἄλωος
εἶθαρ ἀνέπνευσεν καμάτου βίῃ· αὐτὰρ ὁ γαίης
ῥίζαν ἐρυσάμενος τὸ μὲν ἕρκεϊ θρύψεν ὀδόντων
θηλάζων, τὸ δὲ πέσκος ἑῷ περὶ κάββαλεν ἕλκει.
550   Ἦ μὴν καὶ πρασίοιο χλοανθέος ἔρνος ὀλόψας
χραισμήσεις ὀφίεσσι πιὼν ἀργῆτι μετ' οἴνῳ,
ἥ τε καὶ ἀστόργοιο κατείρυσεν οὔθατα μόσχου
πρωτογόνου, στέργει δὲ περισφαραγεῦσα γάλακτι·
τὴν ἤτοι μελίφυλλον ἐπικλείουσι βοτῆρες,
555 οἱ δὲ μελίκταιναν· τῆς γὰρ περὶ φύλλα μέλισσαι
ὀδμῇ θελγόμεναι μέλιτος ῥοιζηδὸν ἵενται.
    Ἠὲ σύ γ' ἐγκεφάλοιο περὶ σμήνιγγας ἀραιὰς
ὄρνιθος λέψαιο κατοικάδος· ἄλλοτ' ἀμόρξαις
ψυχρὰ πολύκνημον καὶ ὀρίγανον, ἢ ἀπὸ κάπρου
560 ἥπατος ἀκρότατον κέρσαι λοβὸν ὅς τε τραπέζης
ἐκφύεται νεύει δὲ χολῆς σχεδὸν ἠδὲ πυλάων·
καὶ τὰ μὲν ἄρ σύμμικτα πιεῖν ἢ ἀπ' ἄνδιχα βάψας
ὄξεος ἢ οἴνης· πλεῖον δ' ἄκος ἕψεται οἴνῃ.

Deest Π ad v. 541
536 δ' ἐν MR δὲ, δ' οἱ, δ' αὖ cett.   538 ὕδασι GMR -ατι cett.   540 οἴνου
BMP | ἀλύξαις R -οις, -εις, -ειν cett.   543 περιστ(ρ)έφει Ω   546 παρὰ ΠGM
περὶ cett. | ἀλωῆς Ω   548 ἐρυσσάμενος GMPRVv   549 περὶ Π ἐνὶ, τάχα Ω

take the root of the double-flowered ASPHODEL, or else the upper
portion of its stem; often with them too the seed which the
enclosing pod ripens; or else HELXINE, which men call *Clybatis*
and which delights in streams and flourishes ever in water-
meadows. Drink them after crumbling them into a *cotyle* of
Vinegar or of Wine which you have drawn. Even with water 540
you might easily escape death.

Consider now the excellent root of Alcibius's BUGLOSS: its
prickly leaves grow ever thick upon it, and it puts out a coronal
of flowers like violets, but beneath them in the soil the root
grows deep and slender. Alcibius a Male Viper wounded above
the lowest part of his groin as he lay asleep upon a mound of
uncleansed grain by the margin of a piled threshing-floor,
straightway rousing him by the violence of the pain. Whereat
he pulled the root from the ground and first broke it small with
his close-set teeth as he sucked it, and then spread the skin upon
his wound.

Again, if you pluck off the shoots of the sprouting HORE- 550
HOUND and drink them with bright Wine you may ward off
snakes: this is the plant which draws down the udder of a young
cow which mothers not her first-born calf, and anon, swollen
with milk, she cares for it. Herdsmen call it *Meliphyllon*
(honey-leaf), others *Melictaena*, for all about its leaves the bees
lured by the fragrance of honey buzz busily.

Or else you should peel off the thin membranes of the brain
of a domestic FOWL, or pare fine some FIELD BASIL and MARJORAM,
or cut from a BOAR'S LIVER the tip of the lobe which grows 560
from the 'table' and inclines towards the gall-bladder and the
portal fissure. These then you should drink, mixed together or
separate, with a draught of Vinegar or Wine, though a fuller

---

551 χραισμήσαις BGRVv -σης M | σὺν οἱ. ω   **557** περὶξ μήν- ω | σμήριγγας
Σ v.l.   **558** λάӡοιο κατοικίδος ω | ἀμόρξαις Π: cf. Hsch. ὀμόρξαις, -ας, -εις ω
559 ψῆγμα ω Σ v.l. | πολυκνήμου BGMRV   **560** κέρσας BMPR   **562** ἤ ἀπ' Π
ἤ GKMRVv δόθι BP | βάψας Gow κόψ- codd.   **563** ἐ. οἴνης ω

ἐν δὲ φόβην ἐρύσασθαι ἀειθαλέος κυπαρίσσου
565 ἐς ποτόν, ἢ πάνακες, ἢ κάστορος οὐλοὸν ὄρχιν,
ἢ ἵππου τὸν Νεῖλος ὑπὲρ Σάιν αἰθαλόεσσαν
βόσκει· ἀρούρῃσιν δὲ κακὴν ἐπιβάλλεται ἅρπην,
ὅς τε καὶ ἐκ ποταμοῖο λιπὼν ζάλον ἰλυόεντα,
χιλοὶ ὅτε χλοάουσι νεὸς δ' ἀπεχεύατο ποίην,
570 τόσσον ἐπιστείβων λείπει βυθὸν ὁσσάτιόν περ
ἐκνέμεται γενύεσσι παλίσσυτον ὄγμον ἐλαύνων.
τοῦ μὲν ἀποπροταμὼν δραχμῆς βάρος ἰσοφαρίζειν,
ὕδατι δ' ἐμπίσαιο κύτει ἐναολλέα κόψας.

Μηδὲ σύ γ' ἀβροτόνου ἐπιλήθεο, μηδέ τι δάφνης
575 καρποῦ ἀραιοτέρης· μάλα δ' ἂν καὶ ἀμάρακος εἴη
χραισμήεις πρασιῇσι καὶ ἀνδήροισι χλοάζων·
ἐν δὲ τίθει τάμισον σκίνακος νεαροῖο λαγωοῦ
ἢ προκὸς ἠὲ νεβροῖο πάροιθ' ἀπὸ λύματα κόψας,
586 ἠὲ καὶ ἐξ ἐλάφοιο ταμὼν πηρῖνα θοραίην,
ἢ ἐλάφου νηδύν, τὸ μὲν ἄρ καλέουσιν ἐχῖνον,
580 ἄλλοι δ' ἐγκατόεντα κεκρύφαλον· ὧν ἀπερύσας
δραχμάων ὅσσον τε δύω καταβάλλεο μοίρας
τέτρασιν ἐν κυάθοις μέθυος πολιοῦ ἐπιμίξας.

Μηδὲ σέ γε χραίσμη πολίου λάθοι ἠὲ κέδροιο,
ἀρκευθίς, σφαῖραί τε θερειλεχέος πλατάνοιο,
585 σπέρματα βουπλεύρου τε καὶ Ἰδαίης κυπαρίσσου·
587 πάντα γὰρ ἀλθήσει καὶ ἀθέσφατον ἐκ μόγον ὤσει.

Τὴν δὲ μετ' ἐξετέρην θανάτου φύξιν τε καὶ ἀλκήν
φράζεο κουλυβάτειαν ἑλών· τροχαλῷ δ' ἐνὶ λίγδῳ
590 σώχειν, ἐν δέ τέ οἱ κοτύλην πτισάνοιο χέασθαι,
ἐν δὲ δύω κυάθεια παλαισταγέος οἴνοιο,
ἐν δὲ καὶ ἀργέσταο λίπευς ἰσόμοιρον ἐλαίου·
φύρσας δὲ πληγῇσι χολοιβόρον ἰὸν ἐρύξεις.

Deest Π a v. 564
569 νεὸς Gow νέον codd.   575 καρποῦ Bent.   -πὸν codd.   576 πρασιῇσι
Gow -ιῆς, -ιῇ, τε codd.   578 ἠὲ MR ἢ cett.   580 ἀπερύσσας BGMRV

cure will attend Wine. And strip the foliage from the evergreen CYPRESS for a potion, or ALL-HEAL, or the testicle which is fatal to the BEAVER, or that of the RIVER-HORSE which the Nile beyond Saïs with its black soil nurtures, and launches, a ruinous sickle indeed, upon the ploughlands. (For the beast, emerging from the muddy ooze of the river when the pastures grow green and the fallow has put forth grass, tramples and leaves behind 570 a deep track as long as that which it devours with its jaws as it cuts its returning swathe.) From it cut off a drachm's weight to match, and soak in water, shredding all together in a vessel.

And do not forget the WORMWOOD or the berries of the slenderer BAY; very serviceable too would SWEET MARJORAM be, which flourishes in garden-plots and borders. And include CURD from a nimble Leveret or from a Fawn of Roe or Red Deer after separating the impurities, or the seminal purse which you have cut from a Stag, or his paunch, which some indeed call the 'urchin' but others the 'intestinal snood'. Take of them 580 portions of two drachms' weight and throw them into four *cyathi* of old Wine and mix well.

And do not overlook the succour afforded by the HULWORT and the CEDAR-TREE, the JUNIPER BERRY and the catkins of the PLANE that invites to sleep in summer, and the seeds of the BISHOP'S WEED and the CYPRESS of Ida; for all these will heal you and will banish untold suffering.

Next consider another means of escape and protection from death, and take HELXINE and grind it in a round mortar and 590 pour in a *cotyle* of BARLEY GRUEL, adding two *cyathi* of Wine of ancient vintage, adding also an equal portion of gleaming Olive Oil; mix them by pounding and you will keep at bay the poison that bites like gall.

586 transp. Gow   583, 4 ante 587 habet B   584 ἀρκευθίς Scal. -θος codd. | σφαῖρα, -ρη KPVv   589 δ' om. BKP

THERIACA

Ἄγρει δ' ἐξάμορον κοτύλης εὐώδεα πίσσαν,
595 καὶ χλοεροῦ νάρθηκος ἀπὸ μέσον ἦτρον ὀλόψας,
ἠὲ καὶ ἱππείου μαράθου πολυαυξέα ῥίζαν
κεδρίσιν ἐντρίψας, ἐλεοθρέπτου τε σελίνου
σπέρματα· μεστωθὲν δὲ χάδοι βάθος ὀξυβάφοιο.
Ἔνθα καὶ ἱππείου προταμὼν σπερμεῖα σελίνου,
600 δραχμάων δὲ δύω σμύρνης ἐχεπευκέος ἄχθη,
ἐν δὲ θερειγενέος καρπὸν κέρσαιο κυμίνου
στήσας ἠὲ χύδην τε καὶ ἄστατον ἀμφικυκήσας·
πῖνε δὲ μιξάμενος κυάθῳ τρὶς ἀφύξιμον οἴνην.
νάρδου δ' εὐστάχυος δραχμήιον ἄχθος ἑλέσθαι,
605 σὺν δὲ καὶ ὀκταπόδην ποταμοῦ ἀποσυληθέντα
καρκίνον ἐνθρύψαιο νεοβδάλτοιο γάλακτος,
Ἰρίν θ', ἣν ἔθρεψε Δρίλων καὶ Νάρονος ὄχθαι,
Σιδονίου Κάδμοιο θεμείλιον Ἁρμονίης τε
ἔνθα δύω δασπλῆτε νομὸν στείβουσι δράκοντε.
610 λάζεο δ' ἀνθεμόεσσαν ἄφαρ τανύφυλλον ἐρείκην,
ἥν τε μελισσαῖος περιβόσκεται οὐλαμὸς ἕρπων·
καὶ μυρίκης λάζοιο νέον πανακαρπέα θάμνον,
μάντιν ἐνὶ ζωοῖσι γεράσμιον, ᾗ ἐν Ἀπόλλων
μαντοσύνας Κοροπαῖος ἐθήκατο καὶ θέμιν ἀνδρῶν·
615 μὶξ δὲ κονυζῆεν φυτὸν ἔγχλοον ἠδὲ καὶ ἀκτῆς
καυλοὺς ἠνεμόεντας ἰδὲ πτερὰ πολλὰ καὶ ἄνθη
σαμψύχου κύτισόν τε καὶ εὐγλαγέας τιθυμάλλους·
πάντα δὲ λίγδῳ θρύπτε, καὶ ἐν σκαφίδεσσι δοχαίαις
φαρμάσσων μέθυ †κεῖνο† χοὸς δεκάτῃ ἐνὶ μοίρῃ.
620 ἀλλ' ἤτοι γερύνων καναχοὶ περίαλλα τοκῆες
βάτραχοι ἐν χύτρῃσι καθεψηθέντες ἄριστοι
βάμματι· πολλάκι δ' ἧπαρ ἐνὶ σχεδίῃ ποθὲν οἴνῃ,
ἢ αὐτοῦ σίντατο κάρη κακὸν ἄλλοτε νύμφαις
ἐμπισθέν, τοτὲ δ' οἴνου ἐνὶ σταγόνεσσιν ἀρήξει.

Deest Π ad v. 625
595 ἅπαξ BGP   601 δ' ἀθερειγενέος ΚΣ v.l.   604 δ' OSch.   τ' codd. | εὐ-
στάχυος Σ v.l.   -εος R εὐσταθέος cett.   605 ποταμῶν ἄπο G   609 om. P
δράκοντες Gv   612 περιθαλπέα Σ v.l.   613 ἐν αἰζηοῖσι Mein.: cf. 343 |

Take also to the sixth of a *cotyle* fragrant PITCH and cut out the central pith from the green GIANT FENNEL; or grate the full-grown root of HORSE-FENNEL into JUNIPER BERRIES, also the seeds of the marsh-bred CELERY. The full depth of an *oxybaphon* should contain them.

Furthermore cut off the seeds of ALEXANDERS and two drachms' **600** weight of pungent MYRRH: cut too the fruit of CUMMIN that grows in summer and weigh them, or pour in at random and shake up unweighed. Then draw thrice a *cyathus* of Wine and mix with them before drinking. Take to yourself a drachm's weight of fruitful SPIKENARD and with it crumble into fresh-drawn Milk an eight-footed CRAB ravished from the river; some IRIS too which Drilon has fostered and the banks of Naron, the abode of Sidonian Cadmus and Harmonia, where as two fearsome snakes they move about the pastures. Take next the **610** thick-growing HEATH when in flower, round which the thronging bees crawl and feed; take too a young frond of the TAMARISK that bears no fruit, an honoured prophet among mortals, which Apollo of Corope endued with prophetic properties and authority over men; with these green FLEABANE, also wind-blown stems of ELDER, also MARJORAM leaves and blossom in plenty, and TREE-MEDICK and the milky SPURGE. Bray all these in a mortar, and in the containing vessels medicate wine with them and take in one-tenth of a *chous*. But of a **620** truth the tadpoles' all too noisy parents, FROGS, are excellent when boiled with Vinegar in a pot; often the LIVER of the biting SNAKE itself if drunk in common Wine, or the poisonous head administered sometimes in water, at other times in a small quantity of Wine, will help you.

αἰὲν 'A. Steph. Byz. 375.9   **614** μαντείας Steph. Byz. | ὁρόπειος Σ v.l. -αῖος Steph. Byz. v.l.   **616** πτίλα Bernard: cf. 524   **619** πῖνε Keydell   **622** Σχερίη, Σχεδίη Σ v.ll.

625 Μὴ σύ γ᾽ ἑλιχρύσοιο λιπεῖν πολυδευκέος ἄνθην,
κόρκορον ἢ μύωπα, πανάκτειόν τε κονίλην,
ἥν τε καὶ Ἡράκλειον ὀρίγανον ἀμφὶς ἕπουσι·
σὺν καὶ ὄνου πετάλειον ὀριγάνῳ, αὖά τε θύμβρης
στρομβεῖα ψώχοιο, κακῆς ἐμφόρβια νούσου.

630 Ἄγρει μὰν ὀλίγαις μηκωνίσι ῥάμνον ἐΐσην
ἑρσομένην, ἀργῆτι δ᾽ ἀεὶ περιδέδρομεν ἄνθῃ·
τὴν ἤτοι φιλέταιριν ἐπίκλησιν καλέουσιν
ἀνέρες οἳ Τμώλοιο παραὶ Γύγαό τε σῆμα
Παρθένιον ναίουσι λέπας, τόθι Κίλβιν ἀεργοί
635 ἵπποι χιλεύουσι καὶ ἀντολαί εἰσι Καΰστρου.
Νῦν δ᾽ ἄγε τοι ῥίζας ἐρέω ὀφίεσσιν ἀρωγούς.
ἔνθα δύω ἐχίεια πιφαύσκεο· τῆς δὲ τὸ μέν που
ἀγχούσῃ προσέοικεν ἀκανθῆεν πετάλειον,
παῦρον ἐπεί, τυτθὸν δὲ καὶ ἐν χθονὶ πυθμένα τείνει.
640 ἡ δ᾽ ἑτέρη πετάλοισι καὶ ἐν καύλοισι θάλεια,
ὑψηλή· ὀλίγῳ δὲ πέριξ καλχαίνεται ἄνθει,
βλαστεῖ δ᾽ ὡς ἔχιος σφεδανὸν δ᾽ ἐφύπερθε κάρηαρ·
τῶν μὲν ἀπ᾽ ἀνδρακάδα προταμὼν ἰσήρεα χραισμεῖν,
ἢ σφέλᾳ ἢ ὅλμῳ κεάσας ἢ ῥωγάδι πέτρῃ.
645 καί τε σύ γ᾽ ἠρύγγοιο καὶ ἀνθήεντος ἀκάνθου
ῥίζεα λειήναιο, φέροις δ᾽ ἰσορρεπὲς ἄχθος
ἀμφοῖν κλώθοντος ἐν ἁρπέζῃσιν ἐρίνου·
λάζεο δ᾽ εὐκνήμοιο κόμην βρίθουσαν ὀρείου
καὶ σπέραδος Νεμεαῖον ἀειφύλλοιο σελίνου,
650 σὺν δὲ καὶ ἀννήσοιο τὸ διπλόον ἄχθος ἀείραι
ῥίζαις ὁλκήεσσαν ὑπὸ πλάστιγγα πεσοῦσαν·
καὶ τὰ μὲν ὀργάζοιο, καὶ εἰν ἑνὶ τεύχεϊ μίξας
ἄλλοτε μέν τ᾽ ἐχίων ὀλοὸν σίνος, ἄλλοτε τύμμα

---

626 ἡμυόεντα ω   627 Ἡ. καὶ ὁ. GKMRVv | ἀμφενέπουσι ω   628 ὀριγάνῳ
Gow -νον codd. -νου OSch.   631 περιτέτροφεν ω | ἄνθη MR -θην Π -θει
cett.   632 om. Π | φιλεταιρίδ᾽ OSch.   638 ἀκανθεῖον Π   639 τε ω
640 πετάλῳ Π | καύλοισι ΠG καλύκεσσι cett.   641 καλχαίνεται ΠG πορφύρεται

You must not neglect the blossom of the sweet GOLD-FLOWER,
nor the BLUE PIMPERNEL with its closed eye, nor the all-healing
MARJORAM, which men honour as *Heracles's Organy*; and with
the Marjoram you should rub small a leaf of POT MARJORAM, and
dry pellets of the SAVORY that muzzle evil disease.

Be sure and take the well-watered RHAMNUS, like to the little 630
Wild Lettuce; it ever clothes itself in blossom of white. The
name whereby men call it is Good Companion, the men who
dwell about the tomb of Tmolus and of Gyges on the steep of
Parthenius, where horses that toil not pasture upon Cilbis, and
where the Caÿster rises.

Attend now and I will tell you of roots that are a help against
Serpents. First, learn the two kinds of VIPER'S BUGLOSS: of one
the prickly leaf is somewhat like Alkanet, since it is small, and
the root which it extends is short and on the ground. The other 640
kind has robust leaves and stalks, is tall, grows purple with
small blossoms all over, and puts out a head like that of a viper
but rough on top. Of these two kinds cut off an equal portion
and use as a remedy after shredding them on a block of wood
or in a mortar or a hollow stone. Also you should make a paste
of the roots of the ERYNGO and the flowering BEARSFOOT, and to
these two add an equal weight of the CAMPANULA that flourishes
about the hedgerows. Take too the heavy foliage of the FIELD-
BASIL upon the mountain and seed of the evergreen CELERY from
Nemea; with them let the double burden of ANISE raise the 650
scale that sinks with the weight of roots. These should you
knead, and having mixed them in a single vessel you may cure
at one time the deadly bane of Male Vipers, at another the

cett. Σ v.l.   **642** βλαστεῖ Gow -τη codd. | κάρηαρ OSch. -ειαρ Π κάρηνον ω
643 χραισμεῖ Gv -μη MR   **645** ἠὲ σύ ω | ἀλθήεντος ω   **646** ῥίζαν ω
647 χλοάοντος Σ v.l.   **648** ὀρείης ω: cf. *Al.* 372   **650** δίξοον Π | ἀείρας ω
652 ἐργάζοιο ΠRv

71

THERIACA

σκορπιόεν, τοτὲ δάχματ᾿ ἐπαλθήσαιο φάλαγγος,
655 τριπλόον ἐνθρύπτων ὀδελοῦ βάρος ἔνδοθεν οἴνης.
    Φράζεο δ᾿ αἰγλήεντα χαμαίλεον ἠδὲ καὶ ὀρφνόν·
δοιοὶ δ᾿ ἀμφὶς ἔασιν· ὁ μὲν ζοφοείδελος ὠπήν
ἤικται σκολύμῳ, τροχεὴν δ᾿ ἀπεχεύατο χαίτην·
ῥίζα δέ οἱ βριαρή τε καὶ αἴθαλος, ἠδ᾿ ὑπὸ κνημοῖς
660 σκοιοῖς ἐντελέθει φυξήλιος ἢ νεμέεσσι.
    τὸν δ᾿ ἕτερον δήεις αἰεὶ πετάλοισιν ἀγαυρόν,
μέσση δ᾿ ἐν κεφαλῇ δύεται πεδόεσσα μολοβρή,
ῥίζα δ᾿ ὑπαργήεσσα μελίζωρος δὲ πάσασθαι.
τῶν δὴ κυανέην μὲν ἀναίνεο, τῆς δ᾿ ἀπὸ φάρσος
665 δραχμαῖον ποταμοῖο πιεῖν ὑδάτεσσι ταράξας.
    Ἄλλην δ᾿ Ἀλκιβίοιο φερώνυμον ἄγρεο ποίην,
δράχμα χερὸς πλήσας, παύρῳ δ᾿ ἐν νέκταρι πίνειν.
τὴν μὲν ὑπὸ σκοπέλοισι Φαλακραίοισιν ἐπακτήρ
Κρύμνης ἄμ πεδίον καὶ ἀνὰ Γράσον ἠδ᾿ ἵνα θ᾿ ἵππου
670 λειμῶνες, σκυλάκεσσιν Ἀμυκλαίῃσι κελεύων,
κνυζηθμῷ κυνὸς οὔλῳ ἐπήισε θυμολέοντος,
ὅς τε μεταλλεύων αἰγὸς ῥόθον ἐν στίβῳ ὕλης
κανθῷ ἐνὶ ῥαντῆρι τυπὴν ἀνεδέξατ᾿ ἐχίδνης·
καὶ τὴν μὲν κλάγξας ἀφ᾿ ἑκὰς βάλε, ῥεῖα δὲ ποίης
675 φύλλα κατέβρυξεν, καὶ ἀλεύατο φοινὸν ὄλεθρον.
    Ἄσαι δ᾿ ἔγχλοα φλοιὸν ἐλαιήεντα κρότωνος
συμμίγδην πετάλοισι μελισσοφύτοιο δασείης,
ἠὲ καὶ ἠελίοιο τροπαῖς ἰσώνυμον ἔρνος
ἢ θ᾿ Ὑπεριονίδαο παλινστρέπτοιο κελεύθους
680 τεκμαίρει γλαυκοῖσιν ἴσον πετάλοισιν ἐλαίης.
αὔτως δὲ ῥίζαν κοτυληδόνος, ἥ τ᾿ ἀνὰ κρυμόν
ῥηγνυμένων ὀλοφυδνὰ διήφυσε ποσσὶ χίμετλα.
δήποτε δ᾿ ἢ βλωθροῖο πυρίτιδος ἔγχλοα φύλλα,
ἢ σκολοπενδρείοιο φέρειν ἀπὸ καυλὸν ἀμήσας.

654 ·τά τε ω   660 σκοιοῖς JGSch. e Σ   σκαι- codd. | ἢ Π   ἐν ω   662 φύεται ω
664 κυάνεον ω   666 αἴρεο ω   667 ἐνὶ MR   om. Kv | πίνοις ω   668 ἐπὶ ω
671 κνυζηθμῷ (κ. οὔλῳ) Bent.   -μὸν κ. -λον codd. | ἐφώρασε Σ v.l.   672 τρίβῳ

Scorpion's wound, at another the bite of the Poisonous Spider,
if you will crumble three obols' weight in Wine.

Consider too the white PINE-THISTLE and the dark kind also.
The two are distinct: the dusky is like the Golden Thistle in
appearance; it puts forth a circle of leaves, its root is strong
and dark, and it grows beneath shady mountain spurs or in 660
glades, shunning the sun. But the other you will find ever in the
pride of its leaves, while the head lies low and bloated in the
middle of them, and its root is whitish and honey-sweet to the
taste. Reject the dark root of these plants, but of the other stir
a piece of a drachm's weight in river water and drink.

Take herbage of another kind that also bears the name of
Alcibius, fill your hand full, and drink in a little Wine. This it was
that when hunting beneath Phalacra's cliffs, on Crymna's plain
and about Grasus, and where lie the meadows of the Horse, 670
as he hallooed to his Amyclaean whelps, he discovered through
the anguished whimpering of his lion-hearted hound; for as it
followed up a goat's trail along some woodland path it had
received the Female Viper's stab in the watering corner of its
eye. And with a howl it flung her off and readily ate the leaves
of this herb and escaped deadly destruction.

Administer plenty of the sappy, oily bark of the CASTOR OIL
TREE, together with the leaves of the thick BALM, or else the
plant whose name is that of the sun's turnings, and which, like 680
the glaucous leaves of the olive, marks the path of the retreating
scion of Hyperion. Take likewise the root of the NAVELWORT,
which in frosty weather draws out the painful chilblains on
the feet of those with broken skin. Sometimes you may take
the green leaves of the tall BINDWEED, or of HART'S TONGUE,
shearing off the stalk. Take too the Phlegyan ALL-HEAL, even

Σ v.l.   673 κανθοῦ Bent.   676 λάζεο δ' ω Σ v.l. | Ἐλαιήεντα Σ v.l
677 μελισσοβότοιο ω   682 ῥηγνυμένοις Bent. | παισὶ ΠV   πᾶσι M

73

THERIACA

685 ἄγρει καὶ πάνακες Φλεγυήιον, ὅ ῥά τε πρῶτος
Παιήων Μέλανος ποταμοῦ παρὰ χεῖλος ἄμερξεν,
Ἀμφιτρυωνιάδαο θέρων Ἰφικλέος ἕλκος,
εὖτε σὺν Ἡρακλῆι κακὴν ἐπυράκτεεν Ὕδρην.
  Εἰ δέ, σύ γε σκύλακας γαλέης ἢ μητέρα λαιδρήν
690 ἀγρεύσαις πρόσπαιον, ἀποσκύλαιο δὲ λάχνην
καρχαλέου καθύπερθε πυρὸς σελάοντος ἀυτμῆς,
τῆς δ' ἐξ ἔγκατα πάντα βαλὼν καὶ ἀφόρδια γαστρός
φύρσον ἁλὸς δίοιο καὶ ἠελίου δίχα τέρσαι
μή τοι ἐνισκήλῃ νεαρὸν σκίναρ ὠκὺς ἀίξας.
695 ἀλλ' ὁπόταν χρειώ σε κατεμπάζῃ μογέοντα,
σῶχε διὰ κνήστι σκελετὸν δάκος, οἷά τ' ἀφαυρόν
σίλφιον ἢ στροφάλιγγα περιξήροιο γάλακτος
οἴνῳ ἐπικνήθων· τὸ δέ τοι προφερέστατον ἄλκαρ
ἐσσεῖται, πάσας γὰρ ὁμῶς ἀπὸ κῆρας ἐρύξει.
700   Πεύθεο δ' εἰναλίης χέλυος κρατέουσαν ἀρωγήν
δάχματος εἶλαρ ἔμεν δολιχῶν ὅσα φῶτας ἀνιγρούς
ἑρπετὰ σίνονται· τὸ δέ τοι μέγ' ἀλέξιον εἴη.
ἤτοι ὅταν βροτολοιγὸν ὑπὲκ πόντοιο χελύνην
αἰγιαλῶν ἐρύσωσιν ἐπὶ ξερὸν ἀσπαλιῆες,
705 τήνδ' ἀνακυπώσας κεφαλῆς ἀπὸ θυμὸν ἀράξαι
μαύλιδι χαλκείῃ, βλοσυρὸν δ' ἐξ αἷμα χέασθαι
ἐν κεράμῳ νεοκμῆτι καμινόθεν, ἐκ δὲ πελιδνόν
οὖρον ἀπηθῆσαι πλαδάον εὐεργέι μάκτρῃ·
ἧς ἔπι δὴ τέρσαιο διατρυφὲς αἷμα κεδάσσας
710 δραχμάων πισύρων μίσγων βάρος· ἐν δὲ κυμίνου
δοιὰς ἀγροτέροιο, καὶ ἐκ ταμίσοιο λαγωοῦ
τετράμορον δραχμῇσι δύω κατάβαλλεο βρῖθος·
ἔνθεν ἀποτμήγων πιέειν δραχμαῖον ἐν οἴνῃ.
  Καὶ τάδε μέν τ' ὀφίεσσιν ἀλεξητήρια δήεις.

686 ἄμερξεν OSch. -σεν codd.   687 ἔρνος ΒΡΣ v.l.   691 καρφαλέου ω |
ἀυτμή Π   693 θείοιο ω | τέρσον ω   694 τοι Μ σοὶ Π τι cett. | ἐπισκή-
λην Π | μὴ σύγ' ἐνὶ σκύλῃ (P) Σ v.l.   696 ῥάκος OSch.   698 ἄλκαρ Σ v.l.
ἄλλων codd.   699 ἀλύξεις ω   701 εἶαρ JGSch.   702 ἀλέξιμον ω: cf. 805,

that which the God of Healing was the first to pluck by the
brim of the river Melas, when ministering to the wound of
Iphicles Amphitryon's son, what time with Heracles he was
burning the evil Hydra.

Now lay sudden hold on the MARTEN's young or their
mischievous mother, and strip their fur over the flame of a 690
fiercely blazing fire, and after rejecting all the inwards and the
stomach's excrements, dress with holy SALT, and then dry away
from the light of the sun, so that its swift shafts do not shrivel
the fresh carcase. But, when necessity comes upon you in
anguish, rub the desiccated beast thoroughly with a rasp as
though it were frail Silphium or a round cake of dried Milk,
grating it into Wine. That will be a most excellent protection,
for you will stave off death in all forms alike.

Learn also that the powerful aid of the SEA-TURTLE is a defence 700
against the bite of all the long, crawling creatures that injure
distressful mortals; and may you find it a strong protection.
Thus, when fishermen draw the murderous Turtle up out of
the sea on to the dry beach, do you, having turned it on its
back, strike the life from its head with a bronze knife and let the
coarse blood pour forth into an earthen jar newly baked in the
furnace; but draw off the livid, thin serum with a well-made
colander and on this dry and break up the clots of blood,
taking for your mixture four drachms by weight. And add two 710
drachms of WILD CUMMIN, and to each two drachms a quarter
by weight of the CURD in a Hare's stomach. From this cut off
one drachm and drink in Wine.

Against Snakes these remedies, you will find, will protect you.

Al. 4   703 βροτολοιγοῦ OSch. | ὑπὲκ OSch. ὑπὲρ codd. | χελύνην OSch.
-ώνην codd.: cf. Al. 555, 558   708 πλαδάον BGKPV -άων M -όον Π -όων
Rv -όοντ' K v.l. | λαέργει ΠGKΣ v.l.   709 ὑπὸ δὴ OSch. ἐπεὶ οὖν JGSch. |
διαδρυφὲς BMPRV | κεά(σ)σας Ω   710 μίσγειν JGSch.   713 οἴνῳ ΠK

715 Ἔργα δέ τοι σίνταο περιφράζοιο φάλαγγος
σήματά τ' ἐν βρυχμοῖσιν· ἐπεί ῥ' ὁ μὲν αἰθαλόεις ῥώξ
κέκληται πισσῆεν, ἐπασσυτέροις ποσὶν ἕρπων·
γαστέρι δ' ἐν μεσάτῃ ὀλοοῖς ἔσκληκεν ὀδοῦσι.
τοῦ δὲ καὶ ἐγχρίμψαντος ἀνουτήτῳ ἴκελος χρώς
720 μίμνει ὅμως, τὰ δ' ὕπερθε φάη ὑποφοινίσσονται,
φρίκη δ' ἐν ῥέθεϊ σκηρίπτεται· αὐτίκα δὲ χρώς
μέζεά τ' ἀνδρὸς ἔνερθε τιταίνεται, ἐν δέ τε καυλός
φύρματι μυδαλέος προϊάπτεται· ἰσχία δ' αὔτως
μάλκῃ ἐνισκήπτουσα κατήριπεν ἔχμα τε γούνων.
725 Ἀστέριον δέ φιν ἄλλο πιφαύσκεο, τεῦ τ' ἐπὶ νώτῳ
λεγνωταὶ στίλβουσι διαυγέες ἐν χροῒ ῥάβδοι·
βρύξαντος δ' ἀίδηλος ἐπέδραμεν ἀνέρι φρίκη,
ἐν δὲ κάρος κεφαλῇ, γούνων δ' ὑποέκλασε δεσμά.
Κυάνεον δέ τοι ἄλλο πεδήορον ἀμφὶς ἀίσσει
730 λαχνῆεν· δεινὸν δὲ φέρει καὶ ἐπὶ χροῒ νύχμα
ὅντινα γυιώσῃ· κραδίη δέ οἱ ἐν βάρος ἴσχει,
νὺξ δὲ περὶ κροτάφοις, ἔμετον δ' ἐξήρυγε δειρῆς
λοιγὸν ἀραχνήεντα· νέμει δέ οἱ ἐγγὺς ὄλεθρον.
Ἀγρώστης γε μὲν ἄλλος, ὃ δὴ λύκου εἴσατο μορφῇ
735 μυιάων ὀλετῆρος· ὀπιπτεύει δὲ μελίσσας,
ψῆνας, μύωπάς τε καὶ ὅσσ' ἐπὶ δεσμὸν ἵκηται.
ἄκμητον δ' ἐπὶ τύμμα φέρει μεταμώνιον ἀνδρί.
Ἄλλο γε μὴν δύσδηρι, τὸ δὴ σφήκειον ἔπουσι,
πυρσὸν ἅλις, σφηκὶ προσαλίγκιον ὠμοβορῆι,
740 ὃς δὴ θαρσαλέην γενεὴν ἐκμάσσεται ἵππου·
ἵπποι γὰρ σφηκῶν γένεσις ταῦροι δὲ μελισσῶν
[σκήνεσι πυθομένοισι λυκοσπάδες ἐξεγένοντο].
τοῦ δὲ καὶ οὐτήσαντος ἐπὶ κρατερὸν θέει οἶδος,
νοῦσοί τ' ἐξέτεραι· μετὰ γούνασι δ' ἄλλοτε παλμός,

Desunt Πv a v. 715.
715 περιφράζοιμι MRV   **716** βρυχμοῖσι BMR   **717** ἐπασσύτερον M -ος P
720 ὕπερθε OSch. ἔνε- codd.   **722** ἔνερθε OSch. ὑπε- codd.   **724** ἐνισκήμ-
πτουσα M -σκίμ- JGSch.: cf. 140, 336 | ἔχμα τε OSch. ἔχματα codd.   **725** τ'

Consider now the operations of the dangerous SPIDER and the symptoms that attend its bite. The one which is the colour of pitchy smoke is named the GRAPE; it moves its feet in succession, and in the centre of its stomach it has hard and deadly teeth. But even when it has fastened on a man, his skin nevertheless remains as though unwounded; yet the eyes above turn reddish 720 and a shivering settles on his limbs, and straightway his skin and his genitals below grow taut, and his member projects, dripping with foul ooze, and at the same time numbness descending upon him overcomes his hips and the support of his knees.

Learn of one different from these—the STARLET, on whose back striped bands gleam radiant on the skin. When it has bitten, a shivering comes unexpectedly upon the victim, a torpor is in his head and breaks the bonds of his knees beneath him.

Another kind is the BLUE SPIDER: it darts about off the ground and is covered with hair. Even on his flesh the victim of this 730 spider carries a terrible wound: his heart is heavy within him and night is about his temples, while from his throat he discharges a deadly vomit like a spider's web; and he thinks that death is near to him.

Yet another is the HUNTSMAN, and he is like the Wolf-Spider in form, the destroyer of blue-bottles; he lies in wait for bees, gall-insects, gadflies, and whatsoever comes into his toils. But the bite he inflicts upon man is painless and without consequence.

But another kind is an aggressive foe, the one men call the WASP-SPIDER, reddish and like the ravenous Wasp, which 740 resembles the horse in its high spirit, for horses are the origin of wasps and bulls of bees [which are engendered in their rotting carcases]. When this creature has inflicted a wound, severe swelling ensues and various forms of sickness, and in some cases

OSch. δ' codd.   727 ἀίδηλον Σ   728 δ' ὑποέκλασε OSch.: cf. 86   δ' ὑπέκ-
KV   δέ θ' ὑπέκ- MR   δέ γ' ὑπέκ- BGP   731 γυιώση B(?)MRV(?) -σει cett.
735 ὀπιπεύει M   738 δὴ Gerhard   δὲ codd.   742 damn. Bent.   744 δ'
add. OSch.   -σιν ἀλ- codd.

THERIACA

745 ἄλλοτε δ' ἀδρανίη· μινύθοντα δὲ τόνδε δαμάζει
ἐσχάτιον κακοεργὸς ἄγων παυστήριον ὕπνος.

Εἰ δ' ἄγε, μυρμήκειον, ὃ δὴ μύρμηξιν ἔικται,
δειρῇ μὲν πυρόεν, ἄζῃ γε μὲν εἴσατο μορφήν,
πάντοθεν ἀστερόεντι περιστιγὲς εὐρέι νώτῳ·
750 αἰθαλέη δ' ἐπὶ τυτθὸν ἀείρεται αὐχένι κόρσῃ·
ἄλγεα δὲ προτέροισιν ἴσα κνώπεσσι πελάζει.

Χειροδρόποι δ' ἵνα φῶτες ἄτερ δρεπάνοιο λέγονται
ὄσπρια χέδροπά τ' ἄλλα μεσοχλόου ἐντὸς ἀρούρης,
ἐνθάδ' ἐπασσύτερα φλογερῇ εἰλυμένα χροιῇ
755 εἴκελα κανθαρίδεσσι φαλάγγια τυτθὰ δίενται.
τοῦ μὲν ὅμως ἔμμοχθον ἀεὶ περὶ δάχμα χέονται
φλύκταιναι, κραδίη δὲ παραπλάζουσα μέμηνε,
γλῶσσα δ' ἄτακτα λέληκε, παρέστραπται δὲ καὶ ὄσσε.

Φράζεο δ' Αἰγύπτοιο τά τε τρέφει οὐλοὸς αἶα
760 κνώδαλα, φαλλαίνῃ ἐναλίγκια τὴν περὶ λύχνους
ἀκρόνυχος δειπνητὸς ἐπήλασε παιφάσσουσαν·
στεγνὰ δέ οἱ πτερὰ πάντα καὶ ἔγχνοα, τοῖα κονίης
ἢ καὶ ἀπὸ σπληδοῖο φαείνεται ὅστις ἐπαύρῃ.
τῷ ἴκελος Περσεῖος ὑποτρέφεται πετάλοισι,
765 τοῦ καὶ σμερδαλέον νεύει κάρη αἰὲν ὑποδρὰξ
ἐσκληκός, νηδὺς δὲ βαρύνεται· αὐτὰρ ὁ κέντρον
αὐχένι τ' ἀκροτάτῳ κεφαλῇ τ' ἐνεμάξατο φωτός,
ῥεῖα δέ κεν θανάτοιο καὶ αὐτίκα μοῖραν ἐφείη.

Εἰ δ' ἄγε, καὶ κέντρῳ κεκορυθμένον ἀλγινόεντι
770 σκορπίον αὐδήσω καὶ ἀεικέα τοῖο γενέθλην.
τῶν ἤτοι λευκὸς μὲν ἀκήριος οὐδ' ἐπιλωβής,
πυρσὸς δ' ἐν γενύεσσι θοὸν προσεμάξατο καῦσον
ἀνδράσιν αἰθαλόεντα· περισπαίρουσι δὲ λώβαις
οἷα πυρίβλητοι, κρατερὸν δ' ἐπὶ δίψος ὄρωρεν.

Desunt v et ad v. 767 Π
746 κακοεργὸς OSch. -ον codd. | ἄγων G ἄγον cett. | ὕπνος OSch. -ον codd.
748 πυρόεις Philum. 15.3 -όειν Mein. 749 πάντοθε δ' OSch. 750 αὐχένι
JGSch. -να codd. 752 ἄνευ Erot. 93.20 754 εἰλημένα BP 758 παρ-

a quivering, in others powerlessness in the knees; and the wasting man is overcome by an evil sleep that brings the final alleviation.

The ANTLET—now mark—which in truth resembles the Ant, has a fiery neck, though its body is dust-coloured; its broad and spangled back is all speckled, and its dusky head is raised but little 750 on its neck, yet it inflicts as much pain as the spiders aforenamed.

Where men go plucking with their hands, not using sickles, gathering pulse and other legumes amid the fields while still green, there in swarms, wrapped in fiery colour and like to blister-beetles, dart small SPIDERS. But for all their size around the troublesome bite of one blisters always rise, and the mind wanders and is crazed; the tongue shrieks disordered words and the eyes squint.

Consider now monsters which the grim land of Egypt fosters, like the Moth which the evening meal-time brings in to flutter 760 round the lamps. All the wings are dense and are covered with down, even as a man appears who may chance to touch dust or ashes. Such in appearance, it is reared among the leaves of Perseus's tree. Its terrible head nods ever in grim fashion and is hard, and its belly is heavy; its sting it plants in the top of a man's neck or on his head, and it may easily and on the spot bring the doom of death.

Come now, and I will speak of the SCORPION, armed with 770 an agonizing sting, and of its disgusting brood. The white kind is harmless and does no hurt. But the red inflicts a swift and burning fever on men's mouths, and the victims struggle convulsively beneath the wound as though caught by fire, and there rises a mighty thirst. The black kind on the other hand, when it

εστράφαται Bent.   761 ἀπήλασε BKP   762 ἔγχνοα G² -χλοα cett. |
κονίης JGSch. -ίλης codd.   764 τῇ JGSch.: cf. v. 210f. | Περσῆος GR
766 κέντρον Bent. -ρῳ codd.   772 κατεμάξατο Π   773 περιπλάζονται
Σ v.l. | λώβη ω

THERIACA

775 αὐτὰρ ὅ γε ʒοφόεις ἄραδον κακὸν ὥπασε τύψας
ἀνδρί· παραπλῆγες δὲ καὶ ἄφραστοι γελόωσιν.
ἄλλος δὲ χλοάων τε, καὶ ὁππότε γυῖον ἀράξῃ
φρῖκας ἐπιπροΐησι, κακὴ δ' ἐπὶ τοῖσι χάλαʒα
εἴδεται ἐμπλάʒουσα καὶ ἢν μέγα Σείριος ἄʒῃ·
780 τοίη οἱ κέντροιο κοπίς, τοιῷ δ' ἐπὶ κέντρῳ
σφόνδυλοι ἐννεάδεσμοι ὑπερτείνουσι κεραίης.
ἄλλος δ' ἐμπέλιος — φορέει δ' ὑπὸ βοσκάδα νηδύν
εὐρεῖαν, δὴ γάρ τε ποηφάγος αἰὲν ἄητος,
γαιοφάγος — βουβῶσι τυπὴν ἀλίαστον ἰάπτει,
785 τοίη οἱ βούβρωστις ἐνέσκληκεν γενύεσσι.
τὸν δ' ἕτερον δήεις ἐναλίγκιον αἰγιαλῆι
καρκίνῳ ὃς μνία λεπτὰ ῥόθον τ' ἐπιβόσκεται ἅλμης.
ἄλλοι δὲ ῥοικοῖσιν ἰσήρεες ἄντα παγούροις
γυῖα βαρύνονται· βαρέαι δ' ἐσκλήκασι χηλαί,
790 οἷά τε πετραίοισιν ἐποκριόωσι παγούροις·
τῶν δὴ καὶ γενεὴν ἐξέμμορον εὖτε λίπωσι
πέτρας καὶ βρύα λεπτὰ πολυστίοιο θαλάσσης.
τοὺς ἁλὸς ἐξερύουσι δελαστρέες ἰχθυβολῆες,
αὐτίκα δ' ἀγρευθέντες ἐνὶ γρώνῃσιν ἔδυσαν
795 μυοδόκοις, ἵνα τέκνα κακοφθόρα τῶνδε θανόντων
σκορπίοι ἐξεγένοντο καθ' ἕρκεα λωβητῆρες.
τὸν δὲ μελίχλωρον· τοῦ μὲν προμελαίνεται ἄκρη
σφόνδυλος, ἄσβεστον δὲ νέμει πολυκήριον ἄτην.
ἔχθιστος δ' ὅ τε ῥαιβὰ φέρει φλογὶ εἴκελα γυῖα
800 ἀνδράσι, νηπιάχοις δὲ παρασχεδὸν ἤγαγεν αἶσαν·
οἷς δὴ καὶ νώτοισι περὶ πτερὰ λευκὰ χέονται
μάστακι σιτοβόρῳ ἐναλίγκια, τοί θ' ὑπὲρ ἄκρων
ἱπτάμενοι ἀθέρων λεπυρὸν στάχυν ἐκβόσκονται
Πήδασα καὶ Κισσοῖο κατὰ πτύχας ἐμβατέοντες.

Deest v
775 ὥρορε Π (ex 774)   776 σπαίροντες τελέθουσι Σ v.l.   778 φρῖκος MRV
779 ἢν Π εἰ ω | ἄʒει BGKPR   782 δ' ὑπὸ Π δέ τε ω   785 οἱ om. ΠΚ ἡ MR
787 λεπτὰ OSch. λειπτα Π λευκὰ ω: cf. 792   788 δὲ ῥοικοῖσιν Π Gal. 18.1.538
δ' αὖ ῥαιβοῖσιν ω agn. Gal.   791 post 792 habent MRV   792 λευκὰ

has struck, causes a fearful agitation in a man: victims go out
of their wits and laugh without reason. But another kind is
greenish, and when it strikes a limb it inflicts shivering fits,
and after them a horrid eruption appears, even though the Dog-
Star burn scorching hot. Such in effect is the sharp edge of its 780
sting, and behind such a sting nine-jointed vertebrae extend
above its head. Another is livid; it carries beneath it a broad and
hungry belly, for in truth it is ever an insatiable eater of grass and
of earth; and it deals a stroke incurable upon the groin, so
ravenous the hunger in its hard jaws. But another kind you will
find like the crab on the sea-shore, which feeds in the delicate
seaweed and the noisy surf. Others again, like the bandy-legged
common crab to look at, are heavy-limbed and their weighty
claws are hard, and serrated as in the rock-haunting crabs. It 790
is from them that they have their allotted being, whenever they
quit the rocks and the delicate wrack of the pebble-strewn sea.
The fishermen with their baits draw them from the salt water;
but directly they are caught they slip into mouseholes, and there
the Scorpions, the deadly offspring of these dead crabs, are
born, to work ruin from wall and fence. Learn too of the HONEY-
COLOURED SCORPION: its end joint is black at the tip, and it
dispenses doom unassuageable and most deadly. But the worst
enemy of man is the one whose crooked legs are like fire: to 800
children it instantly brings death. Upon its back white wings
unfold themselves like those of the corn-devouring locusts,
which flitting over the tops of the corn feed on husked grain,
and haunt Pedasa and the vales of Cissus.

MRV: cf. 787 | πολυστίοιο OSch.: cf. 950, Al. 466 -στείοιο ΠΣ v.l. -ρροίζοιο
ΩΣ v.l. -φλοίσβοιο Σ v.l.   796 om. M   797 μὲν Π γὰρ Ω: cf. 809
799 δ' ὅ τε OSch. δ' ὅγε Ω δέ τε Π   801 οἱ Π | λευκὰ ΠΣ πυκνὰ Ω
802 σιτοβόρῳ Et. M. 216.9 -φάγῳ codd.

THERIACA

805 Οἶδά γε μὴν φράσσασθαι ἀλέξια τοῖο βολάων,
οἷά περ ἐκ βέμβικος ὀρεστέρου ἠὲ μελίσσης,
ᾖ τε καὶ ἐκ κέντρου θάνατος πέλει εὖτε χαράξῃ
ἄνδρα πέριξ σίμβλοιο πονεύμενον ἠὲ καὶ ἀγροῖς·
κέντρον γὰρ πληγῇ περικάλλιπεν ἐμματέουσα,
810 κέντρον δὲ ζωήν τε φέρει θάνατόν τε μελίσσαις·
Οἶδά γε μὴν καὶ ἴουλος ἃ μήδεται ἠδ᾽ ὀλοὸς σφήξ,
πεμφρηδὼν ὀλίγη τε καὶ ἀμφικαρὴς σκολόπενδρα,
ᾖ τε καὶ ἀμφοτέρωθεν ὀπάζεται ἀνδράσι κῆρα,
νήιά θ᾽ ὡς σπέρχονται ὑπὸ πτερὰ θηρὶ κιούσῃ·
815 τυφλήν τε σμερδνήν τε βροτοῖς ἐπὶ λοιγὸν ἄγουσαν
μυγαλέην, τροχιῇσιν ἐνιθνήσκουσαν ἀμάξης.
σῆπά γε μὴν πεδανοῖσιν ὀμὴν σαύροισιν ἀλύξαις,
καὶ σαλαμάνδρειον δόλιον δάκος αἰὲν ἀπεχθές,
ᾖ τε καὶ ἀσβέστοιο διὲκ πυρὸς οἶμον ἔχουσα
820 ἔσσυται †ἀκμήνησ† καὶ ἀνώδυνος· οὐδέ τί οἱ φλόξ
σίνεται ἀσβέστη ῥαγόεν δέρος ἄκρα τε γυίων.
ναὶ μὴν οἶδ᾽ ὅσα πόντος ἁλὸς ῥόχθοισιν ἑλίσσει,
σμυραίνης δ᾽ ἔκπαγλον· ἐπεὶ μογερούς ἁλιῆας
πολλάκις ἐμπρήσασα κατεπρήνιξεν ἐπάκτρου
825 εἰς ἅλα φυζηθέντας ἐχετλίου ἐξαναδῦσα.

· · · · · · · · · ·

εἰ ἔτυμον κείνην γε σὺν οὐλοβόροις ἐχίεσσι
θόρνυσθαι προλιποῦσαν ἁλὸς νομὸν ἠπείροισι.
τρυγόνα μὴν ὀλοεργὸν ἁλιρραίστην τε δράκοντα
οἶδ᾽ ἀπαλέξασθαι· φορέει γε μὲν ἄλγεα τρυγών
830 ἦμος ἐν ὁλκαίοισι λίνοις μεμογηότα κέντρῳ
ἐργοπόνον τύψῃσιν, ἢ ἐν πρέμνοισι παγείη
δενδρείου τό τε πολλὸν ἀγαυρότατον θαλέθῃσι·

Deest v ad v. 812
805 φράσσασθαι M φράσα- cett. | τοῖο MRV τοῖα Π τοῖσι cett.   807 om.
MRV   808 σίμβλοιο ΠV -οισι cett. | ἢ καχύροισι Π   809 γὰρ ω μὲν Π·
cf. 797 | ἐμματέουσα ω   810 fort. damnandus   817 πεδανοῖσιν ὀμὴν Salmasius
-σι δομὴν codd. | ἀλύξεις BKPR¹v   818 ἐπαχθές Π   820 ἔσσεται Π | ἀκμήνης Π

I can tell you however of remedies against the Scorpion's
strokes, just as·for those of the Buzzer from the hills, or of the Bee,
whose death follows from its very sting when it has stabbed
a man as he labours around the hive or in the fields; for as it
implants its sting, it leaves it in the wound, and to the Bee the **810**
sting is both life and death. Yes, and I know too the devices of
the WOODLOUSE, and of the deadly WASP, and of the tiny TREE-
WASP, and of the two-headed CENTIPEDE, which from both ends
can bestow death upon a man, and as the creature moves there
speed beneath it as it were the winged oars of a ship; also of
the blind and fearsome SHREWMOUSE, which brings destruction
upon men and meets its death in the wheel-tracks of carts. You
should certainly avoid the SEPS, which resembles the squat
lizards; and that treacherous and ever detestable beast the
SALAMANDER, which makes its way through unquenchable fire
[unharmed] and without pain; nor does the unquenchable **820**
flame injure its tattered skin or its extremities. Furthermore
I have knowledge of all the creatures that the sea whirls amid its
briny surges, and the horror of the MURRY, since many a time
has it sprung up from the fish-box and striking them with panic
has hurled toiling fishermen from their boat to seek refuge in
the sea... if it be true that this creature couples with deadly-
biting Vipers on the land, forsaking its salt pasturage. Again,
from the death-dealing STING-RAY and the ravening SEA-SNAKE
I can protect you. The STING-RAY causes trouble when it
strikes with its sting the toiler labouring at his hauled drag-nets; **830**
or if the sting is fixed in the trunk of some tree which is
flourishing in full pride, then, as though the tree were stricken by

-μηνος ω   ἄκμητος JGSch. | οἱ om. Π   **821** ῥακόεν JGSch.   **822** ῥοθίοισιν ω:
cf. *Al.* 289, 390   **823** μυραίνης ω Ath. 7.312 D   **824** ἐμβρύξασα ω (ἐκβ-
GAth.) | ἐπάκτρων ω   **825** post h.v. lacunam stat. JGSch.   **826** εἰ ΠAth.
εἴ γ' GKMv   εἰ δ' BPRV | οὐλοβόροις ΠAth.   ἰοβ- ω   **830** μεμογηκότα BKPv
832 τό γε ω | ἀφαυρότατον τελέθησι ω

THERIACA

τοῦ μὲν ὑπὸ πληγῆσιν ἅτ' ἠελίοιο δαμέντος
ῥίζαι σὺν δέ τε φυλλὰς ἀποφθίνει, ἀνδρὶ δὲ σάρκες
835 πυθόμεναι μινύθουσι· λόγος γε μὲν ὥς ποτ' Ὀδυσσεύς
ἔφθιτο λευγαλέοιο τυπεὶς ἁλίου ὑπὸ κέντρου.
Οἷσιν ἐγὼ τὰ ἕκαστα διείσομαι ἄρκια νούσων.
δὴ γὰρ ὅτ' ἀγχούσης θριδακηίδα λάζεο χαίτην,
ἄλλοτε πενταπέτηλον, ὅτ' ἄνθεα φοινὰ βάτοιο,
840 ἄρκτιον, ὀξαλίδας τε καὶ ὁρμενόεντα λυκαψόν,
κίκαμα τόρδειλόν τε περιβρυές, ἐν δὲ χαμηλήν
ῥεῖα πίτυν, φηγοῦ τε βαθὺν περὶ φλοιὸν ἀράξας,
σὺν δ' ἄρα καυκαλίδας τε καὶ ἐκ σταφυλίνου ἀμήσας
σπέρματα καὶ τρεμίθοιο νέον πολυειδέα καρπόν·
845 ἢ ἔτι καὶ φοινίσσον ἁλὸς καταβάλλεο φῦκος,
ἀχραές τ' ἀδίαντον, ἵν' οὐκ ὄμβροιο ῥαγέντος
λεπταλέη πίπτουσα νοτὶς πετάλοισιν ἐφίζει.
εἰ δ' ἄγε καὶ σμυρνεῖον ἀειβρυὲς ἢ σύ γε ποίης
λευκάδος ἠρύγγου τε τάμοις ἀθερηίδα ῥίζαν
850 ἄμμιγα καχρυφόρῳ λιβανωτίδι· μηδ' ἀπαρίνη
μηδ' ἔτι κουλυβάτεια περιβρίθουσά τε μήκων
θυλακὶς ἢ ἐπιτηλὶς ἐπὶ χραίσμησιν ἀπείη.
σὺν δὲ κράδης κυέουσαν ἀποτμήξαιο κορύνην,
ἢ αὐτοὺς κόκκυγας ἐρινάδος, οἵ τε πρὸ ἄλλης
855 γογγύλοι ἐκφαίνουσιν ἀνοιδείοντες ὀπώρης.
λάζεο καὶ πυράκανθαν ἰδὲ φλόμου ἀργέος ἄνθην,
ἄμμιγα δ' αἰγίλοπός τε χελιδονίου τε πέτηλα,
δαύκειον, ῥίζαν τε βρυωνίδος, ἢ καὶ ἔφηλιν
θηλυτέρης ἐχθρήν τε χρόης ὠμόρξατο λεύκην.
860 ἐν δὲ περιστερόεντα κατασμώξαιο πέτηλα,
ἢ καὶ ἀλεξιάρης πτόρθους ἀπαμέργεο ῥάμνου·
μούνη γὰρ δρήστειρα βροτῶν ἀπὸ κῆρας ἐρύκει.
ναὶ μὴν παρθενίοιο νεοδρέπτους ὀροδάμνους,

Deest Π a v. 833 ad v. 848
837 fort. ante h.v. lacuna statuenda   852 ἐπεπλεῖτις Π   854 ἐρινάδας (?) Π
856 ἀργεος ΠG marg.   ἄρρενος cett.   857 αἰγίλιπός ω   858 ἴзας ω

the fierce beams of the sun, its roots and with them its leafage wither; on a man his flesh rots and wastes away. Indeed the story tells how Odysseus of yore perished from the baneful sting of this monster from the sea.

Now will I rehearse the several remedies for these afflictions. You should take at one time the leaves, like wild-lettuce, of ALKANET, at another POTENTILLA, or the crimson flowers of the BRAMBLE; BEARWORT, SORREL, and the long-stemmed VIPER'S 840 HERB, CICAMUM, the luxuriant HARTWORT, and you may well include GROUND-PINE and thick bark which you have broken off from the OAK TREE; with them too HEDGE-PARSLEY, and seeds gathered from the CARROT, and the fresh and variegated berries from the TEREBINTH. Moreover you should store up the purple ORCHELLA-WEED from the sea, and the unspotted MAIDEN-HAIR, on whose leaves the fine moisture falling from the bursting rainstorm does not settle. Note too, you should cut the ever-blooming CRETAN ALEXANDERS or the tufted root of the DEAD-NETTLE and of the ERYNGO, together with the fruit-bearing 850 ROSEMARY FRANKINCENSE. Let there be present also CLEAVERS and HELXINE and the heavy-headed POPPY, CAPSULED or HORNED, to protect you. Cut off also a budding shoot of the FIG-TREE or the actual fruit of the WILD FIG which appears orbed and swelling before other fruit. Take too the FIERY THORN and the blossoms of the bright MULLEIN, and with them leaves of HAVER-GRASS, and CELANDINE, WILD CARROT, and the root of BRYONY, which wipes away freckles and the rash abhorrent to women's skin. Powder also the leaves of VERVAIN, or pluck the twigs of 860 the protective RHAMNUS, for by itself it is efficacious to ward off death from a man. Again, gather freshly plucked branches of FEVERFEW, BLUE PIMPERNEL, or HART'S TONGUE, or take a portion

859 θηλυτέρης ΠΒΡ   -ρων cett. | τε om. ΒΡ | χρόης OSch.   χροὸς GMR   χροιῆς ΒΚΡν   χλης Π   861 ἀπαμείρεο Π   862 δρήστειρα Σ v.l.   νή- ΩΣ v.l. μηστῆρα Π   863 νεοθρεπτοῖ Π

κόρκορον ἢ πεταλῖτιν ἀμέργεο, πολλάκι μίλτου
865 Λημνίδος ἢ πάσῃσι πέλει θελκτήριον ἄταις.
δήποτε καὶ σικύοιο τάμοις ἐνιπευκέα ῥίζαν
ἀγροτέρου· νηδὺν δὲ καὶ ἐμβρίθουσαν ἀνίης
ἤμυνεν καὶ καρπὸς ἐυρρήχου παλιούρου·
σὺν καὶ ἀκανθοβόλος χαίτη, νεαλεῖς τ' ὀρόβακχοι
870 σίδης ὑσγινόεντος ἐπιμύοντας ὀλόσχους
αὐχενίους ἵνα λεπτὰ πέριξ ἐνερεύθεται ἄνθη·
ἄλλοτε δ' ὕσσωπός τε καὶ ἡ πολύγουνος ὄνωνις,
φύλλα τε τηλεφίλοιο, νέον τ' ἐν βότρυσι κλῆμα,
ἀγλῖθες, καὶ καρπὸς ὀρειγενέος κορίοιο,
875 ἢ καὶ λεπτοθρίοιο πολύχνοα φύλλα κονύζης.
πολλάκι δ' ἢ πέπεριν κόψας νέον ἢ ἀπὸ Μήδων
κάρδαμον ἐμπίσαιο· σὲ δ' ἂν πολυάνθεα γλήχων
στρύχνον τ' ἠδὲ σίνηπι κακηπελέοντα σαώσαι.
ἄγρει καὶ πρασιῆς χλοερὸν πράσον, ἄλλοτε δ' αὐτῆς
880 σπέρμ' ὀλοὸν κνίδης ἤ θ' ἑψίη ἔπλετο κούροις·
σὺν καί που νιφόεν σκίλλης κάρη, αὖά τε βολβῶν
σπείρεα, καὶ καυλεῖον ὁμοκλήτοιο δράκοντος,
ῥάμνου τ' ἀσπαράγους θαμνίτιδος, ἠδ' ὅσα πεῦκαι
ἀγρότεραι στρόμβοισιν ὑπεθρέψαντο ναπαῖαι.
885 εἰ δέ, σύ γ' ἐκ ποίης ἀβληχρέος ἔγχλοα ῥίζαν
θηρὸς ἰσαζομένην τμήξαις ἰοειδέι κέντρῳ
σκορπίου, ἠὲ σίδας Ψαμαθηίδας, ἅς τε Τράφεια
Κῶπαί τε λιμναῖον ὑπεθρέψαντο παρ' ὕδωρ,
ᾗπερ Σχοινῆός τε ῥόος Κνώποιό τε βάλλει,
890 ὅσσα θ' ὑπ' Ἰνδὸν χεῦμα πολυφλοίσβοιο Χοάσπεω
πιστάκι' ἀκρεμόνεσσιν ἀμυγδαλόεντα πέφανται·
καυκαλίδας, σὺν δ' αἰθὰ βάλοις φιμώδεα μύρτα,

Deest Π a v. 885
864 κόρκορον (cf. 626) ἢ πεπλεῖτιν ἀναδρέα Π   865 ἄταις OSch. -της codd.
866 ἐχεπευκέα ω: cf. 600   867 ἐμ. ἴησι Π   870 σίδης δ', θ', ω | ὑσγινόεντος
Bent. -τας codd. | ἐπιμύοντας OSch. e Σ ἐπημ- codd. | ὀρόσχους Π   873 τηλε-
φίλοιο Π -φύλλοιο ΒΡ -φίοιο cett.   875 πολύχνοα Σ v.l. Ath. 2.66E -χροα Π
-θρονα ωΣ v.l. | φοινίζης (pro φ.κ.) Π   876 πέπεριν GMRV -ρήν Π -ρι cett.

of Lemnian RUDDLE, which is soothing in all afflictions. Sometimes too you may cut the bitter root of the SQUIRTING
CUCUMBER; to a stomach even sore oppressed with anguish
also the fruit of the prickly PALIURUS affords relief; so too its
spiky leaves, and the young fruits of the POMEGRANATE with 870
scarlet on its neck-like, closing sepals where it reddens about
the slender flowers; at another time HYSSOP and the many-
branched REST-HARROW and the leaves of LOVE-IN-ABSENCE and
the fresh tendril on the GRAPE CLUSTER, CLOVES OF GARLIC, and
the seed of the mountain-born CORIANDER, or even the downy
leaves of the delicate FLEABANE. Often too you may cut off
some fresh PEPPER or Persian GARDEN-CRESS and administer it
in a drink; and the flowering PENNYROYAL and DEADLY NIGHT-
SHADE and MUSTARD too may save one in evil plight. Take
also the green LEAK from the garden-plot, or else the hurtful
seed of the NETTLE itself with which boys play tricks. With 880
these too perhaps the snow-white head of a SQUILL and the
dried coats of PURSE-TASSELS and the stalk of the dragon's
namesake, and the shoots of the shrubby RHAMNUS, and what
the wildwood PINES in the valleys nourish at the heart of their
cones. Look you, you should lop the green root of the feeble
herb SCORPIUS that men liken to the poisonous sting of the
beast, or WATERLILIES from Psamathe, and those which Traphea
and Copae foster by the waters of their lake, wherein discharge
the streams of Schoeneus and Cnopus, and the PISTACHIO NUTS 890
which look like almonds upon the boughs by the Indian flood
of the roaring Choaspes. Collect HEDGE-PARSLEY and the red-
brown, astringent MYRTLE-BERRIES and slips of SAGE and of the

Ath.: cf. *Al.* 332, 607   **878** τρύχνον Π: cf. 74   **879** αἱρεῖ Π | χαράον πρά-
σον Π | αὔης Bernard   **883** ἀσφαράγους Π   **884** ναπαίαις, -οις, -ης ὦ
887 Ψαμαθηιὰς Bent. | τε Τράφεια Lobeck (τε Τρόφ- Σ v.l.) τρέφει αἶα codd.
891 φιττάκι' ἀ. ἀμυγδαλέοισιν ὅμοια. γράφεται δὲ καὶ βιστάκια...ἀμύγδαλα
ὄντα π. Ath. 14. 649 D

THERIACA

κάρφεά θ' ὁρμίνοιο καὶ ἐκ μαράθου βρυόεντος,
εἰρύσιμόν τε καὶ ἀγροτέρου σπερμεῖ' ἐρεβίνθου
895 σὺν χλοεροῖς θάμνοισι βαλὼν βαρυώδεα ποίην.
ναὶ μὴν καὶ σίσυμβρα πέλει μειλίγματα νούσων,
σὺν δὲ μελιλλώτοιο νέον στέφος, ἠδ' ὅσα χαύνης
οἰνάνθης βρύα λευκὰ καταψήχουσι νομῆες,
ὅσσα τε λυχνὶς ἔνερθεν ἐρευθήεις τε θρυαλλίς
900 καὶ ῥόδον ἠδ' ἴα λεπτὸν ὅσον σπερμεῖον ἀέξει.
ἢ καὶ πουλύγονον λασίων ὑπάμησον ἰάμνων,
ψίλωθρον, καρπόν τε πολυθρήνου ὑακίνθου,
ὃν Φοῖβος θρήνησεν ἐπεί ῥ' ἀεκούσιος ἔκτα
παῖδα βαλὼν προπάροιθεν Ἀμυκλαίου ποταμοῖο,
905 πρωθήβην Ὑάκινθον, ἐπεὶ σόλος ἔμπεσε κόρσῃ
πέτρου ἀφαλλόμενος νέατον δ' ἦραξε κάλυμμα.
σὺν δέ τε καὶ τριπέτηλον ὁποῖό τε δάκρυα βάλλοις
τρισσοῖς ὁλκήεσσιν ἰσοζυγέων ὀδελοῖσιν·
ἠὲ σύ γ' ἕρπυλλον κεροειδέα, πολλάκι κρῆθμον,
910 ἢ ποίην κυπάρισσον ἀμέργεο, σὺν δὲ καὶ αὐτοῖς
ἄννησον Λιβυκάς τε ποτῷ ἐνικνήθεο ῥίζας·
ὧν σὺ τότ' ἀμμίγδην, τοτὲ δ' ἄνδιχα πίνεο θρύψας
ἐν κελέβῃ, κεράσαι δὲ σὺν ὀξεῖ, πολλάκι δ' οἴνῃ
ἢ ὕδατι· χραισμεῖ δὲ καὶ ἐνθρυφθέντα γάλακτι.
915 Ἢν δέ σ' ὁδοιπλανέοντα καὶ ἐν νεμέεσσιν ἀνύδροις
νύχμα κατασπέρχῃ, βεβαρημένος αὐτίκα ῥίζας
ἢ ποίην ἢ σπέρμα παρ' ἀτραπιτοῖσι χλοάζον
μαστάζειν γενύεσσιν, ἀμελγόμενος δ' ἀπὸ χυλόν
τύμμασιν ἡμίβρωτα βάλοις ἔπι λύματα δαιτός
920 ὄφρα δύην καὶ κῆρα κατασπέρχουσαν ἀλύξῃς.
Ναὶ μὴν καὶ σικύην χαλκήρεα λοιγέι τύψει
προσμάξας ἰόν τε καὶ ἀθρόον αἷμα κενώσεις,

Deest Π
895 βαλὼν OSch. -λοις codd. 897 μελιλλώτοιο GM²V -ιλώ- cett.
898 καταψήχουσι GR -ψύχ- cett. 900 ὅσον OSch. ὅσα G ἀεὶ cett.
902 πολυθάμνου BP φιλοθρήνου Σ v.l. Tzetz. Ch. 1.300 903 ἀεκούσιον MRV

88

flourishing FENNEL; collect also HEDGE-MUSTARD and the seeds of the WILD CHICK-PEA, including with its green shoots the heavy-smelling leaves. Again, WATER-CRESS alleviates sickness; so too a fresh garland of MELILOT; also the white blossoms of the spongy DROPWORT which shepherds pound in a mortar, and those seeds which the CORN-COCKLE and the red PLANTAIN and the ROSE foster within them, and the tiny seed of the GILLI- 900 FLOWER. Or cut some KNOT-GRASS from the tangled water-meadows, DEPILATORY, and the seed of the mournful HYACINTH, over whom Phoebus wept, since without willing it, hard by the river of Amyclae he slew with a blow the boy Hyacinthus in the bloom of youth; for the iron mass rebounding from a rock smote upon his temple and crushed the sheath beneath it. Mix too some TREFOIL and gum of SILPHIUM equal in scale to the weight of three obols; or else pluck the horn-shaped TUFTED THYME, often too SAMPHIRE or LAVENDAR-COTTON, and 910 along with them grate into some drink ANISE and LIBYAN ROOTS. Having shredded them into a bowl, sometimes together sometimes separately, drink them mixed with Vinegar or else with Wine or Water; these help too when shredded into Milk.

If however some bite should call for haste as you are on your journey and among waterless glades, the moment you are overcome chew with your jaws some roots or leaves or seeds growing by the way, and sucking out the sap, lay the half-eaten remains of the food upon the wounds in order that 920 you may avoid suffering and imminent death.

Again, by applying to some deadly wound a brazen cupping vessel you will drain the poison and the blood together; or by

904 βαλὼν G λαβὼν cett.   908 Ἰσοȝυγέοντ' OSch.   916 βεβαρημένος OSch. -ον codd.   919 ἔπι OSch. ἀπὸ codd.   920 δύην ὀλοοῦ καὶ πότμον θηρὸς ἀ. BKP   921 ἢ μὴν κ.σ.χ. ἠὲ σίνηπυ Ath. 9.366D

ἠὲ κράδης γλαγόεντα χέας ὀπόν, ἠὲ σίδηρον
καυστείρης θαλφθεῖσαν ὑπὸ στέρνοισι καμίνου.
925 ἄλλοτε φορβάδος αἰγὸς ἐνίπλειον δέρος οἴνης
χραισμήσει τημοῦτος ἐπὴν σφυρὸν ἢ χέρα κόψῃ.
ἀσκοῦ ἔσω βαρύθοντα μέσον διὰ πῆχυν ἐρείσεις
ἢ σφυρόν, ἀσκοδέταις δὲ πέριξ βουβῶνας ἑλίξεις
εἰσόκε τοι μένος οἴνου ἀπὸ χροὸς ἄλγος ἐρύξῃ.
930 δήποτε καὶ βδέλλας κορέσαις ἐπὶ τύμμασι βόσκων,
ἢ ἀπὸ κρομμυόφι στάζων ὀπόν, ἄλλοτε δ᾽ οἴνης
μίγδην ἐν πυράθοισι χέας τρύγα φυρήσασθαι
ἢ ὄξευς, νεαλεῖ δὲ πάτῳ περὶ τύψιν ἑλίξαις.
Ὄφρα δὲ καὶ πάσῃσιν ἀλεξητήριον ἄταις
935 τευξάμενος πεπύθοιο, τό τοι μέγα κρήγυον ἔσται
ἦμος ὅτε θρόνα πάντα μιῇ ὑπὸ χειρὶ ταράξῃς,
ἐν μὲν ἀριστολόχεια, καὶ ἴριδος ἐν δέ τε νάρδου
ῥίζαι, χαλβανίδες τε σὺν αὐαλέοισι πυρέθροις
εἶεν, δαυκείου τε παναλθέος, ἐν δὲ βρυώνης,
940 σὺν δέ τε ῥίζεα χαῦνα νεωρυχέος γλυκυσίδης
κάρφεά τ᾽ ἐλλεβόρου μελανόχροος, ἄμμιγα δ᾽ ἀφρός
λίτρου· σὺν δὲ κύμινα χέαις βλαστόν τε κονύζης,
ἄμμιγα δ᾽ ἀγροτέρης σταφίδος λέπος· ἴσα δὲ δάφνης
σπερμεῖα κύτισόν τε κατακνήθειν τε χαμηλόν
945 ἱππεῖον λειχῆνα, καὶ ἐν κυκλάμινον ἀγείρας.
ἐν καὶ μήκωνος φιαρῆς ὀπόν, ἀμφὶ καὶ ἄγνου
σπέρματα βάλσαμόν τε καὶ ἐν κινάμοιο βαλέσθαι,
σὺν καὶ σφονδύλειον ἁλός τ᾽ ἐμπληθέα κύμβην,
ἄμμιγα καὶ τάμισον καὶ καρκίνον· ἀλλ᾽ ὁ μὲν εἴη
950 πτωκός, ὁ δ᾽ ἐν ποταμοῖσι πολυστίοισι νομάζων.
καὶ τὰ μὲν ἐν στύπεϊ προβαλὼν πολυχανδέος ὅλμου

Deest Π
925 δέρας G   927 μέσου OSch. | ἐρείσεις Gow -σας codd. -σαι OSch.
928 ἐλίσσεις Σ v.l.   930 κορέσεις GKP   931 στάξει B -ειν P -εις Bent.
933 ὄξευς OSch. -ξους codd.: cf. Al. 321, 366, al.   935 τευξόμενος OSch.
936 μιᾷ BGKPv | ταράξαις G -ξας KPv   938 αὐαλέοισι v -έοις τε MRV(?)

pouring on the milky juice of the FIG, or by using an iron heated
in the heart of a hot furnace. Sometimes the skin of a grazing
goat filled with Wine will be of service at a time when the
wound is in ankle or hand. You will fix the sufferer in the
wineskin to the mid forearm or ankle and wind the fastening
cord about the groin or armpit until the strength of the Wine
has drawn out the pain from the flesh. At times moreover let
LEECHES feed on wounds and drink their fill. Or drip ONION 930
JUICE, or else pour Lees of Wine or of Vinegar, upon SHEEP'S
DROPPINGS, make a paste, and plaster the wound with the fresh
dung.

But that you may with instruction compound a general
panacea,—it will be very serviceable after you have mixed all
the simples together—let there be BIRTHWORT, root of IRIS and
of SPIKENARD, of ALL-HEAL too with dried PELLITORY, of all-
curing WILD CARROT, and of BLACK BRYONY, and with them 940
the spongy roots of a freshly dug PEONY, sprigs of the BLACK
HELLEBORE, and mingled with them NATIVE SODIUM CARBONATE.
Pour in too CUMMIN and a sprig of FLEABANE mixed with the
husks of STAVESACRE; and grate down an equal quantity of the
BAY'S BERRIES and TREE-MEDICK and the lowly HORSE-MOSS, and
gather in some CYCLAMEN. Cast in also the juice of the gleaming
POPPY, and over all the seeds of the AGNUS CASTUS, BALSAM too
and some CASSIA, and with them COW-PARSNIP and a bowlful
of SALT, mingling them with CURD and a CRAB; but the former
should come from a Hare, the latter should be a dweller in 950
pebbly streams. Now all these you should throw into the belly

---

-έαισι G -έεσσι BKP   940 ριζέα G -ʒία cett.: cf. 646, Al. 69, 145, 588
942 λίτρου OSch. vί- cett.: cf. Al. 327, 337, 532   944 σπερμεῖον Hermann |
κατακνήθειν Kv -θην cett. | χαμηλόν Gow -λήν codd.   945 ἀγείρᾳς Kv
946 νεαρῆς BGP   947 βαλσάμου Stephanus   950 πολυστίοισι OSch.: cf.
Al. 466 -στείοισι codd. -μνίοισι Σ v.l.

THERIACA

μάξαι λαϊνέοισιν ἐπιπλήσσων ὑπέροισιν·
αἶψα δ᾽ ἐπ᾽ αὐαλέοισι χέας ἀπαρινέα χυλόν
ἄμμιγα συμφύρσαιο, καταρτίζοιο δὲ κύκλους
955 δραχμαίους πλάστιγγι διακριδὸν ἄχθος ἐρύξας,
οἴνης δ᾽ ἐν δοιῆσι χαδεῖν κοτύλῃσι ταράξας.
Καί κεν Ὁμηρείοιο καὶ εἰσέτι Νικάνδροιο
μνῆστιν ἔχοις, τὸν ἔθρεψε Κλάρου νιφόεσσα πολίχνη.

Deest Π
952 μάξαι R νά- cett.   954 om. V   955 διασταδὸν Σ v.l.   958 κολώνη
Tzetz. Exeg. ad Il. 131.14 Herm.

of a capacious mortar, kneading them with the blows of stone pestles. And on the dry ingredients pour at once the juice of CLEAVERS and mix well together; then prepare round cakes of a drachm each, limiting the weight precisely with a balance; then shake them up in two *cotylae* of Wine and drink.

So now you will treasure ever the memory of the Homeric Nicander, whom the snow-white town of Clarus nurtured.

ΝΙΚΑΝΔΡΟΥ ΑΛΕΞΙΦΑΡΜΑΚΑ

Εἰ καὶ μὴ σύγκληρα κατ' Ἀσίδα τείχεα δῆμοι
τύρσεσιν ἐστήσαντο τέων ἀνεδέγμεθα βλάστας,
Πρωταγόρη, δολιχὸς δὲ διάπροθι χῶρος ἐέργει,
ῥεῖά κέ τοι ποσίεσσιν ἀλέξια φαρμακοέσσαις
5 αὐδήσαιμ' ἅ τε φῶτας ἐνιχριμφθέντα δαμάζει.
ἢ γὰρ δὴ σὺ μὲν ἄγχι πολυστροίβοιο θαλάσσης
Ἄρκτον ὑπ' ὀμφαλόεσσαν ἐνάσσαο ἦχί τε Ῥείης
Λοβρίνης θαλάμαι τε καὶ ὀργαστήριον Ἄττεω·
αὐτὰρ ἐγὼ τόθι παῖδες ἐυζήλοιο Κρεούσης
10 πιοτάτην ἐδάσαντο γεωμορίην ἠπείρου
ἐζόμενοι τριπόδεσσι πάρα Κλαρίοις Ἑκάτοιο.
Ἀλλ' ἤτοι χολόεν μὲν ἰδὲ στομίοισι δυσαλθές
πυνθείης ἀκόνιτον, ὃ δή ῥ' Ἀχερωίδες ὄχθαι
φύουσιν τόθι χάσμα δυσέκδρομον Εὐβουλῆος
15 ἄστυρά τε Πριόλαο καταστρεφθέντα δέδουπε.
τοῖο δὲ πάντα χαλινὰ καὶ οὐρανόεσσαν ὑπήνην
οὖλά θ' ὑποστύφει χολόεν ποτόν, ἀμφὶ δὲ πρώτοις
εἰλύεται στέρνοισι κακῇ ἀλάλυγγι βαρῦνον
φῶτ' ἐπικαρδιόωντα· δύῃ δ' ἐπιδάκνεται ἄκρον
20 νειαίρης, ἄκλειστον ἀειρόμενον στόμα γαστρός,
τεύχεος ἣν κραδίην ἐπιδορπίου οἱ δὲ δοχαίην
κλείουσι στομάχοιο, πύλη δ' ἐπικέκλιται ἀρχαῖς
πρῶτα κόλων ὅθι πᾶσα βροτῶν ἅλις ἐμφέρεται δαίς.
αἰεὶ δ' ἐκ φαέων νοτέων ὑπολείβεται ἱδρώς,
25 ἡ δὲ κυκαομένη τὰ μὲν ἔβρασεν ἤλιθα νηδύς
πνεύματα, πολλὰ δ' ἔνερθε κατὰ μέσον ὀμφαλὸν ἴζει·
κράατι δ' ἐν βάρος ἐχθρόν, ὑπὸ κροτάφοισι δὲ παλμός

CODICES: Π ω= BGMPRVv
_____
Deest Π
TITULUS: Ἀντιφάρμακα Σ v.l. Et. M. 241.12, 256.55 περὶ θανασίμων φαρμάκων
Σ v.l.

ALEXIPHARMACA

Even though the peoples from whom you and I, Protagoras, have derived our births did not set up the walls of their strong towers side by side in Asia, and a great space separates us, yet I can easily instruct you in the remedies for those draughts of poison which attack men and bring them low. You indeed have made your home by the tempestuous sea beneath bossy Arctus, where are the caverns of Lobrinian Rhea and the place of the secret rites of Attes; while I dwell where the sons of the far-famed Creusa divided among themselves the richest portion 10 of the mainland, settling by the tripods of Apollo in Clarus.

You must, to be sure, learn of the ACONITE, bitter as gall, deadly in the mouth, which the banks of Acheron put forth. There is the abyss of the Wise Counsellor whence few escape, and there the towns of Priolas fell crashing in ruins.

All the drinker's jaws and the roof of his mouth and his gums are constricted by the bitter draught, as it wraps itself about the top of the chest, crushing with evil choking the man in the throes of heartburn. The top of the belly is gripped with pain— the swelling, open mouth of the lower stomach, which some 20 call the 'heart' of the digestive vessel, others the 'receiver' of the stomach—and the gate is closed immediately upon the beginning of the intestines where a man's food in all its abundance is carried in. And all the while from his streaming eyes drips the moisture; and his belly sore shaken vainly throws up wind, and much of it settles below about his mid-navel; and in his head is a grievous weight, and there ensues a rapid throbbing

11 ἐзόμενοι MRV -νος cett. Σv.l.   21 ἐπιδορπίου OSch. -ιον codd. Gal. 5.275
25 κυκαομένη Headlam -καωμ- v -κοωμ- BP ταρασσομένη GMRV

πυκνὸς ἐπεμφέρεται, τὰ δὲ διπλόα δέρκεται ὄσσοις
οἷα χαλικραίη νύχιος δεδαμασμένος οἴνῃ.
30 ὡς δ᾽ ὁπότ᾽ ἀγριόεσσαν ὑποθλίψαντες ὀπώρην
Σιληνοὶ κεραοῖο Διωνύσοιο τιθηνοί
πρῶτον ἐπαφρίζοντι ποτῷ φρένα θωρηχθέντες
ὄθμασι δινήθησαν ἐπισφαλεροῖσι δὲ κώλοις
Νυσαίην ἀνὰ κλιτὺν ἐπέδραμον ἀφραίνοντες,
35 ὣς οἵγε σκοτόωσι κακῇ βεβαρηότες ἄτῃ.
τὴν μέν τε κλείουσι μυοκτόνον, ἢ γὰρ ἀνιγρούς
παμπήδην ὕρακας λιχμήμονας ἠρήμωσεν·
οἱ δέ τε παρδαλιαγχές, ἐπεὶ θήρεσσι πελώροις
πότμον βουπελάται τε καὶ αἰγινομῆες ἔθεντο
40 Ἴδης ἐν νεμέεσσι Φαλακραίη ἐνὶ βήσσῃ,
πολλάκι θηλυφόνον καὶ κάμμαρον· ἐν δ᾽ Ἀκοναίοις
δηλήειν ἀκόνιτον ἐνεβλάστησεν ὀρόγκοις.
τῷ καί που τιτάνοιο χερὸς βάρος ἔσσεται ἄρκος
πιμπλαμένης ὅτε νέκταρ ἐύτριβι κιρρὸν ἀφύσσῃς
45 μετρήδην — κοτύλη δὲ πέλοι καταμέστιος οἴνης—
σὺν δὲ καὶ ἁβροτόνοιο ταμὼν ἄπο καυλέα θάμνου
ἢ χλοεροῦ πρασίοιο τὸ δὴ μελίφυλλον ὑδεῦσι·
καί τε σὺ ποιήεντος ἀειθαλέος χαμελαίης
βλάστην πηγάνιόν τε πόροις, ἐν βάμματι σίμβλων
50 σβεννὺς αἰθαλόεντα μύδρον γενύεσσι πυράγρης,
ἠὲ σιδηρήεσσαν ἄπο τρύγα τήν τε καμίνων
ἔντοσθεν χοάνοιο διχῇ πυρὸς ἤλασε λιγνύς·
ἄλλοτε δὲ χρυσοῖο νέον βάρος ἐν πυρὶ θάλψας
ἠὲ καὶ ἀργυρόεν θολερῷ ἐνὶ πώματι βάπτοις.
55 πολλάκι δ᾽ ἡμιδαὲς χειρὸς βάρος αἴνυσο θρίων
παῦρα χαμαιπίτυος, τότ᾽ ὀνίτιδος αὖον ὀρείης
ἠὲ νέον ῥάδικα πολυκνήμοιο κολούσας,

Deest Π ad. v. 34
32 ἔτ᾽ ἄφρ. Bent. 33 ὄμμασι BPR 34 ἐπέδραμον ΠΒΡν ὑπ- cett. 36 μέν
τοι ΠΒΡν: cf. 498 37 παμβλήδην Π | λιχμήρεας ω 38 πορδαλιαγχές ω
40 νεμέεσσι ΠΒΡν κνημοῖσι cett. | Φαλακραίη...βήσσῃ Π -αίαις, -αίης...-σαις ω

beneath his temples, and with his eyes he sees things double, like a man at night overcome with unmixed wine. And as when 30 the Silens, the nurses of the horned Dionysus, crushed the wild grapes, and having for the first time fortified their spirits with the foaming drink, were confused in their sight and on reeling feet rushed madly about the hill of Nysa, even so is the sight of these men darkened beneath the weight of evil doom. This plant men call also *Mouse-bane*, for it utterly destroys troublesome, nibbling mice; but some call it *Leopard's-choke*, since cowherds and goatherds with it contrive the death of those great beasts amid the glades of Ida in the vale of Phalacra. Again 40 they name it *Woman-killer* and *Crayfish*. And the deadly Aconite flourishes amid the Aconaean mountains.

For one so poisoned GYPSUM to the weight of a handful will perhaps be a protection, if you draw thereto tawny Wine in due measure with the Gypsum reduced to fine powder—let it be a full *cotyle* of Wine—and add stalks of WORMWOOD, cutting them from the shrub, or of bright green HOREHOUND which they call *Honeyleaf*; administer also a shoot of the herbaceous, evergreen SPURGE-OLIVE and RUE, quenching in vinegar and honey a red-hot lump of metal between the jaws 50 of the fire-tongs, or DROSS OF IRON which the flame of the fire has separated within the melting-pot in the furnace; or sometimes just after warming in the fire a lump of gold or silver you should plunge it in the turbid draught. Or again you should take leaves, half a handful's weight, of the GROUND PINE; or a dry sprig of POT MARJORAM from the hills, or cut a fresh spray

41 κάμμορον Σ   **42** δηλήειν OSch.   θηλήειν Π   -είην cett. | ἀνεβλάστησεν Ѡ
43 βάθος Π: cf. 55 | ἕ. ἄλκαρ BG v.l. PRv   **45** μετρηδόν Ѡ | πέλοι ΠΜ   -λει
cett.   **49** πλοις ἐνὶ Ѡ   **50** σβεννύς τ᾽ BPRv   **51** σιδηρείεσσαν Π
54 ἀργύρεον Ѡ   **55** ἡμιδεὲς Scal. | βάθος Π: cf. 43

ALEXIPHARMACA

τέτρασιν ἐν κυάθοισι χαδεῖν μελιανθέος οἴνης·
ἢ ἔτι μυελόεντα χαλικρότερον ποτὸν ἴσχοις
60 ὄρνιθος στρουθοῖο κατοικάδος εὔθ᾽ ὑπὸ χύτρῳ
γυῖα καταθρύπτῃσι βιαζομένη πυρὸς αὐγή·
καί τε βοὸς νέα γέντα περιφλίοντος ἀλοιφῇ
τηξάμενος κορέσαιο ποτῷ εὐχανδέα νηδύν.
ναὶ μὴν βαλσάμοιο τότ᾽ ἐν σταγόνεσσι γάλακτος
65 θηλυτέρης πώλοιο χέαις ὀπόν, ἄλλοτε νύμφαις,
ἔστ᾽ ἂν ὑπὲκ φάρυγος χεύῃ παναεργέα δόρπον.
πολλάκι δ᾽ ἢ σκίνακος δερκευνέος ἢ ἀπὸ νεβροῦ
πυετίην τμήξαιο πόροις δ᾽ ἐν νέκταρι φύρσας·
ἄλλοτε καὶ μορέης ἄπο ῥίζεα φοινηέσσης
70 ὅλμου ἐνὶ στύπεϊ προβαλὼν καὶ ὀμήρεα κόψας
οἴνῳ, ἐνεψηθέντα πόροις καμάτοισι μελίσσης·
καί κεν ἐπικρατέουσαν ἀπεχθέα νοῦσον ἀλάλκοις
φωτός, ὁ δ᾽ ἀσφαλέεσσι πάλιν μετὰ ποσσὶν ὁδεύοι.
Δεύτερα δ᾽ αἰγλήεντος ἐπιφράζευ πόσιν ἐχθρήν
75 κιρναμένην ὀλοοῦ ψιμυθίου ἥ τε γάλακτι
πάντοθεν ἀφρίζοντι νέην εἰδήνατο χροιήν
πελλίσιν ἐν γρώνῃσιν ὅτ᾽ εἴαρι πῖον ἀμέλξαις.
τοῦ μὲν ὑπὲρ γένυάς τε καὶ ἧ ῥυσαίνεται οὖλα
ἀφρὸς ἐπιστύφων ἐμπλάσσεται, ἀμφὶ καὶ ὁλκός
80 τέτρηχε γλώσσης, νέατος δ᾽ ὑποκάρφεται ἰσθμός,
ξηρὰ δ᾽ ἐπιλλύζων ὀλοῇ χελλύσσεται ἄτῃ,
ἀβλεμὲς ἢ γὰρ κεῖνο πέλει βάρος· αὐτὰρ ὁ θυμῷ
ναυσιόεις ὀλοοῖσιν ὑποτρύει καμάτοισι·
πολλάκι δ᾽ ἐν φαέεσσιν ἄλην ἑτερειδέα λεύσσων
85 ἄλλοτε δ᾽ ὑπναλέος ψύχει δέμας, οὐδ᾽ ἔτι γυῖα
ὡς τὸ πάρος δονέει, καμάτῳ δ᾽ ὑποδάμναται εἴκων.

Deest Π a v. 74
58 τέτρασιν δ᾽ Π | μελιηδέος οἴνου ω   61 βιαζομένη Π -νης ω | αὐγή Scal.
-γῆς ω -γαῖς Π   62 περιφλίοντος ΠΜR -φλιδόωντος cett.   63 εὐχανδέα G
ἐν χ- Π ἐγχ-, ἐνιχ- cett.   64 μὴν βαλσάμοιο ΠΜR μ. καὶ β. ΒΡ μ. καὶ βλασάμ-
cett.: cf. Th. 947   65 χέαις Π χέας, χέων ω   66 ἔστ᾽ Bent. εὖτ᾽ codd. |

of FIELD BASIL, and cover them in four *cyathi* of honey-sweet Wine. Or you may take some broth, still meaty and undiluted, made from a domestic fowl when the forcible glow of the fire 60 beneath the pot reduces the body to pieces. Also you should render down the fresh meat of an ox abounding in fat and satisfy the stomach to its full capacity with the soup. Again, sometimes you should pour the juice of BALSAM into some drops of Milk from a young girl, or else into water, until the patient discharges from his throat the undigested food. Sometimes too you should cut out the CURD from the stomach of the nimble beast that sleeps open-eyed (hare), or of a Fawn, and give it mixed in Wine; at other times cast the roots of the purple MULBERRY into the hollow of a mortar, bray them mingled with Wine, 70 and give them boiled in the labours of the Bee. Thus may you ward off loathsome sickness though it threaten to master a man, and he may once again walk on unfaltering feet.

In the second place consider the hateful brew compounded with gleaming, deadly WHITE LEAD whose fresh colour is like milk which foams all over when you milk it rich in the spring-time into the deep pails. Over the victim's jaws and in the grooves of the gums is plastered an astringent froth, and the furrow of the tongue turns rough on either side, and the depth 80 of the throat grows somewhat dry, and from the pernicious venom follows a dry retching and hawking, for this affliction is severe; meanwhile his spirit sickens and he is worn out with mortal suffering. His body too grows chill, while sometimes his eyes behold strange illusions or else he drowses; nor can he bestir his limbs as heretofore, and he succumbs to the over-mastering fatigue.

ὑπὲρ Π   67 δ' ἢ Zon. 477 (Et. M. 256.56) δὲ codd.   69 ῥιζέα ΠG -ία cett.: cf. Th. 940 | φοινικοέσσης ω   72 ἐπαχθέα ω   78 ῥυσσαίνεται GVv: cf. 181 79 ἐμπλάσσεται BPRv ἐμπάσσ- GV ἐμφράσσ- MR² | καὶ MR δὲ cett. 81 ἐπιλλύζων V -λίζων cett.   82 ἐκεῖνο BPRv   83 ναυσιόεις GM ναυτ-cett. | ὑποτρύζει Bent.

ALEXIPHARMACA

τῷ καὶ πρημαδίης ἢ ὀρχάδος εἶαρ ἐλαίης
ἢ ἔτι μυρτίνης σχεδίην δεπάεσσιν ὀρέξαις
ὄφρ' ἂν ὀλισθήνασα χέῃ κακὰ φάρμακα νηδύς·
90 ἠὲ σύ γ' οὐθατόεντα διοιδέα μαζὸν ἀμέλξας
ῥεῖα πόροις, φιαρὴν δὲ ποτοῦ ἀποαίνυσο γρῆυν.
καί τε σύ γ' ἢ μαλάχης ῥαδάμους ἢ φυλλάδα τήξας
χυλῷ ἔνι κλώθοντι κακηπελέοντα κορέσσαις.
πολλάκι σήσαμα κόπτε, πόροις δ' ἐν νέκταρι καὶ τά·
95 ἠὲ σὺ κληματόεσσαν ἐν ὕδατι πλύνεο τέφρην
θαλπομένην, τὸ δὲ ῥύμμα νεοπλεκέος καλάθοιο
κόλποις ἰκμήνειας, ὁ γάρ τ' ἀναδέξεται ἰλύν.
καί τε κατατριφθέντα μετ' ἀργήεντος ἐλαίου
σκλήρ' ἀπὸ περσείης κάρυα βλάβος οὖλον ἐρύξει,
100 Περσεὺς ἥν ποτε ποσσὶ λιπὼν Κηφηίδα γαῖαν,
αὐχέν' ἀποτμήξας ἅρπῃ γονόεντα Μεδούσης,
ῥεῖα Μυκηναίῃσιν ἐνηέξησεν ἀρούραις,
Κηφῆος νέα δῶρα, μύκης ὅθι κάππεσεν ἅρπης,
ἄκρον ὑπὸ πρηῶνα Μελανθίδος ἔνθα τε Νύμφη
105 Λαγγείης πόμα κεῖνο Διὸς τεκμήρατο παιδί.
πολλάκι δ' ἐνθρύψειας ἐν ὀπταλέῃσιν ἀκοσταῖς
Γερραίης λιβάνοιο χύσιν περιπηγέα θάμνοις·
καί τε σύ γ' ἢ καρύης ἄπο δάκρυον ἢ ἀταλύμνου,
ἢ πτελέης ὅ τε πολλὸν ἀεὶ καταλείβεται ὄσχαις,
110 κόμμινά τε χλιόεντι ποτῷ ἐπαρωγέα τήξαις,
ὄφρα τὰ μέν τ' ἐρύγῃσι τὰ δ' ἐφητοῖσι δαμασθεὶς
ἀλθήσῃ ὑδάτεσσιν ὅτ' ἰκμήνῃ δέμας ἱδρώς.
καὶ κεν ὅγ' ἄλλοτε δόρπα δεδεγμένος ἄλλοτε δ' οἴνης
πιοτέρης κορέοιτο, καὶ ἀκλέα πότμον ἀλύξαι.
115 Μὴ μὲν κανθαρίδος σιτηβόρου εὖτ' ἂν ὀδώδῃ
κεῖνο ποτὸν δέξαιο χυτῇ ἐναλίγκια πίσσῃ·

Deest Π ad v. 107
87 πρημαδίην MR   91 φέροις MR²V²   92 καί τε σύ OSch.
κ. δὲ σ. GM κ. σὺ δέ V | ἠδὲ, εἰ δὲ, σύ cett. | ῥαδάμους Mein. ex Hsch. -άλους G -άμνους cett.
99 ξήρ' Σ v.l. | οὖλον Page οἶον codd.   105 Λαγγείη GV   106 ὀπταλέῃσιν
GV (-οισιν V) ἀσταλ- Μ ἀυαλ- BRv αὐκλ- Ρ   107 φύσιν Π   109 κατα-

100

Give the patient at once a cupful of oil of the PREMADIA- or ORCHIS- or MYRTLE-OLIVE, so that the stomach being lubricated may void the evil drug; or else you may readily milk the 90 udder's swelling teat and give it him; but skim the oily surface from the draught. And you may infuse sprigs or leaves of the MALLOW in fresh sap and dose the sufferer with as much as he can take. Or again pound SESAME seeds and administer them also in Wine; or else heat and cleanse in water the ashes of VINE TWIGS, and strain the lye through the interstices of a newly woven basket, for this will retain the sediment. Moreover if you rub down the hard stones of the PERSEA in gleaming Olive Oil, they will ward off injury—the persea which once on 100 a time Perseus, when his feet bore him from the land of Cepheus and he had cut off the teeming head of Medusa with his falchion, readily made to grow in the fields of Mycenae (it was a recent gift of Cepheus) on the spot where the scabbard-chape of his falchion fell, beneath the topmost summit of Melanthis, where a Nymph revealed to the son of Zeus the famed spring of Langea. Or else you should break up in roasted Barley the sap which congeals upon the FRANKINCENSE bushes of Gerrha; also as helpful you should dissolve in warm water the tears from the WALNUT-TREE or from the PLUM or those which ever drip in plenty on the ELM-TWIGS, and drops of GUM, so that he 110 may vomit up part of the poison, and part render wholesome as he yields to the hot water when the sweat moistens his body. And again he might sate himself with a meal which he has taken or with strong Wine and so escape an inglorious death.

When a liquid smells of the corn-eating BLISTER-BEETLE, that is to say, like liquid pitch, refuse it, for on the nostrils it weighs

λείβεται BGPRv -λείπεται MV -λείεται Π | ὤσχαις G   110 κόμμι τὰ δὲ ῶ |
χλιόεντι ΠV -όωντι cett. χλιδόωντι G v.l.   111 δαμάσ(σ)ας HPv   114 κορέσαιτο BPR²v | ἀλκέα ΠGRV   115 σιτηβόρου ΠGMR σιτοβ- BPv σιτηφάγου V
116 δέξαιτο OSch.

πίσσης γὰρ ῥώθωσιν ἄγει βάρος, ἐν δὲ χαλινοῖς
οἷά τε δὴ καρφεῖα νέον βεβρωμένα κέδρου.
αἱ δ' ὁτὲ μὲν πλαδόωντι ποτῷ ἐπὶ χείλεσι δηχμόν
120 τεύχουσιν τοτὲ δ' αὖτε περὶ στόμα νείατα γαστρός·
ἄλλοτε καὶ μεσάτη ἐπιδάκνεται ἄλγεσι νηδύς
ἢ κύστις βρωθεῖσα· περιψαύουσι δ' ἀνῖαι
θώρηκος τόθι χόνδρος ὑπὲρ κύτος ἕζετο γαστρός·
αὐτοὶ δ' ἀσχαλόωσιν, ἄλη δέ φιν ἤθεα φωτός
125 ἄψυχος πεδάει, ὁ δ' ἀελπέα δάμναται ἄταις,
οἷά τε δὴ γήρεια νέον τεθρυμμένα κάκτου
ἠέρ' ἐπιπλάζοντα διαψαίρουσι πνοῇσι.
τῷ δὲ σὺ πολλάκι μὲν γληχὼ ποταμῇσι νύμφαις
ἐμπλήδην κυκεῶνα πόροις ἐν κύμβεϊ τεύξας,
130 νηστείρης Δηοῦς μορόεν ποτὸν ᾧ ποτε Δηώ
λαυκανίην ἔβρεξεν ἀν' ἄστυρον Ἱπποθόωντος
Θρηίσσης ἀθύροισιν ὑπὸ ῥήτρησιν Ἰάμβης.
δήποτε δ' ἢ σιάλοιο καρήατος ἠὲ καὶ ἀμνοῦ
ἀμμίγδην σπεράδεσσιν ἐυτροχάλοισι λίνοιο,
135 ἠὲ νέον κορσεῖα ταμὼν κερόεντα χιμαίρης,
ἢ ἔτι που χηνὸς μορόεν ποτὸν αἴνυσο χύτρου,
ἐς δ' ἔμετον κορέσαιο, τὰ δ' ἀθρόα νειόθι βράσσοι
ἐμματέων ἔτ' ἄπεπτα πύλη μεμιασμένα δόρπα.
πολλάκι δ' ἐν κλυστῆρι νέον γλάγος οἰὸς ἀμέλξας
140 κλύζε, τὰ δ' ἤλιθα γαστρὸς ἀφόρδια κεινώσειας·
ἄλλοτ' ἀλυσθαίνοντι ποθὲν γάλα πῖον ἀρήξει·
ἠὲ σύ γ' ἀμπελόεντα γλυκεῖ ἔνι καυλέα κόψαις
χλωρά, νέον πετάλοισι περιβρίθοντα κολούσας·
ἠὲ μελισσάων καμάτῳ ἔνι παῦρα μορύξαις
145 σκορπιόεντα χαδὼν ψαθυρῆς ἐκ ῥίζεα γαίης
αἰὲν κεντρήεντα· πόη γε μὲν ὕψι τέθηλεν
οἵη περ μολόθουρος, ἔνισχνα δὲ καυλέα βάλλει.

121 ἄλγει Π   122 παραψαύουσι Π   123 γαστρός om. Π   126 πάππου ω
127 -ουσιν ἀέλλαις ω   129 κύμβεσι MRV | τῆξας Keydell   130 ν. Μητρὸς μ.
Headlam   131 λαυκανίην ΠG λευκ- cett.   132 ῥήτροισι ΠΜ   134 ἐυτρο-

like pitch and in the mouth like freshly eaten berries of the
juniper. Sometimes in a weak infusion these creatures produce
a biting sensation upon the lips, or again deep down about the 120
mouth of the stomach; at other times the middle of the belly
or the bladder is gnawed and seized with griping pains, while
discomfort attacks men where the cartilage of the chest rests over
the hollow of the stomach. And the victims are distressed in
themselves: swooning delusions hold in bondage what is
human in them, and the victim is brought down unexpectedly
by pain, like the freshly scattered thistledown which roams the
air and is fluttered by every breeze.

At times administer to the patient doses of PENNYROYAL mixed
with river water, making a posset of them in a mug. This was 130
the rich draught of the fasting Deo; once with this did Deo
moisten her throat in the city of Hippothoon by reason of the
unchecked speech of Thracian Iambe. At other times take from
your pot and mix with the round seeds of FLAX a rich draught
brewed from the head of a HOG or of a LAMB or from the horned
head of a GOAT which you have but lately cut off, or even, maybe, from a GOOSE, and give it until the man is sick; and let him
by tickling his throat stir up in the gullet below the entire mass
of polluted food still undigested. At times you should draw the
fresh milk of a SHEEP in a clyster-pipe, administer a clyster 140
and so empty the useless faeces from the bowel. At another
time a draught of creamy MILK will help the sufferer; or you
should lop the green tendrils of the VINE when they are fresh-
burdened with leaves and chop them up in GRAPE-SYRUP; or
take from crumbling soil the ever sting-shaped roots of SCORPIUS
and steep in the Bees' produce. The plant grows high like
asphodel but sheds its stalks when withered. Also you should

χάλοιο ὦ   135 κεράεντα ὦ   137 βράσσοις, -σαις ὦ   138 ἐμμαπέως Π:
cf. 536 | πύλης Π   141 τόθεν Π   142 ἐν Π   144 ἔπι Π   145 ταμὼν
ψαφαρῆς ὦ

καί τε σὺ δραχμάων πισύρων βάρος αἴνυσο γαίης
Παρθενίης τὴν Φυλλὶς ὑπὸ κνημοῖσιν ἀνῆκεν,
150 Ἰμβρασίδος γαίης χιονώδεος ἥν τε κεράστης
ἀμνὸς Χησιάδεσσι νέον σημήνατο Νύμφαις
Κερκέτεω νιφόεντος ὑπὸ σχοινώδεσιν ὄχθαις·
ἢ καὶ σειραίοιο πόσιν διπλήθεα τεύξαις,
σὺν δέ τε πηγανόεντας ἐνιθρύψειας ὁράμνους
155 ὀργάζων λίπεϊ ῥοδέῳ θρόνα· πολλάκι χραίνοις
ἰρινέῳ τό τε πολλὸν ἐπαλθέα νοῦσον ἔτευξεν.
    Ἤν γε μὲν οὐλόμενόν γε ποτὸν κορίοιο δυσαλθές
ἀφραδέως δεπάεσσιν ἀπεχθομένοισι πάσηται,
οἱ μέν τ᾽ ἀφροσύνῃ ἐμπληγέες οἷά τε μάργοι
160 δήμια λαβράζουσι παραπλῆγές θ᾽ ἅτε Βάκχαι
ὀξὺ μέλος βοόωσιν ἀταρμύκτῳ φρενὸς οἴστρῳ.
τῷ μέν τ᾽ ἐξ ἐδανοῖο πόροις δέπας ἔμπλεον οἴνης,
Πράμνιον αὐτοκρηές, ὅπως ὑπετύψατο ληνοῦ,
ἢ νύμφαις τήξαιο βαλὼν ἁλὸς ἔμπλεα κύμβην,
165 πολλάκι δ᾽ ὀρταλίχων ἀπαλὴν ὠδῖνα κενώσας
ἀφρὸν ἐπεγκεράσαιο, θοοῦ δορπήια κέπφου·
τῷ γὰρ δὴ ζωήν τε σαοῖ, καὶ πότμον ἐπισπεῖ
εὖτε δόλοις νήχοντα κακοφθόρα τέκν᾽ ἁλιήων
οἰωνὸν χραίνωσιν, ὁ δ᾽ ἐς χέρας ἔμπεσε παίδων
170 θηρεύων ἀφροῖο νέην κλύδα λευκαίνουσαν.
καί τε σύ γ᾽ ἀγλεύκην βάψαις ἰόεντα θάλασσαν,
ἥν τε καὶ ἀτμεύειν ἀνέμοις πόρεν Ἐννοσίγαιος
σὺν πυρί· καὶ γὰρ δὴ τὸ πνοαῖς συνδάμναται ἐχθραῖς.
πῦρ μὲν ἀείζωον καὶ ἀχύνετον ἔτρεσεν ὕδωρ
175 ἀργέστας· καί ῥ᾽ ἡ μὲν ἀκοσμήεσσα φιλοργής
δεσπόζει νηῶν τε καὶ ἐμφορέων αἰζηῶν,
ὕλη δ᾽ ἐχθομένοιο πυρὸς κατὰ θεσμὸν ἀκούει.
ναὶ μὴν ἀτμένιόν τε κεραιόμενον λίπος οἴνῃ

Deest Π a v. 157
148 καὶ δὲ ω   149 ἦν ω | επι Π   150 αἴης ω   153 διπλήρεα BPRv
157 οὐλομένοιο π. OSch.   158 πάσωνται MR   165 ἀλαλὴν Σ v.l.

104

take four drachms' weight of PARTHENIAN EARTH which Phyllis
brings forth under her mountain-spurs, the snow-white earth 150
of the Imbrasus which a horned lamb first revealed to the
Chesiad Nymphs beneath the rush-grown river-banks of snow-
capped Cercetes. Or brew a drink of boiled-down MUST of
twice that quantity, and into it shred some sprigs of RUE,
kneading the herbs with ROSE-OIL, or sometimes soak it in
IRIS-OIL, which has often cured an illness.

If however a man thoughtlessly taste from loathsome cups
a draught, deadly and hard to remedy, of CORIANDER, the
victims are struck with madness and utter wild and vulgar 160
words like lunatics, and like crazy Bacchanals bawl shrill songs
in frenzy of the mind unabashed. To such a case you should
administer a cupful of hedanian WINE, 'Pramnian', unmixed,
just as it gushed from the vat. Or cast a cupful of SALT into water
and let it dissolve. Or else you should empty the fragile EGG of
a chicken and mix with it the SEA-FOAM upon which the swift
petrel feeds. It is with this that it sustains life, and also meets
its doom, when the fishermen's destructive children assail with
their tricks the swimming fowl; and it falls into the boys' hands
as it chases the fresh and whitening surge of foam. Do you also 170
draw from the bitter, violet-hued sea—the sea, which, with
fire too, the Earth-Shaker has enslaved to the winds. For fire is
vanquished by hostile blasts: the undying fire and the expanse
of waters tremble before the north-west winds; though the
unruly sea, swift to anger, lords it over ships and over the men
who perish in it, while to the rule of the abhorred fire the forest
is obedient. Again, common OIL mingled with Wine or a drink

167 ἐπισπεῖ MV -σποι var. acc. cett.   173 δὴ πνοιαῖς BPRv   176 ἐμ-
πορέων Bent. | ἁλιήων BPR

ἢ χιόνι γλυκέος μίγδην πόσις ἄλγος ἐρύξει,
180 ἦμος ὑπὸ ζάγκλησι περιβρίθουσαν ὀπώρην
ῥυσαλέην ἐδανοῖο καὶ ἐκ ψιθίης ἐλίνοιο
κείροντες θλίβωσιν, ὅτε ῥοιζηδὰ μέλισσαι,
πεμφρηδών, σφῆκές τε καὶ ἐκ βέμβικες ὄρειαι
γλεῦκος ἄλις δαίνυνται ἐπὶ ῥαγέεσσι πεσοῦσαι,
185 πιοτέρην ὅτε βότρυν ἐσίνατο κηκὰς ἀλώπηξ.

Καί τε σὺ κωνείου βλαβόεν τεκμαίρεο πῶμα·
κεῖνο ποτὸν δὴ γάρ τε καρήατι φοινὸν ἰάπτει
νύκτα φέρον σκοτόεσσαν· ἐδίνησεν δὲ καὶ ὄσσε,
ἴχνεσι δὲ σφαλεροί τε καὶ ἐμπλάζοντες ἀγυιαῖς
190 χερσὶν ἐφερπύζουσι· κακὸς δ' ὑπὸ νείατα πνιχμός
ἴσθμια καὶ φάρυγος στεινὴν ἐμφράσσεται οἶμον·
ἄκρα δέ τοι ψύχει, περὶ δὲ φλέβες ἔνδοθι γυίων
ῥωμαλέαι στέλλονται· ὁ δ' ἠέρα παῦρον ἀτύζει
οἷα κατηβολέων, ψυχὴ δ' Ἀιδωνέα λεύσσει.
195 τὸν μέν τ' ἢ λίπεος κορέοις ἢ ἀμισγέος οἴνης
ὄφρα κεν ἐξερύγῃσι κακὴν καὶ ἐπώδυνον ἄτην,
ἠὲ σύ γε κλυστῆρος ἐνεὶς ὁπλίζεο τεῦχος·
πολλάκι δ' ἢ οἴνης ἀμιγῆ πόσιν, ἢ ἀπὸ δάφνης
Τεμπίδος ἢ δαυχμοῖο φέροις ἐκ καυλέα κόψας
200 ἢ πρώτη Φοίβοιο κατέστεφε Δελφίδα χαίτην,
ἢ πέπερι κνίδης τε μίγα σπερμεῖα λεήνας
νείμειας, τοτὲ νέκταρ ὀπῷ ἐμπευκέι χράνας·
δήποτε δ' ἰρινέου θυέος μετρηδὸν ὀρέξαις
σίλφιά τ' ἐνθρυφθέντα μετ' ἀργήεντος ἐλαίου·
205 ἐν δὲ μελιζώρου γλυκέος πόσιν, ἐν δὲ γάλακτος
ἀφριόεν νέμε τεῦχος ὑπὲρ πυρὸς ἠρέμα θάλψας.

Καί κεν λοιγήεντι παρασχεδὸν ἄχθος ἀμύνοις
τοξικῷ, εὖτ' ἀχέεσσι βαρύνηται ποτῷ ἀνήρ.
τοῦ καὶ ἔνερθε γλῶσσα παχύνεται, ἀμφὶ δὲ χείλη

Deest Π
181 ῥυσαλέην GV ῥυσσ- cett.: cf. 78   184 ῥάγεσσι Bent.   190 πνιχμός
OSch. πνιγ- codd.: cf. 365   192 δ' ἐπιψύχει BPRv δέ οἱ ψ. Klauser:

of GRAPE-SYRUP mixed with snow will stay the pain, what time 180
the reapers with their pruning-hooks lop the heavy, wrinkled
vintage of the hedanian and the psithian vine and crush it, while
with a humming sound bees and the tree-wasp, wasps and
buzzers from the hills fall upon the grapes and feast their
fill of sweetness, and the mischievous fox ravages the richer
clusters.

Take note too of the noxious draught which is HEMLOCK, for
this drink assuredly looses disaster upon the head bringing the
darkness of night: the eyes roll, and men roam the streets with
tottering steps and crawling upon their hands; a terrible 190
choking blocks the lower throat and the narrow passage of the
windpipe; the extremities grow cold; and in the limbs the
stout arteries are contracted; for a short while the victim draws
breath like one swooning, and his spirit beholds Hades.

Give the patient his fill of OIL or of unmixed WINE until he
vomit up the evil, painful poison; or prepare and insert a clyster;
or else give him draughts of unmixed WINE, or cut and bring
him twigs of SWEET BAY or BAY OF TEMPE (this was the first 200
plant to crown the Delphian locks of Phoebus); or else pound
some PEPPER with NETTLE SEEDS and administer them, or again
infuse Wine with the bitter JUICE OF SILPHIUM. Sometimes you
may offer him a measure of scented IRIS-OIL and SILPHIUM
shredded in with gleaming OIL. Also give him a draught of
honey-sweet GRAPE-SYRUP, and a foaming vessel of MILK which
you have slightly warmed over the fire.

There are even means of promptly averting the oppression
caused by deadly ARROW-POISON, when a man is overcome with
anguish from drinking it. First, his tongue begins to thicken

cf. 282, 341, 343   193 ῥωγαλέαι Bent. | ἀτύzει BPV Et. M. 168.9   ἀτίzει
Rv Et. M. v.l.   ἀλύzει ΜΣ v.l.   ἀλέξει G   199 δαυχνοῖο Bergk: cf. Th. 94
208 ποτοῦ JGSch.

210 οἰδαλέα βρίθοντα περὶ στομάτεσσι βαρύνει,
ξηρὰ δ' ἀναπτύει, νεόθεν δ' ἐκρήγνυται οὖλα·
πολλάκι δ' ἐς κραδίην πτοίην βάλε, πᾶν δὲ νόημα
ἔμπληκτον μεμόρηκε κακῇ ἐσφαλμένον ἄτῃ·
αὐτὰρ ὁ μηκάζει μανίης ὕπο μυρία φλύζων,
215 δηθάκι δ' ἀχθόμενος βοάᾳ ἅ τις ἐμπελάδην φώς
ἀμφιβρότην κώδειαν ἀπὸ ξιφέεσσιν ἀμηθείς,
ἢ ἅτε κερνοφόρος ζάκορος βωμίστρια Ῥείης,
εἰνάδι λαοφόροισιν ἐνιχρίμπτουσα κελεύθοις,
μακρὸν ἐπεμβοάᾳ γλώσσῃ θρόον, οἱ δὲ τρέουσιν
220 Ἰδαίης ῥιγηλὸν ὅτ' εἰσαΐωσιν ὑλαγμόν·
ὡς ὁ νόου λύσσῃ ἐσφαλμένα βρυχανάαται
ὠρυδόν, λοξαῖς δὲ κόραις ταυρώδεα λεύσσων
θήγει λευκὸν ὀδόντα παραφρίζει δὲ χαλινοῖς.
τὸν μὲν καὶ δεσμοῖσι πολυπλέκτοισι πιέξας
225 νέκταρι θωρήξαιο, καὶ οὐ χατέοντα κορέσκων
ἦκα βιησάμενος· διὰ δὲ στόμα βρῦκον ὀχλίζοις
ὄφρ' ἂν ὑπεξερύγῃσι δαμαζόμενος χερὶ λώβην·
ἠὲ σὺ βοσκαδίης χηνὸς νέον ὀρταλιχῆα
ὕδασιν ἐντήξαιο πυρὸς μεμορημένον αὐγαῖς·
230 καί τε σὺ μηλείης ῥηχώδεος ἄγρια κάρφη
οὔρεσιν ἐνθρεφθέντα πόροις ἀπὸ σίνεα κόψας,
ἢ ἔτι καὶ κλήροισιν ἐπήβολα τοῖά περ ὧραι
εἰαριναὶ φορέουσιν ἐνεψιήματα κούραις,
ἄλλοτε δὲ στρούθεια, τοτὲ βλοσυροῖο Κύδωνος
235 κεῖνο φυτὸν Κρήτηθεν ὃ δή ῥ' ἐκόμισσαν ἄναυροι·
πολλάκι δὴ σφύρῃσιν ἅλις ἐναολλέα κόψας
ὕδασιν ἐμβρέξαιο, νέην δ' ὀσμήρεα γληχώ
σπέρμασι μηλείοισι βάλοις ἐνομήρεα φύρων·
καί τε σύ γε ῥοδέης θυόεν μαλλοῖσιν ἀφύσσων
240 παῦρα λίπος στάξειας ἀνοιγομένοις στομάτεσσιν,

Deest Π
212 πτοίη Page 214 μυκάζει BP: cf. Th. 432 218 εἰκάδι Σ v.l. | λειοφόροισιν
MRVv¹ 221 νόου OSch. νόον codd. | βραυκανάαται BPR²v Σ v.l. 224 πολυ-

from the root and weighs upon the lips which are heavy and 210
swollen about the mouth; he suffers from a dry expectoration,
and his gums break open from the base. Often too his heart is
smitten with palpitations, and it is his fate that all his wits are
stunned and overthrown by the evil poison; and he makes
bleating noises, babbling endlessly in his frenzy; often too in his
distress he cries aloud even as one whose head, the body's master,
has just been cut off with the sword; or as the acolyte with her
tray of offerings, Rhea's priestess, appearing in the public highways on the ninth day of the month, raises a great shout with her
voice, while the people tremble as they hearken to the horrible 220
yelling of the votary of Ida. Even so the man in his frenzy of
mind bellows and howls incoherently, and as he glances sidelong
like a bull, he whets his white teeth and foams at the jaws.

You must even bind him fast with twisted ropes and make
him drunk with WINE, with gentle force filling him to satiety
even against his will; then force his gnashing teeth apart in
order that under your mastering hand he may vomit up the
deadly stuff. Or divide up and boil till soft over a bright fire
the young GOSLING of a free-feeding Goose; you should also 230
give him the wild fruit of the rough-barked APPLE-TREE grown
upon the hills after cutting off the inedible parts; or even those
kinds that pertain to the fields, such as the spring seasons bring
forth for girls to sport with; or again PEAR-QUINCES, or else the
famed fruit of the grim Cydon, which Cretan torrents have
fostered. Or sometimes, after sufficiently pounding all these with
a mallet, you should soak them in water and then throw in some
fresh and fragrant PENNYROYAL and stir in together with APPLE-
PIPS. Also you may soak up some fragrant ROSE-OIL or IRIS-OIL
into wool and let it drip into his parted lips. Yet hardly may a 240

στρέπτοισι BPR   230 τρηχώδεος Σ v.l.   236 καὶ ἀολλέα BPv   239 γε MV
γ᾽ ἢ cett. | ῥοδέης M   -έοις cett.   -έου JGSch.

ἠὲ καὶ ἰρινέοιο· μόλις δέ κε μυρί' ἐπιτλάς
ἤμασιν ἐν πολέεσσιν ἀκροσφαλὲς ἴχνος ἰήλαι
ἀσφαλέως πτοιητὸν ἔχων ἑτεροπλανὲς ὄθμα.
τῷ μὲν Γερραῖοι νομάδες χαλκήρεας αἰχμάς
245 οἵ τε παρ' Εὐφρήταο ῥόον πολέοντες ἀρούρας
χραίνουσιν· τὰ δὲ πολλὸν ἀναλθέα τραύματα τεύχει
σάρκα μελαινομένην, πικρὸς δ' ὑποβόσκεται Ὕδρης
ἰός, σηπόμενον δὲ μύδῳ ἐκρήγνυται ἔρφος.
Ἢν δὲ τὸ Μηδείης Κολχηίδος ἐχθόμενον πῦρ,
250 κεῖνό τις ἐνδέξηται ἐφήμερον, οὗ περὶ χείλη
δευομένου δυσάλυκτος ἰάπτεται ἄμμιγα κνηθμός
οἶά τ' ὀπῷ νιφόεντι κράδης ἢ τρηχέι κνίδῃ
χρῶτα μιαινομένοις ἢ καὶ σπειρώδεϊ κόρσῃ
σκίλλης ἥ τ' ἔκπαγλα νέην φοινίξατο σάρκα.
255 τοῦ καὶ ἐπισχομένοιο περὶ στόμαχον βάρος ἵζει
πρῶτον ἐρεπτόμενον, μετέπειτα δὲ λοιγέι συρμῷ
ῥιζόθεν ἑλκωθέντα, κακὸν δ' ἀποήρυγε δειρῆς,
259 σὺν δέ τε καὶ νηδὺς μεμιασμένα λύματα βάλλει
258 ὡς εἴ τε κρεάων θολερὸν πλύμα χεύατο δαιτρός.
260 ἀλλὰ σὺ πολλάκι μὲν χαίτην δρυὸς οὐλάδα κόψας,
πολλάκι καὶ φηγοῖο πόροις ἀκύλοισιν ὁμαρτῇ,
ἠὲ σύ γε βδήλαιο νέον γλάγος ἔνδοθι πέλλης·
αὐτὰρ ὁ τοῦ κορέοιτο καὶ ἐν στομάτεσσιν ἐρύξας.
ἢ μὴν πουλυγόνοιο τοτὲ βλαστήματ' ἀρήξει,
265 ἄλλοτε δὴ ῥιζεῖα καθεψηθέντα γάλακτι.
σὺν δὲ καὶ ἀμπελόεις ἕλικας ἐνθρύπτεο νύμφαις,
ἴσως καὶ βατόεντα περὶ πτορθεῖα κολούσας.
καί τε σὺ γυμνώσειας εὐτρεφέος νέα τέρφη
καστηνοῦ, καρύοιο λαχυφλοίοιο κάλυμμα,
270 νείαιραν τόθι σάρκα περὶ σκύλος αὖον ὀπάζει

Desunt Π ad v. 249, M a v. 245
241 μόλις OSch. μόγις codd.   243 om. M | ὄμμα BPR   244-8 post 208
locandos cens. JGSch.: cf. fr. 100 adn.   246 τὸ δὲ BPV¹   249 ἐχθρόμενον Π
251 ἔνδοθι κν. ω   253 μιαινομένοις JGSch. -νος codd. (μαιν- Π)   255 ἐπεσ-

man after countless sufferings at the end of many days launch
with safety his unsteady steps, while his startled gaze roams this
way and that. This is the poison with which the nomads of
Gerrha and they who plough their fields by the river Euphrates
smear their brazen arrow-heads. And the wounds, quite past
healing, blacken the flesh, for the stinging poison of the Hydra
eats its way in, while the skin, turning putrid with the infection,
breaks into open sores.

But if a man taste the loathsome fire of Colchian Medea,
the notorious MEADOW-SAFFRON, an incurable itching assails 250
his lips all over as he moistens them, such as comes upon
those whose skin is defiled with the snow-white juice of the
Fig-tree or by the stinging Nettle or by the many-coated head
of the Squill, which fearfully inflames the flesh of children. But
if he retain the poison, there settles in his gullet a pain which at
first eats into it and presently lacerates it from below with
desperate retching as he disgorges the poison from his throat;
and at the same time the belly also voids the polluted scourings,
even as a carver pours off the turbid water in which the meat
was washed.

Now sometimes you should cut and administer the crinkled 260
leaves of the OAK, or else those of the VALONIA OAK together
with the acorns; or you should draw fresh MILK in a pail and
then let the man swallow his fill of the Milk after retaining it
in his mouth. At times to be sure shoots of KNOT-GRASS will
help, or else the roots boiled in Milk. You should also infuse
VINE-TENDRILS in water, or equally well shoots of BRAMBLE
which you have chopped. Further, you should strip the green
hulls of a well-grown CHESTNUT-TREE that cover the thin-
skinned nut where the dry husk encloses the inner flesh of the 270

χυμένοι Π   256 πρῶτ' ἀνερεπτόμενον (ἀναρ-) ω   258, 9 trai. Bent.
261 ὀμήρῃ ω   Ἰσήρῃ G v.l.   263 ἐρύξει, -ξαι ω   265 δὴ ΠGP   δὲ cett. |
καταψηχθέντα, -ψυχ- ω   269 λαχυφλοίοιο ΠGΣ v.l.   ταχυ- V   τασυ- R
δασυ- BPvΣ

δυσλεπέος καρύοιο τὸ Καστανὶς ἔτρεφεν αἶα.
ῥεῖα δὲ νάρθηκος νεάτην ἐξαίνυσο νηδύν
ὅς τε Προμηθείοιο κλοπὴν ἀνεδέξατο φωρῆς·
σὺν δὲ καὶ ἑρπύλλοιο φιλοζώοιο πέτηλα
275 εὐφίμου τ᾽ ἀπὸ καρπὸν ἅλις καταβάλλεο μύρτου·
ἢ καί που σιδόεντος ἀποβρέξαιο κάλυμμα
καρπείου, μιγάδην δὲ βαλὼν ἐμπίσεο μήλοις
ὄφρ᾽ ἂν ἐπῇ στῦφόν τι ποτῷ, νοῦσον δὲ κεδάσσεις.
Ἰξιόεν δέ σε μή τι δόλῳ παρὰ χείλεσι πῶμα
280 οὐλόμενον λήσειεν ὅ τ᾽ ὠκιμοειδὲς ὄδωδε.
τοῦ μὲν ὑπὸ γλώσσης νέατος τρηχύνεται ὁλκός
νέρθεν ἐπιφλεγέθων, τὸ δέ οἱ ἐμπλάζεται ἦτορ·
λυσσηθεὶς γλῶσσαν δὲ καταπρίει κυνόδοντι,
δὴ γὰρ ὅγ᾽ ἔμπληκτος φρένα δάμναται· ἀμφὶ δὲ δοιούς
285 εἰκῇ ἐπιφράσσουσα πόρους τυφλώσατο νηδύς
ὑγρῶν τε βρωτῶν τε, καταπνίγουσα δὲ πνεῦμα
ἐντὸς ὑποβρομέει, ὀλίγῳ δ᾽ ἐνελίσσεται ὄγμῳ
πολλάκι δὴ βροντῇσιν ἀνομβρήεντος Ὀλύμπου
εἰδόμενον, τοτὲ δ᾽ αὖτε κακοῖς ῥόχθοισι θαλάσσης
290 οἵοις πετραίῃσιν ὑποβρέμεται σπιλάδεσσι.
τῷ καὶ στρευγομένῳ περ ἀνήλυθεν ἐκ καμάτοιο
πνεῦμα μόλις, πόσιες δὲ παραυτίκα λύματ᾽ ἔχευαν
φαρμακόεις ᾧσιν ἀλίγκια τοῖά τε βοσκάς
ὀρταλὶς αἰχμῇσιν ὑπευνασθεῖσα νεοσσοῖς
295 ἄλλοτε μὲν πληγῇσι νέον θρομβήια γαστρός
ἔκβαλεν ἐν μήνιγξιν ἀνόστρακα, πολλάκι νούσῳ
δαμναμένη δύσποτμον ὑπὲκ γόνον ἔκχεε γαίῃ.
τῷ μέν τ᾽ εὐβραχέος ἀψινθίου ἄλγος ἐρύξει
ἐνστῦφον πόμα κεῖνο νεοθλίπτῳ ὑπὸ γλεύκει·

Deest M ad v. 276
273 ὥστε Π | πυρὸς ἀ. φωρήν JGSch. | φωρός Σ v.l. ut vid.   277 μίγδην ω:
cf. 349 | μύρτοις ω   278 ἐπῇ Gow στῦφόν τι OSch. ἐπιστύφοντι ω -στύ-
ψαντι Π | κεδάσσαις ω   280 οὐλοφόνον ω Zon. 1112   282 ἐμπάζεται ΠΡ
ἀμπ- OSch.   284 ὅτ᾽ Π   286 καταπνείουσα Π   287 ὄγμῳ ΠGMV ὁλκῷ

nut so hard to peel which the land of Castanea brings forth.
You may suitably extract the inmost pith of the GIANT FENNEL
which received the spoils of Prometheus's thieving, and at the
same time throw in a quantity of leaves of the evergreen
TUFTED THYME and of the berries of the styptic MYRTLE; or you
might perhaps soak the rind of the POMEGRANATE, and steep it
with APPLES in a mixture until there is added to the draught
something astringent, and you will dispel the sickness.

Beware lest by craft there pass undetected on the lips a deadly
drink brewed with the CHAMAELEON-THISTLE, which has a smell 280
like that of Basil. The furrow of the victim's tongue grows rough
at the base and inflamed from below, and his heart wanders
within him. In his frenzy he gnaws his tongue with his dog-
teeth, for at times his madness overmasters his wits, while the
stomach blinds with wanton obstruction the two channels of
liquid and solid food, and rumbles with the wind it has penned
within, which circulating in a confined track often seems like
the thunder of stormy Olympus, or again like the wicked
roaring of the sea as it booms beneath rocky cliffs. Distressed 290
though he is, despite his efforts scarce can the wind escape
upward; yet medicinal draughts can at once make him void
egg-shaped stools, like the shell-less lumps which the free-
feeding fowl, when brooding her warlike chicks, sometimes
under stress of recent blows drops from her belly in their
membranes; sometimes under stress of sickness she will cast out
her ill-fated offspring upon the earth.

The familiar astringent draught of WORMWOOD steeped in
freshly pressed GRAPE-SYRUP will check his pain; sometimes too 300

---

cett.   **288** δὲ, δ' ἐν, βρ. ⍵   **289** εἰδόμενον OSch. -ος codd.   **290** οἵοις
Bent. οἵοης Π οἷος ⍵   **292** πόσιος παρ. Π   **294** ὑπευνηθεῖσα ⍵   **295** νέα
Bent. | θρόμβοις ἀνα γ. Π   **296** om. V | ἀνόστρακα Gow   -όστεα codd.
297 μαρναμένη GMRVv | δύσπεπτον ⍵   **298** εὐβραχέος ΠG -βρεχ- cett. |
ἀρήξει GMVv   **299** νεοθλίπτῳ OSch. -θλήπτῳ Π -θρίπτῳ ⍵

300 καί ποτε ῥητίνην τερμινθίδα, πολλάκι πεύκης,
πολλάκι καὶ πίτυος γοερῆς ἀπὸ δάκρυα τμήξαις
Μαρσύου ᾗχί τε Φοῖβος ἀπὸ φλόα δύσατο γυίων·
ἡ δὲ μόρον πολύπυστον ἐπαιάζουσα κατ᾿ ἄγκη
οἴη συνεχέως ἀδινὴν ἀναβάλλεται ἠχήν.

305 ἆσαι δ᾿ ἢ πολίοιο μυοκτόνου ἀργέος ἄνθην,
ἢ ἔτι καὶ ῥυτῆς πεδανὰς ἀπαμέργεο βλάστας,
νάρδον, λιμναίου τε χαδὼν ἀπὸ κάστορος ὄρχιν·
ἢ ὀδελὸν κνηστῆρι κατατρίψαιο χαρακτῷ
σιλφίου, ἄλλοτε δ᾿ ἴσον ἀποτμήξειας ὁποῖο·

310 πολλάκι δ᾿ ἀγροτέρης τραγοριγάνου ἠὲ γάλακτος
πηγνυμένου κορέοιτο νεημέλκτη ἐνὶ πέλλῃ.
Ἣν δέ τις ἀφροσύνη ταύρου νέον αἷμα πάσηται,
στρευγεδόνι προδέδουπε δαμαζόμενος καμάτοισιν
ἦμος πιλνάμενον στέρνοις κρυσταίνεται εἶαρ

315 ῥεῖα θρομβοῦται δὲ μέσῳ ἐνὶ τεύχεϊ γαστρός·
φράσσονται δὲ πόροι, τὸ δὲ θλίβεται ἔνδοθι πνεῦμα
αὐχένος ἐμπλασθέντος, ὁ δὲ σπαδόνεσσιν ἀλύων
δηθάκις ἐν γαίῃ σπαίρει μεμορυχμένος ἀφρῷ.
τῷ μέν τ᾿ ἢ ὀπόεντας ἀποκραδίσειας ἐρινούς

320 ὄξει δ᾿ ἐμπίσαιο, τὸ δ᾿ ἀθρόον ὕδατι μίξαις
συγκεράων νύμφας τε καὶ ἐνστῦφον ποτὸν ὄξευς·
ἠὲ καὶ ἐκβδήλαιο καταχθέος ἕρματα γαστρός.
καί τε σὺ πυετίην ὀθόνης πολυωπέϊ κόλπῳ
φύρσιμον ἠθήσαιο, τοτὲ προκός, ἄλλοτε νεβροῦ

325 ἢ ἐρίφου, τοτὲ δ᾿ ἂν σὺ καὶ εὐσκάρθμοιο λαγωοῦ
αἰνύμενος μογέοντι φέροις εὐαλθέ᾿ ἀρωγήν.
ἠὲ λίτρου στήδην ὀδελοῦ πόρε τριπλόον ἄχθος
εὐτριβέος, κίρνα δὲ ποτῷ ἐν δεύκεϊ Βάκχου,
ἐν καὶ σιλφιόεσσαν ὁποῖό τε μοιρίδα λίτρην,

301 τμῆξαι ω   305 ἄνθη Π Et. Gen. B 250: cf. 529, Th. 625, 856   306 ἀπα-
μέργεο BPv ἀνα- GMRV ἀπαμέλγεος Π   308 καταστρέψαιο Π | χαρακτῷ PG
-τρῷ cett.   309 ἄλλοτ᾿ ὄλιζον BPVv   310 ἀγροτέρης Et. M. 763.32,
Zon. 1742 αὐαλέης codd. | ἠδὲ Zon.   312 μέλαν ω   314 πιανόμενον Π

you may cut up the resin of the TEREBINTH-TREE, or else the tears of the CORSICAN PINE, or again of the ALEPPO PINE which makes moan on the spot where Phoebus stripped the skin from the limbs of Marsyas; and the tree, lamenting in the glens his far-famed fate, alone utters her passionate plaint unceasingly. Give him also plenty of the flowers of the bright HULWORT, fatal to mice, or strip the low-growing shoots of RUE, and SPIKENARD, and take also the testicle of the BEAVER that dwells in the lake; or rub down an obol of SILPHIUM with a toothed scraper, or else cut off the same quantity of its gum. Sometimes too he may be 310 given his fill of the wild GOAT'S MARJORAM, or of MILK just curdling in the pail after milking.

But if a man in his folly taste the fresh blood of a BULL he falls heavily to the ground in distress, overmastered by pain, when, as it reaches the chest, the blood congeals easily, and, in the hollow of his stomach, clots; the passages are stopped, the breath is straitened within his clogged throat, while, often struggling in convulsions on the ground, he gasps bespattered with foam.

You should cut off for him some juicy WILD FIGS, soak in 320 VINEGAR, and then mingle the whole with water, stirring together the water and the astringent draught of Vinegar; or drain away the burden of his surcharged belly. Also you should strain through a porous bag of fine linen some stirred CURD either from a Fawn of Roe or Red Deer or from a Kid; or again if you take some from the nimble Hare you will bring healing and help to the sufferer. Or give him three obols' weight of well-powdered SODA, and mix it in a sweet draught of Wine; mix too a *litra* with equal parts of SILPHIUM

318 σπαίρει ΠVv σκαί- cett. | μεμορυχμένος M -υγμένος cett.: cf. 330, 375
319 μὲν δὴ Π   320 ἐμμίξαιο Π | ὕδασι μίξας Ω   322 ἐκφλοίοιο Ω -φλύοιο
Toup | ἐρύματα M (fort. ἐρ-)   324 τοτὲ ΠGM   ποτὲ cett.   327 λίτρου ΠGM
νί- cett.: cf. 337, 532, Th. 942   328 ἐνὶ Ω   ἐνδευκέι OSch.

330 καὶ σπέραδος κραμβῆεν ἄδην μεμορυχμένον ὄξει·
ἇσαι δὲ ῥάδικα κακοχλοίοιο κονύζης,
ἢ πέπεριν τά τε βλαστὰ κατασμώξαιο βάτοιο,
καί κεν πηγνυμένοιο χύσιν διὰ ῥεῖα κεδάσσαις
ἠὲ διαθρύψειας ἐν ἄγγεσιν ἑστηυῖαν.
335 Μὴ μὲν ἐπαλγύνουσα πόσις βουπρήστιδος ἐχθρῆς
λήσειεν, σὺ δὲ φῶτα δαμαζόμενον πεπύθοιο.
ἡ δ' ἤτοι λίτρῳ μὲν ἐπιχρώζουσα χαλινά
εἴδεται ἐμβρυχθεῖσα βαρύπνοος· ἀμφὶ δὲ γαστρός
ἄλγεα δινεύοντα περὶ στομάτεσσιν ὄρωρεν,
340 οὖρα δὲ τυφλοῦται, νεάτη δ' ὑπὸ κύστις ὀρεχθεῖ,
πᾶσα δέ οἱ νηδὺς διαπίμπραται ὡς ὁπόθ' ὕδρωψ
τυμπανόεις ἀνὰ μέσσον ἀφυσγετὸς ὀμφαλὸν ἴζει,
ἀμφὶ δέ οἱ γυίοις τετανὸν περιφαίνεται ἔρφος.
ἡ καί που δαμάλεις ἐριγάστορας ἄλλοτε μόσχους
345 πίμπραται ὁππότε θῆρα νομαζόμενοι δατέονται,
τούνεκα τὴν βούπρηστιν ἐπικλείουσι νομῆες.
τῷ δὲ καὶ εὐκραδέος τριέτει ἐν νέκταρι μίξαις
συκῆς αὐανθεῖσαν ἅλις πόσιν ὀμφαλόεσσαν,
ἢ ἔτι καὶ σφύρῃ μιγάδην τεθλασμένα κόψας
350 ἐν πυρὶ τηξάμενος πορέειν ἀλκτήρια νούσων.
καί κε μελιζώροιο νέον κορέσαιο ποτοῖο
ἀνέρα λαιμάσσοντα, τοτὲ γλάγος εἰν ἑνὶ χεύας·
πολλάκι φοίνικος ψαφαρὸν καταμίσγεο καρπόν,
ἄλλοτε δ' αὐαλέας δὴν ἀχράδας, ἢ ἀπὸ βάκχης,
355 ἢ ἀπὸ μυρτίνης, ὁτὲ μυρτίδας οἰνάδι βάλλων.
ἢ ὅγε καὶ θηλῆς ἅτε δὴ βρέφος ἐμπελάοιτο
ἀρτιγενές, μαστοῦ δὲ ποτὸν μοσχηδὸν ἀμέλγοι,
οἵη τ' ἐξ ὑμένων νεαλὴς ὑπὸ οὔθατα μόσχος

Deest Π a v. 335 ad v. 347
330 ἅλις ω | μεμορυχμένον ΠΜ -ρυγ- cett.: cf. 318, 375   331 δὲ ΠGM δὴ
cett. | κακοφλοίοιο ω   332 πέπερι Π: cf. 607, Th. 876 | τά τε β. Π ἢ β. GMRVv
βλάστας τε ΒΡ | κατατμήξαιο Π   334 ἑστηκυῖαν ΠG   335 ἀπαλγύνουσα
ΜRV   342 ἀφυσγετὸν ΒGP   345 π. ἐσχατιῇσιν ὅταν καυλεῖα φάγωσιν

and of its Gum, and seed of CABBAGE soaked thoroughly in 330
VINEGAR. And give him a sprig of FLEA-BANE with its ill-
coloured leaves. Or you should bruise some PEPPER and buds of
the BRAMBLE-BUSH; then you will easily dissipate a mass of
congealing blood, or break it up if it has lodged in the vessels.

Do not let the agonising drink of the hateful BUPRESTIS escape
your knowledge; and you should recognise a man overcome
by it. In truth, when bitten, its contact with the jaws seems that
of Soda; it has an evil smell; and all about the mouths of the
stomach arise shifting pains; the urine is stopped and the lowest 340
part of the bladder throbs, while the whole belly is inflated, as
when a tympanitic dropsy settles in abundance about the mid
navel, and all over the man's limbs the skin is visibly taut. This
creature too, I fancy, causes swelling in plump-bellied heifers
or calves, whenever they bite it as they graze. For this reason
herdsmen name it *Buprestis* (cow-inflater).

Mix for the patient a draught of well-dried NAVEL-FIGS from
a flourishing tree in Wine three years old; or you might also
crush them together with a mallet, dissolve them over a fire, 350
and give as an antidote to his sickness. And when he recovers
his appetite give him again his fill of this honey-sweet drink,
sometimes adding MILK to the mixture; or else cast in and mix
with Wine the dry fruit of the DATE-PALM or WILD PEARS that
have long been dried, or the fruit of the common PEAR, or of
the CORDATE PEAR, or sometimes MYRTLE-BERRIES; or let him
even, like a new-born child, put his lips to the nipple, and
calf-like draw a draught from the breast, even as a new-born
calf fresh from the womb, butting the udder, forces out the

BPRv Σ v.l. | δατέωνται G   347 τοῖς δὲ Σ v.l.   τῷ καὶ ω | εὐκραδέης, -ίης
ω Σ v.l. | τριπετεῖ GP   -τῇ BMRVv Σ v.l. | μίξαις om. Π   348 συκέης OSch.
-κων codd.   349 μίγδην Π: cf. 277   350 φορέειν Π | νούσου Bent.
352 λαιμώσσοντα, μαι- ω | χεύας OSch. -αις ω -σας Π   354 αὐαλέης δ.
ἀχράδος ω   355 βάλλοι Π   358 οὔθατα GMRV   -τι cett.

βράσσει ἀνακρούουσα χύσιν μενοεικέα θηλῆς.

360 ἄλλοτε πιαλέης πόσιος χλιαροῖο κορέσκοις,
ἐς δ' ἔμετον βιάοιο καὶ οὐ ποθέοντά περ ἔμπης
χειρὶ βιαζόμενος ἠὲ πτερῷ, ἢ ἀπὸ βύβλου
στρεβλὸν ἐπιγνάμψαιο ταμὼν ἐρυτῆρα φάρυγγος.
Ἢν δ' ἐπιτυρωθῇ νεαρὸν γάλα τεύχεϊ γαστρός,
365 δὴ τοτὲ τόνδε πνιχμὸς ἀθροιζομένοιο δαμάζει.
τῷ δ' ἤτοι τρισσὰς πόσιας πόρε, μέσσα μὲν ὄξευς
δοιὰς δὲ γλυκέος, στεγανὴν δ' ὑποσύρεο νηδύν·
ἢ ἔτι καὶ Λιβύηθε ποτῷ ἐγκνήθεο ῥίζας
σιλφίου, ἄλλοτ' ὁποῖο, νέμοις δ' ἐν βάμματι τήξας·
370 πολλάκι δὲ θρύπτειραν ἐπεγκεράσαιο κονίην,
ἠὲ νέον βρυόεντα θύμου στάχυν· ἄλλοτ' ἀμύνει
βότρυς ἐυκνήμοιο μίγα βρεχθέντος ἐν οἴνῃ·
ἐν καί που ταμίσοιο ποτὸν διεχεύατο θρόμβους,
καὶ χλοεραὶ μίνθης ἄπο φυλλάδες ἠὲ μελίσσης
375 ἠὲ καὶ ἐνστύφοντι ποτῷ μεμορυχμέναι ὄξευς.
Ἀλλ' ἄγε δὴ φράζοιο δορύκνιον, οὔ τε γάλακτι
ὠπῇ τε βρῶσίς τε παρὰ στομάτεσσιν ἔικται·
τῷ δ' ἤτοι λυγμοὶ μὲν ἀηθέσσοντες ὁμαρτῇ
αὐχέν' ἀνακρούουσιν, ὁ δ' ἀχθόμενος στόμα γαστρός
380 πολλάκι μὲν δαίτην ἀπερεύγεται αἱματόεσσαν,
ἄλλοτε νηδυίων θολερὴν μυξώδεα χεύει
τηνεσμῷ ὡς εἴ τε δυσέντερος ἀχθόμενος φώς·
δήποτε τειρόμενος καμάτοις κάρφουσι δέδουπε
γυῖα δαμείς· οὐ μὲν ποθέει ξηρὸν στόμα δεῦσαι.
385 τῷ δὲ σὺ πολλάκι μὲν γλάγεος πόσιν, ἄλλοτε μίγδην
ῥεῖα γλυκὺ νείμειας ἀλυκρότερον δεπάεσσι·
καί τε καὶ ὄρνιθος φιαρῆς πυρὶ τηκομένη σάρξ
θωρήκων ἤμυνεν ἐυτρεφέων βρωθεῖσα·

---

359 βράσσει OSch. -ττει codd.: cf. 137   **360** λιαροῖο Π   **361** χατέοντα ω
362 βινσάμενος Π | ἢ καὶ π. ω   **363** στρεβλὸν Πν   στρεπτὸν cett. | ἐπη-
νέψαιο Π | κακῶν ω   **364** ἐπιθρομβωθῇ νεαλὲς (ι)   **365** ποτε τόνδε τε
πνιγμὸς ω   **370** ῥύπτειραν G | κονίλην ω   **373** ἢν καὶ Π   **375** ἐν στυ-

quickening flow from the teat. Or else you may give him his 360 fill of some warm and greasy drink and compel him to vomit, unwilling though he be, forcing him with your fingers or with a feather; or cut and twist from papyrus a curved throat-tickler.

But if fresh MILK turn cheesy in the hollow of a man's stomach, then, as it collects, suffocation overcomes him. Give him three draughts, one of VINEGAR between two of GRAPE-SYRUP, and purge his costive bowels. Or further, grate into a draught the root of SILPHIUM from Libya, or else some of its gum, and administer it dissolved in Vinegar. Or again, you 370 may add to the mixture dispersive LYE or a fresh-blooming sprig of CRETAN THYME. Sometimes the clustered fruit of the EUCNEMUS well-steeped in Wine is a help. Also a drink of CURD, they say, disperses the clots; so too the green leaves of MINT mixed either with a draught of HONEY or with an astringent one of VINEGAR.

Consider now the THORN-APPLE, whose aspect and whose taste upon the lips are like milk. At once unwonted retchings agitate the throat of the drinker, and by reason of the pain at the mouth of his stomach he either vomits up his food stained with 380 blood, or else he voids it, foul and full of mucus, from his bowels, like one suffering from the spasms of dysentery. Sometimes worn out with the parching struggle his limbs give way and he falls to the ground, yet has no wish to moisten his dry mouth.

You must either administer draughts of MILK, or else perhaps GRAPE-SYRUP, slightly warmed and mixed with it in his cup. Moreover the flesh from the plump breast of a sleek FOWL,

φόεντι Σ | μεμορυγμέναι ὦ: cf. 318, 330   376 δορύχνιον Π Et. M. 283.38 v.l.
377 περὶ ὦ Et. Gen. B 92   378 ἤτοι ΠMR   ἤδη cett.   381 νηδύων ΠPVv
383 δήν ποτε Π   384 στ. βρέξαι ὦ   385 γάλατος Π   386 ῥεῖ
ἀποτὸν Π

119

ἤμυνεν καὶ χυλὸς ἅλις κύμβῃσι ῥοφηθείς,
390 ὅσσα τε πετρήεντος ὑπὸ ῥόχθοισι θαλάσσης
κνώδαλα φυκιόεντας ἀεὶ περιβόσκεται ἀγμούς·
ὧν τὰ μὲν ὠμὰ πάσαιτο, τὰ δ' ἐφθέα, πολλὰ δὲ θάλψας
ἐν φλογιῇ. στρόμβων δὲ πολὺ πλέον, ἢ ἔτι κάλχης,
κηραφίδος, πίνης τε καὶ αἰθήεντος ἐχίνου
395 δαῖτες ἐπαλθήσουσιν ἰδὲ κτένες· οὐδέ τι κῆρυξ
†δὴν ἔσεται† τήθη τε γεραιρόμενα μνίοισι.
Μηδέ σέ γ' ἐχθομένη λήθῃ πόσις — οὐ γὰρ ἄιδρις—
Φαρικοῦ, ἢ γναθμοῖσιν ἔπι βαρὺν ὤπασε μόχθον.
τὴν ἤτοι γευθμῷ μὲν ἰσαιομένην μάθε νάρδῳ,
400 ἤνυσε δὲ σφαλερούς, ὁτὲ δ' ἄφρονας, ἐν δὲ μονήρει
ῥηιδίως ἀκτῖνι βαρὺν καταναίρεται ἄνδρα.
ἀλλὰ σὺ πολλάκι μὲν σταδίην εὐανθέα νάρδου
ῥιζίδα θυλακόεσσαν ὀπάζεο τήν τε Κίλισσαι
πρηόνες ἀλδαίνουσι παρὰ πλημμυρίδα Κέστρου,
405 ἄλλοτε δὲ σμυρνεῖον ἐυτριβές. αἴνυσο δ' αὐτήν
ἴριδα λειριόεν τε κάρη τό τ' ἀπέστυγεν Ἀφρώ,
οὕνεκ' ἐριδμαίνεσκε χρόης ὕπερ, ἐν δέ νυ θρίοις
ἀργαλέην μεσάτοισιν ὀνειδείην ἐπέλασσε
δεινὴν βρωμήεντος ἐναλδήνασα κορύνην.
410 πολλάκι δὲ σκύλαιο κάρη, περὶ δ' αἴνυσο λάχνην
κέρσας εὐήκει νεόθεν ξυρῷ, ἐν δέ νυ θάλψαις
ἤια κριθάων νεοθηλέα φυλλάδα τ' ἰσχνήν
πηγάνου ἥν τ' ὤκιστα βορῇ ἐπεσίνατο κάμπη,
βάμματι δ' ἐνδεύσαιο καὶ εὖ περὶ κόρσεα πλάσσοις.
415 Μηδὲ συοσκυάμῳ τις ἀιδρήεντα κορέσκοι
νηδύν, οἷά τε πολλὰ παρασφαλέες τεύχονται,
ἠὲ νέον σπείρημα καὶ ἀμφίκρηνα κομάων
κοῦροι ἀπειπάμενοι ὀλοήν θ' ἑρπηδόνα γυίων,

390 πετρήεσσιν BP   392 δάσαιο Π   -αιτο OSch. | πολλάκι θ. ω   394 καὶ
ῥαφίδος Π | πίνης ΠΜ   πίννης cett.   395 ἀπαλθήσουσιν Π: cf. Th. 654
396 γεραιρόμενα Toup   γεραιό- codd.   γεραινό- Σ   397 ἐχθομένου
ἄνθηι π. Π   402 στήδην Bent.: cf. 327   403 ῥιζάδα BPR   405 αἴνετο Π

softened on the fire and eaten, can be a help; so too is GRUEL if
swallowed by the bowlful; also the creatures which beneath 390
the roaring of the rocky sea ever feed about the weed-clad
crags: some of these he should devour raw, others boiled,
many of them after broiling over a fire; but dishes of SEA-
SNAILS or of the PURPLE LIMPET, of CRAYFISH and PINNA and
of the brown SEA-URCHIN will be far more helpful, and
SCALLOPS; neither...the TRUMPET-SHELL or SEA-SQUIRTS that
revel in the seaweed.

Let not the hateful draught of PHARICUM escape your memory
—for you are not ignorant of it: it causes grievous suffering
in the jaws. Know that to the taste it is like spikenard; but
it sends men reeling or sometimes out of their senses, and in 400
a single day it can easily kill a strong man.

Now you may either weigh out and administer some of the
purse-like root of the fair-flowering MOUNTAIN NARD which the
headlands of Cilicia nourish by the brimming Cestrus, or else
well-ground CRETAN ALEXANDERS. Take also the IRIS itself and
the head of the LILY, abhorred of Aphrodite, seeing that it was
her rival for colour; wherefore in the midst of its petals she
attached a thing of shame to vex it, making to grow there the
shocking yard of an ass. Or else you may shave his head, and 410
having cut the hair from the roots with a keen-edged razor,
take it, and after heating along with it fresh BARLEY-MEAL and the
dry leaves of RUE, which in its feeding the caterpillar is quickest
to spoil, soak in Vinegar and plaster thickly about his temples.

Let no man in ignorance fill his belly with HENBANE, as men
often do in error, or as children who, having lately put aside
their swaddling-clothes and head-bindings, and their perilous

ἄλλοτε M   409 ἐναλδήσασα GMRVv -ανθήσασα Π   410 post 412 habent ὠ
411 ἔρσας Π   412 νεοθηλέα BGP -θήλατα Π νεοηλέα cett.   414 πάσσοις Π
415 μὴ μὲν ὑοσκυάμῳ ὠ   416 σπέρχονται ὠΣv.l.   417 ἀμφίκρηνα OSch.
-κρήμνα Π -κάρηνα ὠ   418 θ' om. Π

121

ὀρθόποδες βαίνοντες ἄνις σμυγεροῖο τιθήνης
420 ἡλοσύνῃ βρύκουσι κακανθέεντας ὁράμνους,
οἷα νέον βρωτῆρας ὑπὸ γναθμοῖσιν ὀδόντας
φαίνοντες τότε κνηθμὸς ἐνοιδέα δάμναται οὖλα.
τῷ δ' ὁτὲ μὲν καθαρὴν γλάγεος πόσιν ἄλθεα πίσαις,
ἄλλοτε βουκέραος χιληγόνου ὅ ῥα κεραίας
425 εὐκαμπεῖς πετάλοισιν ὑπηνεμίοισιν ἀέξει,
ἀτμενίῳ μέγ' ὄνειαρ ὅτ' ἐμπλώῃσιν ἐλαίῳ.
ἠὲ σύ γ' αὐαλέον κνίδης σπόρον, ἄλλοτε δ' αὐτήν
νείμαις ὠμόβρωτον ἄδην ἀνὰ φυλλάδ' ἀμέλξαι,
κίχορα καρδαμίδας τε καὶ ἣν Περσεῖον ἔπουσιν,
430 ἐν δέ τε νάπειον ῥάφανόν θ' ἅλις, ἐν δέ τε λεπτάς
ἄμμιγα κρομμύων γηθυλλίδας· ἤρκεσε δ' ἄτην
εὐάγλις κώδεια νέον σκορόδοιο ποθεῖσα.
    Καί τε σὺ μήκωνος κεβληγόνου ὁππότε δάκρυ
πίνωσιν, πεπύθοιο καθυπνέας· ἀμφὶ γὰρ ἄκρα
435 γυῖα καταψύχουσι, τὰ δ' οὐκ ἀναπίτναται ὄσσε
ἀλλ' αὔτως βλεφάροισιν ἀκινήεντα δέδηεν·
ἀμφὶ καὶ ὀδμήεις καμάτῳ περιλείβεται ἱδρώς
ἀθρόος, ὠχραίνει δὲ ῥέθος, πίμπρησι δὲ χείλη,
δεσμὰ δ' ἐπεγχαλάουσι γενειάδος, ἐκ δέ τε παῦρον
440 αὐχένος ἑλκόμενον ψυχρὸν διανίσσεται ἄσθμα·
πολλάκι δ' ἠὲ πελιδνὸς ὄνυξ μόρον ἢ ἔτι μυκτήρ
στρεβλὸς ἀπαγγέλλει, ὁτὲ δ' αὖ κοιλώπεες αὐγαί.
ἄσσα σὺ μὴ δείδιχθι, μέλοιο δὲ πάμπαν ἀρωγῆς
οἰνάδι καὶ γλυκόεντι ποτῷ κεκαφηότα πιμπλάς
445 τινθαλέῳ· τοτὲ δ' ἔργα διαθρύψαιο μελίσσης
ἄμμιγα ποιπνύων Ὑμησσίδος αἵ τ' ἀπὸ μόσχου
σκήνεος ἐξεγένοντο δεδουπότος ἐν νεμέεσσιν·

419 ἄνευ ΠG | μογεροῖο ω   420 βρύκουσι Gow -κωσι codd. | κακανθήεντας
BPv -ήσαντας GMRV κακ' ἀλθήεντας Π   422 φύοντες Bent. | post h.v. fort.
statuenda lacuna   423 γλάγεος καθαρὴν Π | ἤλιθα ω | πίσαις Gow πίνειν ω
πώμοις Π   424 χιληγόνου ΠΣ v.l. Et. M. 207.38 σιτη- ΩΣ v.l. κεβλη- G v.l.,
Σ v.l.: cf. 433 | ὅρρα codd.   427 αὐαλέης Π | αὐτῶν Π   428 ἀμέλξαι G¹MRV

crawling on all fours, and walking now upright with no anxious nurse at hand, chew its sprays of baleful flowers through 420 witlessness, since they are just bringing to light the incisor teeth in their jaws, at which time itching assails their swollen gums.

Give the patient either pure MILK to drink as a remedy or else FENUGREEK, which is grown for fodder and puts forth curving horns amid its windswept leaves—a great boon when it floats in common OIL. Or else you should give him dried NETTLE SEED, or even the raw leaves of the Nettle itself in plenty to suck, or CHICORY and GARDEN-CRESS and what they call PERSEUM, and 430 besides these, MUSTARD and RADISHES in plenty, and mingled with them slender SPRING ONIONS. A head of GARLIC with well-grown cloves just taken in a drink also averts disaster.

Learn further that when men drink the tears of the POPPY, whose seeds are in a head, they fall fast asleep; for their extremities are chilled; their eyes do not open but are bound quite motionless by their eyelids. With the exhaustion an odorous sweat bathes all the body, turns the cheeks pale, and causes the lips to swell; the bonds of the jaw are relaxed, and through 440 the throat the laboured breath passes faint and chill. And often either the livid nail or wrinkled nostril is a harbinger of death; sometimes too the sunken eyes.

Of all these symptoms you must not be afraid, but devote yourself entirely to succour, filling the failing man with boiling-hot WINE and GRAPE-SYRUP. Or else make haste to break in pieces the labour of the Bee of Hymettus. (Bees were born

-ξας v² ἀμίξαι Π ἀμέρξαι G² -ξας BPv¹ 430 νάπειον MR -ειαν cett.
431 κρομμυόφιν Bent.: cf. Th. 931 433 καὶ δὲ ω 437 καὶ ΠGMR δὲ cett.
439 ἐπεγχελάουσι γενειάδες ἐς Π 443 ἀλλὰ σὺ Klauser | δείδιθι ω 445 ποτὲ
ω | διαθρύψαιο BG -ψιε Π -θρέψαιο P -τρέψ- MR -θρύπτοιο Vv 446 Ὑμητ-
τίδος ω

ἔνθα δὲ καὶ κοίλοιο κατὰ δρυὸς ἐκτίσσαντο
πρῶτόν που θαλάμας συνομήρεες, ἀμφὶ καὶ ἔργων
450 μνησάμεναι Δηοῖ πολυωπέας ἤνυσαν ὄμπας
βοσκόμεναι θύμα ποσσὶ καὶ ἀνθεμόεσσαν ἐρείκην.
452 δήποτε δ᾽ ἢ ῥοδέοιο νέον θύος εὔτριχι λήνει,
455 ἠὲ καὶ ἰρινόεν, τοτὲ δ᾽ αὖ μορόεντος ἐλαίης,
453 ὀχλίζων κυνόδοντα, τότ᾽ ἡμύουσι χαλινοῖς,
454 ἐνθλίβοις, μαλλὸν δὲ βαθὺν κεκορημένον ἕλκοι.
456 αἶψα δὲ τόν γ᾽ ἑκάτερθε διὰ ῥέθος ἔγρεο πλήσσων,
ἄλλοτε δ᾽ ἐμβοόων, τοτὲ δὲ κνώσσοντα σαλάσσων,
ὄφρα κατηβολέων ὀλοὸν διὰ κῶμα κεδαίῃ,
τῆμος δ᾽ ἐξερύγῃσιν ἀλεξόμενος κακὸν ἄλγος.
460 σπεῖρα δ᾽ ἐνὶ χλιαρῷ λίπεϊ, πρὸ δὲ νέκταρι, βάπτων
τρῖβε καὶ ἐκθέρμαινε ποτῷ ἐψυγμένα γυῖα,
ἄλλοτε δ᾽ ἐν δροίτῃ κεράων ἐμβάπτεο σάρκας,
αἶψα δὲ τινθαλέοισιν ἐπαιονάασθε λοετροῖς
αἷμ᾽ ἀναλυόμενοι τετανόν τ᾽ ἐσκληκότα ῥινόν.
465 Εἰδείης δὲ λαγοῖο κακοφθορέος πόσιν αἰνήν,
οὐλομένην, τὸν κῦμα πολυστίου τέκεν ἅλμης.
τοῦ δ᾽ ἤτοι λοπίδων μὲν ἰδὲ πλύματος πέλει ὀδμή,
γευθμὸς δ᾽ ἰχθυόεις νεπόδων ἅτε σαπρυνθέντων,
ἠὲ καὶ ἀρρύπτων ὁπόταν λοπὶς αὐξίδα χραίνῃ.
470 ὃς δ᾽ ἤτοι ῥυπόεις μὲν ὑπ᾽ ὀστλίγγεσσιν ἀραιαῖς
τευθίδος ἐμφέρεται νεαλὴς γόνος ἢ ἅτε τεύθου,
οἷά τε σηπιάδος φυξήλιδος ἥ τε μελαίνει
οἶδμα χολῇ δολόεντα μαθοῦσ᾽ ἀγρώστορος ὁρμήν.
τῶν ἤτοι ζοφόεις μὲν ἐπὶ χλόος ἔδραμε γυίοις
475 ἰκτερόεις, σάρκες δὲ περισταλάδην μινύθουσι
τηκόμεναι, ὁ δὲ δόρπα κατέστυγεν · ἄλλοτε ῥινός

449 θαλάμας ΠGM -μους cett. | συνομηρέας GMR 450 ὤπασαν Μ | ὄμπνας ΒΡ
451 ἠνεμόεσσαν Σ v.l. 452 λήνει ΠGM λίνῳ cett. 455 trai. Gow | Ἰρινέου ω |
ἐλαίου GM 453 καὶ ἡμύουσι Ρ¹ καὶ εἰμ- ΒΡΡ² | χαλινούς ΜΡ 454 κεκορεσμένον ω | ἕλκοι Gow -κοις codd. 457 ὀτὲ ω | παλάσσων ΒΡν 458 κεδαίῃ
OSch. -ης Π κεδάσσῃ ω 459 ἀφυξόμενος Π 460 χλοερῷ ω 462 ἐμβάλλεο

from the carcase of a calf that had fallen dead in the glades, and
there in some hollow oak they first, maybe, united to build
their nest, and then, bethinking themselves of work, wrought 450
round it in Demeter's honour their many-celled combs, as with
their feet they gathered thyme and flowering heath.) There are
times when, prizing open his dog-teeth, or into his drooping
jaws, you should squeeze with a tuft of fleecy wool some fresh,
fragrant ROSE-OIL or IRIS-OIL or again oil of the sleek OLIVE; and
let him drain a thick flock saturated with it. And forthwith
rouse him with slaps on either cheek, or else by shouting, or
again by shaking him as he sleeps, in order that the swooning
man may dispel the fatal drowsiness and may then vomit,
ridding himself of the grievous affliction. And dip cloths first 460
in WINE and then in warm OIL, and rub and chafe his chilled
limbs with the liquid; or again, mix them in a bath-tub and dip
his body in it, and at once immerse him in the hot bath and so
thaw his blood and soften his taut, dry skin.

Also you should learn to know the dire and fateful drink of
the deadly SEA-HARE, offspring of the waves of the pebbly sea.
Its odour is that of fishes' scales and of the water in which they
have been scoured; its taste is fishy like that of rotten fish, or of
unwashed when scales taint the dish. A sordid creature with its 470
slim tentacles, it resembles the new-born young of the calamary
or of the octopus or the fugitive cuttlefish, which stains the
sea black with its gall directly it perceives the fisherman's
crafty assault. Over the limbs of the poisoned spreads the
dusky pallor of jaundice, and piecemeal their flesh melts away
and dwindles, and food is utterly loathsome. At times the

MR | σάρκα Ѡ   463 ἐπαι(ο)νάασθαι Ѡ -νάσαιο Scal.   464 ἀναλυόμενος Ѡ
465 κακοφθαρέος Π | π. ἔμπης Ѡ   466 πολυστίον Π: cf. Th. 792   467 λεπίδων
BPR: cf. Th. 154   469 ἀπλύντων MRV   471 ἢ ἀπὸ Π   472 ἢ ἅτε σ. Ѡ
473 δολόεντι Bent.   475 περισταλάδην Bent. e Σ -στολ- codd.

ἄκρον ἐποιδαίνων σφυρὰ πίμπραται, ἀμφὶ δὲ μήλοις
ἄνθε᾽ ἅτε βρυόεντα κυλοιδιόωντος ἐφίζει.
δὴ γὰρ ἐφωμάρτησεν ὀλιζοτέρη ῥύσις οὔρων,
480 ἄλλοτε πορφυρέη, τότ᾽ ἐπὶ πλέον αἱμάσσουσα.
πᾶς δὲ παρὰ δρακέεσσι φανεὶς ἐχθαίρεται ἔλλοψ,
αὐτὰρ ὁ ναυσιόεις ἀλίην ἐμυσάξατο δαῖτα.
τῷ μὲν Φωκήεσσαν ἅλις πόσιν ἐλλεβόροιο
νείμειας, τοτὲ δάκρυ νεοβλάστοιο κάμωνος,
485 ὄφρα ποτὸν νέποδός τε κακοῦ ἐκ φύρματα χεύῃ·
ἄλλοτε βρωμήεντος ἀμελγόμενος γάλα πίνοι,
ἠὲ χύτρῳ τήξας μαλάχης λιπόωντας ὀράμνους·
καί ποτε κεδρινέης πελάνου βάρος ἔμμορε πίσσης,
βρύκοι δ᾽ ἄλλοτε καρπὸν ἅλις φοινώδεα σίδης
490 Κρησίδος, οἰνωπῆς τε καὶ ἣν Προμένειον ἔπουσι,
σὺν δὲ καὶ Αἰγινῆτιν, ὅσαι τ᾽ ἐσκληκότα κάρφη
φοίνι᾽ ἀραχνήεντι διαφράσσουσι καλύπτρῃ·
ἄλλοτε δ᾽ οἰνοβρῶτα βορὴν ἐν κυρτίδι θλίψαις
ὡς εἴ περ νοτέουσαν ὑπὸ τριπτῆρσιν ἐλαίην.
495 Ἢν δέ τις ἀζαλέῃ πεπιεσμένος αὐχένα δίψῃ
ἐκ ποταμοῦ ταυρηδὸν ἐπιπροπεσὼν ποτὸν ἴσχῃ
λεπτὰ διαστείλας παλάμῃ μνιώδεα θρῖα,
τῷ μέν τε ῥοιζηδὰ φιλαίματος ἐμπελάουσα
ῥύμῃ ἅλις προὔτυψε ποτοῦ μέτα χήτεϊ βρώμης
500 βδέλλα πάλαι λαπαρή τε καὶ ἱμείρουσα φόνοιο.
ἢ ὅθ᾽ ὑπὸ ζοφερῆς νυκτὸς κεκαλυμμένος αὐγάς
ἀφραδέως κρωσσοῖο κατακλίνας ποτὸν ἴσχῃ
χείλεσι πρὸς χείλη πιέσας, τὸ δὲ λαιμὸν ἀμείψῃ
κνώδαλον ἀκροτάτοισιν ἐπιπλῶον ὑδάτεσσι,
505 ταὶ μὲν ἵνα πρώτιστον ὀχλιζομένας ῥόος ὤσῃ
ἀθρόα προσφύονται ἀμελγόμεναι χροὸς αἷμα,

Desunt Π a v. 483 ad v. 495, BP a v. 497 ad v. 503
479 ῥύσις Page : cf. 599   κρίσις codd.   482 ἐμυσάξατο Bent. ἐμυδά- ω ἀνεμύ-
ξατο Π ἀπε- OSch.   483 Φωκήεσσαν G²Σ v.l. φοινή- cett.   487 ῥυπόων-
τας BP   488 ἔμπορε Scal.   491 δὲ Vv om. cett. | τ᾽ ἐσκληκότα Gv τὰ
σκληρέα cett.   494 νοτέουσαν GMR ν(ε)οτ(τ)εύου- cett.   495 αὐαλέῃ ω :

surface of the flesh swells and grows puffy about the ankles; the
eyes are swollen, and as it were luxuriant blossoms settle upon
the cheeks. For there follows a scantier flow of urine, which
is sometimes red, at others still more bloody in colour. Then **480**
the sight of every fish is hateful to his eyes and in his disgust
he loathes food from the sea.

Give the patient a sufficient draught of Phocian HELLEBORE or
the gum of new-grown SCAMMONY in order that he may void
both the draught and the filth of the evil fish; or else he should
milk a SHE-ASS and drink the milk, or he should dissolve smooth-
skinned sprigs of the MALLOW in a pot. Then again he is given
an obol's weight of CEDAR PITCH; or else let him eat his fill of the
scarlet fruit of the POMEGRANATE, the Cretan kind, the wine- **490**
red, and the sort they call *Promenean*, also that from Aegina, and
all those which partition hard, red grains into sections by
a covering like a spider's web. Or else you should squeeze the
flesh of GRAPES through a strainer, like olives oozing beneath
the presses.

But if a man whose throat is constrained by parching thirst fall
on his knees and draw water from a stream like a bull, parting
with his hand the delicate, moss-like plants, then, approaching
eagerly along with the water there rushes upon him in its
desire for food the blood-loving LEECH, long flaccid and yearn- **500**
ing for gore. Or when a man's eyes are shrouded beneath dark
night, and without thinking he drinks from a pitcher, tipping
it up and pressing his lips to its, the creature floating on the
surface of the water passes down his throat. At the point to
which first the stream drives and collects them, the Leeches
fasten on in numbers and suck the body's blood, settling now

cf. *Th.* 339   **498** τοῦ ω | τοι ρ. Π: cf. 36   **499** μέτα χήτεϊ OSch.   μετὰ
χείλει ω   -λεσι Π   **500** πάλαι OSch.   παραὶ codd. | λαμυρή Knox
501 ζοφέης ω   **502** ἴσχοι Π   **505** ταὶ Bent.   τὰς codd. | ὀχλιζόμενος ρ.
σώσει Π

ἄλλοτε μέν τε πύλησιν ἐφήμεναι ἔνθα τε πνεῦμα
αἰὲν ἀθροιζόμενον στεινοῦ διαχεύεται ἰσθμοῦ,
ἄλλοτε δὲ στομίοισι πέριξ ἐπενήνοθε γαστρός
510 ἀνέρα πημαίνουσα, νέην δ' ἐπενείματο δαῖτα.
τῷ σὺ τότ' ἐν δεπάεσσι κεραιόμενον ποτὸν ὄξευς
νείμειας, ποτὲ δαῖτα συνήρεα χιονόεσσαν,
πολλάκι κρυστάλλοιο νέον βορέησι παγέντος.
ἠὲ σὺ γυρώσαιο καθαλμέα βώλακα γαίης
515 ναιομένην, θολερὴν δὲ πόσιν μενοεικέα τεῦχε·
ἢ αὐτὴν ἅλα βάπτε, τότ' ἠελίοισι δαμάζων
εἶθαρ ὀπωρινοῖσι, τότ' ἠνεκὲς ἐν φλογὶ θάλψας.
πολλάκι δ' ἢ ἅλα πηκτὸν ὁμιλαδόν, ἢ ἁλὸς ἄχνην
ἐμπίσαις τήν τ' αἰὲν ἀνὴρ ἁλοπηγὸς ἀγείρει
520 νειόθ' ὑφισταμένην ὁπόθ' ὕδασιν ὕδατα μίξῃ.
    Μὴ μὲν δὴ ζύμωμα κακὸν χθονὸς ἀνέρα κήδοι
πολλάκι μὲν στέρνοισιν ἀνοιδέον, ἄλλοτε δ' ἄγχον,
εὖτ' ἐπὶ φωλεύοντα τραφῇ βαθὺν ὁλκὸν ἐχίδνης
ἰὸν ἀνικμαῖνον στομίων τ' ἀποφώλιον ἄσθμα.
525 κεῖνο κακὸν ζύμωμα τὸ δή ῥ' ὑδέουσι μύκητας
παμπήδην, ἄλλῳ γὰρ ἐπ' οὔνομα κέκριται ἄλλο.
ἀλλὰ σύ γ' ἢ ῥαφάνοιο πόροις σπειρώδεα κόρσην,
ἢ ῥυτῆς κλώθοντα περὶ σπάδικα κολούσας·
πολλάκι καὶ χαλκοῖο πάλαι μεμογηότος ἄνθην,
530 ἄλλοτε κληματόεσσαν ἐν ὀξεῖ θρύπτεο τέφρην·
δήποτε ῥιζάδα τρῖβε πυρίτιδα βάμματι χραίνων
ἠὲ λίτρον, τοτὲ φύλλον ἐναλδόμενον πρασιῇσι
καρδαμίδος, Μῆδόν τε καὶ ἐμπρίοντα σίνηπυν·
σὺν δὲ καὶ οἰνηρὴν φλογιῇ τρύγα τεφρώσαιο
535 ἠὲ πάτον στρουθοῖο κατοικάδος· ἐκ δὲ βαρεῖαν
χεῖρα κατεμματέων ἐρύγοι λωβήμονα κῆρα.

508 δια(ν)ίσσεται ω   511 τῷ ΠG καὶ cett.   513 βορέαο Π   515 θολερὴν
ΠG v.l. Μ Σ v.l.   θαλ- cett. | τεύξαις ω   517 φλογὶ ΠGM   πυρὶ cett.   520 μίξει
ΠV   524 ἀνικμαῖνον OSch. -ιχμ- Π -ικμάζων Σ v.l.   ἀποπνεῖον ω   525 κακὸν
ΠG   ποτὸν cett.   526 ἄλλως Π | κέκληται ἄλλῳ Π   528 κλωσθέντα Π | ῥάδικα

at the entrance where the breath always gathers to pour through
the narrow pharynx, and sometimes one clings about the mouths
of the stomach inflicting pain, and swallows a fresh repast.   510

You should administer to the patient a draught of VINEGAR
mixed in his cup, and sometimes with it SNOW to eat, or ICE fresh
frozen by the north winds. Or you should dig up some moist,
brackish SOIL and brew therewith a turbid potion to give him
strength; or draw actual SALT WATER, and either warm it at once
beneath the late summer sun or heat it steadily over a fire. Or
else you should give him ROCK SALT in plenty or the SALT
FLAKES which a salter ever gathers as they settle at the bottom 520
when he mingles water with water.

Let not the evil ferment of the soil injure a man; it will often
swell up in his chest, at other times it will choke him, when it
is fostered over the Viper's coil deep in its lair, sucking up the
monster's venom and the noxious breath from its mouth. This
is the evil ferment which they call *Fungi* in general, for to
different kinds different names have been assigned.

Now do you cut off either the head of a CABBAGE with its
coats of leaves or the green fronds of RUE, and administer them.
Or else crumble the BLOOM OF COPPER that has had long use,
or ashes of the VINE in VINEGAR. Sometimes grate the root of 530
BINDWEED or some SODA into an infusion of Vinegar, or a leaf
of the CRESS which grows in garden-plots; and CITRON too, and
the biting MUSTARD. You should also reduce to ashes in the fire
the lees of WINE or the droppings of the domestic FOWL, and then
let the man thrust his hand hard down his throat and vomit up
the deadly poison.

Σ v.l.   530 θρύπτεο ΠGM ῥύπτεο cett.   531 ῥιзάδα ΠMPR -ίδα cett. |
ῥαίνων ω   532 ἢ λ. Π: cf. 327   533 ἐμπριόεντα GP | σίνηπυν ΠMR -πι
cett.   535 βαθεῖαν Bent.   536 ἐρύκοις ω: cf. 137, 8 | λωβήτορα ω

Ἢν δὲ λιπορρίνοιο ποτὸν δυσάλυκτον ἰάψῃ
φαρμακίδος σαύρης πανακηδέος ἢν σαλαμάνδρην
κλείουσιν, τὴν οὐδὲ πυρὸς λωβήσατο λιγνύς,
540 αἶψα μὲν ἐπρήσθη γλώσσης βάθος, ἂψ δ' ὑπὸ μάλκης
δάμνανται, βαρύθων δὲ κακὸς τρόμος ἄψεα λύει ·
οἱ δὲ περισφαλόωντες ἅτε βρέφος ἑρπύζουσι
τετραποδί · νοεραὶ γὰρ ἀπὸ φρένες ἀμβλύνονται ·
σάρκα δ' ἐπιτροχόωσαι ἀολλέες ἄκρα πελιδναί
545 σμώδιγγες στίζουσι κεδαιομένης κακότητος.
τῷ δὲ σὺ πολλάκι μὲν πεύκης ἀπὸ δάκρυ' ἀμέρξας
τενθρήνης ἀνάμιγδα πόροις ἐν πίοσιν ἔργοις,
ἠὲ χαμαιπίτυος βλαστήμονος ἄμμιγα κώνοις
φύλλα καθεψήσειας ὅσους ἐθρέψατο πεύκη ·
550 ἄλλοτε δὲ σπέραδος κνίδης μυλοεργέι μίσγων
τερσαίνοις ὀρόβοιο παλήματι · καί ποτε κνίδην
ἑψαλέην κρίμνοισι παλυνάμενος ψαθυροῖσιν
εὖ λίπεϊ χραίνοιο, βορῆς δ' ἀέκοντα κορέσκοις.
ναὶ μὴν ῥητίνη τε καὶ ἱερὰ ἔργα μελίσσης
555 ῥίζα τε χαλβανόεσσα καὶ ὤεα θιβρὰ χελύνης
ἀλθαίνει τότε νέρθε πυρὸς ζαφελοῖο κεραίης ·
556a ἀλθαίνει καὶ γέντα συὸς φλιδόωντος ἀλοιφῇ
ἀμμίγδην ἀλίοιο καθεψηθέντα χελύνης
γυίοις ἤ τ' ἀκιρῇσι διαπλώει πτερύγεσσιν,
ἄλλοτε δ' οὐρείης κυτισηνόμου ἤν τ' ἀκάκητα
560 αὐδήεσσαν ἔθηκεν ἀναύδητόν περ ἐοῦσαν
'Ερμείης · σαρκὸς γὰρ ἀπ' οὖν νόσφισσε χέλειον
αἰόλον ἀγκῶνας δὲ δύω παρετείνατο πέζαις.
καί τε σύ γ' ἢ γερύνων λαιδροὺς δαμάσαιο τοκῆας
ἄμμιγα δὲ ῥίζας ἠρυγγίδας, ἢ καὶ ἐπαρκές

---

538 πανακηδέος OSch. -κιδ- Π πολυκηδ- ω   540 βάρος Π   541 δάμναται
ἐμβαρύθων ω   542 περισφαλέοντες ω   543 τετράποδες ω   544 ἐπι-
τροχόωσιν ω   545 στάζουσι ω Σ ν.l.   546 δάκρυα μόρξα(ι)ς BPRv δ. τμή-
ξα(ι)ς GM   549 τ' ἔθρ. MR   551 παλήατι GM   552 ἀψαλέην Π |
παλυνόμενος GM | ψαθυροῖσιν OSch. -ρῆσιν Π -φαροῖσιν ω   553 εὖ Π σὺν

But if hurt come from a draught, hard to cure, of the sorcerer's Lizard, slippery-skinned and utterly reckless, which they call the SALAMANDER, and which not even a fierce flame can harm, then on a sudden the base of the tongue is inflamed and 540 then the victims are overcome with chill, and a fearful trembling burdens and loosens their joints. They stagger and crawl upon all fours like an infant, for the faculties of the mind are utterly blunted, and livid weals spreading thick over the skin blotch the extremities as the poison is diffused.

Give the sufferer frequent doses of the tears stripped from the PINE-TREE mingled with the Bee's rich produce; or boil down the leaves of the budding GROUND-PINE together with the cones which the PINE puts forth. And sometimes mix the NETTLE'S 550 seed with the finely ground meal of BITTER VETCH, and dry them. Sometimes too you should sprinkle cooked NETTLES with crumbling BARLEY-GROATS, dress well in OIL, and force the patient to eat in plenty even against his will. Again, PINE-RESIN and the sacred produce of the Bee and the root of ALL-HEAL and the delicate eggs of the TORTOISE are curative when you mix them on a hot fire; curative too the flesh of a HOG abounding in fat when boiled down together with the limbs of the SEA-TURTLE which swims at large with weak flippers; or else with those of the mountain TORTOISE that feeds on tree-medick, the creature that Hermes the Gracious endowed with a voice 560 though voiceless, for he separated the chequered shell from the flesh and extended two arms from its edges. Further, either you should bend to your service the TADPOLES' impudent parents and ERYNGO roots with them, or you should throw into a pot

GM ἐν cett.   555 χελώνης ω: cf. 557   556, 6a in marg. habet G   556a om. V | φλιόωντος ἀλοιφήν Π   557 ἀλίοισι Π | χελύνης ΠG¹ -ώνης cett.: cf. 555 558 ἤ τ' ἄκρησι Σ v.l.   ἤ ταχινῆσι ω   562 παρετείνετο Πν   564 ἤ Π ἐν ω | καὶ G   δὲ καὶ BP   δὲ cett.

565 θάλπε βαλὼν χύτρῳ σκαμμώνιον. οἶσι κορέσκων
ἀνέρα καὶ θανάτοιο πέλας βεβαῶτα σαώσεις.
Ἢν γε μὲν ἐκ φρυνοῖο θερειομένου ποτὸν ἴσχῃ,
ἢ ἔτι καὶ κωφοῖο λαχειδέος ὅς τ' ἐνὶ θάμνοις
εἴαρι προσφύεται μορόεις λιχμώμενος ἔρσην,
570 τῶν ἤτοι θερόεις μὲν ἄγει χλόον ἠΰτε θάψου,
γυῖα δὲ πίμπρησιν, τὸ δὲ συνεχὲς ἀθρόον ἄσθμα
572 δύσπνοον ἐκφέρεται παρὰ χείλεσι δ' ἐχθρὸν ὄδωδεν.
578 αὐτὰρ ὅ γ' ἄφθογγός τε καὶ ἐν δονάκεσσι θαμίζων
πολλάκι μὲν πύξοιο χλόον κατεχεύατο γυίοις,
580 ἄλλοτε δ' ὑγραίνει χολόεν στόμα· καί ποτε λυγμοί
ἀνέρα καρδιόωντα θαμειότεροι κλονέουσι·
δὴν δὲ κατικμάζων ἄγονον σπόρον ἄλλοτε φωτός,
583 πολλάκι θηλυτέρης, σκεδάων γυίοισι τέλεσκε.
573 ἀλλὰ σὺ τῷ βατράχοιο καθεφθέον ἠὲ καὶ ὀπτήν
574 σάρκα πόροις, ὁτὲ πίσσαν ἐν ἡδέι μίγμενος οἴνῃ·
575 καί τε σπλὴν ὀλοοῖο κακὸν βάρος ἤρκεσε φρύνης,
576 λιμναίης φρύνης πολυηχέος ἥ τ' ἐπὶ φύκει
577 πρῶτον ἀπαγγελέουσα βοᾷ θυμάρμενον εἶαρ.
584 ναὶ μὴν τοῖς ὁτὲ νέκταρ ἀφυσγετὸν ἐν δεπάεσσι
585 χεύαις εἰς ἔμετον δὲ καὶ οὐ χατέοντα πελάζοις,
ἠὲ πίθου φλογιῇ θάλψας κύτος αἰὲν ἐναλθῆ
ἀνέρα θερμάσσαιο, χέαι δ' ἀπὸ νήχυτον ἱδρῶ·
καί τε καὶ αὐξηρῶν δονάκων ἀπὸ ῥιζέα κόψας
οἴνῃ ἐπεγκεράσαιο, τὰ δή ῥ' ὑποτέτροφε λίμνη
590 οἰκείῃ τόθι λεπτὰ διὲκ ποσὶν ἑρπετὰ νήχει,
ἠὲ φιλοζώοιο κυπείριδος ἠὲ κυπείρου,
αὐτόν τ' ἠνεκέεσσι τρίβοις πανάπαστον ἐδωδῆς
καὶ πόσιος ξήραινε, κατατρύσαιο δὲ γυῖα.

565 ἀμμώνιον Π | κορέσκοις Π   567 ἴσχη G -ης cett. Σ v.l.   568 λεχειδέος
MR λαχιδ- BP | ὅς ποτε Π   572 ὀδωδεῖ Π   581 θαμειότεροι MR θαμ(ε)ινό-
cett.   583 κεδάων Π | τελίσκει ω   573-7 transp. Gow   573 καθεφ-
θέον OSch.: cf. 392   κατεφθέος Π καθεψέος ω (-ψίοιο M) | ὀπτῆς Bent.

a sufficient quantity of SCAMMONY and cook it. With these feed
the sick man to satiety, and though he be near to death, you will
save him.

If a man imbibe a draught from the sun-loving TOAD or from
the dumb and green-hued TOAD which in the springtime clings
to the bushes, sleek, and licking up the dew, one of them, the 570
sun-lover, induces a pallor like fustic and causes swellings in
the limbs while the breath issues continually in long gasps and
forced, and smells foul at the mouth. Whereas the voiceless one 578
that frequents the reeds sometimes diffuses the yellowness of
boxwood over the limbs, and sometimes bedews the mouth 580
with a flow of bile. Sometimes too a man suffers from heartburn, and persistent hiccups convulse him. And it causes the
seed, now of man now of woman, to drip on, and often
scattering it over their limbs it renders it infertile. But you 573
should give the patient the flesh of a FROG boiled or roasted;
sometimes PITCH which you have mixed with sweet WINE. And
the spleen of the deadly TOAD averts the grievous oppression—
the vocal Toad of the fen, which cries on the sedge, the first
harbinger of delightful spring. Further, for such patients you 584
should sometimes pour out WINE in abundance, cup after cup,
and induce the man to vomit, reluctant though he be; or else
heat over a fire a big-bellied vessel and keep the sick man
always warm, and let him sweat profusely. Also you should
clip and mix with WINE the roots of tall-growing REEDS which
are nourished by the Toads' native marsh, where as tiny 590
creatures they swim about with their feet, or roots of the life-
loving GALINGALE, female and male; and dry the man's body by
ceaseless exercise, keeping him from all food and drink, and
exhaust his limbs.

575 φρύνης om. Π -νοῦ Bent.   576, 7 fort. eiciendi   576 πολυάλγεος Π |
ἐνὶ OSch.   577 ἀπαγγέλλουσα ω   586 ἀναλθῆ ΜΣ v.l.   587 φαρμάσ-
σαιο Π   588 αὖ ξηρῶν MRV   ἢ ξ. Σ v.l.   αὐχμηρῶν JGSch.   589 οἴνῳ ω |
ὑπεγκεράσαιο Π   590 οἰκίει Π

Ἐχθραλέον δέ σε μή τι λιθάργυρος ἀλγινόεσσα
595 λήσειεν τότε γαστρὶ πέσῃ βάρος, ἀμφὶ δὲ μέσσον
πνεύματ' ἀνειλίσσοντα κατ' ὀμφάλιον βρομέῃσιν,
οἷά περ εἰλίγγοιο δυσαλθέος ὅς τε δαμάζει
ἀνέρας ἀπροφάτοισιν ἐνιπλήσσων ὀδύνῃσιν.
οὐ μὲν τῶν γ' οὔρων ἄνυται ῥύσις, ἀμφὶ δὲ γυῖα
600 πίμπραται, αὐτάρ που μολίβῳ εἰδήνατο χροιή.
τῷ δ' ὀτὲ μὲν σμύρνης ὀδελοῦ πόρε διπλόον ἄχθος,
ἄλλοτε δ' ὁρμίνοιο νέην χύσιν, ἄλλοτε κόψαις
οὐρείην ὑπέρεικον, ὅθ' ὑσσώπου ὀροδάμνους,
πολλάκι δ' ἀγριόεντα κράδην, σπέραδός τε σελίνου
605 Ἴσθμιον, ᾧ θ' ὑπὸ κοῦρον ἀλίβλαπτον Μελικέρτην
Σισυφίδαι κτερίσαντες ἐπηέξησαν ἀέθλους.
ἠὲ σύ γ' ἐν πέπεριν ῥυτῇ συνομήρεα φώξας
οἴνῳ ἐνιτρίψαιο, κακῆς δ' ἀπερύκεο νούσου·
κύπρου τε βλαστεῖα νεανθέα, πολλάκι σίδης
610 πρωτόγονον κυτίνοιο πόροις ἀνθήμονα καρπόν.
[Μὴ μὲν δὴ σμῖλον σὺ κακὴν ἐλατηίδα μάρψαις
Οἰταίην, θανάτοιο πολυκλαύτοιο δότειραν,
ἥν τε καὶ ἐμπλείουσα χαλικροτέρη πόσις οἴνης
οἵη ἐπαλθήσειε παρὰ χρέος ἡνίκα φωτός
615 ἴσθμια καὶ φάρυγος στεινὴν ἐμφράσσεται οἶμον.
Καὶ τὰ μὲν οὖν Νίκανδρος ἑῇ ἐνικάτθετο βίβλῳ
μοχθήεντα μύκητα παρ' ἀνέρι φαρμακόοντα.
πρὸς δ' ἔτι τοῖς Δίκτυννα τεῆς ἐχθήρατο κλῶνας
Ἥρη τ' Ἰμβρασίη μούνη στέφος οὐχ ὑπέδεκτο,
620 κάλλεος, οὕνεκα Κύπριν, ὅτ' εἰς ἔριν ἠέρθησαν
ἀθάναται, κόσμησεν ἐν Ἰδαίοισιν ὄρεσσι—
τῆς σύ γ' ἀπ' εὐύδροιο νάπης, εὐαλθὲς ὄνειαρ,
καρπὸν πορφυρόεντα συναλδέα χειμερίῃσιν

Deest Π a v. 611
594 ἐχθομένη ω   597 εἰλειοῖο Π   598 ἐπαΐσσων GM   599 τό γ' Π τῶν
GM   600 χροιήν ω   604 κράδης Π   605 ᾧ ποτε G | ἀλίβλαπτον ΠG² -βαπ-
cett.   606 ἀέθλοις GMPR   607 πέπερι GP | ῥυσίμῳ ἐνομήρεα κόψας ω

Also do not neglect LITHARGE, which brings suffering when its hateful burden sinks into the stomach and wind circulates and rumbles about the mid navel, as in a violent colic which overpowers men, smiting them with sudden pains. The victi.. 's flow of urine fails; then the limbs swell and the skin has the 600 appearance of lead.

Give the patient either a double obol's weight of MYRRH or a fresh infusion of SAGE, or else cut him HYPERICUM from the hills, or sprigs of HYSSOP, or again a spray of the WILD FIG and seed of CELERY from the Isthmus, beneath which the sons of Sisyphus buried the youthful Melicertes, slain by the sea, and established games. Or else you should roast PEPPER along with RUE and grate them into WINE, and so rescue him from deadly sickness. You should also give him fresh buds of HENNA, or the firstling fruit of the POMEGRANATE with the 610 flower still upon it.

[See that you do not pluck the dangerous, pine-like YEW of Oeta: it is the giver of lamentable death, and only a copious draught of unmixed WINE can bring instant help when it chokes the pharynx and the narrow passage of a man's throat.]

[Some remedies medicinal for a man against noxious Fungi Nicander in fact set down in his book, but in addition to these (the MYRTLE) whose twigs Dictynna abhors, and which Hera of the Imbrasus alone receives not for her garland, seeing that it adorned the Cyprian queen on mount Ida, when the 620 goddesses were roused to compete in beauty with one another— from this in some watered glade take as a healing boon the scarlet fruit that waxes and is warmed with the wintry rays of

611-28 damn. OSch.   612 πολυκλαύστοιο BMR   616 ἐνικάτθετο MR   ἐγκ-
cett.   617 φαρμακόοντα Gow   -όεντα codd.   618 τοῖς OSch. e Σ   τοι GM
σοι cett.   619 ῞Ηρη Spanheim   -ρης codd. | Ἰμβρασίη B   -ίης cett.   620 ἠέρθη-
σαν GM   ἠερέθ- RV   ἠρέθισσαν BPv   622 εὐαλθὲς MR   -αλδὲς cett.: cf. 326

ἠελίου θαλφθέντα βολαῖς δοίδυκι λεήνας,
625 χυλὸν ὑπὲρ λεπτῆς ὀθόνης ἢ σχοινίδι κύρτῃ
ἐκθλίψας πορέειν κυάθου κοτυληδόνα πλήρη—
ἢ πλεῖον, πλεῖον γὰρ ὀνήιον· οὐ γὰρ ἀνιγρόν
πῶμα βροτοῖς—τόδε γάρ τε καὶ ἄρκιον αἴ κε πίῃσθα.]
Καί κ' ἔνθ' ὑμνοπόλοιο καὶ εἰσέτι Νικάνδροιο
630 μνῆστιν ἔχοις, θεσμὸν δὲ Διὸς ξενίοιο φυλάσσοις.

Deest Π
625 ὑπαὶ G   626 ἐκθλίψας πορέειν Bent.   -ψαντα πορεῖν codd.   628 τόδε
BG   τότε cett.   629 καί κεν ἔθ' GM

the sun, and pounding them with a pestle strain the juice over
fine linen or with a rush sieve and administer a cup containing
a *cyathus*—or more, for a larger dose is serviceable since this
draught is not harmful to men—for that is in fact sufficient cure
if you drink it.]

And now hereafter you will treasure the memory of Nicander
the singer, and observe the command of Zeus, Protector of **630**
Friendships.

FRAGMENTS

OETAICA

16

Ath. vii. 282 F: Νίκανδρος δ' ἐν δευτέρῳ Οἰταϊκῶν φησι·

πομπίλος ὃς ναύτῃσιν ἀδημονέουσι κελεύθους
μηνῦσαι φιλέρωσι καὶ ἄφθογγός περ ἀμύνων.

18

Ath. vii. 329 A: τῶν δὲ ἰώπων μνημονεύει Νίκανδρος ἐν β'
Οἰταϊκῶν·

ὡς δ' ὁπότ' ἀμφ' ἀγέλῃσι νεηγενέεσσιν ἰώπων
ἠὲ φάγροι ἢ σκῶπες ἀρείονες ἠὲ καὶ ὀρφός.

THEBAICA

19

Σ Th. 214: Παμβώνια δὲ ὄρη τῆς Μεγαρικῆς, ὡς αὐτὸς ἐν
τρίτῳ τῶν Θηβαϊκῶν·

τείχεά τε προλιπόντες ὑπὲρ Παμβωνίδας ὄχθας
ἐσσύμενοι Μεγαρῆος ἐνευνάσσαντο δόμοισι.

SICELIA

21

Steph. Byz. s.v. ΖΑΓΚΛΗ: Νίκανδρος ἐν τῷ η' Σικελίας·

καί τις καὶ Ζάγκλης ἐδάη δρεπανηίδος ἄστυ.

16.2 μήνυσεν Dobree | ἀμύνων Gesner -νω A
18. β' Οἰταϊκῶν Dind. Βοιωτιακῶν A   2 ἠὲ Headlam ἦ A

138

OETAICA

16

Nicander in the second book of his *Oetaica* says

Pilot-fish, who would show the way to amorous sailors in their sore distress, succouring them voiceless though he be.

18

Sprats are mentioned by Nicander in the second book of his *Oetaica*:

And as when around the shoals of new-born sprats sea-breams or the larger cod-fish or a sea-perch.

THEBAICA

19

The Pambonian mountains are in Megaris, as Nicander himself says in the third book of his *Thebaica*:

And leaving the walls, over the Pambonian hills they sped and laid them to sleep in the halls of Megareus.

SICELIA

21

ZANCLE: Nicander in the eighth book of his *Sicelia*:

And one learnt also of the city of Zancle the sickle-shaped.

21. η': v.ll. ζ', δεκάτῳ

22

Σ *Th.* 382: τὴν μάλκην … αὐτὸς Νίκανδρος ὁτὲ μὲν ἐπὶ ψύχους ὁτὲ δ' ἐπὶ τοῦ ναρκᾶν κέχρηται· καὶ ἐπὶ μὲν τοῦ ψύχους ἐν τῇ Σικελίᾳ τὸν τρόπον τόνδε·

ὄμβρῳ τε κρυμῷ τε, δέμας τότε δάμνατο μάλκη

ἐπὶ δὲ τοῦ ναρκᾶν μόνον ἐν τοῖς Κιμμερίοις εἶπεν.

EUROPIA

26

Steph. Byz. *s.v.* ῎ΑΘΩΣ: ὄρος Θράκης, ἀπὸ ῎Αθω γίγαντος, ὡς Νίκανδρος πέμπτῳ τῆς Εὐρωπείας·

καί τις ῎Αθω τόσον ὕψος ἰδὼν Θρήικος ὑπ' ἄστροις
ἔκλυεν αὐδηθέντος ἀμετρήτῳ ὑπὸ λίμνη
ὄσσαν· ἀπ' οὖν χείρεσσι δύο ῥίπτεσκε βέλεμνα,
ἠλιβάτου προθέλυμνα Καναστραίης πάρος ἀκτῆς.

27

Σ *Th.* 460: τῆς Ζώνης … μέμνηται καὶ οὗτος ὁ Νίκανδρος·

τῷ μὲν ὑπὸ Ζωναῖον ὄρος δρύες ἀμφί τε φηγοί
ῥιзόθι δινήθησαν ἀνέστησάν τε χορείην
οἷά τε παρθενικαί.

22.1 δέμας τότε δάμνατο Lobeck δέματ' ὅτε δ. G δ. ὁ. δάμνονται P δέσμαθ' ὅτ' ἐδάμνοντο K δ. ὅτε θάμναντο V | μάλκη Gow μᾶλλον codd.

22

The word *malke* Nicander himself uses sometimes in the sense
of 'cold' and sometimes in the sense of 'growing numb'; and
in the sense of 'cold' he uses the word thus in his *Sicelia*:

With both rain and frost, when the body was overcome with
cold,

but in his *Cimmerians* he uses it only in the sense of 'growing
numb'.

EUROPIA

26

ATHOS: a mountain in Thrace, so named after the giant Athos,
as Nicander in the fifth book of his *Europia* says:

And one beholding Thracian Athos towering up beneath the
stars, heard his voice as he shouted beneath the fathomless lake.
So with his hands he hurled two missiles wrenched erewhile
from the steep promontory of Canastrum.

27

And in another passage our author Nicander mentions Zone:

Therefore beneath the Zonaean mount oak-trees and ilexes
all about were whirled from their roots and began to dance
as maidens do.

26.2 αὐδηθέντος Hermann οὐ δ- codd. οὐδήεντος Headlam 3 ὅσσαν·
ἀπ' οὖν OSch. ὃς ἀναποῦν codd.
27.1 τῷ OSch. τό, τά, καί codd. 2 χορείην OSch. -αν codd.

OPHIACA

31

Ael. N.A. x. 49: Νίκανδρος· λέγει δὲ

οὔκ ἔχις οὐδὲ φάλαγγες ἀπεχθέες οὐδὲ βαθυπλήξ
ἄλσεσιν ἐνζώει σκορπίος ἐν Κλαρίοις,
Φοῖβος ἐπεί ῥ' αὐλῶνα βαθὺν μελίῃσι καλύψας
ποιηρὸν δάπεδον θῆκεν ἑκὰς δακετῶν.

32

Ael. N.A. xvi. 28: ὁ δὲ (Ψύλλος) τῷ νοσοῦντι παρακλίνεται γυμνῷ γυμνός, καὶ τοῦ χρωτός οἱ τοῦ ἰδίου προσανατρίψας τὴν ἰσχὺν τὴν συμφυῆ, εἶτα μέντοι τοῦ κακοῦ πεποίηκε τὸν ἄνθρωπον ἐξάντη. ἀποχρῶν δὲ ἄρα ὑπὲρ τούτου εἴη ἂν μάρτυς καὶ Νίκανδρος ὁ Κολοφώνιος λέγων,

ἔκλυον ὡς Λιβύης Ψύλλων γένος οὔτε τι θηρῶν
αὐτοὶ κάμνουσιν μυδαλέῃσι τυπαῖς
οὓς Σύρτις βόσκει θηροτρόφος, εὖ δὲ καὶ ἄλλοις
ἀνδράσιν ἤμυναν τύμμασιν ἀχθομένοις
οὐ ῥίζαις ἔρδοντες, ἑῶν δ' ἀπὸ σύγχροα γυίων,

καὶ τὰ ἐπὶ τούτοις.

HETEROEUMENA

43

Steph. Byz. s.v. ΑΣΠΑΛΑΘΕΙΑ: πόλις Ταφίων. Νίκανδρος Ἑτεροιουμένων πρώτῃ·

Ἀσπαλάθεια βοήροτος.

31.2 ἐνζώει Bernhardy ἐν ζώοις codd.

OPHIACA

31

And Nicander says:

No viper, nor harmful spiders, nor deep-wounding scorpion inhabit the glades of Clarus, for Apollo veiled its deep grotto with ash-trees and purged its grassy floor of noxious creatures.

32

The Psyllian lies down naked beside the sick man also naked, and applying to him by friction the innate power of his own skin, renders him free of the poison. And Nicander of Colophon should be sufficient witness to the fact, when he says:

I have heard how the race of Psylli in Libya suffer not at all themselves from the festering wounds inflicted by the creatures that are nurtured by beast-infested Syrtis, and are well skilled also to succour other men when grievously bitten; not working with simples, but from their own limbs, skin touching skin—

and so on.

HETEROEUMENA

43

ASPALATHEA: a town of the Taphians. Nicander in Book I of the *Heteroeumena*:

Aspalathea ploughed by oxen.

32.1 Λιβύης Bergk   Λίβυες codd.   **3** v.l. θινοτρόφος

FRAGMENTS

50

Ath. iii. 82 A: μνημονεύει δ' αὐτῶν (τῶν ἐν Σιδοῦντι μήλων)
καὶ Νίκανδρος ἐν Ἑτεροιουμένοις οὕτως·

αὐτίχ' ὅγ' ἢ Σιδόεντος ἠὲ Πλείστου ἀπὸ κήπων
μῆλα ταμὼν χνοάοντα τύπους ἐνεμάσσετο Κάδμου.

59

Ath. vii. 305 D: Νίκανδρος δ' ἐν τετάρτῳ Ἑτεροιουμένων
φησίν·

ἢ σκάρον ἢ κίχλην πολυώνυμον.

62

ΣΜ Eur. Hec. 3: Νίκανδρος δὲ Εὐριπίδῃ συνδραμὼν τὴν
Ἑκάβην φησὶ Κισσέως·

ἔνθ' Ἑκάβη Κισσηίς, ὅτ' ἐν πυρὶ δέρκετο πάτρην
καὶ πόσιν ἑλκηθεῖσα παρασπαίροντα θυηλαῖς,
εἰς ἅλα ποσσὶν ὄρουσε καὶ ἣν ἠλλάξατο μορφήν
γρήιον, Ὑρκανίδεσσιν ἐειδομένην σκυλάκεσσιν.

GEORGICA

68

Ath. iii. 126 B: (Νίκανδρος) ἐν τῷ προτέρῳ τῶν Γεωργικῶν
ἐμφανίζων τὴν τοῦ χόνδρου χρῆσιν καὶ μύστρον ὠνόμασε
διὰ τούτων·

ἀλλ' ὁπότ' ἢ ἐρίφοιο νεοσφάγος ἠὲ καὶ ἀρνός
ἢ αὐτοῦ ὄρνιθος ἐφοπλίζηαι ἐδωδήν,
χίδρα μὲν ἐντρίψειας ὑποστρώσας ἐνὶ κοίλοις

50.2 χνοάοντα Jacobs χλο- A | ἐνεμάσσετο Dind. νεμέσσατο A
62.2 ἑλκηθεῖσα Cobet -θεῖσαν Μ | θυηλαῖς Cobet θηλαῖς Μ   3 ποσσὶν ὄρουσε
Cobet ποσὶν ὥρουσε Μ   4 Ὑρκανίδεσσιν Hermann ὑρνακίδεσιν Μ | ἐειδο-
μένην Hermann -νον Μ | σκυλάκεσσιν Cobet -εσιν Μ

144

50

Nicander too in his *Heteroeumena* speaks thus of them (the apples of Sidus):

Straightway he cut Cadmean characters with deep impress upon downy apples from the gardens of Sidus or of Pleistus.

59

Nicander in the fourth book of his *Heteroeumena* says:

Either parrot-wrasse or wrasse of many names.

62

And Nicander concurs with Euripides in calling Hecabe the daughter of Cisseus:

Whereat Hecabe, daughter of Cisseus, when as a captive she beheld her home in flames and her husband gasping out his life beside the sacrificial victims, leaped into the sea and changed her aged form, which took the semblance of a Hyrcanian hound.

GEORGICA

68

Nicander in the first book of his two *Georgica* showing the use of groats also mentions the word *mystron* [spoon hollowed out of bread] in the following words:

But when you prepare for eating a freshly-killed kid or lamb or even a chicken, sprinkle the bottom of hollow vessels with unripe wheaten groats and pound them down; then stir up

68. 1 καὶ JGSch. κεν codd.   2 ἐφοπλίζηαι Dind. -ʒεαι epitt. -εσθαι A
3 ἐντρίψειας OSch. ἐκτ-, εἰστ- codd. | ἐνὶ JGSch. δ' ἐνὶ codd.

FRAGMENTS

ἄγγεσιν, εὐώδει δὲ μιγῆ ἀνάφυρσον ἐλαίῳ,
5 ζωμὸν δὲ βρομέοντα †καταντλας†...

...πνῖγε δὲ πῶμα
ἀμφιβαλών, φωκτὸν γὰρ ἀνοιδαίνει βαρὺ κρῖμνον·
ἠρέμα δὲ χλιάον κοίλοις ἐκδαίνυσο μύστροις.

69

Ath. ii. 52 E: φηγοὶ Πανὸς ἄγαλμα,
φησὶ Νίκανδρος ἐν β΄ Γεωργικῶν.

70

Ath. (a) (1-5) ix. 369 B: Νίκανδρος δ' ἐν τοῖς Γεωργικοῖς τῆς
βουνιάδος μνημονεύει· (b) (4-18) iv. 133 DE: ὅτι δ' ἤσθιον διὰ
ἀναστόμωσιν καὶ τὰς δι' ὄξους καὶ νάπυος γογγυλίδας
σαφῶς παρίστησι Νίκανδρος ἐν δευτέρῳ Γεωργικῶν λέγων
οὕτως· (c) (16) ix. 366 D: σίνηπυ δ' ὠνόμασε Νίκανδρος ὁ
Κολοφώνιος...ἐν δὲ τοῖς Γεωργικοῖς·

γογγυλίδας σπείροις δὲ κυλινδρωτῆς ἐφ' ἅλωος
ὄφρ' ἂν ἴσαι πλαθάνοισι χαμηλοτέροις θαλέθωσι·
βουνιὰς †ἀλλ' εἴσω ῥαφάνοις εἴσω λαθαρωκοί†.
γογγυλίδος δισσὴ γὰρ ἰδ' ἐκ ῥαφάνοιο γενέθλη
5 μακρή τε στιφρή τε φαείνεται ἐν πρασιῆσι.
καὶ τὰς μέν τ' αὖηνον ἀποπλύνας βορέησι,
προσφιλέας χειμῶνι καὶ οἰκουροῖσιν ἀεργοῖς·
θερμοῖς δ' ἱκμανθεῖσαι ἀναζώουσ' ὑδάτεσσι.
τμῆγε δὲ γογγυλίδος ῥίζας κατακαρφέα φλοιόν
10 ἦκα καθηράμενος λεπτουργέας, ἠελίῳ δέ
αὐήνας ἐπὶ τυτθόν, ὅτ' ἐν ζεστῷ ἀποβάπτων
ὕδατι, δριμείη πολέας ἐμβάπτισον ἅλμη·
ἄλλοτε δ' αὖ λευκὸν γλεῦκος συστάμνισον ὄξει

68. 4 ἀνάφυρσον OSch. ἅμα φ. codd. 5 καταντλάσαι OSch., qui lacunam
statuit 7 δὲ epitt. δ' ἐν A | χλιαρὸν Cas. | ἐκδαίνυσο Kaibel -νεο A ἐξαίρεο
epitt.
70. 2 χαμηλοτέροις Gow -ραι codd. 3 ῥάφανος κείσθω OSch. 6 τ' αὖ.

146

together with fragrant oil. And when the broth seethes, pour it over them...but smother by clapping on the lid, for as it stews the coarse meal swells. And when it simmers gently, eat it with hollow scoops of bread.

69

Oaks, the delight of Pan,

says Nicander in the second book of the *Georgica*.

70

(*a*) Nicander in his *Georgica* mentions the French turnip. (*b*) And that to whet the appetite they also ate turnips treated with vinegar and mustard Nicander makes plain in the second book of his *Georgica*, saying... (*c*) Nicander of Colophon mentioned mustard [in *Th.* 921] and in his *Georgica*.

But sow turnips on a threshing-floor levelled with a roller, so that they may grow to the shape of low kneading-tables. The French turnip...for two stocks, turnip and French turnip, both of them long and solid, are to be seen in our garden-plots. French turnips you should wash and dry in the north winds; they are welcome in winter to those who stay idle indoors, and if soaked in hot water they revive. But the roots of the turnip you should cut into fine slices after gently washing the dry outer skin, and then let them parch for a little while in the sun; or else dip a number of them in boiling water, and then plunge them into bitter brine; or again pour white must and vinegar into the same vessel in equal quantities, and then

Gow θ' αὖ. codd. | ἀποπλύνας Bernard -βλύν -A **9** κατακαρφέα OSch. καὶ ἀκαρφέα codd. **10** ἠελίῳ Mus. -ιος A **12** δριμείη Bernard -μύη A | ἅλμη Mus. -μηνι A **13** γλεῦκος Mus. γλυκεῖ A

147

ἶσον ἴσῳ, τὰς δ᾽ ἐντὸς ἐπιστύψας ἁλὶ κρύψαις.
15 πολλάκι δ᾽ ἀσταφίδας προχέας τριπτῆρι λεήναις
σπέρματά τ᾽ ἐνδάκνοντα σινήπυος. εἶν ἑνὶ δὲ τρύξ
ὄξεος ἰκμάζουσα καὶ †ὠμοτέρην ἐπὶ κόρσην
ὥριον ἁλμαίην ἄμυσαι κεχρηόσι δαίτης†

71

Ath. ix. 371 b: Νίκανδρος δ᾽ ἐν δευτέρῳ Γεωργικῶν φησιν·

ἐν δέ τε καὶ μαράθου καυλὸς βαθύς, ἐν δέ τε ῥίζαι
πετραίου, σὺν δ᾽ αὐτὸς ἐπαυχμήεις σταφυλῖνος,
σμυρνεῖον σόγκος τε κυνόγλωσσός τε σέρις τε·
σὺν καὶ ἄρου δριμεῖα καταψήχοιο πέτηλα
ἠδ᾽ ὅπερ ὄρνιθος κλέεται γάλα.

72

Ath. ix. 372 e: Νίκανδρος ὁ Κολοφώνιος ἐν τῷ δευτέρῳ τῶν
Γεωργικῶν μνημονεύει ταύτης τῆς χρήσεως, σικύας ὀνο-
μάζων τὰς κολοκύντας· οὕτως γὰρ ἐκαλοῦντο, ὡς πρότερον
εἰρήκαμεν· λέγει δ᾽ οὕτως·

αὐτὰς μὴν σικύας τμήγων ἀνὰ κλώσμασι πείραις
ἠέρι δὲ ξήρανον· ἐπεγκρεμάσαιο δὲ καπνῷ,
χείμασιν ὄφρ᾽ ἂν δμῶες ἅλις περιχανδέα χύτρον
πλήσαντες ῥοφέωσιν ἀεργέες, †ἔνθα τε μέτρια†
5 ὄσπρια πανσπερμηδὸν ἐπεγχεύῃσιν ἀλετρίς.
τῇ ἔνι μὲν σικύης ὅρμους βάλον ἐκπλύναντες,
ἐν δὲ μύκην σειράς τε πάλαι λαχάνοισι πλακείσας
αὐοτέροις †καυλοῖς τε μιγήμεναι εὐφαοριζῃ†.

70. 15 ἀσταφίδας Bernard -δος A
71. 1 τε Bernard τι A | ἐν δέ τε Bernard οὐδ᾽ ἔτι A   2 πετραίου Schweig.
-ρίου A | ἐπαυχμήεις OSch -μείην A   3 σμυρνεῖον JGSch. -νίον A   5 κλέεται
Dind. καλέεται A: cf. Th. 104

immerse them in it and cover with salt. Again, you may pound raisins and the mordant seed of mustard with a pestle and pour them in. And at the same time moist lees of vinegar....

71

Nicander in the second book of his *Georgica* says:

And along with them a tall stem of fennel, along with them too roots of stone sperage, and even the slatternly carrot as well, Cretan alexanders, and sow-thistle, and hound's tongue, and endive; with them pound also the bitter leaves of cuckoo-pint and the plant which is called 'bird's milk'.

72

Nicander of Colophon in the second book of his *Georgica* makes mention of this practice, calling *kolokyntae* [gourds] 'sikyae', for, as we have said before, that was what they used to be called. And this is what he says:

But as to the gourds themselves, when you cut them, put cords through them and dry them in the open air. Then hang them up in the smoke so that in winter your servants may fill a sufficiently ample pot and may gobble them up with no need to work...the woman who grinds corn pours in pulse of all kinds. Into it men cast strings of gourds after a thorough cleansing, and mushrooms too, and ropes long since plaited of dried vegetables....

72. 1 τμήγων Schweig. τμητῶν A   4 ἀεργέες Mus. -γὲς A   5 poṣt h v. fort. lacuna statuenda   7 σειράς Schweig. σιρ- A   8 αὐοτέροις Wilam. αὐλ- A

73

Ath. ix. 395 c: Νίκανδρος ἐν δευτέρῳ Γεωργικῶν τῶν
Σικελικῶν μνημονεύων πελειάδων φησί·

καί τε σύ γε θρέψαιο Δρακοντιάδας διτοκεύσας
ἢ Σικελὰς μεγάροισι πελειάδας· οὐδέ φιν ἅρπαι
οὐδ' ὄφις ὀστρακέοις λωβήσιμοι ἐξενέπονται.

74

Ath. xv. 683 A–684 F: Νίκανδρος ἐν δευτέρῳ Γεωργικῶν
καταλέγων καὶ αὐτὸς στεφανωτικὰ ἄνθη καὶ περὶ Ἰωνιάδων
Νυμφῶν καὶ περὶ ῥόδων τάδε λέγει·

ἀλλὰ τὰ μὲν σπείροις τε καὶ ὅσσ' ὡραῖα φυτεύοις
ἄνθε' Ἰαονίηθε. γένη γε μὲν ἴασι δισσά,
ὠχρόν τε χρυσῷ τε φυὴν εἰς ὦπα προσεικές,
ἄσσα τ' Ἰωνιάδες Νύμφαι στέφος ἀγνὸν Ἴωνι
5 Πισαίοις ποθέσασαι ἐνὶ κλήροισιν ὄρεξαν.
ἤνυσε γὰρ χλούνηνδε μετεσσύμενος σκυλάκεσσιν,
Ἀλφειῷ καὶ λύθρον ἑῶν ἐπλύνατο γυίων   B
ἑσπέριος, Νύμφῃσιν Ἰαονίδεσσι νυχεύσων.
αὐτὰρ ἀκανθοβόλοιο ῥόδου κατατέμνεο βλάστας
10 τάφροις τ' ἐμπήξειας, ὅσον διπάλαιστα τελέσκων—
πρῶτα μὲν Ὠδονίηθε Μίδης ἅπερ Ἀσίδος ἀρχήν
λείπων ἐν κλήροισιν ἀνέτρεφεν Ἡμαθίοισιν
αἰὲν ἐς ἑξήκοντα πέριξ κομόωντα πετήλοις·
δεύτερα Νισαίης Μεγαρηίδος· οὐδὲ Φάσηλις
15 οὐδ' αὐτὴ Λεύκοφρυν ἀγασσαμένη ἐπιμεμφής,   C
Ληθαίου Μάγνητος ἐφ' ὕδασιν εὐθαλέουσα.
κισσοῦ δ' ἄλλοτε κλῶνας ἐυρρίζου καπέτοισι,
πολλάκι δὲ στέφος αὐτὸ κορυμβήλοιο φυτεύσαις

73. 2 Σικελὰς Mus. -λικὰς A | μεγάροισι JGSch. -ροιο A | ἅρπαι Heringa
αρσαι A   3 ὄφις ὀστρακέοις OSch. εφινοστρακεοι A | λωβήσιμοι OSch. νωμ- A |
ἐξενέπονται Heringa -νίπ- A
74. 1 ὅσσ' OSch. ὡς A   2 ἄνθε' OSch. -θη A   3 προσεικές Kaibel τρο-

73

Nicander in the second book of his *Georgica* speaking of Sicilian doves says

And you should rear in your home Dracontian doves which lay two eggs at a time, or doves of Sicily; for it is said that neither kites harm them, nor (?) snakes their eggs.

74

Nicander in the second book of his *Georgica*, likewise enumerating flowers which are suitable for wreaths, speaks of the Ioniad Nymphs and of roses as follows:

But the flowers of Ionia you should sow, and all such as come to full growth you should transplant. Of gilliflowers there are two kinds, one is yellow and like gold to look upon; the others, those which the Ioniad Nymphs proffered in their yearning as a pure chaplet to Ion in the lands of Pisa; for, pursuing a wild boar with his hounds, he had overtaken it, and in Alpheus's stream he washed the bloodstains from his limbs at eve before passing the night with the Ioniad Nymphs.

But from the thorny rose you should cut shoots and plant 10 them in trenches making them two full palms in length. First, those which Midas of Odonia, when he forsook his kingdom in Asia, raised in the lands of Emathia, ever crowned with full sixty petals in a ring. Second, the roses of Nisaea by Megara; neither is Phaselis nor the city which reveres the White-browed Goddess to be spurned, the flourishing city by the waters of Magnesian Lethaeus.

Sometimes plant shoots of the strong-rooted ivy in trenches, sometimes even a spray of the white-berried ivy from Thrace,

σειδες A   8 Νύμφῃσιν OSch. -αισιν A   9 βλαστά OSch.   10 ὅσον Mein.
ὁδόν A | διπάλαιστα τελέσκων Scal. -λεστα -σχων A   11 ᾿Ωδονίηθε Schweig.
-ησθε A   12 ᾿Ημαθίοισιν Weston ημματ- A   14 Νισαίης Canter -σέης A
15 ἀγασσαμένη Schweig. -νης A   17 κλῶνας Cas. -νες A

151

Θράσκιον ἢ ἀργωπὸν ἠὲ κλαδέεσσι πλανήτην·
20 βλαστοδρεπῆ δ᾽ ἐχυροῖο, καὶ εἰς μίαν ὄρσεο κόρσην
σπεῖραν ὑπὸ σπυρίδεσσι νεοπλέκτοισι καθάπτων
ὄφρα δύο κροκόωντες ἐπιζυγέοντε κόρυμβοι
μέσφα συνωρίζωσιν ὑπερφιάλοιο μετώπου   D
χλωροῖς ἀμφοτέρωθεν ἐπηρεφέες πετάλοισιν.
25 σπέρματι μὴν κάλυκες κεφαληγόνοι ἀντέλλουσιν,
ἀργήεις πετάλοισι κρόκῳ μέσα χροιισθεῖσαι,
ἃ κρίνα λείρια δ᾽ ἄλλοι ἐπιφθέγγονται ἀοιδῶν,
οἱ δὲ καὶ ἀμβροσίην, πολέες δέ τε χάρμ᾽ Ἀφροδίτης·
ἤρισε γὰρ χροιῇ· τὸ δέ που ἐπὶ μέσσον ὄνειδος
30 ὅπλον βρωμήταο διεκτέλλον πεφάτισται.   E
Ἶρις δ᾽ ἐν ῥίζῃσιν ἀγαλλιὰς ἢ θ᾽ ὑακίνθῳ
αἰαστῇ προσέοικε χελιδονίοισι δὲ τέλλει
ἄνθεσιν ἰσοδρομεῦσα χελιδόσιν, αἵ τ᾽ ἀνὰ κόλπῳ
φυλλάδα νηλείην ἐκχεύετον, ἀρτίγονοι δέ
35 εἴδοντ᾽ ἡμύουσαι ἀεὶ κάλυκες στομίοισιν·
σὺν καὶ ἅπερ τ᾽ ὀξεῖα χρόη, λυχνὶς ἠδὲ θρυαλλίς,
οὐδὲ μὲν ἀνθεμίδων κενεὴ γηρύσεται ἀκμή
οὐδὲ βοάνθεμα κεῖνα τά τ᾽ αἰπύτατον κάρη ὑψοῖ,
φλόξ τε θεοῦ αὐγῇσιν ἀνερχομέναις ἰσάουσα.
40 ἔρπυλλον δὲ †φριαλευσοτεν βώλοισι† φυτεύσεις,   F
ὄφρα κλάδοις μακροῖσιν ἐφερπύζων διάηται
ἠὲ κατακρεμάῃσιν ἐφιμείρων ποτὰ νυμφέων.
καὶ δ᾽ αὐτῆς μήκωνος . . .
                        . . . ἀπὸ πλαταγώνια βάλλοις,
ἄβρωτον κώδειαν ὄφρα κνώπεσσι φυλάξῃ·
45 φυλλάσιν ἦ γὰρ πάντα διοιγομένῃσιν ἐφίζει
ἑρπετά, τὴν δὲ δρόσοισιν εἰσκομένην βοτέονται
κώδειαν καρποῖο μελιχροτέρου πλήθουσαν.   684A

20 βλαστοδρεπῆ δ᾽ ἐχυρῷῷ Wilam. βλαστοδρεπιδεχυτοιο A | ὄρσεο JGSch.
ὄρεο A   22 κόρυμβοι Canter -βοις A   23 μέσφα Mein. μέσσα A   25 σπέρ-
ματι μὴν OSch. -τίνην A | ἀντέλλουσιν Brodaeus ἀντελέουσιν A   28 τε OSch.
γε A   31 θ᾽ OSch. δ᾽ A   32 τέλλει Canter τίλλει A   33 κύκλῳ Wilam.
34 ἀρτίγονοι Cas. -νον A   35 εἴδοντ᾽ Cas. εἴδοντ᾽ ετ᾽ A   36 ἅπερ OSch.

or else the white kind or that with wandering tendrils. They should be plucked as young shoots, and you should strengthen 20 and make them to grow into a single head, fastening the twisted ends deep in freshly plaited baskets in order that two golden clusters may unite and be linked right up to the flaunting crown, the green foliage sheltering them on either side.

From seed no doubt spring the cupped flowers (lilies) that put forth heads, whose petals are white, whose centres saffron-stained. These some poets style *krina*, and others *leiria*, others again *ambrosia*, and many *Aphrodite's Joy*, for the lily rivalled the hue of her skin. But the thing of shame uprising in its midst has been named the yard of a braying ass. 30

The iris however is grown from roots—the dwarf iris and that which is like the mourning hyacinth but grows with blossoms swallow-hued, keeping pace with the swallows' coming; and both kinds put forth in folds their ruthless leaves, and the new-born flower-cups seem ever to have drooping lips. So too grow the flowers of dazzling hue, corn-cockle and plantain; nor shall the camomile in bloom be counted nought, nor the well-known ox-eyes which uplift their head so high, nor the wallflower that vies with the rising beams of the Sun-god. But tufted thyme you will plant on...in order that, as 40 its long sprays creep forward, the wind may blow through them or that it may hang downwards in its desire for draughts of water.

But of the poppy itself...cast away the petals, in order that you may preserve its capsule undevoured by caterpillars, for in truth all creeping things settle upon the petals as they open and feed upon the capsule which is like dewdrops, full as it is

περ A | τ' ὀξεῖα χρόη Mein. τοξια χροίη A | ἠδὲ Wilam. οὐδὲ A 38 επυτα-τον κορη A corr. Schweig. | ὑψοῖ Cas. ὑψοῦ A 39 τε Schweig. δὲ A | ἰσάουσα Kaibel αουσα A 40 δ' ὀφρύεσσιν, ὅτ' ἐν Gow | βουνοῖσι Merkel 42 ἐφιμείρων Scal. ἐφ' μιρων A 43 lacunam statuit OSch. 45 φυλ-λάσιν Schweig. φυλασσιν A

θρίων δ' οἰχομένων ῥέα μὲν φλόγες, ἄλλοτε ῥιπαί
πῆξαν σάρκα τυπῆσι· τὰ δ' οὐ βάσιν ἐστήριξαν
50 †οὔτε τι παι† βρώμην ποτιδεγμένα· πολλάκι δ' ἴχνη
στιφροῖς ὠλίσθηναν ἐνιχρίμψαντα καρείοις.
. . . .
ἀδρύνει δὲ βλαστὰ βαθεῖ' ἐν τεύχεϊ κόπρος
σαμψύχου λιβάνου τε νέας κλάδας ἠδ' ὅσα κῆποι   B
ἀνδράσιν ἐργοπόνοις στεφάνους ἔπι πορσαίνουσιν
. . . .
55 ἢ γὰρ καὶ λεπταὶ πτερίδες καὶ παιδὸς ἔρωτες
λεύκη ἰσαιόμενοι, ἐν καὶ κρόκος εἴαρι μύων,
κύπρος τ' ὀσμηρόν τε σισύμβριον ὅσσα τε κοίλοις
ἄσπορα ναιομένοισι τόποις ἀνεθρέψατο λειμών
κάλλεα, βούφθαλμόν τε καὶ εὐῶδες Διὸς ἄνθος,
60 χάλκας, σὺν δ' ὑάκινθον ἰωνιάδας τε χαμηλάς   C
ὀρφνοτέρας, ἃς στύξε μετ' ἄνθεσι Περσεφόνεια.
σὺν δὲ καὶ ὑψῆέν τε πανόσμεον, ὅσσα τε τύμβοι
φάσγανα παρθενικαῖς νεοδουπέσιν ἀμφιχέονται,
αὐτάς τ' ἠιθέας ἀνεμωνίδες ἀστράπτουσαι
65 τηλόθεν ὀξυτέρησιν ἐφελκόμεναι χροιῆσι.
πᾶς δέ τις ἢ ἐλένειον ἢ ἀστέρα φωτίζοντα   D
δρέψας εἰνοδίοισι θεῶν παρακάββαλε σηκοῖς
ἢ αὐτοῖς βρετάεσσιν, ὅτε πρώτιστον ἴδωνται·
πολλάκι θερμία καλά, τοτὲ χρυσανθὲς ἀμέργων
70 λείριά τε στήλησιν ἐπιφθίνοντα καμόντων
καὶ γεραὸν πώγωνα καὶ ἐντραπέας κυκλαμίνους
σαύρην θ' ἢ χθονίου πέφαται στέφος Ἡγεσιλάου.

48 δ' οἰχ- Schweig. διοιχ- A | ῥιπαί JGSch. ρειπη A   49 πῆξαν OSch.
πλῆ- A | σάρκα τυπ- JGSch. σαρκοτυπ- A   50 οὐδ' ἔμπα Wilam.   51 ὠλίσ-
θηναν OSch. -ησαν A | post h.v. lacunam statuit Gow   52 βαθεῖ' ἐν τ. κόπρος
OSch. βαθεῖ ἐν τ. καρπόν A   54 post h.v. lacunam statuit Gow   56 ιαρι
μυιων A corr. Cas.   57 κοίλοις Porson   κ' οιαοις A   58 ναιομένοισι Mein.
νεομ- A: cf. Al. 515 | τόποις Cas. πότ- A   59 εὐειδὲς OSch.   60 ιωνιάδας Scal.

of honey-sweet fruit. But when the petals are gone, the heat or else the buffeting winds easily harden the flesh, and the creatures get no firm foothold when they hope to find food, and often 50 their footsteps slip when they essay the solid heads. . . .

A good depth of manure in the pot brings on the shoots of marjoram and the young sprigs of the frankincense-tree, and all other plants which gardens furnish to make chaplets for toiling men. . . .

Yes, and delicate ferns and the acanthus which resembles the white poplar, and the crocus which closes in the spring, henna too and scented bergamot-mint and all other lovelinesses that unsown a meadow rears in hollow, watered spots, ox-eye and fragrant flower-of-Zeus, chrysanthemums and also hyacinth 60 and low-growing violets, dark, and abhorred of Persephone among flowers. And of their company are the towering all-scent and the cornflags which encircle the graves of virgins lately dead, and sparkling anemones which with their dazzling colours lure living maidens from afar.

And everybody plucks elecampane or gleaming blue-daisy and sets it down by the roadside shrines of gods or upon the statues themselves, as soon as he sees them, gathering sometimes, too, fair lupins, or else the gold-flower and lilies that fade upon 70 the tombstones of the dead, and salsify with its grey beard, and modest cyclamens and garden-cress, which men call the garland of the Netherworld Captain.

-νιδας A   62 ὑψήεντα ταπανος μεον A   corr. Mein.   63 νεοχουπαισιν A corr. Mein.   64 αὐτάς Gow   -ταί A | ἠιθέας OSch.   -θειαι A   65 post h.v. ἐν ἐνίοις δὲ γράφεται ἐφελκόμεναι φιλοχροιαῖς A   68 ὅτε Mein.   ἄτε A   69 θερμία Wilam.   θελ. . μια A   70 λείριά Canter   λίριάς A | στήλησι OSch. -λεσιν A   72 Ἡγεσιλάου Salmasius   -λίου A

75

Ath. ii. 51 D: καὶ Νίκανδρος δὲ ἐν Γεωργικοῖς ἐμφανίζει καὶ ὅτι
πρότερον τῶν ἄλλων ἀκροδρύων φαίνεται (τὸ συκάμινον),
μορέην τε καλεῖ τὸ δένδρον ἀεὶ ὡς καὶ οἱ Ἀλεξανδρεῖς·

καὶ μορέης, ἣ παισὶ πέλει μείλιγμα νέοισι
πρῶτον ἀπαγγέλλουσα βροτοῖς ἡδεῖαν ὀπώρην.

76

Ath. ii. 54 D: λόπιμον κάρυόν τε
Εὐβοέες, βάλανον δὲ μετεξέτεροι καλέσαντο,
Νίκανδρός φησιν ὁ Κολοφώνιος ἐν Γεωργικοῖς.

78–9

Ath. ii. 60 E–61 A: φύονται δὲ οἱ μύκητες γηγενεῖς καί εἰσιν
αὐτῶν ἐδώδιμοι ὀλίγοι· οἱ γὰρ πολλοὶ ἀποπνίγουσιν...
Νίκανδρος δ' ἐν Γεωργικοῖς καταλέγει καὶ τίνες αὐτῶν εἰσιν
οἱ θανάσιμοι, λέγων

ἐχθρὰ δ' ἐλαίης
ῥοιῆς τε πρίνου τε δρυός τ' ἀπὸ πήματα κεῖται

. . . .

οἰδαλέων σύγκολλα βάρη πνιγόεντα μυκήτων.
φησὶ δὲ καὶ ὅτι

συκέης ὁπότε στέλεχος βαθὺ κόπρῳ
5 κακκρύψας ὑδάτεσσιν ἀειναέεσσι νοτίζοις,
φύσονται πυθμέσσιν ἀκήριοι· ὧν σὺ μύκητα
θρεπτὸν μή τι χαμηλὸν ἀπὸ ῥίζης προτάμοιο.
[τὰ δ' ἄλλα οὐκ ἦν ἀναγνῶναι.]

(79)   καί τε μύκητας ἀμανίτας τότ' ἐφεύσεις,
φησὶν ὁ αὐτὸς Νίκανδρος ἐν τῷ αὐτῷ.

78. 2 post h. v. lacunam statuit Gow   **3** οἰδαλέων Kaibel -λέα codd. |
σύγκολλα Cas. συκ- codd.   **8** epitomatoris verba

75

And Nicander besides in his *Georgica* explains also that it (the mulberry) appears earlier than other fruits, and he always calls the tree *morea*, as do the Alexandrian writers too.

And of the mulberry, which is the delight of little boys and is the harbinger to man of the pleasant season of fruit.

76

The Euboeans named it (i.e. the sweet chestnut) *lopimon* and *karyon*, but others *balanos*,

says Nicander of Colophon in his *Georgica*.

78–9

And fungi are generated from the soil, and only a few of them are edible, for the majority choke the eater.... And Nicander in his *Georgica* states also which are the deadly ones, and says

Horrid pains are in store from the olive and from the pomegranate and the holm-oak and the oak... the choking weight of puffy fungi that cling to...

And he says also,

When you bury the foot of a fig-tree deep in dung and moisten it with a constant flow of water, there will grow on the roots fungi of the harmless kind. You may gather any of these cultivated on the root, but not those which grow on the ground.

[The remainder could not be read.]

(79) And then you will cook some champignons with them, says Nicander in the same passage.

80

Ath. ii. 71 D: Νίκανδρος Γεωργικοῖς·

σὺν καὶ φοίνικος παραφυάδας ἐκκόπτοντες
ἐγκέφαλον φορέουσι νέοις ἀσπαστὸν ἔδεσμα.

81–2

Ath. iii. 72 A: Νίκανδρος ἐν Γεωργικοῖς·

σπείρειας κυάμων Αἰγύπτιον, ὄφρα θερείης
ἀνθέων μὲν στεφάνους ἀνύσῃς τὰ δὲ πεπτηῶτα
ἀκμαίου καρποῖο κιβώρια δαινυμένοισιν
ἐς χέρας ἠιθέοισι πάλαι ποθέουσιν ὀρέξῃς.
5 ῥίζας δ᾽ ἐν θοίνῃσιν ἀφεψήσας προτίθημι.

ῥίζας δὲ λέγει Νίκανδρος τὰ ὑπ᾽ Ἀλεξανδρέων κολοκάσια
καλούμενα· ὡς ὁ αὐτός·

(82) κυάμου λέψας κολοκάσιον ἐντμήξας τε.

83

Ath. iii. 92 D: Νίκανδρος δ᾽ ὁ Κολοφώνιος ἐν Γεωργικοῖς τάδε
τῶν ὀστρέων καταλέγει·

ἠὲ καὶ ὄστρεα τόσσα βυθοὺς ἅ τε βόσκεται ἅλμης,
νηρῖται στρόμβοι τε πελωριάδες τε μύες τε,
γλίσχρ᾽ ἁλοσύνης τέκνα, καὶ αὐτῆς φωλεὰ πίνης.

84

Ath. ix. 366 D: σίνηπυ δ᾽ ὠνόμασε Νίκανδρος ὁ Κολοφώνιος
...ἐν δὲ τοῖς Γεωργικοῖς· σπέρματα δ᾽ ἐνδάκνοντα σινήπυος
(=fr. 70. 16) καὶ πάλιν

κάρδαμ᾽ ἀνάρρινόν τε μελάμφυλλόν τε σίνηπυ.

80. 1 παραφυάδας Mus. -δα codd.
81. 1 κυάμων Mein. -μον codd.   2 ἀνύσῃς Mein. ἀνύῃς codd.   4 χέρας
Mus. χεῖρας codd.   6 κυάμου Cas. -μους codd.

80

Nicander in his *Georgica* says

At the same time they lop off the side-growths of the date-palm and bear away the 'cabbage', which children delight to eat.

81–2

Nicander in his *Georgica* says

Of beans sow the Egyptian, so that in summer you may contrive garlands with its flowers, and that, when the pods of ripe fruit have fallen off, you may hand them to youths who have long craved for them as they feast. But the tubers I boil down and serve at banquets.

What Nicander calls 'tubers' Alexandrian writers call *colocasia*; as the same writer has it

(82) Having stripped the colocasium from its bean and shredded it into....

83

And Nicander of Colophon in his *Georgica* enumerates the following kinds of shell-fish:

Or all such shell-fish also as feed in the depths of the brine—sea-snails and whelks and clams and mussels, the clinging children of the sea-goddess, and the den of the pinna itself.

84

Nicander of Colophon mentions mustard and in his *Georgica* says, And the mordant seeds of mustard.

And again:

Garden-cress and pepper-grass and the dark-leaved mustard.

83. 2 πελωριάδες Mus. -ίδες A   3 γλίσχρ' 'Α.τ. Bothe   γλίσχραι τ' ἀλλὰ σύνες τε codd.
84. 2 κάρδαμ' ἀνάρρινόν Cas.   κάρδαμον ἄρρινόν A

85

Ath. ix. 370A: Νίκανδρος δ' ἐν Γεωργικοῖς·

λείη μὲν κράμβη, ὁτὲ δ' ἀγριὰς ἐμπίπτουσα
σπειρομέναις πολύφυλλος ἐνηβῆσαι πρασιῆσιν
ἢ οὔλη †καὶ τύριος ὀθάμνιτις† πετάλοισιν
ἢ ἐπιφοινίσσουσα καὶ αὐχμηρῇσιν ὁμοίη
5 βατραχέη Κύμη τε κακόχροος ἢ μὲν ἔοικε
πέλμασιν οἶσι πέδιλα παλίμβολα κασσύουσιν,
ἢν μάντιν λαχάνοισι παλαιόγονοι ἐνέπουσιν.

86

Ath. ii. 35A: τὸν οἶνον ὁ Κολοφώνιος Νίκανδρος ὠνομάσθαι
φησὶν ἀπὸ Οἰνέως.

Οἰνεὺς δ' ἐν κοίλοισιν ἀποθλίψας δεπάεσσιν
οἶνον ἔκλησε.

87

Ath. ii. 49F: Νίκανδρος

μῆλον ὃ κόκκυγος καλέουσι.

90

Σ Th. 349: ἀμορβεύειν γὰρ τὸ ἀκολουθεῖν καὶ ὑπηρετεῖν.
Νίκανδρος ἐν ἑτέρῳ·

βουκαῖοι ζεύγεσσιν ἀμορβεύουσιν ὀρήων.

91

Σ Al. 298: εἴωθε γὰρ τὰ πικρὰ καὶ δριμέα στύφοντα καλεῖν.
τοὺς γοῦν ὄμφακας ἐπιστύφοντας ἔφη

ὄμφακες ἡνίκα χεῖλος ἐπιστύφουσι ποθεῖσαι.

85. 2 σπειρομέναις Gow (-ης Wilam.) -νη A | ἐνήβησε Schweig. 3 καπυροῖ-
σιν Jacobs κατάπυρσος OSch. | ὁραμνῖτις OSch. 4 ἢ Cas. ηκαι A

85

Nicander in his *Georgica* says:

The cabbage is smooth, but at times the wild form may intrude into sown gardens and flourish with an abundance of leaves, either the curled kind... with leaves, or the green, which turns red and looks parched, and the ill-coloured Cumaean which is like the soles wherewith men cobble second-hand sandals. This men of an older generation style a prophet for vegetables.

86

Nicander of Colophon says that wine (*oinos*) was so called after Oineus:

And Oineus squeezed it out into hollow cups and called it *oinos*.

87

Nicander,

The fruit they call the cuckoo's.

90

The word ἀμορβεύειν signifies 'to attend' and 'to minister to'. Nicander in another work writes:

Oxherds attend to the teams of mules.

91

For he habitually calls bitter, pungent things 'astringent'. For example, he describes unripe grapes as 'drawing up', 'astringent'.

When a draught of unripe grapes draws up the lip.

90 ἐν ῾Ετεροιουμένοις Bernhardy

CYNEGETICA [?]

98

Etym. Mag. 395.36: ΕΥΡΙΝΩΝ ΚΥΝΩΝ ΚΑΙ ΣΚΥΛΑΚΩΝ . . . καὶ
Νίκανδρος,

Ἄρτεμις εὐρίνων ἑσμὸν ἄγει ⟨σκυλάκων⟩.

100

Etym. Mag. 712.42: Νίκανδρος ἐν τοῖς Ἀλεξιφαρμάκοις
ἐπιλίζοντας ὀιστούς
τοῦ λίγξε τὸ θέμα θελήσας εἰπεῖν ἔφθειρε τὴν τοῦ ἤχου
μίμησιν.

HYMN TO ATTALUS [?]

104

Vita Nicandri in Σ *Th.*:

Τευθρανίδης, ὧ κλῆρον ἀεὶ πατρώιον ἴσχων,
κέκλυθι μηδ᾽ ἄμνηστον ἀπ᾽ οὔατος ὕμνον ἐρύξῃς,
Ἄτταλ᾽, ἐπεί σεο ῥίζαν ἐπέκλυον Ἡρακλῆος
ἐξέτι Λυσιδίκης τε περίφρονος, ἣν Πελοπηίς
Ἱπποδάμη ἐφύτευσεν ὅτ᾽ Ἀπίδος ἤρατο τιμήν.

EPIGRAMS

105

Anth. Pal. vii. 435: ΝΙΚΑΝΔΡΟΥ

Εὐπυλίδας, Ἐράτων, Χαῖρις, Λύκος, Ἄγις, Ἀλέξων,
ἐξ Ἰφικρατίδα παῖδες, ἀπωλόμεθα
Μεσσάνας ὑπὸ τεῖχος· ὁ δ᾽ ἕβδομος ἄμμε Γύλιππος
ἐν πυρὶ θεὶς μεγάλαν ἦλθε φέρων σποδιάν,
Σπάρτᾳ μὲν μέγα κῦδος, Ἀλεξίππᾳ δὲ μέγ᾽ ἄχθος
ματρί· τὸ δ᾽ ἒν πάντων καὶ καλὸν ἐντάφιον.

98.1 σκυλάκων suppl. Sylburg

CYNEGETICA [?]

98

OF KEEN-SCENTED HOUNDS AND WHELPS . . . So too Nicander,
Artemis brings her pack of keen-scented ⟨whelps⟩.

100

Nicander in the *Alexipharmaca*,
  whizzing arrows,
by choosing to use the present tense of λίγξε destroyed the
imitation of the sound.

HYMN TO ATTALUS [?]

104

Scion of Teuthras, who dost ever hold the heritage of thy
fathers, hearken and thrust not away from thine ear my hymn
out of mind; for I have heard, O Attalus, that thy stock dates
back to Heracles and sage Lysidice, whom Hippodame the wife
of Pelops bore when he had won the lordship of the Apian land.

EPIGRAMS

105

NICANDER

We, Eupylidas, Eraton, Chaeris, Lycus, Agis, Alexon, six
sons of Iphicratidas, fell beneath the wall of Messana. The
seventh, Gylippus, laid our bodies on the pyre, and with the
ashes of so many came bringing to Sparta great renown, to our
mother Alexippa great sorrow. For all, one burial and a glorious.

104.4 ἐξέτι OSch. εἰσέτι codd. | Λυσιδίκης JGSch. λυσιακῆς codd. **5** Ἱππο-
δάμη G 'Ἱπποδάμει' cett.

106

Anth. Pal. vii. 526: ΝΙΚΑΝΔΡΟΥ ΚΟΛΟΦΩΝΙΟΥ

Ζεῦ πάτερ, Ὀθρυάδα τίνα φέρτερον ἔδρακες ἄλλον
ὃς μόνος ἐκ Θυρέας οὐκ ἐθέλησε μολεῖν
πατρίδ᾽ ἐπὶ Σπάρταν, διὰ δὲ ξίφος ἤλασε πλευρᾶν
'δοῦλα' καταγράψας 'σκῦλα κατ᾽ Ἰναχιδᾶν';

107

Anth. Pal. xi.7: ΝΙΚΑΝΔΡΟΥ

Οὐδεὶς τὴν ἰδίην συνεχῶς, Χαρίδημε, γυναῖκα
κινεῖν ἐκ ψυχῆς τερπόμενος δύναται·
οὕτως ἡ φύσις ἐστὶ φιλόκνισος †ἀλλότριος χρώς†
καὶ ζητεῖ διόλου τὴν ξενοκυσθαπάτην.

INCERTAE SEDIS FRAGMENTA

108

Parthen. 34: Νίκανδρος μέντοι τὸν Κόρυθον οὐκ Οἰνώνης
ἀλλὰ Ἑλένης καὶ Ἀλεξάνδρου φησὶν γενέσθαι, λέγων ἐν
τούτοις·

ἠρία τ᾽ εἰς Ἀίδαο κατοιχομένου Κορύθοιο
ὅν τε καὶ ἁρπακτοῖσιν ὑποδμηθεῖσ᾽ ὑμεναίοις
Τυνδαρὶς αἴν᾽ ἀχέουσα κακὸν γόνον ἤρατο βούτεω.

109

Σ *Th.* 215: Ῥυπαῖον... ἐστὶ τῆς Αἰτωλίας, ὡς Νίκανδρος
περί τινων εἰς Αἰτωλίαν ἐρχομένων διηγούμενος·

δι᾽ αἰπεινήν τε κολώνην
Οἰωνοῦ Ῥύπης ⟨τε⟩ πάγον κατ᾽ Ὀανθίδα λίμνην
στείχοντες Ναύπακτον ἐς Ἀμφιδύμην τ᾽ ἐπέλαζον.

107. ΝΙΚΑΡΧΟΥ Plan.   3 ἀλλοτριόχρως Toup   4 ξενοκυσθαπάτην OSch.
-κυστ- *A.P.*

106

NICANDER OF COLOPHON

Father Zeus, what man nobler than Othryadas hast thou seen? He would not return alone from Thyrea to his home in Sparta, but drove his sword through his side after he had traced the words 'Spoils captured from the sons of Inachus'.

107

NICANDER

Nemo, Charideme, semper uxorem suam cum plena voluptate subigitare potest, adeo natura titillationem appetit...et furtiva adulteria usque quaque quaerit.

FRAGMENTS OF UNSPECIFIED POEMS

108

Nicander however asserts that Corythus was the son not of Oenone but of Helen and Alexander, in these words:

And the sepulchre of Corythus who went down to Hades, and whom the daughter of Tyndarus, for all she was mated in stolen wedlock, reared to her bitter sorrow, the base offspring of the shepherd.

109

The Rhypaean mountain...is in Aetolia, as Nicander says, discoursing of certain people who came to Aetolia:

Passing over the steep hill of Oeonus and Rhype's mount by the lake of Oanthe they drew near to Naupactus and Amphidyme.

108.1 εἰς L. Legrand εἰν cod.   3 καλὸν Mein. κακοῦ OSch.
109.2 τε add. JGSch. | κατ' OSch. καὶ codd. | 'Οανθίδα Mein. 'Ονθίδα codd.

110

Vita Nicandri in Σ *Th.*: υἱὸν δέ φησιν αὐτὸν Δαμαίου οὕτω λέγων·

αἰνήσεις υἷα πολυμνήστοιο Δαμαίου.

111

Porphyr. *Quaest. Hom.* 92 Νίκανδρος,

ἐϋκτιμένην Μαραθῶνα.

112

Suidas *s.v.* ΕΥΡΥΒΑΤΟΣ: ...οἱ δὲ τὸν Κέρκωπα τὸν ἕτερον...
Νίκανδρος·

†αἰγίνεον† Εὐρύβατον πανουργότατον.

110

He calls himself the son of Damaeus in these words:

Thou wilt commend the son of the memorable Damaeus.

111

Nicander:

Well-built Marathon.

112

Eurybatus... according to some, one of the two Cercopes...
Nicander:

...most rascally Eurybatus.

NOTES

THERIACA

ANALYSIS

I. 1-7, *Proem*: Hermesianax, I will tell you of poisonous creatures, of their bites, and how to cure them.

II. 8-20, Reptiles and other plagues sprung from the blood of the Titans. Artemis, Orion, and the Scorpion. 21-34, There are means of protection. 35-56, Fumigation; 57-79, Repellent herbs; 80-97, Repellent herbal unguents. 98-114, An unguent made from snakes. 115-20, Female snakes more dangerous than male. 121-44, Dangerous seasons.

III. 145-492, SNAKES. 145-56, the Seps. 157-89, the Asp, 190-208, and the Ichneumon. 209-57, the Viper. 258-81, the Cerastes. 282-308, the Blood-letting Snake, 309-19, and Helen of Troy. 320-33, the Sepedon. 334-42, the Dipsas, 343-58, and the Ass. 359-71, the Chersydrus. 372-83, the Amphisbaena. 384-95, the Scytale. 396-410, the Basilisk. 411-37, the Dryinas. 438-47, the Dragon, 448-57, and the Eagle. 458-82, the Cenchrines. 483-7, the Gecko and Demeter. 488-92, Harmless reptiles.

IV. 493-714, HERBAL AND OTHER ANTIDOTES. 493-508, Fresh Herbs, particularly Centaury. 509-19, Birthwort. 520-27, Clover. 528-40, Compound remedies: Fustic, Agnus Castus, Savin, Rue, Savory, Asphodel, Helxine. 541-9, Bugloss, as used by Alcibius. 550-56, Horehound. 557-73, Chicken's brain, Field Basil, Marjoram, Boar's liver, Cypress, All-heal, Testicle of the Beaver, of the Hippopotamus. 574-82, Wormwood, Bay, Sweet Marjoram, Curd, Deer's scrotum or paunch. 583-7, Hulwort, Cedar, Juniper, Catkins of the Plane, Bishop's Weed, Cypress. 588-93, Helxine, Barley. 594-8, Pitch, Fennel, Juniper, Celery. 599-624, Alexanders, Myrrh, Cummin, Spikenard, River Crab, Iris, Heather, Tamarisk, Fleabane, Elder, Marjoram, Tree Medick, Spurge, Frogs, Snake's liver or head. 625-9, Gold Flower, Blue Pimpernel, Marjoram, Savory. 630-35, Rhamnus. 636-55, Roots to cure snake-bite: Viper's Bugloss, Eryngo, Bear's Foot, Campanula, Basil, Celery, Anise. 656-65, Pine-Thistle. 666-75, Plant discovered by Alcibius. 676-88, Castor-Oil Tree, Balm, Heliotrope, Navelwort, Bindweed, Hart's Tongue, All-heal (as used by Apollo). 689-99, Flesh of the Marten. 700-14, Blood of the Turtle, Wild Cummin, Curd.

V. 715-68, SPIDERS. 715-24, the Grape-spider. 725-8, the Starlet. 729-33, the Blue spider. 734-7, the Huntsman. 738-46, the Wasplet. 747-51, the Antlet. 752-8, Spiders in crops. 759-68, the Cranocolaptes.

VI. 769-804, SCORPIONS. 769-85, five species, 786-96, two crablike species, 797-804, two more species.

VII. 805-36, OTHER DANGEROUS CREATURES. Bees, Wasps, Myriopods, Shrews, the Seps Lizard, the Salamander, the Murry, the Sting Ray.

VIII. *837–956*, GENERAL REMEDIES. *837–914*, a catalogue of 82 herbs. *915–20*, Measures in emergency. *921–9*, Cupping, Fig-Juice, Cautery, Application of Wine. *930–33*, Leeches, Onion-Juice, Sheep's Droppings. *934–56*, a Panacea.

IX. *957–8*, *Sphragis*: Treasure the memory of Nicander.

NOTES

3 Hermesianax. See Introd. p. 7.

8 φαλάγγια: Aristotle (*H.A.* 622 b 28) distinguishes φ. from ἀράχνια, a word not used by N. Pliny (*N.H.* 11.79) says *araneorum…plura sunt genera…phalangia ex eis appellantur quorum noxii morsus*, but this distinction is not made by Aristotle, whom he seems otherwise to be following.

10 ff. Σ, remarking that no such lore is to be found in Hesiod, cite Acusilaus for the statement that πάντα τὰ δάκνοντα sprang from the blood of Typhon, who, if not a Titan, belongs to that order of beings. Other authors however, though much later, also credit Hesiod with having described the gigantomachy (see Lobeck *Agl.* 567). The suggestion in 13 seems to be that Artemis, whose mother, Leto, was a daughter of the Titan Coeus (Hes. *Th.* 404), could thus call cousins with the scorpion summoned to punish Orion. For this story see Arat. 635 ff. In Ap. Rh. 4.1513, Luc. 9.700 snakes are born from drops of Medusa's blood.

According to Σ Melisseeis is that part of Helicon on which Hesiod received instruction from the Muses (*Theog.* 22). Permessus, one of their bathing places (*ib.* 5), is a stream flowing from Helicon into Lake Copais (Strab. 9.407).

13 χαλαζήεντα: as Page points out, the scorpion owes this surprising epithet to the eruption of the skin, χάλαзα, produced by its sting (778).

18 For the proverbial scorpion under the stone see Pearson on Soph. *fr.* 37.

26 ἀνυλήεντα: *C.Q.* 45.98. On the analogy of ἀνομβρήεις (*Al.* 288) the adj. might mean *wooded*.

30 *C.Q.* 45.110.

35 ff. The protective fumigation of Cato's camp by the Psylli (Nic. *fr.* 32) is described in Luc. 9.915 ff.

37 ἐγγαγίδα πέτρην is *lignite* or *wood-coal* (cf. Diosc. 5.128, Plin.*N.H.* 36.141). It was commonly known as Γαγάτης (sc. λίθος) from Γάγας or Γάγαι, a river and town on the south coast of Lycia where it was found. See C. Müller *Geogr. Gr. Min.* 1.492.

39 πολυσχιδέος: the correct botanical term is *pinnate*. Βλῆτρον in L-S⁹ is *Aspidium filix-mas*, said by Brenning to be extremely rare in Greece; Sibthorp preferred *A. aculeatum*. Perhaps no special kind is intended.

45 f. Plin. *N.H.* 33.94 *calx aqua accenditur et Thracius lapis, idem oleo restinguitur*; and so [Arist.] *Mir.* 833 a 23, where it is said to be called also σπίνος. Theophr. *fr.* 2.13 makes a similar statement about σπίνος. Possibly quicklime is meant, though Pliny distinguishes the two. Pliny ascribes the same properties to his *Gagates lapis* in virtually the same words (*N.H.* 36.141), and Dioscorides, who has more than one use for γαγάτης λίθος, says that the virtues of Θρᾳκίας are the same (5.128 f.).

49 [Arist.] *Mir.* 841 a 28 (copied by Ael. *N.A.* 9.20, Steph. Byz. 570.13) states that the river Pontus is 'in that part of Thrace which is called the country of the

171

Sinti and Maedi', and that it brings down stones with the properties mentioned. It seems however a strange source for material which burns on contact with water.

51ff. The lines are imitated by Virgil (G. 3.414). For χαλβάνη, *galbanum*, in this connexion see also Diosc. 3.83, Plin. *N.H.* 12.126, Luc. 9.916; for cedar Plin. *N.H.* 24.19.

ἄκνηστις: *Urtica pilulifera* is the commonest kind of nettle in Greece (Brenning).

60 Σ explain καιτήεσσαν to mean μεγάλην καὶ ὑψηλήν, connecting it with κῆτος. See however Pfeiffer on Call. *fr.* 639.

67 ἀργεννήν: cf. Rhian. *fr.* 54 οὔρεος ἀργεννοῖο περὶ πτύχας, *C.Q.* 45.98.

74 σκύρα: οἱ δὲ τὸ ἐρυθράδιόν φασιν, Σ—that is presumably ἐρευθέδανον (ἐρυθρόδ-), madder, *Rubia tinctorum*, Diosc. 3.143.

80 For εἰ thus used cf. 689, 747, 885.

85 Silphium, rendered *laserwort* by L-S⁹, was an umbelliferous plant with a reddish, translucent root of which the juice had medicinal virtues, while the leaves and stalk were in great demand as a vegetable and as a condiment in sauces. It had a sharp but not disagreeable scent. Though a purgative, sheep and goats grew fat upon it. It is first mentioned in Hdt. 4.169 and was the special product of Cyrene, which derived a considerable profit from its export. It figures on the coins, and the 'Arcesilas' kylix (6th cent. B.C., Laconian) shows the king supervising its weighing, packing, and stowing in the hold of a ship (Pfuhl *Mal.u. Zeichn. d. Gr.* 3.45). By the 1st cent. B.C. the supply had begun to fail, and a century later Pliny deplored its total disappearance. Efforts made to cultivate it in the Peloponnese and Ionia were unsuccessful. Other but inferior kinds were said to grow in Parthia and Syria. It has been identified with *Narthex asa foetida* and *Ferula tingitana*, but its precise nature is still unknown. See *RE* 3 A 103.

86 On the widespread belief in the deterrent or even destructive effect of human saliva see *Harv. Stud.* 8.24.

87f. βάμματι: at *Al.* 49, 369, 414, 531 Σ assert that βάμμα means *vinegar*, or gloss it ὄξος. This seems right, and we assume that it applies also here and in 622. Cf. *C.Q.* 45.99.

Diosc. 2.60 also recommends κάμπαι αἱ ἐπὶ τῶν λαχάνων γεννώμεναι as a deterrent, but prescribes them rubbed on in oil.

94 δαυχμοῦ: cf. *Al.* 199, *C.Q.* 45.100.

102 Σ hesitate over the amount: τὸ τρίτον μέρος τοῦ δεκάτου τῆς δραχμῆς· τὸ τρίτον δέ ἐστι τῆς δεκάδος τρεῖς καὶ τρίτον. ἢ τριπλάσιον τῆς δεκάδος, τουτέστι τριάκοντα δραχμάς. See Appendix II.

103f. *C.Q.* 45.110. The feminines seem to be due to some abstract substantive implied, e.g. θλίψις, στάξις, στύψις.

109 Call. *fr.* 286 αὖτις ἀπαιτίζουσαν ἐὴν εὐεργέα λάκτιν, where, as here, the noun is said to mean *ladle*. If so, ταράσσειν will mean *stir*.

116 Cels. 5.27.10 *illud ignorari non oportet omnis serpentis ictum et ieiuni et ieiuno magis nocere.*

122f. The heliacal rising of the Pleiads early in May marks the beginning of the harvest and of the sailing season. See Hes. *W.D.* 383, A. W. Mair *Hesiod* 136, Smith *Dict. of Antiquities* 1.219.

As Σ Arat. 172 remark on this passage, the Bull is only head and shoulders and should therefore have no tail. See however Housman on Manil. 2.199.

125 διψάς: cf. 334 n.

128 ff. Hdt. 3.109 reports the savagery both of the mating echidna and of her young, who eat their way out of the womb. Ael. *N.A.* 1.24 repeats both stories but at 15.16 withdraws the second on the authority of Theophrastus, who apparently held that the mother burst asunder in parturition. Aristotle, who is well-informed about reproduction in vipers (*H.A.* 558a 25, *al*), mentions neither story, though [Arist.] *Mir.* 846b 18 retails both, apparently from N. or his source. Cf. *Hermes* 65.367. The belief is discussed at some length by Sir Thomas Browne (*Pseudodoxia* iii.16).

139 ff. For the hostility of deer and snakes see Opp. *Cyn.* 2.233, *Hal.* 2.289, Ael. *N.A.* 2.9, *Et. M.* 326.2, Plin. *N.H.* 8.118, *al*. Most of the passages mentioned refer, as does N. in 144, to the effect of the stag's breath, and Σ, after some wild guesses, suggest ὁ διὰ τῶν ῥωθώνων ἀποσπασμός as the meaning of σκαρθμός in 139. The word however should, and elsewhere does, mean *prancing*, and both deer and goats kill snakes by trampling them under their sharp hoofs; see W. H. Hudson *Naturalist in La Plata* ch. 11, *The Field* 1951, p. 789. Goats are said to eat their victims; we do not know that this is recorded of deer, but according to Hudson the deer of South America hate and kill snakes. In that country the strong scent of the deer is held to be repellent to snakes, and the references to the stag's breath perhaps indicate a similar belief in antiquity. Cf. also *Bodl. Quart. Rec.* 3.289.

142 νεβροτόκοι is apparently used substantivally for ἔλαφοι: see *C.Q.* 45.105.

147 Σ are in doubt whether δίψιος means *thirsty* because frequenting dry places, or *thirst-causing* by its bite—like the διψάς in 340.

σήψ: snakes in general, Brenning; unidentifiable, Gossen-Steier. See *Philol.* 83.359. Pausanias (8.4.7) describes a σήψ which he has seen as small, ash-coloured, spotted: flat head, narrow neck, large belly, short tail: moves like a cerastes (266 n.). According to H. O. Lenz *Zool. d. alt. Gr.* 465 this should be the south-European viper. Σήψ is a lizard in 817: in Philum. 23 it is apparently the snake which N. calls σηπεδών (320 n.). Luc. 9.723 *ossaque dissoluens cum corpore tabificus seps* perhaps echoes N.'s line; the sequelae of its bite are elaborated by Lucan in 762 ff.

153 We understand this to refer only to the colour of the snail or its shell. Κόχλος commonly denotes a shellfish and, if N. means *snail*, requires definition; but the gen. αἴης in place of χερσαίοις is hard to parallel.

154 We take κύκλον to be the coiled body of the snake.

158 ἀσπίδα: *Naia haie* (Brenning, Gossen-Steier), *Vipera aspis*[1] (Keller)—the common hooded cobra of Africa. Philum. 16 distinguishes three varieties by their size and colour. The name refers to the expansion of the neck into a 'hood'. See on this snake *Philol.* 83.370, Keller *Ant. Tierwelt* 2.295, and for ἄνυδρός *C.Q.* 45.98.

163 ἐπιλλίζουσα: *C.Q.* 45.102. The word usually means *wink*, but snakes have no eyelids.

173 OSch. printed ἢ περὶ μ., where περί would have, we suppose, to mean *exceedingly*.

[1] *Vipera aspis* is a European viper, but Keller adds *die ägyptische Aspis*.

NOTES

179 Text doubtful. OSch. printed ὑπὸ σπείρης but did not say what he understood it to mean.

184 In venomous snakes the poison-duct does not run into the base of the fang but opens near by, and the venom is prevented from escaping by a fold of mucous membrane to which N. here refers. See H. Noguchi *Snake Venoms* 58f., also Ael. *N.A.* 9.4.

187ff. For these symptoms, with which the medical writers agree (e.g. Philum. 16.3), see also Ap. Rh. 4.1522ff., Lucan 9.815ff.

200ff. Arist. *H.A.* 612a15, Opp. *Cyn.* 3.433, Mair *ad loc.*, *Philol.* 83.371.

209 ἔχις, ἔχιδνα: *Vipera ammodytes* (Gossen-Steier), also *Pelias berus* and *Vipera aspis* (Brenning). *Vipera ammodytes*, common in south-east Europe, has over the nostrils a scaly appendage as described in 212f. (see Gadow *Amphibia and Reptiles* fig. 173), but no doubt the word includes other vipers, of which there are several species. The common European viper (*V. berus*) varies much in colour and pattern, but the males are usually smaller than the females and have darker markings on lighter ground-colour (Gadow *op. cit.* 641).

According to Ael. *N.A.* 10.9 some regarded ἔχιδνα as differing in species from ἔχις, but they are classed together in Philum. 17; and here, as in 129ff., are plainly male and female. The snake which bit St Paul in Melita (*Act. Ap.* 28.3) was an ἔχιδνα, from whose bite the natives expected him μέλλειν πίμπρασθαι ἢ καταπίπτειν ἄφνω νεκρόν.

214f. The Scironian rocks are on the borders of Attica and Megaris; for the Pambonian hills see *fr.* 19 n.; Rhype is a mt. in Aetolia (cf. *fr.* 109); Corax, a mt. on the east border of Aetolia; Aselenus, a mt., in Locris according to Σ, or near Trachis according to *Et. M.* 153.4. Cf. *fr.* 6 n.

218 Αἰσαγέης ὄρος αἰπύ appears (between Clarus and Samos) in a geographical list at *H. Hom.* 3.40. It is not mentioned elsewhere. Cercaphus, mentioned in Lyc. 424, is said by Σ there to be a mountain near Colophon. Both places may therefore have been familiar to N. Bucarterus is otherwise unknown.

224 μάσσων i.e. than the ἔχιδνα.

226 πεδανή: cf. 289, 817, *Al.* 306; *C.Q.* 45.107.

232ff. No viper has more than two functioning poison-fangs, the reserve fangs only becoming functional when these are shed or lost. It has no other teeth in the upper jaw; the small teeth in the lower jaw and palate are mainly used in swallowing, and would be the less likely to mark the skin since we understand that a viper, unlike a cobra, does not normally grip its victim when it strikes. N. makes a similar mistake about the Cerastes (261 n.); here his misinformation is possibly due to some confusion with snakes of the Opisthoglypha order which have two or three grooved fangs on either side of the upper jaw. On 234 see *C.Q.* 45.110.

237 Paraphrased, according to Σ, from Numenius (ὑπόχλωρόν γε μὲν ἕλκος | κυκλαίνει. τὸ δὲ πολλὸν ἀνέδραμεν αὐτόθεν οἶδος).

256 Also, according to Σ, from Numenius (ῥέθεσίν γε μὲν εἴδετ' ἐπ' ἰχώρ | ἠερόεις, τοτὲ δ' αὖ μολίβῳ ἐναλίγκιον εἶδος | ἀμφὶ ἑ κυδαίνει χάλκη ἴσον—ἐναλίγκιος Morel, κυκλαίνει JGSch.).

257 ἄνθεσι χάλκου: *C.Q.* 45.98. Probably blue, like copper sulphate, or green, like verdigris, is meant; cf. however *Al.* 529 n.

174

258 **κεράστην**: Cerastes cornutus (Gossen-Steier), C. Aegyptiacus (Brenning), Vipera cerastes (Keller)—a difference of nomenclature only. Philum. 18: one to two cubits in length, sand-coloured, slender tail, two horns, makes a rustling sound as it moves owing to arrangement of scales στοιχηδόν, moves πλαγίως.

260 In 213 however we were told that European vipers were horned.

261 The Cerastes has two 'horns' only: cf. 232 n.

263 For the word ἀματροχιή see Call. fr. 383.10, Pfeiffer ad loc.

266 C.Q. 45.113. Here and in 294 ff. N. is describing the crotaline or 'sidewinding' movement of the Cerastes, which advances by throwing its body forward in a series of loops, and leaves as its track in dust or sand a series of parallel lines, disconnected and oblique to the direction in which the snake is moving.

268 OSch. thought that ἄκατος was the hull of the merchantman rather than a second vessel, and it is not plain why a second should be mentioned unless N. is thinking of the discontinuity of movement in the Cerastes or the yawing of a towed boat.

279 **ἐμφέρεται**: cf. Al. 471, C.Q. 45.101.

282 **αἱμορροῖς**: Vipera latastei, Gossen-Steier; a form of Cerastes, Brenning. Philum. 21: sand-coloured, three palms in length, slender tail, sluggish and moves straight forward, spotted black and white, makes a whistling sound as it moves owing to roughness of scales (cf. 296 f.). It will be noted that N. disagrees with Philumenus as to the coloration and movement of this snake, and the crotaline movement which he ascribes to it, suitable to a sandy habitat, is less so to that given in 283 f. Haemorrhage, haematemesis, and haematuria are common sequelae of snake-bite (Osler and McCrae Syst. of Medicine 1.261). Lucan (9.806) describes them with gusto in the victim of a Haemorrhois.

N.'s Haemorrhois is an Egyptian snake (309) described in so much detail that an identification should be easy. Professor James Gray, whom we consulted, referred our inquiry to Mr H. W. Parker of the British Museum, who writes:

'An awkward problem. The Haemorrhois would appear to have possessed these characters—supra-orbital horns [291, 322], rustling scales [297], sidewinding locomotion [294] and strongly haemorrhagic venom [301]. Aspis cerastes (Linn.: formerly Cerastes cornutus) possesses the first three and the right geographical distribution. Its venom however is reported by Corkill (1935, Notes on Sudan Snakes) to be abnormal among viperine venoms in being almost devoid of haemorrhagic effects. It is further disqualified by the fact that Nicander recognizes a Cerastes as another snake distinct from his Haemorrhois and there is no other sidewinding, rustling, horned snake in Egypt.

'Echis carinata possesses the last three of the characters listed above for Haemorrhois, and also has the right geographical distribution; but is disqualified through lack of a supra-orbital horn. Nicander's description however seems odd in regard to the horn. A supra-orbital horn is such an uncommon feature among snakes that possession of it by a Haemorrhois might have been expected to have been one of its most striking features and been singled out for description as such. Instead it is only referred to obliquely as a landmark for the eye. Can it be that the word translated as "horn" may also mean the supra-orbital or supraciliary region? If that were so I should unhesitatingly plump for Echis.

'The only other snake of the region with supra-orbital horns is *Pseudocerastes fieldi*. This species, at present only known from the Sinaic Transjordan region, may have extended into Egypt in Trojan times; it probably sidewinds and its venom is probably haemorrhagic but it has no rustling scales. The latter is such an unlikely character for Nicander to have observed that the fact of his doing so carries conviction.'

We fear that the horns are beyond dispute, but they are peculiar to N. (see 291 n.), and a hypothesis that N. was embellishing his authority, or that his authority was mistaken, would cause us no grave discomfort.

285 Klauser (*Diss. Vind.* 6.19) wished to translate εἰλυθμὸν ἔχεσκεν *ubi convolvitur*.

291 f. Σ paraphrase the ms text ὑπὲρ νιφόεντα φάη κέρατα δοιὰ μετώπῳ ἔγκειται, but it is difficult to believe that νιφόεντα does not agree with κέρατα, and the eyes of snakes are not white. The Haemorrhois is not usually credited with horns, but they are implied again in 322; cf. Ael. *N.A.* 15.13, which follows N. or his source.

We translate λογάδες *irises* since snakes have no whites in their eyes. The eyes of locusts are, we understand, coloured like their bodies; these vary, and N.'s description is not very helpful.

297 The meaning is plain but the form of the sentence uncomfortable. Perhaps one should write either ὑποψοφέει...διέρπων, or ὑποψοφέων, κ.χ. οἷα δι', ἔρπει.

313 Thonis was at the Canobic mouth of the Nile (Diod. 1.19, Strab. 17.800, Steph. Byz.), and named after the king who received Helen and Menelaus in Egypt (Hdt. 2.113; cf. *Od.* 4.228).

εὐνῇ: perhaps rather *crushed by his bedding*.

316 Aelian (*N.A.* 15.13) adds that with some purpose unknown to him Helen removed τὸ φάρμακον from the spine.

According to *Et. M.* 328.17 the plant ἐλένειον (cf. *fr.* 74.66) sprang from tears shed on this occasion by Helen; according to Ael. *N.A.* 9.21 it was given to Helen by Polydamna, wife of Thonis, to rid the island of Pharos of snakes. Either story, or both, may well derive from N. (see p. 204).

320 σηπεδόνος: unidentifiable (Gossen-Steier, Brenning). Not mentioned by Philumenus, but seems to be the snake he calls σήψ (see 147 n.). He describes it (23) as up to two cubits in length, tapering; moves slowly and straight forward, flat head, spotted white all over; and he includes ἀλφοειδὴς χρόα and ῥύσεις τριχῶν among the sequelae of a bite (cf. 328 ff.).

322 ἔμπλην: C.Q. 45.101.

334 διψάδος: *Cerastes vipera*, Gossen-Steier; *Vipera prester*, Brenning. Philum. 20: a cubit in length, tapering, spotted black and yellow all over, very narrow head: called by some of the θηριακοὶ καύσων ὄφις. Luc. *Dips.* 4 ὄφις οὐ πάνυ μέγας, ἐχίδνῃ ὅμοιος. According to Sostratus *ap.* Ael. *N.A.* 6.51 it is white with two black marks on the tail. For the effects of its bite see also Lucan 9.737.

342 The sense is clear, but ἐξέρρηξε χέη δέ, printed and ineffectively defended by OSch., seems incredible. We have suggested a more normal syntax, but in ℗2 ε is preceded by traces of a letter which do not favour either ξ or τ but rather λ, α, or possibly χ or μ.

343 ff. According to Ael. *N.A.* 6.51 the legend which follows was handled by Sophocles (*fr.* 362 P.), Dinolochus, Ibycus, Aristias, and Apollophanes.

345-53 The acrostic signature was detected by Lobel (*C.Q.* 22.114) who pointed out that ΣΙΚΚΝΔΡΟΣ at *Al.* 266 ff. must be an attempt at another. Cicero (*de Div.* 2.111) found *in quibusdam Ennianis* the acrostic Q. ENNIUS FECIT. ΔΙΟΝΥΣΙΙΟΥ at Dion. Per. 112 ff. provides a later parallel, for which see *RE* 5.917. According to Phot. *Bibl.* 8 b 27 the opening letters of 12 books of Philostorgius formed an acrostic of his name. If anyone should be inclined to believe, on the testimony of Σ Dion. Thr. 568.27 Hilgard, that the *Theriaca* is a supposititious work by a later writer, this signature should be sufficient refutation. It may be noted that it is placed in the most ornamental passage of the whole poem whereas *Al.* 266 ff. is in no way memorable.

359 χερσύδροιο: Laticauda laticaudata, L. colubrina, Gossen-Steier; *Tropidonotus natrix*, Lenz (*Zool. d. alt. Gr.* 448), Keller. The first identification is seemingly based on a mistaken belief that Philumenus calls this a sea-snake. *Tropidonotus natrix*, the common grass-snake, as Brenning remarks, is not venomous. Philum. 24: called ὕδρος as a water-snake, χέρσυδρος on land, when its venom is more concentrated (cf. Quint. Sm. 9.385). Resembles a small ἀσπίς except that it lacks the flattened neck (i.e. the hood). According to Solin. 2.33 common in Calabria.

See on this snake *Philol.* 83.380. Virgil's Calabrian snake (*G.* 3.425 ff.) *notis longam maculosus grandibus aluum* is not named, but the description otherwise follows N. on the χέρσυδρος. Conington in his preface to the *Georgics* translated 366–71: *At first under the wide-throated lake wages truceless war with the frogs, but when Seirius dries up the water, and the dregs at the bottom of the lake are seen, appears that moment on land, adust and bloodless, warming his grim form in the sun, and hissingly with out-darted tongue makes a thirsty furrow as he goes.* He added modestly *I am not sure that I have in all cases rightly interpreted the words, as in a writer like Nicander there is room for considerable differences of opinion.*

368 τρύγη: perhaps *there is a harvest upon.* But cf. *C.Q.* 45.114.

372 ἀμφίσβαιναν: (on the form of the word see 384 n.) *Typhlops vermicularis*, Gossen-Steier; fabulous, Lenz (*Zool. d. alt. Gr.* 451), Brenning. Philum. 27: resembles the σκυτάλη, of equal girth throughout so that head and tail cannot be distinguished, differs from σκυτάλη in moving either end foremost. The latter belief, though not mentioned by N., is implicit both in the head at either end and in the name ἀμφίσβαινα. It seems likely that some real snake was known by this name (cf. *RE* 11.1969), and it is perhaps worth note that there are oriental snakes reports of whose behaviour may have contributed to its fabulous attributes. Ditmars *Snakes of the World* 159 (of the Doliophis): *They crawl slowly away, keeping the head close to the ground. The retreat, however, is a rearguard action in which the tail solely figures. It is reared upward, then bent slightly in the direction of the object of fright. Being blunt, curved in at just the right angle, then slowly waved...it awesomely looks like a threatening head awaiting a chance to bite. And as a keen touch to the spectacle, the 'throat' of the simulated head is bright red....Strangely enough several harmless snakes inhabiting the same regions, and being of similar size and form, as well as colouration, affect the same antics as if seeking defence in imitating their poisonous neighbours.*

377 ff. The sense of the ms text is plain, but in Ψ1 the word βοτῆρες in the scholia suggests that the lemma (missing) had that word and not βατῆρα or the v.l. βοτῆρα at the end of 377—the ὀροιτύποι skin the amphisbaena as herdsmen peel a stick. With the reading βατῆρα Antigonus is reported by Σ to have explained that the men wrapped the skin of the snake round a stick and warmed their hands on it. *Fr.* 34 records a different use for an amphisbaena's skin on a stick, but it is difficult to see how Antigonus extracted such a meaning from this passage. Pliny *N.H.* 30.85 quotes N. for the body or skin of the snake as a cure for *perfrictiones*, and continues *quin immo arbori quae caedatur adalligata non algere caedentis faciliusque sic caedere.* Possibly this is from some other source, but Morel (*Philol.* 83.354) suggested that Pliny may have equated ῥάδιξ in 378 with *radix* and concluded that tree-felling was involved. Cf. *fr.* 35.

πολυστεφέος: *C.Q.* 45.108. The scholia in *p. Ox.* 2221 have καθὸ καὶ ἐν τοῖς | . . .]το ὅλον στέφανον, and though quite irrelevant an ornamental reference to Olympic garlands should perhaps be preferred. This adj. presents difficulties at 490 also.

384 σκυτάλην: unidentifiable (Gossen-Steier, Brenning). Philum. 27 (see 372 n.): cf. Plin. *N.H.* 32.54, Lucan 9.717. The form ἀμφίσφαινα is not accidental in Ϸ1 since it is twice repeated in the commentary. Perhaps therefore it should be accepted here and introduced in 372. Ἀμφίσμαινα is recognized in Hsch., -ίσθμαινα in *Et. M.*

385 The Scytale's tail is probably useless in contrast to the amphisbaena's, which has a head at the end.

391f. The text presented by the mss is intelligible, but the papyrus throws doubt on its correctness; for if ἀκρεμόνας is right, there is no room for ἔρνος at the end of the line, and the papyrus had something other than ἄψεα in 392. Lobel wrote ἔρ[νεα βάλλῃ and supposed the phrase to refer not to snakes but to plants. It seems also possible that ἐρπετά was wrongly repeated from 390. The fragmentary commentary in the papyrus throws no light on the problem.

397 The snake meant is the βασιλίσκος—either fabulous or an Agame (a lizard), Gossen-Steier; fabulous, Brenning. Philum. 31: three palms in length, pointed head, colour ξανθός. Philumenus plainly follows the same authority as N. Pliny (*N.H.* 8.78) says that the habitat of the *basiliscus* is Cyrenaica and that it has a white spot on its head like a *diadema*; Galen (14.233) that it is ὑπόξανθος and has three protuberances on its head. See on this snake *RE* 3.100, 11.1965, *Philol.* 83.367.

403 Philum. 31 (of the victims of the βασιλίσκος) συμβαίνει φλόγωσις ὅλου τοῦ σώματος. From parallel passages in medical writers it would seem that πίμπρημι has this sense at *Al.* 540 (where see n.) also, but elsewhere (*Th.* 306, *Al.* 345, 438, 477, 571, 600) means *cause swelling.* Cf. *C.Q.* 45.107.

406 Σ quote Euphor. *fr.* 89 ὑετόμαντις ὅτε κρώξειε κορώνη (which N. is apparently imitating) and Arat. 963. Add Arat. 1022, Hor. *C.* 3.17.12.

411 δρυΐνας = χέλυδρος: *Vipera berus?* Gossen-Steier (but χέλυδρος *Tropidonotus tessellatus*), *Vipera lebetina?* Brenning. Philum. 25 (δρυΐνας): common on Hellespont, live in roots of oaks, stink, two cubits long, stout-bodied, very rough scales which harbour μυίας τὰς χαλκοπτέρους. These destroy the snake. Virg. *G.* 2.214 *nigris exesa chelydris creta.* See *Philol.* 83.378, 383.

416 μολουρίδας: 'A creature like a locust or, as some say, like a black-beetle' (Σ): cf. *Et. Gen.* B 218. It is more likely to bear the same relation to μόλουρος at 491 as βατραχίς bears to βάτραχος, and μόλουρος is a snake, or at any rate a reptile. Cf. *C.Q.* 45.104.

417 μύωπος: see 736 n.

418 φηγοῦ: a species of oak not certainly identified, perhaps the Valonia oak (see

RE 3.972, 5.2030). For want of a single word we have used the generic name, and neither N. nor the dryinas is likely to have been particular as to the species.

419 *C.Q.* 45.115. The translation is insecure.

420 ἀρπεδές: *Et. M.* 148.15 expresses the opinion that N. uses this word ἀντὶ ἐπιτάσεως μόνης. Cf. Antim. *fr.* 5 Wyss.

421 ὕδρῳ: i.e. χερσύδρῳ: see 359 n.

425 It was the stench from Philoctetes's wound which caused him to be marooned in Lemnos (Procl. *Chrest.* 104 Allen, *al.*). The snake to which he owed it is most commonly called a hydrus, but cf. *Philol.* 83.381.

438 δράκοντα: *Python sebae*, Gossen-Steier; fabulous, Brenning. Philum. 30: non-poisonous, numerous in Aethiopia and Lycia, black, yellow, or ashen in colour, from five to thirty cubits or more in length, scaled all over, large eyes with protuberances over them, an appendage below chin, wide gape, prominent tongue, teeth like those of wild boar.

Python sebae is a tropical and South African snake. Perhaps the Indian *P. molurus* contributes to the non-fabulous background of this creature, but the capture of a thirty cubit snake for Ptolemy Philadelphus is recorded at length in Diod. 3.36; cf. Plin. *N.H.* 8.37. The *dracones* in Luc. 9.727 are plainly fabulous.

440 Pelethronius is a valley of Pelion particularly connected with the Lapithae. See *RE* 19.270.

443 πίονα: *C.Q.* 45.107. *Bulging* is perhaps as likely.

456 ἀτέλεστα: apparently borrowed from Arat. 678 ἀτέλεστα διωκομένοιο λαγωοῦ.

457 Call. *fr.* 374 ὄμμασι λοξὸν ὑποδράξ | ὀσσομένη.

458 ff. The island of Hephaestus is Lemnos; Σάμος here, as in *Il.* 24.78, 753 (cf. 13.12), Samothrace; ʿRhescynthus, according to Σ, a Thracian mountain on which was a temple of Hera; Zone a town in Thrace (Hdt. 7.59, *al.*); Zerynthus another, with a cave sacred to Hecate or Rhea (Σ Lyc. 77, Steph. Byz.). For the oaks of Orpheus see *fr.* 27.

The punctuation of 460 is OSch.'s. Klauser (*Diss. Vind.* 6.71) retained the comma before ἑκάς, which he wished to translate *contra*.

463 κεγχρίνεω: *Zamenis gemonensis*, Gossen-Steier; *Pelias berus*, *Vipera ammodytes*, or more probably fabulous, Brenning. Philum. 26: κ. or ἀκοντίας, two cubits long, tapering, χλωρός, particularly on belly (hence name, from κέγχρος, or because fierce in season of millet); also called ἀκοντίας from its rapidity of movement. Ἀκοντίας in N. (*Th.* 491) is a harmless snake; in Ael. *N.A.* 8.13 a χέρσυδρος which launches itself on its prey from a tree; cf. Plin. *N.H.* 8.85. In Luc. 9.822 a *iaculus* does this with so much force that it goes straight through its victim's head. Κεγχρίας in Philum. 22 is another name for ἀμμοδύτης (sand-coloured with black spots); *cenchris* in Luc. 9.712 a spotted snake distinguished from *ammodytes*.

469 Cf. Arat. 149 ἠελίοιο θερείταταί εἰσι κέλευθοι.

472 Mosychlus according to Σ and Hsch. is a hill in Lemnos. Σ are in some doubt whether Saüs is there or in Samothrace, and Lyc. 78 with Σ favours Samothrace.

483 ff. According to Ant. Lib. 24, where N. (*fr.* 56) is named as the authority, Ascalabus jeered at the eagerness with which the fasting Demeter drank the posset given her by his mother Misme, and she threw the dregs over him, turning him into a gecko. Her hostess is here Metaneira, wife of Celeüs, king of Eleusis, and according to Σ it was Metaneira's son Ambas who was turned into the gecko.[1] Whatever the origin of Demeter's cult-title Ἀχαιά, N. pretty plainly connects it with her sorrows (ἄχη) for the loss of her daughter. Καλλίχορον is the well at Eleusis over which the temple of the goddess was built (see *RE* 10.1631).

484 ἀσκαλάβου: the word no doubt covers all the species of gecko known to the Greeks: see Keller *Ant. Tierwelt* 2.278. They are quite harmless and cannot even bite hard, though Aristotle (*H.A.* 607a 27) asserted that in parts of Italy the bite was fatal. The sequelae according to Philum. 13 are continuous pain and a blanching of the skin round the wound.

490ff. πολυστεφέας: *C.Q.* 45.108. According to Σ, τοὺς πολλοὺς στεφάνους ἔχοντας καὶ γραμμάς (i.e. ringed or banded), which may be right. Cf. 377 n.

Of the snakes mentioned in these lines ἔλοψ, λίβυς, and μόλουρος are unidentified. For μύαγρος Gossen-Steier suggest *Vipera ursinii*, and Brenning has no suggestion. For ἀκοντίας (*Zamenis gemonensis*, Gossen-Steier; *Eryx jaculus* Brenning) see 463 n. Τυφλώψ is according to Brenning the blind-worm (*Anguis fragilis*); Gossen-Steier hesitate between *Blanus cinereus* (another lizard) and *Typhlops vermicularis*, Keller favours this or *T. flavescens*.

Philumenus (22) recommends for victims of the μύαγρος the same treatment as for those of the ἀμμοδύτης, but does not describe the snake. Of ἔλοψ he says (28) that he finds no description παρὰ τοῖς θηριακοῖς, but that its bite produces gastric spasms which should be treated with diuretics and stomachic sedatives. Ἀκοντίας he regards as another name for κεγχρίνης (see 463 n.). The others he does not mention.

491f. φορέονται: or perhaps *all the Darters [etc.] which move about harmlessly.*

494 On the ground that N. nowhere instructs us in the proper time to gather simples, OSch. wrote ὥρην, *rizotomicas rationes*, but these are not discussed either, and seasons are at any rate indicated in some cases (498, 506, 610, 612).

500 Χείρωνος ῥίζαν: centaury.

505 Πελεθρόνιον: 440 n.

509 ἀριστολόχεια: *Aristolochia parvifolia* is said by Brenning to be the commonest species in Greece, while *A. pallida* is the most efficacious.

516 The best boxwood came from Paphlagonia and Corsica (Theophr. *H.P.* 3.15.5, Plin. *N.H.* 16.71). Oricus in Epirus had a reputation for terebinths, but not elsewhere for box unless at Virg. *Aen.* 10.136 *inclusam buxo aut Oricia terebintho* the adj. goes with both nouns.

526 κύμβοιο τραπεζήεντος: in the sense of *cup* N. uses both τὸ κύμβος (*Al.* 129) and ἡ κύμβη (*Th.* 948, *Al.* 389). According to Σ ὁ κύμβος is here equivalent to ὀξύβαφον; cf. Hsch. κύμβη· νεὼς εἶδος καὶ ὀξύβαφον. This may be right, for ὀξύβαφον denotes a quarter of a κοτύλη (cf. 598) and a precise measure would be welcome here. We do not understand τραπεζήεντος, which Σ seem to assert makes the meaning ὀξύβαφον plain.

529 θάψου, *Rhus cotinus,* was the source of a yellow dye (Zante fustic) mentioned at *Al.* 570, on which see *RE* 5A 1281. But cf. Introd. p. 24. Θαψία, *Thapsia garganica,* of which the root contains a sharp, milky sap, was used as a remedy for various complaints; see Theophr. *H.P.* 9.9.1, 5, 6, Diosc. 4.153, Plin. *N.H.* 13.124.

[1] On the relation of these accounts to Ov. *Met.* 5.451 ff. see *Philol.* 59.54, *Rhein. Mus.* 90.249.

530 λευκανθέος: *bright-* rather than *white-flowered*, since white is seldom seen (Brenning). The flowers are normally pale violet.

531 νῆριν: savin is a shrub yielding a volatile oil used in medicine. But see Introd. p. 24. Brenning and Wellmann (Diosc. 4.81 *app. crit.*) interpret it as = νήριον, *Neriuṁ oleander.* Flower and leaves were a remedy for θηρίων δήγματα Diosc. *l.c.*

534 διανθέος: *C.Q.* 45.100. The stamens and pistil were regarded as an inner flower. See 869 n., Theophr. *H.P.* 1.13.2.

537 ἑλξίνην: see Introd. p. 24. The plant is named twice in Dioscorides, and identified by L–S⁹ at 4.39 as *convolvulus*, but at 4.85 as *pellitory*. Neither is suitable here as both plants prefer dry places. Another possible candidate, *Helxine soleirolii*, does not appear in Halacsy *Conspectus flor. Gr.* and is said now to be confined to Corsica and Sardinia where it grows beside mountain streams. See H. A. Weddell *Monogr. de la famille des urticées* 530 (= *Arch. du Mus. d'Hist. Nat., Paris*, 9).

541 Cf. 666 n.

550 Here, as at *Al.* 47, N. is distinguishing the πράσιον called μελίφυλλον and by similar names from μελαμπράσιον and the πράσιον called φιλοφαρές. See Diosc. 3.103 ff., Gow on Theocr. 4.25.

559 ff. N. is describing the left central lobe of a boar's liver: it is triangular, lies close to the gall-bladder, and points downwards (νεύει) from the diaphragm (presumably the meaning of τράπεζα here). It is nearer to the commencement of the portal fissure (πυλάων) than to the diaphragm itself.

565 οὐλοόν: it was supposed that castoreum, a strong-scented secretion of the beaver used in medicine, was contained in its testicles (see, e.g., Diosc. 2.24, Plin. *N.H.* 32.27), and also that the beaver castrated itself to avoid death at the hands of hunters. N.'s adjective does not necessarily imply the second belief, but it was widespread. See Mayor on Juv. 12.34.

566 Cf. Diosc. 2.23.

572 We take this to mean that a drachm's weight of the last ingredient is required, to match the same amount (which has not been stated) of those previously mentioned.

577 τάμισος or πυετία (*Al.* 68) is curdled milk taken from the stomach of young animals of various species and used as a coagulant in cheese-making. See Gow on Theocr. 7.16.

578 Cf. *Al.* 324. Προκὸς τοῦ τέκνου τῆς δορκάδος, Σ, which seems right here though πρόξ may sometimes mean *fallow deer*, which are represented on the coins of Proconnesus. Cf. *C.Q.* 45.105.

579 f. Arist. *H.A.* 507 b 2 συνήρτηται δ' αὐτῇ (τῇ κοιλίᾳ τῇ μεγάλῃ) πλησίον τῆς τοῦ στομάχου προσβολῆς ὁ καλούμενος κεκρύφαλος ἀπὸ τῆς ὄψεως· ἔστι γὰρ τὰ μὲν ἔξωθεν ὅμοιος τῇ κοιλίᾳ, τὰ δ' ἐντὸς ὅμοιος τοῖς πλεκτοῖς κεκρυφάλοις· μεγέθει δὲ πολὺ ἐλάττων ἐστὶν ὁ κεκρύφαλος τῆς κοιλίας. τούτου δ' ἔχεται ὁ ἐχῖνος, τὰ ἐντὸς ὢν τραχὺς καὶ πλακώδης, τὸ δὲ μέγεθος παραπλήσιος τῷ κεκρυφάλῳ.

N. or his authority fails to distinguish between reticulum (κεκρύφαλος) and many-plies (ἐχῖνος).

586 There is plainly some dislocation. JGSch. placed 586 after 582, where it is inappropriate. We have joined it to 578 f., which mention similar ingredients and where the homoearchon would account for its omission. In this connexion Pliny (*N.H.* 28.150) mentions in the same sentence (*cerui*) *testes uel genitale* and *uenter*. OSch. without transposing marked a lacuna after 585. Diosc. 2.41 recommends αἰδοῖον ἐλάφου taken in wine against viper-bite.

605 f. The freshwater crab, *Thelphusa fluviatilis*, occurs in many ancient medical recipes (e.g. Diosc. 2.10, Plin. *N.H.* 32.53). All crabs have eight legs in addition to their claws, and N.'s epithet is ornamental not distinctive.

607 Drilon and Naron are rivers in Illyria (see Strab. 7.316f.). On Cadmus's connexion with those parts see *RE* 10.1466.

614 Corope is in Thessaly, near Pagasae: Orope according to Steph. Byz. in Euboea. According to Σ Scythians and Magi used tamarisk in divination, and they record similar lore from other places.

619 *C.Q.* 45.114. The text printed is unintelligible, and we have provisionally translated that suggested in the apparatus. It is however possible that something has fallen out after 618. Σ throw no light on the passage. Eutecnius paraphrases ἐν σκαφίδι οἴνου προσπλεκομένου συνανακιρνάσθω, ὁ δὲ οἶνος μέτρον ἔστω δέκατόν που χοός. R. Keydell (*Quaest. Metr. de Epic. Recent.*, Berlin, 1911) proposed πῖνε. This is nearer to the tradition, and there are in this part of the poem several prescriptions addressed not as usual to the physician but to the patient (507, 527, 551, 562, 665, 667, 713). It would not however account for the paraphrase.

620 Aratus, of whom N. may be thinking, calls frogs (947) πατέρες γυρίνων. Cf. *Al.* 563.

622 βάμματι: 87 n.

626 κόρκορον: cf. 864, *J. Phil.* 33.201.

628 OSch., reading ὀριγάνου, said the meaning was *folium* ὀριγάνου ὀνίτιδος. Cf. *C.Q.* 45.106.

630 ῥάμνον: see Introd. p. 24. Φιλεταιρίς (-ριον), which N. gives, as a synonym, appears at Diosc. 4.8. and Plin. *N.H.* 25.64 and 99 as another name for πολεμώνιον, *Hypericum olympicum*, 'Cheiron's all-heal'. But its flowers are not white and it bears no resemblance to μηκωνίς, 'wild lettuce'. Or ῥάμνος may signify *Rhamnus cathartica*, 'common buckthorn', which thrives in hedges and woods and was formerly used as a diuretic and strong purgative; but its resemblance to wild lettuce is no closer, and since N. says no word about its properties or how it is to be used, its identification must remain uncertain.

633 ff. The tomb of Gyges, the Mermnad king of Lydia, is mentioned by Hipponax (*fr.* 15 Bk) among the monuments of the country. Tmolus, more commonly a mountain or a town, is here presumably the Lydian king who bequeathed his kingdom to his wife Omphale (Apoll. 2.6.3.), but nothing is known of his tomb. Παρθένιον λέπας· ἀκρωτήριον τῆς Λυδίας (Σ), but the name is not elsewhere recorded from these parts. Κίλβις· ὄρος Λυδίας ἢ τόπος ἢ ποταμός (Σ). The Cayster rises, according to Pliny (*N.H.* 5.115), *in Cilbianis iugis*: there was a river Κίλβος and a δῆμος Κιλβιανῶν in the district, and Strabo (13.629) mentions a Κιλβιανὸν πεδίον, πολύ τε καὶ συνοικούμενον εὖ καὶ χώραν ἔχον σπουδαίαν, which is perhaps what N. refers to.

639 Theophr. *H.P.* 7.8.3. classes ἄγχουσα among ἐπιγειόφυλλα, and N. seems to refer to this characteristic.

642 *C.Q.* 45.114. According to Σ σφεδανόν means τραχὺ καὶ σκληρὸν καὶ σφιγκτόν. The plant owes its name to the supposed resemblance of its seeds to a snake's head. They are however noticeably rough on the surface, and τραχύ is presumably right.

647 κλώθοντος: cf. *Al.* 93 n.

648 εὐκνήμοιο: if this = πολύκνημον it signifies 'field basil', *Zizyphora capitata*. (Brenning prefers *Calamintha clinopodium*.)

650 f. *C.Q.* 45.105.

656 χαμαίλεον cf. *J.H.S.* 56.5.

658 σκολύμῳ: cf. *J.H.S.* 56.6.

666 ff. Cf. 541. Presumably some species of bugloss is the plant meant (*Echium sericeum*, Brenning).

Alcibius seems to be mentioned only in these two places and Σ have no information about him. Phalacra is a summit of Mt Ida; Crymne and Grasus, otherwise unknown, must therefore be in the Troad, and Σ, though presumably guessing, may be right in explaining the Horse to be the Wooden Horse. Diosc. 4.24, 27 mention two plants useful in snake-bite called 'Ἀλκιβιάδειον. One is another name for a form of ἄγχουσα or ὀνοχειλές, the other of ἔχιον. Presumably these are the same as N.'s pair, but in such a context Alcibiades is as obscure as Alcibius.

670 For Amyclean (i.e. Spartan) hounds see Arist. *H.A.* 574b 26, Xen. *Cyn.* 10.4, Virg. *G.* 3.44, 405, Hor. *Epod.* 6.5, Nemes. *Cyn.* 107, *al.* According to Arist. *H.A.* 607a 3 they were a cross between dog and fox.

676 ἆσαι: cf. *Al.* 305, 331, *C.Q.* 45.99.

678 I.e. ἡλιοτρόπιον, *heliotrope*.

685 ff. Heracles's assistant against the Hydra is elsewhere Iolaus, not his father Iphicles, and the variant ἔρνος, though ill-supported, should perhaps be preferred since it restores Iolaus to the story. He cauterized the monster's necks as Heracles cut off the heads. (Eur. *Ion* 195, Apoll. 2.5.2)

The geography is obscure. The Hydra's habitat was the swamp of Lerna in Argolis. Phlegya was the name of a Boeotian town, the Phlegyae of a people commonly associated with Thessaly, Boeotia, and Phocis; less commonly with Epidaurus or Arcadia (see *RE* 20.267). Melas is a common river-name, one river so called being near Trachis. Perhaps, as Σ suggest, Asclepius, who by one account was grandson of Phlegyas, practised at Delphi. According to Σ the wound was caused by the Hydra's blood.

689 The γαλέη is the domestic animal—γαλῆ κατοικίδιος Diosc. 2.25, where the same prescription is given. Galen (12.362) mentions other complaints for which it was prescribed but says that he has never tried it.

697 στροφάλιγγα: perhaps what Theocritus (1.58) calls τυρόεντα μέγαν λευκοῖο γάλακτος.

703 See *Al.* 558 n. If N. called the χελύνη βροτολοιγός he was probably thinking of the man-eating tortoise of the Scironian cliffs (see Call. *fr.* 296).

708 μάκτρη should mean *kneading-trough*, but we do not see how this should be used as a filter.

709 *C.Q.* 45.115. The ingredients of this prescription are plain; the meaning of the words, which may be corrupt, very doubtful. Diosc. 2.79 merely recommends turtle-blood, drunk in wine with τάμισος from a hare, and cummin for θηριοδήγματα καὶ φρυνοῦ πόσιν.

716 ῥώξ: *Lycosa palustris* L., Sprengel; *Lathrodectus tredecimguttatus*, Kobert, Steier. The latter is the Italian and Corsican malmignatte, of which a black variety, sometimes called *L. erebus*, extends as far east as the Caspian (Vellard *Venin d. Araignées* 24). Taschenberg refuses to believe that it is an identifiable spider, and thinks it may be a millepede, but is in difficulties with the resemblance to a grape. Philum. 15 says that the ῥάγιον is round in form, black, small-footed, with mouth beneath belly. Cf. Plin. *N.H.* 29.86.

717 πισσῆεν is strangely placed if it qualifies αἰθαλόεις, but we do not see how else to construe it.

718 ἔσκληκεν: cf. 766, 785, 789, *Al.* 491, *C.Q.* 45.108. N. seems to use this word in reference to chitinous parts of spiders and scorpions, with a sense rather of *hard* than *dry*. A spider's 'teeth' are in the front mid-line of the prosoma, which N. or his authority perhaps took for its stomach.

722 For these symptoms see Plin. *N.H.* 24.62, Ael. *N.A.* 17.11, Philum. 15.6.

725 ἀστέριον: *Lathrodectus conglobatus*, Kobert, Steier; *Tetragnatha extensa*, Sprengel; a tarantula, Lichtenstein; *T. stellata*, Taschenberg. The first is sometimes known as the Greek malmignatte, but is held by T. Thorell to be merely an age-variety of *L. tredecimguttatus*, on which see 716 n. He remarks of this genus *colour and markings can be very variable in one and the same species* (*Synonyms of European Spiders* 508)—a point which may help to explain the multiplicity of dangerous spiders distinguished by N.; see Introd. p. 23. For ἀστέριον cf. Plin. *N.H.* 29.86.

729 κυάνεον: *Clubiona holoserica* Deg., Sprengel; a solpuge, Lichtenstein; unidentifiable, Steier, Taschenberg. Cf. Plin. *N.H.* 29.86.

733 ἀραχνήεντα: similarly ἀραχνιῶδες γάλα Arist. *H.A.* 622 b 12, οὖρον Hippocr. *Coac.* 571. The meaning is perhaps *full of filaments*.

734 ἀγρώστης: *Aranea speciosa* L., Lichtenstein; *Lycosa tarantula*, Menge; *Linyphia triangularis* Cl., Sprengel; a wolf-spider, Steier, Taschenberg.

On λύκοι see Arist. *H.A.* 623 a 1, Philum. 15.2. The wolf-spiders of modern zoologists, unlike the λύκος of Philumenus, and all but the first of the species so named by Aristotle, do not make webs.

736 ψῆνας: the gall-insect, or fig-wasp (*Cynips psenes* L. See Arist. *H.A.* 557b 26, *RE* 6.2129); μύωψ, mentioned at 417, a horse-fly (*Tabanus.* See Arist. *H.A.* 528b 31, 552a 29), but perhaps includes other stinging flies.

738 σφήκειον: *Aranea saccata* L., Lenz, Brenning; *A. retiaria*, Sprengel; unidentifiable, Steier. Lichtenstein and Taschenberg take it for an insect, suggesting respectively *Asilus crabroniformis* and *Scolia haemorrhoidalis*. Cf. Plin. *N.H.* 29.86 *etiamnum deterior a crabrone pinna tantum differens. hic et ad maciem perducit.*

741 ff. These lines are very puzzling, and if they were mutually consistent there would be some temptation to expel both. As they stand they assert that bulls are born of bees, and λυκοσπάδες is unintelligible, whereas the familiar βουγονία myth (on which see *C.R.* 58.14) tells of bees generated from oxen, and is followed by N. himself in *Al.* 446. Σ refer λυκοσπάδες to the bees, which the text does not permit, and assert that it means 'generated from corpses torn by wolves', and OSch. wrote ταύρων δὲ μέλισσαι. If N. really called bees λ. it would be less far-fetched to treat λυκο- as referring not to wolves but to the wolf-spider of 734 which preys on flies, but as between bulls and bees the former would seem more suitably so described, and μελίσσας...ἐγγεννῶσι or ἐγγείνοντο (*Il.* 19.26) might also be considered. Line 741 however is quoted in the form presented by the mss in Σ *Al.* 446, and without an author's name in *A.P.* 9.503, Simplic. *ad* Arist. *Phys.* 191 b 18, Suidas *s.vv.* βούπαις, ἵππος: and Varro (*R.R.* 3.16.4) quotes from Archelaus the line ἵππων μὲν σφῆκες γενεὰ μόσχων δὲ μέλισσαι which must be imitated by or from N. As these facts discourage emendation we have preferred to eject 742. The translation gives the general sense of the line but shirks λυκοσπάδες.

747 μυρμήκειον: *Salticus formicarius*, Keller; *Galeodes araneoides* Koch, Brenning. Many varieties of spiders mimic ants (J. Crompton *The Spider* 175), but Dr M. Pryor informs us that the description fits *Mutilla europea*, which has a red 'neck' (prothorax) and two conspicuous white spots on the thorax. It is not a spider but an insect, the female wingless, common in the Mediterranean area, parasitic on humble-bees, and capable of inflicting a painful sting. It is not unlike an ant in appearance. Lichtenstein said *ohne Zweifel die Puppe des Termes foetale oder einer ähnlichen Species*. Taschenberg (who also thought of *Mutilla*) commented *so erkläre ich das, wie vieles andere, was er schreibt, für Nonsens*. Cf. Plin. *N.H.* 29.87, Philum. 15.3.

748 πυρόεν: for Meineke's πυρόειν see *Al.* 42 n.

752ff. J. H. Fabre *Life of the Spider* (1912) p. 2: *In the neighbourhood of Pujaud, not far from Avignon, the harvesters speak with dread of Theridion lugubre...according to them her bite would lead to serious accidents*. The name seems to be an alias of the Corsican malmignatte (see 716 n.), of which Vellard (*Venin des Araignées* 14) records plagues in Spain and *nombreux accidents, dont plusieurs mortels, parmi les moissonneurs*. The range of this spider, and the danger to which it exposes harvesters makes an identification here tempting. On the other hand neither the appearance nor the symptoms produced by it (for which see Vellard *op. cit.* 20) much resemble those of N.'s φαλάγγια. Brenning said *eine Mylabris-art, nach Schauenstein M. Cichorii Fabr. und M. variegata*: on which Taschenberg remarked that the first was a Chinese, the second a non-existent, species. Lichtenstein thought the 'spiders' might be *Lytta syriaca* L.; Taschenberg also suggested a beetle—*Telephorus* or *Malachius*. It is perhaps just worth noting that Galen (19.731) mentions φαλάγγια as a substitute for κανθαρίδες.

755 N. prescribes for cantharides poisoning at *Al.* 115. Diosc. 2.61 mentions as the most potent variety αἱ ποικίλαι μηλίνας ἐγκαρσίους ζώνας ἔχουσαι ἐν τοῖς πτεροῖς, ἐπιμήκεις τὸ σῶμα, ἁδραί, ἐμπίμελοι ὡς αἱ σίλφαι, and adds that the self-coloured kind are less efficacious. This is apparently not the Spanish Fly of the modern pharmacopoeia but according to Keller *Meloë cichorei*, and to Gossen *Lytta dives* (Brullé).

759 According to Σ this creature is the κρανοκολάπτης, and their notes disclose that it is also called κεφαλοκρούστης, that it has four wings, and a sting beneath its head concealed by its neck, and that according to Sostratus ἐν τῷ περὶ βλητῶν καὶ δακέτων it frequents the persea-tree and if drowned in oil is remedial. It has wings and sting, and should therefore not be a spider, but its position between spiders and scorpions suggests that N. so regarded it, and Philumenus (15) includes the κρανοκολάπτης among φαλάγγια (see Introd. p. 23). He says of it that it ὑπόμηκές ἐστι καὶ ἔγχλωρον, τὸ δὲ κέντρον ἔχει ὑπὸ τὸν τράχηλον, and that it attacks the head and neighbouring parts. Diosc. 1.129 (of the Persea) ἐφ' οὗ καὶ τὰ λεγόμενα κρανοκόλαπτα φαλάγγια εὑρίσκεται, μάλιστα δὲ ἐν τῇ Θηβαΐδι. So far as we are aware no identification has been suggested, though Taschenberg thought that some butterfly was the object of needless alarm. It is perhaps worth note that winged scorpions also are reported from these parts (801 n.). For the persea-tree see *Al.* 99 n.

760 On the word φάλλαινα, which Σ assert to be Rhodian in this sense, see *Glotta* 6.194.

762 στεγνά: ἀντὶ τοῦ ὑμενώδη, ὡς τῶν ἀκρίδων (Σ), but the following words show that this creature is not hymenopterous but lepidopterous and we take the adj. to mean something like *felted*. Cf. *C.Q.* 45.108.

771 According to Steier *Scorpio europaeus* Latr., but see Introd. p. 21.

772 ἐν γενύεσσι: or possibly *the scorpion with red on its jaws*, but we understand the thirst in 774 to be caused by the inflammation of the victim's mouth. According to Steier this scorpion is *Buthus occitanus* Amour.

775 According to Steier *Androctonus ater*.

777f. We know of no suggested identification for this scorpion, nor for those in 782, 786. In 778f. the hailstone-like eruption (χάλαζα) is perhaps, like the shivering, unexpected in the dog-days.

781 ἐννεάδεσμοι: ἀντὶ τοῦ πολύδεσμοι (Σ). Scorpions have in fact tails consisting of five segments and the sting. Cf. Introd. p. 21.

785 Cf. 718 n.

786ff. According to D. W. Thompson *Gloss. Gk Fishes* καρκίνος is a generic name for crabs, and includes πάγουρος, the common crab, *Cancer pagurus*. The first of the two crabs here mentioned will be some smaller species found among the seaweed and on shore.

791ff. For the generation of scorpions from crabs see Ov. *Met.* 15.369, Plin. *N.H.* 9.99, and for similar fables *RE* 3 A 1807.

797 According to Steier *Androctonus (Buthus) australis*.
The acc. apparently depends upon δήεις (786).

801 According to Paus. 9.21.6 a Phrygian brought to Ionia a scorpion with wings like those of an ἀκρίς. Large, winged scorpions appear in an unveracious account of India from Megasthenes (Strab. 15.703), they are reported in Libya by Strab. 17.830, Luc. *Dips.* 3, and in Ael. *N.A.* 16.42 Pammenes claims to have encountered in Egypt winged scorpions with two stings. For a representation of one see Keller *Ant. Tierwelt* 2.479. No scorpion has wings, and if some insect is the basis of these stories it has not been identified. Cf. 759 n.

802 We suppose τοὶ θ' to be the locusts, not the flying scorpions, and so Σ. Eutecnius however takes the other view.

804 Pedasa was in Caria near Halicarnassus (see *RE* 19.26). More than one place named Cissus is known (*RE* 11.522), but none in or very near Caria. The best known is near Thessalonica, but Asia Minor seems more probable in this context, and many places prolific in ivy may have been so called.

806 βέμβικος: see *Al.* 182 n.

811f. ἴουλος and σκολόπενδρα are mentioned together as wingless insects at Arist. *H.A.* 523 b 18. The first, glossed ὄνος in Hsch. (cf. Plin. *N.H.* 29.136), is no doubt a woodlouse of one or more species; the second a centipede, perhaps *Scolopendra forficata* L. or *S. morsitans* (Keller *Ant. Tierwelt* 2.481). The woodlouse is of course harmless, but the bite of some centipedes is poisonous. For πεμφρηδών see *Al.* 182 n. N. compares the centipede's legs to the oars of a ship. Conversely Lycophron (23) calls ships ιουλόπεзοι.

815 Aristotle (*H.A.* 604 b 19) says only that the bite of the shrewmouse is dangerous to draught animals as causing blisters; but cf. Plin. *N.H.* 8.227, 29.88, [Diosc.] *Ther.* 8, Ael. *N.A.* 2.37, Philum. 33. These superstitions have extended into modern times; cf. *C.Q.* 45.96.

816 Plin. *N.H.* 8.227 *idem* (sc. *mures aranei*) *ubicunque sunt, orbitam si transiere, moriuntur*—apparently misunderstanding N. He means, as Σ and Aelian say, that the shrews fall into the ruts and cannot get out.

817 σῆπα, here distinguished as a lizard from the snake of 147, is said in Diosc. 2.65, Plin. *N.H.* 29.102 to be another name for Χαλκιδική σαύρα, *Chalcis*. Philumenus (34), who couples Χαλκιδική σαύρα with the salamander (presumably following the same authority as N.), says that according to Soranus the bite of the lizard produces a blister with blackening and sepsis round it. Σ equate σήψ with χαλκίς, which, they say, is four palms long and has bronze lines on its back, and in Arist. *H.A.* 604 b 23 there is a χαλκίς, called also з1γνίς, shaped like a small lizard and coloured like οι τυφλῖνοι ὄφεις, whose bite is dangerous to draught animals.

Gossen-Steier from these and a few immaterial references produce three lizards—*Tropidosaurus algira* (Philum.), *Chalcides tridactylus* (Nic., Diosc., Plin.), *Ablepharus pannonicus* (Arist.). We should have thought one enough, and in any case N. and Philumenus should go together. All these lizards are harmless, but so are the salamander and the gecko.

818 For the salamander see *RE* I A 1821, Keller *Ant. Tierwelt* 2.318. For earlier references to its fire-resisting capacities, Arist. *H.A.* 552 b 16, Theophr. *fr.* 3.60. The creature is harmless, but according to Philum. 34 its bite produces a painful scab. At *Al.* 537 N. describes, and prescribes for, the symptoms occasioned by a draught prepared from one; cf. Plin. *N.H.* 29.74 *inter omnia uenenata salamandrae scelus maximum est. cetera enim singulos feriunt nec plures pariter interimunt,... salamandra populos pariter necare improuidos potest.* Pliny has much else to say to the discredit of the salamander. See also Ael. *N.A.* 2.31, 9.28.

823 σμυραίνης: *Muraena helena*: see D. W. Thompson *Gloss. Gk Fishes* 162. D. S. Jordan *Fishes* 371 *A live Moray, four to six feet long, [is] often able to drive men out of a boat.* Its bite is poisonous, though the nature of the toxin is uncertain: see H. M. Evans *Sting-fish and Seafarer* 91.

825f. We suppose ἐχέτλιον to be the well in the boat into which the fish are thrown as they are caught.

OSch., punctuating with a comma at the end of 825, improbably supposed these lines to explain the murry's purpose in emerging. We cannot construe them in their present context, but it should be said that Athenaeus, who is talking of the mating of murry and viper, quotes 823-7 as they stand in the mss.

The details of this union are described at length in Opp. *Hal.* 1.554; see also Ath. 4.136 B, Ael. *N.A.* 1.50, 9.66, Plin. *N.H.* 9.76, 32.14. Ath. 7.312 B and Σ 823 cite Andreas (physician to Ptolemy IV) as contradicting the tale.

828 τρυγόνα: the sting-ray, *Trigon pastinaca*, common in the Mediterranean. It has a long and poisonous spike in the tail. Cf. Opp. *Hal.* 2.470 ff., H. M. Evans *Sting-fish and Seafarer* 43.

δράκοντα: the weever (*Trachinus draco* and other species), which has a poisonous spine and dorsal fin. Cf. Opp. *Hal.* 2.459 (where see Mair), H. M. Evans *Sting-fish and Seafarer* 25.

831 ff. For the effect of the sting on trees see Opp. *Hal.* 2.488, Ael. *N.A.* 2.36, *al.* According to Philum. 37 if a τρυγών has stung a man and the sting is then driven into a tree, preferably an oak, the man recovers and the tree dies.

835 Odysseus was killed by his son Telegonus, who was using a spear tipped with the sting of a ray which his mother Circe had given him; or, according to Aeschylus (*fr.* 275), by a heron which dropped the sting on him. On these stories, which perhaps derive from the θάνατος ἐξ ἁλός prophesied by Teiresias for Odysseus at *Od.* 11.134, see D. W. Thompson *Gloss. Gk Fishes* 271, Mair on Opp. *Hal.* 2.497, *RE* 17.1991.

837 We do not understand οἶσιν, which Σ explain to mean ἐφ' οἶστισιν— presumably *besides*. Perhaps an antecedent has been lost—e.g. δάχμασι πημαίνουσι κινώπετα μυρία φῶτας.

The portentous list of simples which follows (838–914) does not fulfil the apparent promise of 837, for N. only once (867) condescends to tell us in what complaints these will be useful; and having disclosed in 876 f. how two of them are to be administered, forgets this detail again until his catalogue is almost at an end (907 ff.).

841 The mss write τ' ὄρδειλον. If τόρδειλον is right it is presumably another form of τόρδυλον: τόρδιλον, which should perhaps be preferred, appears in Diosc. 3.54.

843 καυκαλίδας: L-S⁹ define as *Tordylium apulum*, but since *Tordylium* (*hartwort*) was mentioned in 841, this can hardly be the meaning here. We have preferred Mr Raven's suggestion of *hedge-parsley*.

852 θυλακίς: *C.Q.* 45.103. Dioscorides (4.65) says of μήκων κερατῖτις, καρπὸν ...καμπύλον ὥσπερ κέρας ὅμοιον τῷ τῆς τήλιδος, ὅθεν καὶ ἐπωνόμασται: cf. *Al.* 424 n. Page suggests that Π's ἐπεπλεῖτις and πεπλεῖτις (864) conceal genuine variants. Neither word is known, but πεπλίς and πεπλίον are other names for μήκων ἀφρώδης (Ps.-Diosc. 4.168).

862 Σ explain the v.l. νήστειρα to mean *taken fasting*. OSch. wrote δὴ σπεῖρα— *de vimine ῥάμνου intelligo ad arcendas serpentes circumligato*.

864 Lemnian μίλτος, a substance frequently prescribed by ancient physicians, is a silicate of aluminium and iron, of which the exact analysis will be found in *Rev. Arch.* 3rd ser. 27.321.

869 ff. *C.Q.* 45.106. In 871 ἄνθη means the stamens and pistil left after the petals have fallen from the sepals or perianth. So διανθής of annuals and other flowers: cf. 534 n.

872 ὕσσωπος: according to Thiselton-Dyer (*J. Phil.* 33.199) this is not hyssop (though so translated in L-S⁹) but marjoram. Cf. *Al.* 603.

873 τηλεφίλοιο: From Σ Theocr. 3.29 may be taken to mean *poppy* or else some shrub-like plant with a spiral seed-pod.

877 κάρδαμον: cf. *J. Phil.* 34.293.

882 I.e. of δρακόντιον, *edderwort*.

886 σκορπίου: for this plant, which we have been content to leave as *scorpius*, at least half a dozen equivalents have been suggested. Wellmann, comparing Diosc.4.76, thinks that it may be aconite, *Doronicum pardalianches*. Cf. Theophr. *H.P.* 9.13.6.

887f. Psamathe is a spring (Σ, Plin. *N.H.* 4.25), Traphea a town (Steph. Byz.), in Boeotia, Copae a town on the shore of Lake Copais. Schoeneus and Cnopus are the names of streams in Boeotia, the latter identified by Σ with the Ismenus, which however seems to have flowed into Lake Halice rather than Copais.

890f. N. is distinguishing the Indian Choaspes (which is a tributary of the Kabul River) from the more famous Persian. Theophrastus (*H.P.* 4.4.7) describes the pistachio in similar terms, but knows it only by hearsay. Dioscorides, who also recommends the nuts for snake-bite (1.124), says they came from Syria.

892 OSch. wished to alter καυκαλίδας because they have been mentioned already at 843. But N. may well have been negligent in so long a list, especially if he was compiling from more than one source. Cf. *Al.* 198 n.

894f. Klauser (*Diss. Vind.* 6.20) proposed (as an alternative remedy to OSch.'s βαλών) to read εἰρύσιμον δέ and to regard βαρυώδεα ποίην as in apposition to what precedes.

902 ψίλωθρον: this may be the equivalent of ἄμπελος λευκή (or ἀγρία). *Bryonia cretica*, bryony, of which the root was used as a depilatory, Theophr. *H.P.* 9.20.3. We translate ὑακίνθου *hyacinth*, without prejudice; but see *fr.* 74.31 n.

903 For the myth of Hyacinthus see Apoll. 1.3.3, 3.10.3, Frazer *ad ll.*

911 Λιβυκὰς ῥίζας: i.e. σίλφιον. See 85 n.

915 ἀνύδροις: the implication seems to be that chewing will serve if there is no water to make a paste or infusion.

921 The remedies which follow are no longer suitable for emergency use, and we assume that they are not, as in the preceding paragraph, intended to be applied by the victim to himself.

927f. In 928 βουβῶνας must include μασχάλας, as Σ imply. The translation therefore adds them. The arm or leg is inserted by the neck of the skin, which is then fastened round it, and it is held immersed to the right depth in the wine—if we have translated 927 correctly.

941 See *Al.* 483 n.

943 ἀγροτέρης στ. λέπος: Dioscorides (4.152) and modern writers mention the seeds of stavesacre as emetic, purgative, and anthelmintic, but say nothing of the husks or rind (λέπος).

949 τάμισον: see 577 n.

950 See 605 n.

957 There was a Ὁμήρειον at Colophon (which was among the places claiming Homer as a townsman), and Pasquali (*Stud. It.* 20.89) supposed N.'s adjective to mean that he belonged to a guild or society associated with it. It seems however not inappropriate to a self-satisfied poet writing hexameters with an archaic vocabulary. Cf. *fr.* 14 n.

958 A variation of Κλάρος αἰγλήεσσα in *H. Hom.* 3.40. It seems unnecessary to suppose with Pasquali (*Stud. It.* 20.83) that Clarus is here the eponymous hero of the place, and that N. means Colophon. Cf. Introd. p. 5.

ALEXIPHARMACA

ANALYSIS

The poem enumerates twenty-two substances, animal, vegetable, and mineral, which are deadly or injurious to man. The three kinds are arranged in no special order, but with each he adopts a uniform method, describing first the effects produced by the poison, and then the antidotes to be employed.

I. 1–11, *Proem*: Nicander to Protagoras; I will tell you of poisons and their antidotes.

II. 12–628, Poisons. 12–73, Aconite. 74–114, White Lead. 115–56, Blister-Beetle. 157–85, Coriander. 186–206, Hemlock. 207–48, Arrow-poison. 249–78, Meadow Saffron. 279–311, Chameleon-Thistle. 312–34, Bull's Blood. 335–63, Buprestis. 364–75, Curdling Milk. 376–96, Thorn-Apple. 397–414, Pharicum. 415–32, Henbane. 433–64, Opium. 465–94, Sea-Hare. 495–520, Leeches. 521–36, Fungi. 537–66, Salamander. 567–93, Toads. 594–610, Litharge. [611–15, Yew-tree. 616–28, Fungi.]

III. 629–30, *Sphragis*: Treasure the memory of Nicander.

NOTES

1 ff. Νίκανδρός ἐστιν ὁ λέγων Κολοφώνιος Πρωταγόρᾳ Κυζικηνῷ (Σ).

5 ἅ τε: the antecedent is φάρμακα concealed in the preceding adj. Cf. *Th.* 818 σαλαμάνδρειον... δάκος... ἤ τε....

7 f. We accept the view of J. H. Voss (on Cat. 63.5) that Ἄρκτος is here the mountain, called in Ap. Rh. 1.941, 1150, Strab. 12.575 Ἄρκτων ὄρος, on which part of Cyzicus stands. On the assumption that Ἄρκτος means the pole Σ are put to very far-fetched explanations of the adjective. Cf. *C.Q.* 45.106.

According to Σ, Λόβρινον is a mountain at Cyzicus, but the name is otherwise unknown. For the cult of Cybele at Cyzicus see *RE* 11.2287.

9 παῖδες K.: the Ionians, for Ion, their ancestor, was son of Creusa and Xuthus (Apoll. 1.7.3).

11 See Introd. p. 5.

13 ff. According to Ap. Rh. 2.780 Priolas was a prince of the Mariandyni, son of Dascylus, and killed by the Mysians (see however Roscher 3.2991). Apollonius (2.720 ff.), from whom N. is perhaps borrowing, places in these parts an ἄκρη Ἀχερουσίς, a σπέος Ἀΐδαο, and προχοαὶ ποταμοῦ Ἀχέροντος. On Eubuleus (or -lus) as a euphemistic name for Hades see *RE* 6.864. According to Σ aconite sprang from the vomit of Cerberus who, when dragged out of Hades by Heracles, could not stand the light and was sick; cf. Plin. *N.H.* 27.4. This story derives from the Ξένιος of Euphorion (*fr.* 37), to whom N. may be indebted in this context.

18 *An. Bekk.* 374.11 ἀλάλυγγι πνιγμῷ, ἀπορίᾳ, δυσπνοίᾳ.

19 ff. In this very troublesome passage we take νείαιρα to be used substantivally

190

in the sense of *stomach* or of some larger part of the trunk which includes the stomach (cf. Call. *fr.* 43.15), and στόμα γαστρός to define ἄκρον νειαίρης. The objection to taking ν. adjectivally with γαστρός, which would seem much more natural, is that ν. στόμα γ., *mouth of the lower stomach*, could hardly mean anything but the pylorus, whereas κραδίη (as δοχαίη also implies) means the cardiac entrance. This meaning of καρδία is insisted upon by Galen (5.274), who cites this and other passages in illustration, and though it is possible, it is not, we think, likely that N. has confused the two openings. Στόμα γαστρός seems to mean the cardiac opening in 120, 379; in 339, 509, where plurals are used, both cardiac and pyloric may be meant. The latter is here called πύλη. We are doubtful as to the meaning of ἀειρόμενον (20) and πρῶτα (23).

23 We have attempted to construe ἅλις, but this word seems often in *Al.* to have little or no meaning. See, for example, 483, 499. Similar difficulties are not infrequently presented by νέον and ῥεῖα.

25 For ταράσσειν as a gloss to κυκᾶν see, e.g., *Et. M.* 548.43, Hsch., Suid., Σ Ar. *Equ.* 363, 866.

30 *C.Q.* 45.97.

34 For Nysa, the mythical birthplace of Dionysus, see *RE* 17.1628.

38 For panthers and παρδαλιαγχές see Arist. *H.A.* 612a 7, Ael. *N.A.* 4.49. According to Diosc. 4.76 the root was used for poisoning baits for panthers and other animals.

40 *Th.* 666 n.

41 Aconae is a town near Heraclea in Bithynia, in the country of the Mariandyni (cf. 13 n.) according to a convincing conjecture in Theophr. *H.P.* 9.16.4, where we are told that the best and most plentiful supplies of ἀκόνιτον come from those parts though it grows also in Crete and Zacynthus. Aconite is called θηλυφόνον according to Pliny (*N.H.* 27.4) because, *constat...tactis quoque genitalibus feminini sexus anima-lium eodem die inferre mortem*: cf. Theophr. 9.18.2. The name κάμμαρος is apparently derived from the shape of the roots: cf. Diosc. 4.76f., Theophr. *l.c.*, *J.H.S.* 56.4.

42 On the n. termination -ειν see Hermann *Orphica* 705, J. U. Powell *Coll. Al.* 131 (*Eleg. Adesp.* 1.7); cf. *Th.* 748.

47 See *Th.* 550 n.

49 πηγάνιον: according to Theopompus (*fr.* 200 M.) the inhabitants of Heráclea were wont to take rue before going out as a prophylactic against the loving-cups of aconite proffered them by their tyrant Clearchus. For βάμμα σίμβλων see *Th.* 87 n. N. means the mixture of honey and vinegar called elsewhere ὀξυμελί-κρητον and ὀξύμελι.

56 παῦρα: cf. 144, 240; *C.Q.* 45.115. We cannot construe the word in these places. *Little by little*, appropriate in 144 and 240, seems excluded by this.

62 Cf. 557, Call. *fr.* 322 γέντα βοῶν μέλδοντες.

64 For the prosody of βάλσαμον cf. *Th.* 947.

65 Νέας γυναικός φησι, καὶ οὐ πώλου ἵππου. ὅτι δὲ χρήσιμον τὸ γυναικεῖον γάλα καὶ Ἐρασίστρατος μαρτυρεῖ ἐν τῷ περὶ θανασίμων, Σ. Cf. 356 n., Diosc. 2.70.6, Gal. 6.775, 12.265, *al.*, Plin. *N.H.* 28.72.

68 πυετίη is the same as τάμισος, on which see *Th.* 577 n.

79 ὀλκός: γλώσσης ὁ. occurs again at 281. N. constantly uses ὀλκός of the

NOTES

trailing body of a snake, and Page suggests that in these two places the phrase denotes the whole snake-like tongue.

93 κλώθοντι: Σ explain absurdly τῷ ὡς νῆμα κλωθομένῳ χυλῷ. Our translation is tentative. The verb occurs again at *Th.* 647, *Al.* 528 and in the latter place is glossed χλωρὸν θάλλοντα καὶ χλοάζοντα. Cf. *C.Q.* 45.103.

99 ff. Οἶον seems meaningless. OSch. wrote οἶον and explained it from Hsch. οἶα· τὰ δεινά. Αἰολεῖς, but this is Musurus's correction of οἰατά· δυνά. Αἰέν or αἰνόν might also be considered.

On the persea-tree, identified as *Mimusops Schimperi,* see *RE* 19.941, A. Engler *Monogr. Afr. Pfl. Fam.* 8.76 and Pl. 30, *J. Phil.* 34.87. According to Theophr. *H.P.* 4.2.5, who says that its stone is not as hard as that of a plum, it was a native of Egypt, but Abyssinia and Arabia are its probable home. The country of Cepheus, Andromeda's father, was variously located in the East (see *RE* 11.224), but N. probably derives the statement that Perseus brought the tree to Egypt from Callimachus (*fr.* 655, where see Pfeiffer).

Medusa's neck is γονόεις because Chrysaor and Pegasus sprang from it.

103 The derivation of Μυκῆναι from μύκης goes back to Hecataeus (*fr.* 360 M.).

104f. Melanthis is otherwise unknown; Langia only as a spring at Nemea in Stat. *Th.* 4.717, unless it is the πηγὴ Λαγκία mentioned without indication of site in Paus. 3.21.2.

107 Gerrha was an important town on the Arabian coast of the Persian Gulf (Strab. 16.766, 778, *RE* 7.1270).

108 δάκρυον: so at 108, 301, 546 and *Th.* 907 for *gum* or *resin.*

112 *C.Q.* 45.97.

115 κανθαρίδος: see *Th.* 755 n.

σιτηβόρου: distinguishing κανθαρίδες from this source from other beetles so called: Diosc. 2.61 κανθαρίδες εἰς ἀπόθεσιν εὔθετοι αἱ ἀπὸ τοῦ σίτου.

119ff. *C.Q.* 45.107. Στόμα γαστρός is presumably the cardiac opening, as in 379; cf. 19 n.

130 μορόεν: cf. 136, 455, 569. The meaning of this obscure adj. is discussed in *C.Q.* 45.104.

131f. For Hippothoon see *RE* 8.1924. He is said by Σ and Σ Eur. *Or.* 964 to be Metaneira's husband. She is more commonly the wife of Celeüs, as in *Th.* 486, and in *H. Hom.* 2.96ff., the earliest source for the story of Iambe, whose jokes cheered Demeter so that she broke her fast.

138 For πύλη = *throat* see 507.

144 See 56 n.

145f. Cf. Theophr. *H.P.* 9.13.6, 18.2.

148 Phyllis is an ancient name for Samos. Imbrasus is a river, called also Parthenius (cf. 618 n.), Cercetes a mountain, in the island. The Chesiad Nymphs are presumably, like Ocyrhoe in a fragment of Ap. Rh. (*ap.* Ath. 7.283 E), children of Imbrasus and Chesias, and attendant on Artemis, who is called Χησιάς (and Ἰμβρασίη) in Call. *H.* 3.228, Χήσιον being, according to Σ there, an ἀκρωτήριον τῆς Σάμου: Chesius in Plin. *N.H.* 5.135 is a river.

'Samian earth' is described in Theophr. *fr.* 2.62f., and would seem to have been a kind of clay. Dioscorides (5.153) mentions two kinds, one called also κολλούριον, the other ἀστήρ, and recommends it for various disorders: cf. Gal. 12.178. The legend of the horned lamb, which excites the incredulity of Σ, seems otherwise unrecorded, but Suid. *s.v.* ἐπὶ τὰ Μανδροβόλου is possibly relevant.

157 κόριον, here described as a dangerous poison, is curative at *Th.* 874, though it is not there said how it is to be used. According to Diosc. 3.63 it is a vermifuge and aphrodisiac, but in large doses deranges the mind, and Galen (14.139) prescribes τοῖς χλωρὸν κορίαννον πιοῦσι. The belief that coriander may be injurious, though shared by later herbalists (e.g. Culpeper), is said to be without foundation.

159 οἱ μέν: the change of number is characteristic of N. Μέν might seem to imply that other alternative sequelae were to be mentioned and that a lacuna should be marked after 161. The other authorities however ([Diosc.] *Alex.* 9, Paul. Aeg. 5.40, Scribon. 185), though they add that the victim's body smells of coriander, agree on frenzy and offer no alternative.

160 δήμια according to Σ means ἐν τῷ δήμῳ, but according to [Diosc.] *Alex.* 9 (and Paul. Aeg. 5.40) victims of κόριον λαλοῦσι μετ' αἰσχρολογίας.

161 ἀταρμύκτῳ: elsewhere only in Euphorion (*fr.* 124), who applies it to ὄμμα.

162 ἑδανοῖο: *C.Q.* 45.100. The name occurs again in 181, there accompanied by 'psithian' which Σ, perhaps guessing, assert to be another name for 'Pramnian'. The original meaning of all these words is lost, but Pramnian and perhaps psithian wine was dry, and presumably 'hedanian' was so also.

166f. Aristotle (*H.A.* 620a 13) gives a similar account of the κέπφος. The rendering *petrel* is traditional but unsupported by evidence.

If ἐπισπεῖ is what N. wrote he presumably took the Homeric πότμον ἐπισπεῖν (*Il.* 7.52, *Od.* 4.562, *al.*) to contain a pres. inf.

172-7 N.'s digressions are mostly mythological ornamentation (e.g. *Al.* 100 ff., 302 ff., 560 ff., 605 f.), and these lines seem totally irrelevant to the context. *Th.* 740 ff., *Al.* 448 ff. however are little less so.

178 ἀτμένιον, applied to oil again in 426, is said by Σ to mean *prepare laboriously*, or *by slaves*. We suppose it to mean *such as slaves use.* Cf. *C.Q.* 45.99.

182 ff. On the vines see 162 n. The insects appear all to be bees or wasps. Πεμφρηδών is called ὀλίγη at *Th.* 812 and is here said by Σ to be wasp-like, larger than an ant but smaller than a bee, black and white, and nesting in hollow oaks. Βέμβιξ is said by Σ here to be a wasp-like bee sometimes called βόμβυξ, and at *Th.* 805 to be black and wasp-like. In Plin. *N.H.* 11.75 bombyx is a large Assyrian species of bee or wasp. One might guess the word to be equivalent here to βομβύλιος, and to denote a bumble-bee. Βέμβιξ and πεμφρηδών are mentioned together as stinging insects in Epiphan. 1.301 C.

185 N. is copying the fox in the vineyard who in Theocr. 1.48 ἀν' ὄρχως | φοιτῇ σινομένα τὰν τρώξιμον.

187 *C.Q.* 45.109.

193 ἠέρα παῦρον ἀτύζει: perhaps *draws short breaths*, but the meaning of ἀτύζει is obscure. Βλέπει ἢ ἕλκει ὅ ἐστι σπᾷ τὸν ἀέρα καὶ ὀλίγον ἀναπνεῖ, Σ, *Et. M.* 168.12. ἐὰν ἀτύζων, ἀφροντιστῶν, ἐὰν δὲ ἀτίζων, ἄτη περιφερόμενος, καταπίπτων. οὕτως εὗρον ἐν ὑπομνήματι Νικάνδρου. The verb does not occur elsewhere in N., and *Et. M.* is explaining this passage, which has just been quoted.

197 On the construction see *C.Q.* 45.115.

198 Unmixed wine has already been prescribed in 195. Possibly N. is now paraphrasing a second authority. Cf. 554, *Th.* 892 nn.

199 δαυχμοῖο: *Th.* 94 n.

208 According to Σ τοξικόν is so called either because when taken it is as rapidly fatal as an arrow, or because Parthians and Scythians poison their arrows with it; and those who identify it with hemlock are mistaken. To N. it is plainly a poison used by archers (244), and from its mention at this place it should be a plant, or at least of vegetable origin, though not hemlock, which has been dealt with in 186. Different peoples poisoned their arrows with different substances, whether vegetable (e.g. Plin. *N.H.* 16.51, 25.61, 27.101) or other (e.g. *ib.* 11.279, Ov. *e P.* 4.9.83),[1] but the τοξικόν for the internal consumption of which physicians prescribed must have been a known and familiar poison. Pliny (*N.H.* 6.176) and Pollux (1.138) say that Arabs (cf. 244) poisoned their arrows but do not say with what. Paul. Aeg. 5.30 however classes τοξικόν among ἐρνώδη καὶ λάχανα. Most probably therefore a simple vegetable poison is here meant, though Mercurialis (*de Venen.*, ed. 1588, 40) cited from an apparently unpublished ms of Aelius Promotus a statement that, like φαρικόν (398 n.), it was compound.

209 χείλη...βαρύνει: or perhaps *his lips, which are...oppress him.*

215f. For the shouts of the decapitated see commentators on *Il.* 10.457: cf. Ov. *Met.* 5.104. For ἀμφιβρότην we follow Σ though sceptically (τὴν ὅλον τὸν ἄνδρα συνέχουσαν). E. Goebel (*Jahrb. cl. Phil.* 141.826) proposed to connect the word with βρότος, and translated *wie ein mann heulend herankommt, dem der rings blutende kopf mit schwerten verhauen ist.* For ἐμπελάδην see *C.Q.* 45.101.

217 κερνοφόρος: the κέρνος was a tray to which a number of small cups to contain offerings was attached. See Ath. 11.476E, J. E. Harrison *Proleg.* 158ff., 559.

218 According to Σ the celebrations took place on the 9th of the lunar month: cf. Lobeck *Agl.* 645.

227 δαμαζόμενος χερί: presumably you are to tickle his throat: cf. 138, 362, 535.

228 βοσκάδης presumably means the same as βοσκάς in 293, where it is glossed νομάς, i.e. *fending for itself*, not artificially fed; and that is the meaning of βοσκάς in Aët. 9.30 ('Αθηνᾶ 23.342). But at *Th.* 782 βοσκάς means *greedy*. Cf. *C.Q.* 45.99.

229 *C.Q.* 45.104.

230ff. All the fruits named here have strong astringent qualities.

234 Cydon, whose parentage is variously reported (*RE* 11.2304), was the founder of Cydonia in Crete. The fruit is the quince.

239ff. According to Brenning these oils are emetics.

240 See 56 n.

247 Apparently implying that the plant sprang from the blood of the Hydra, a belief mentioned in Σ 207. OSch.'s view that N. means '*like* the Hydra's venom' seems improbable.

249 On ἐφήμερον see Theophr. *H.P.* 9.16.6, where we are told of a certain antidote.

266ff. See n. on *Th.* 345–53.

271 Καστάναια or Κασθ- is a town or village on the coast of Magnesia (Steph.

---

[1] The arrow-poisons of the world are exhaustively dealt with in L. Lewin *Die Pfeilgifte* (Leipzig, 1923).

Byz., Strab. 9.443) to which, according to *Et. M.* 493.25, the chestnut owes its Greek name. See however *RE* 10.2344.

273 Prometheus concealed and kept alight in a fennel-stalk the fire he had stolen (Aesch. *P.V.* 109).

278 OSch. wrote ἔπι στῦφόν τι, but, if this is right in principle, ἐπῇ is a small change and seems desirable. Bent. and JGSch. supposed two hemistichs missing between ποτῷ and νοῦσον. Zeune proposed νούσημα.

280 οὐλοφόνον (ω) according to Diosc. 3.9.1. is another name for ἰξίας.

293ff. Hens lay shell-less eggs when their diet is deficient in lime. N.'s meaning is so far plain, but it is hard to believe that the ms ἀνόστεα could mean *shell-less*. If 296f. mean merely that they break the eggs they are brooding or drop their eggs away from the nest, N. has lost sight of his human patient, but we do not see what else the lines should mean. On βοσκάς see 228 n.

302 The scene of Marsyas's death was his home, Celaenae, in Phrygia. According to various authorities he was tied to a pine for flaying, and his skin was hung on one, and this no doubt lent point to the pine's sorrow, though Ovid (*Met.* 6.392) does not include trees in his list of mourners. Cf. Luc. *Trag.* 315.

312 On the supposedly poisonous effect of bull's blood see [Diosc.] *Alex.* 25, Plin. *N.H.* 11.222. According to Plut. *Flam.* 20 Midas, Themistocles, and Hannibal committed suicide by drinking it; so, according to Apollonius (*Lex. Hom.* 156.18) did Jason and Midas, and according to Herodotus (3.15) Psammenitus: cf. Soph. *fr.* 178, Ar. *Equ.* 83 (Neil *ad loc.*). Recorded deaths from the blood not willingly self-administered are fewer—Aeson (Apoll. 1.9.27), Smerdis (Ctesias *ap.* Phot. *Bibl.* 37b 27). Roscher thought that the toxic quality of blood from an animal suffering from anthrax might account for the belief (*Jahrb. cl. Phil.* 127.158) but this explanation does not seem very satisfactory, and others are less so (Gruppe *Gr. Myth.* 877, Frazer *Pausan.* 4.175, *C.R.* 25.171).

319 This might perhaps more naturally mean *cut sprays* (κράδαι) *from a figtree in sap,* but it is the fruit which other authorities prescribe for such patients (e.g. Plin. *N.H.* 23.128, [Diosc.] *Alex.* 25, Gal. 14.143).

323 πυετίην: Th. 577 n.

329 λίτρην: a measure used particularly in Sicily and equivalent to about a quarter of the modern litre or 218 grammes: cf. Hultsch *Gr. u. röm. Metrologie*[2] 120 n. 2, 662.

331 κακοχλοίοιο: apparently *ill-coloured*. The epithet (on which Σ make no comment) is inappropriate, but though OSch.'s *folio aspero* (cf. Plin. *N.H.* 20.171) and Brenning's *übel-riechend* (cf. Theophr. *H.P.* 6.2.6, Diosc. 3.121) are correct descriptions, neither sense can well be elicited from κακόχλοος.

335 Plin. *N.H.* 30.30 *buprestis animal est rarum in Italia, simillimum scarabaeo longipedi. fallit inter herbas bouem maxime, unde et nomen inuenit, deuoratumque tacto felle ita inflammat ut rumpat;* cf. Ael. *N.A.* 6.35, Veget. 5.14.10. They are classed in Diosc. 2.61 together with κανθαρίδες and described as εἶδος κανθαρίδων, and Hippocrates mentions them several times for their medical use. Keller (*Ant. Tierwelt* 2.414) does not attempt an identification; Gossen suggests *Meloë variegatus* L.; Lenz *M. proscarabaeus.* JGSch. cited from Bellonius *Obs.* 1.45 the statement that on Mt Athos a stout, pale beetle injurious to cattle when accidentally eaten was called *bupristi*. There was also a plant called βούπρηστις (Theophr. *H.P.* 7.7.3) which no doubt explains the presumably interpolated lection of BPRv in 345.

339 στομάτεσσι: see 19 n.

342 Or, reading ἀφυσγετόν, *settles its filth*. Cf. *C.Q.* 45.99.

344f. See on 335.

356ff. Human milk is no doubt intended, and according to Plin. *N.H.* 28.74 this was prescribed by Aristotle in buprestis-poisoning. Cf. 65 n.

376 δορύκνιον: variously explained as *Convolvulus dorycnium* (Fraas) or as *Solanum melongena* (Sprengel), while at Ps.-Diosc. 4.72 it is synonymous with στρύχνον μανικόν, *Datura stramonium*, 'thorn-apple'. The first and third are described by Dioscorides as narcotics fatal in large doses, and it seems unlikely that N. means either plant. Singer at *J.H.S.* 47.27 declines to attempt an identification.

389 According to Σ χυλός is the broth of the chicken.

390ff. 390f. seem to refer to small fish, shrimps, etc. which swim: 393 ff., with the possible exception of κηραφίδες, to shellfish, on which see D. W. Thompson *Gloss. Gk Fishes* s.vv. There is a somewhat similar list in *fr.* 83. Στρόμβος and κῆρυξ are apparently generic for spiral-shelled varieties: κηραφίς is glossed κάραβος in Hsch. but perhaps wrongly. It is otherwise unknown. Τῆθος we have assumed to be the same as τήθυον (-θεον), but according to Σ they are τὰς ἀγρίας λεπάδας ἃς ἡμεῖς ὠτία λέγομεν.

The text of l. 396 is highly uncertain, for we cannot swallow Σ's explanation that δὴν ἔσεται means πολὺ ἀπέσται ἀντὶ τοῦ ἐκτὸς ἔσται, nor OSch.'s *non delectentur diu muscis* (which would seem to imply ἔστω). JGSch. courageously translated *iuvabunt comesta*. Knox proposed δηλέεται, but both the uncontracted form of the verb and the resulting sentence are unsatisfactory. Possibly some shellfish-name is concealed, and ἡδ' ἔτι κῆρυξ | (νηρεῖται) τ. τε would be nearer the truth.

397 The parenthesis seems pointless, and there is some temptation to translate ἄιδρις *unknown*.

398 **Φαρικόν,** or Φαριακὸν φάρμακον as it is called by Phylarchus *ap.* Ath. 3.81 E, is defined by Hsch. as φάρμακον σύνθετον θανάσιμον, and so Scribon. 195 *dicitur ex conpluribus conponi*, but its ingredients are nowhere disclosed, and a reference in Diosc. 5.6.4 does not help. Σ are in doubt whether it is called after a man or a place (of which they name three). In case one or other explanation is right we print with a capital Φ.

402f. Diosc. 1.9 names Cilicia and Syria as the sources for ἡ ὀρεινὴ νάρδος, καλουμένη δὲ ὑπό τινων καὶ θυλακῖτις καὶ πυρῖτις. The only known Cestrus is the considerable river which rises in Pisidia and flows through Pamphylia to the sea, outside the borders of Cilicia though in the right neighbourhood.

407f. Cf. *fr.* 74.29f. We cannot identify a lily which answers plausibly to this description.

420ff. *C.Q.* 45.115. JGSch. defended βρύκωσι by supposing a line lost before 420 which had contained ὅταν. He also marked a lacuna after 420 which should contain the symptoms of henbane poisoning (one of which he supposed to be itching gums). It is true that lines on this subject might be expected, but between 422 and 423 seems a more suitable place for them.

424 Elsewhere modern editors usually follow Aristarchus (Σ Ap. Rh. 3.37) in writing ὅ ῥα, and at *Th.* 685 this spelling has the support of BKv.

N. is explaining the name βούκερας for fenugreek, more commonly called τῆλις: Plin. N.H. 24.184 *feno Graeco...quod telin uocant, ali carphos, aliqui buceras, ali aegoceras quoniam corniculis semen est simile.* Cf. *Th.* 852 n.

426 ἀτμενίῳ: 178 n.

429 Πέρσειον in Diosc. 4.73 is another name for στρύχνον μανικόν (cf. 376 n.) but in Theophr. *H.P.* 2.2.10, and Posidon. *fr.* 6 M. it is the fruit of the persea-tree, on which see 99 n. N. presumably means the latter. We cannot supply the fem. noun implied in ἥν: cf. *Th.* 103 n.

433 κεβληγόνου: the adj. occurs elsewhere only in Euphor. *fr.* 108, where it is applied to Athena, born from Zeus's head.

443 On the prosody of δείδιθι see Cobet *V.L.* 393.

448–51 This seemingly irrelevant digression is perhaps prompted by the fact that the poppy with its capsule is constantly associated with Demeter; and if the honey is also hers it may for that reason help in the cure.

452ff. *C.Q.* 45.116.

463f. The plural is unwelcome, and unique in similar contexts in N., and Scaliger's correction (with ἀναλυόμενος) should perhaps be accepted in default of a better. Suidas has τινθαλέοισι...τινθαλέοισι κατικμήναιντο λοέτροις, and the anonymous fragment is assigned to the *Hecale* of Callimachus (*fr.* 247). There are no plain Nicander-glosses in Suidas, and it is more likely therefore that N. is borrowing here from Callimachus than that the gloss indicates a variant κατικμήναιο.

465 On λαγὼς θαλάσσιος, *lepus marinus*, see D. W. Thompson *Gloss. Gk Fishes* s.v. It is traditionally and no doubt rightly identified with *Aplysia depilans*, a form of sea-slug which has 'ears' like a hare and emits an acid secretion of bright purple colour. For the superstitious terrors which it inspired see Plin. *N.H.* 32.8.

469 αὐξίδα: *C.Q.* 45.99. The translation of αὐξίς as *dish* is no more than a guess. Σ explain as εἶδος ἰχθύος ὅμοιον θύννῳ (the word elsewhere denotes the young of the tunny), or alternatively σῶμα. Neither explanation seems plausible.

471f. ἐμφέρεται: *C.Q.* 45.101. Τευθίς and τεῦθος are squids, the latter much larger than the former (Arist. *H.A.* 524a25, where see D. W. Thompson)— probably *Loligo vulgaris* and *Todarodes sagittatus*. Σηπιάς (elsewhere -ία) is a cuttle-fish—*Sepia officinalis* and allied species.

473 The ink of the cuttle-fish (usually θολός or ὀλός) seems not to be called gall elsewhere. Plin. *N.H.* 9.84 takes it for blood though its origin had been accurately described by Aristotle (*H.A.* 524b14).

479 Apparently the swellings and eruptions are regarded as a consequence of the defective discharge of urine.

483 Φωκήεσσαν: i.e. from the Phocian Anticyra. See Mayor on Juv. 13.97. White hellebore seems to be meant, of which Diosc. 4.148 says πρωτεύει δὲ ὁ Ἀντικυρικός·...καθαίρει δὲ δι᾽ ἐμέτων ἄγων ποικίλα. Black hellebore, prescribed at *Th.* 941, was principally used as a purgative: see *RE* 8.165.

484 δάκρυ...κάμωνος: Theophr. *H.P.* 9.1.3 τὸ δάκρυον...ἐν ταῖς ῥίζαις... τῆς σκαμμωνίας.

489ff. We cannot throw much light on these pomegranates. 490 apparently indicates two Cretan varieties, the second according to Σ called ἀπό τινος Προμένου Κρητός. This may well be a guess, but we write the adj. with a capital Π on the chance that it is true. Hsch. προμένειοι · ῥοιαί τινες, the only other trace of the word, probably derives from this line. The Aeginetan pomegranates of 491 are not mentioned elsewhere, and we are in doubt whether the following relative clause adds a fourth variety of pomegranate, describes the Aeginetan (in N. the change of number would hardly present a difficulty), or means, as we incline to think, *and any which have the same qualities as the three mentioned.*

Diosc. 1.110 distinguishes three sorts, ἡ γλυκεῖα, ἡ ὀξεῖα, and ἡ οἰνώδης, Pliny (*N.H.* 23.106; cf. 13.112, 15.39) at least nine, but their descriptions do not help, unless indeed N.'s οἰνωπή is Dioscorides's οἰνώδης and Pliny's *uinosa*. This however in Pliny is a sweetish variety, while it is the *acerbum* which he prescribes (23.108) *contra leporem marinum*; and this, in view of 479, squares with Diosc. ἡ δὲ ὀξεῖα... οὐρητική and with his own statement (in 107) that it is diuretic. Moreover 491 plainly distinguishes what is elsewhere called the σκληρόκοκκος from the ἀπύρηνος (Ath. 14.650E, Plin. *N.H.* 23.106 *dulcia quae apyrena alio nomine appellauimus*), to which the *uinosa* comes next in sweetness (cf. Theophr. *H.P.* 4.13.2). It is likely therefore that οἰνωπή refers to the interior of the fruit, φοινώδης to the exterior. Apart from N. and Pliny pomegranates do not seem to be prescribed in these cases.

Much information about pomegranates, though little to the present purpose, will be found in Pallad. 4.10 and J. G. Schneider's notes *ad loc.*; see also Hehn *Kultur-pflanzen*, ed. 6, 233.

493 οἰνοβρῶτα βορήν: perhaps the flesh of the pomegranate rather than grapes.

499 The general sense of the line is clear, the text uncertain. Σ connect χείλεσι with ἐμπελάουσα, and ῥύμη with ποτοῦ. The latter is plausible but difficult to reconcile with OSch.'s correction (which βρώμης appears to necessitate) unless, as seems improbable, μέτα governs ῥύμη. Ῥευμαλέου, *streaming*, would make the same point but the adj., though of a formation favoured by N., is unattested. We cannot translate ἅλις, but this word presents difficulties elsewhere in N. (see 23 n.).

509 στομίοισι: 19 n.

515 ναιομένην: cf. *fr.* 74.58. Lobeck *Rhem.* 353 ναιομένην id est νάουσαν.

520 Fresh water, preferably rain-water, was mixed with sea-water in the evaporating pans (Plin. *N.H.* 2.233, 31.81), and according to Σ removed the smell. For *salinae* see Manil. 5.682, Rut. Nam. 1.475.

524 ἀποφώλιον, which usually means μάταιον, is glossed χαλεπόν in Σ, but in view of 523 N. perhaps means ἀπὸ τοῦ φωλεοῦ. In Eur. *fr.* 996, where the Minotaur is called σύμμικτον εἶδος κἀποφώλιον τέρας (or βρέφος), a connexion with φωλεός (i.e. the Labyrinth) seems again possible. For the poison gathered from snakes by fungi see Plin. *N.H.* 22.95.

528 κλώθοντα: cf. 93 n.

529 χαλκοῖο π. μ. ἄνθην: if we have translated μεμογηότος rightly, presumably verdigris is meant. If however he is thinking of long treatment in the furnace, cuprous oxide or cupric oxide may be intended. The first is red, the second black, and Dioscorides (5.76f.), describing the preparation of a medicament which he calls κεκαυμένος χαλκός from ships' nails treated in a furnace, says that one variety is red, another black. He also describes χαλκοῦ ἄνθος, produced by pouring water on molten copper and κατάπυρρος in colour. Copper sulphate, thrown off when copper sulphide ore is roasted, seems less likely: cf. *Th.* 257 n.

537 λιπορρίνοιο: the sense is uncertain. The meaning *skinless* offered as an alternative by Σ might be expected but would be hard to explain.

538 For lizards in magic see Gow on Theocr. 2.58.

539 Cf. *Th.* 818 n.

540 ἐμπρήσθη: the verb seems here at any rate to mean *inflame* rather :an *inflate* (its plain meaning in 477), and [Diosc.] *Alex.* 4 speaks of γλώσσης φλεγμονή as a sequela of salamander-poisoning. Cf. *Th.* 403 n.

544 But ἄκρα '*valde*' *significat* according to OSch.

547 N. appears to use τενθρήνη as a synonym of μέλισσα. Τενθρηδών in Arist. *H.A.* 629a 31 is rather some species of wasp, but according to Hsch. the word was used also for ἡ ἀγρία μέλισσα.

554 Resin has already been prescribed in 546; see *Th.* 892 n.

556 We do not understand νέρθε πυρός. Σ (who take κεραίης for a noun) say ἄγαν σφοδρῶς ἐν τῇ σποδιᾷ τοῦ κέρατος ἑψηθῆναι.

557a Both Schneiders condemned this verse though the homoearchon fully accounts for its omission in GV, and its resemblance to 62 is not close enough to warrant suspicion. OSch. however, unlike JGSch., included it in his enumeration but instead of calling it 556b called what is here 559 560, and our 560 560b. We have not thought it desirable to renumber the whole poem from this point onwards but have treated the verse which caused the trouble rather than 560 as *extra numerum*.

558ff. N.'s sea-tortoise, mentioned also at *Th.* 703, is no doubt the loggerhead turtle, *Thalassochelys caretta*; his land-tortoise, the common *Testudo graeca*.

563 δαμάσαιο: ἑψήσειας (Σ).

567f. According to Wellmann (*RE* 7.116) these toads are respectively *Bufo vulgaris* and *B. viridis*, but the identification seems insecure, and according to Σ the φρυνὸς κωφός is a frog and not a toad. Cf. 575 n. The allegedly poisonous properties of toads are discussed by Wellmann (*l.c.*).

568 Other interpretations of λαχειδής in Σ are δασύς and μικρός.

573ff. For the transposition see *C.Q.* 45.116.

575ff. This toad presents a difficulty, for its habits and habitat suggest that it is the same as that mentioned in 568f., 578, except that it is vocal while the other is mute. The change of gender, if it is correct, possibly indicates that a different species is meant, but N. is much given to such shifts, we cannot discover that φρυνός and φρύνη are elsewhere differentiated, and Plin. *N.H.* 32.52 *ex isdem his ranis lien contra uenena quae fiant ex ipsis auxiliatur, iocur uero etiam efficacius* encourages the belief that the same toad supplies both poison and antidote. According to Aelian (*N.A.* 17.15: cf. Plin. *N.H.* 32.50) toads have two livers of which one provides the antidote to the other. The difficulty would vanish if 576f. were removed, and we therefore regard that couplet with suspicion; if it were removed 575 might refer to the toad responsible for the particular case of poisoning, or perhaps to both species. We cannot accept Σ's explanation τὸ κακὸν βάρος τὸ ὀλεθρίου ἐκείνου φαρμάκου· τούτου γὰρ λείπει, and we regard ὀλοοῖο as one of the very numerous cases in which N. restricts to two terminations an adj. elsewhere of three (see *C.Q.* 45.97). OSch. printed πολυαλγέος in 576 and imaginatively referred it to the discomforts endured by the toad in winter; Wellmann (*RE* 7.116) thought it alluded to the toad's melancholy cries. If it should in fact be preferred, the pains inflicted on the victim would seem to provide a more probable explanation. Keller *Ant. Tierwelt* 2.310 and Wellmann in *RE* 7.116 (where he seems to distinguish this toad from that mentioned in 568) identified this toad with the fire-bellied toad, *Bombinator igneus*, but according to Gadow *Amphibia and Reptiles* 155 this species is unknown south of the Danube, where its near relative *B. pachypus* replaces it.

586   The treatment prescribed, according to Σ, is ξηροπυρία. The earthenware πίθος is to be heated and the patient placed in it.

591   φιλοζώοιο: *C.Q.* 45.109. According to Theophr. *H.P.* 4.10.5 κύπειρις is πάντων μάλιστα δυσώλεθρον owing to the character of its roots.

592   τρίβοις, which might be supposed to mean *frictions*, is explained by Σ to mean περιπάτοις, *walking exercise*, and we accept this view since [Diosc.] *Alex.* 31 says of those suffering from toad-poisoning δεῖ δὲ αὐτοὺς καὶ ἀναγκάζειν συντόνως περιπατεῖν καὶ τρέχειν.

594   λιθάργυρος: *lead oxide.* Σ assert, on the authority of οἱ περὶ 'Απολλόδωρον, that it was administered in food, μετὰ φακοῦ ἢ πισσίου ἢ πλακοῦντος, its colour rendering it hard to detect.

603   ὑπέρεικον, more commonly ὑπέρικον, is *St John's wort,* a name hardly suitable for a pagan author. For ὕσσωπος see *Th.* 872 n.

605   For the highly confused legend of Melicertes see *RE* 15.514. N. follows the version in which his mother Ino jumped into the sea with him, and the Isthmian games (with victors' garlands of σέλινον) were founded in his honour when his corpse was washed up at the Isthmus.

611-15   The lines were condemned by OSch. for their brevity, the absence of any account of symptoms, and the fact that they are addressed to Protagoras as patient not as doctor (see however *Th.* 619 n.): 615 is borrowed from 191.

616-28   Seem plainly a remedy for fungus-poisoning additional to those mentioned in 527-36, and they were condemned by OSch. JGSch. less plausibly condemned 617 but transferred the whole passage to follow 536. On 617 see *C.Q.* 45.117.

618   Dictynna dislikes myrtle because a branch of it caught in her garments when she was being pursued by Minos (Call. *H.* 3.201). It is often connected with Aphrodite (*RE* 16.1180), but, so far as we are aware, neither the dislike of Hera nor its reason is mentioned elsewhere. Imbrasus is the river in Samos (see on 148) called also Parthenius owing to Hera's having spent her childhood there. She is called 'Ιμβρασίη at Ap. Rh. 1.186.

623f.   Columella (12.38.6), giving instructions for making a concoction of the strained juice of myrtle-berries and honey, adds *sed hoc mense Decembri fieri debebit, quo fere tempore matura sunt myrti semina.*

626   We accept Bentley's correction since the acc. ἐκθλίψαντα following the nom. λεήνας, though printed by OSch., is hardly credible even in an interpolator. N. habitually uses a nom. (never an acc.) with the inf. of command (e.g. *Th.* 95, 122, 506 *al., Al.* 350).

FRAGMENTS

The numbers are those of O. Schneider. Numbers in a bracket, which in some cases follow, are those of such fragments as appear in F. Jacoby *Frag. d. Gr. Historiker* 3 A 87 ff.

AETOLICA

Fr. 1 contains cited words in Ionic prose (see below). It seems probable therefore that this was a prose work[1] and that some fragmentary hexameters in *fr.* 5 (*q.v.*) are an illustrative quotation. There is no reason to suppose that they come from N.'s own poems; see however *fr.* 109.

1 (2)

Ath. 11.477B. From Bk I. Ἐν τῇ ἱεροποιίῃ τοῦ Διδυμαίου Διὸς κισσοῦ σπονδοποιέονται πετάλοισιν, ὅθεν τὰ ἀρχαῖα ἐκπώματα κισσύβια φωνέεται. Cf. Macrob. 5.21.12, Eust. 1632.8.

2 (1)

Ath. 2.296F. From Bk I. Apollo taught prophecy by Glaucus. The latter discovers a magic herb and presently drowns himself.

3 (3)

Harpocrat. *s.v.* Θύστιον. From Bk I. Mentioned as a town in Aetolia.

4 (4)

Phot. *s.v.* Τιτανίδα γῆν. From Bk I. The Titans assisting men.

5 (5)

Σ Ap. Rh. 1.419. From Bk I. Delos called Ortygia from Ortygia in Aetolia. The cited verses (see above) are οἱ δ' ἐξ Ὀρτυγίης Τιτηνίδος ὁρμηθέντες | οἱ μὲν τὴν Ἔφεσον. OSch. attempted to reconstruct two and a half more from the following prose.

6 and 7 (6)

Σ Ap. Rh. 4.57, *Et. M.* 153.4. From Bk 2. Endymion and Selene. According to *Et. M. N.* asserted that the Ἀσέληνα ὄρη (*Th.* 214 n.) were so called because when Selene slept there with Endymion the rest of the world went moonless. Cf. *frr.* 24, 147.

8 (7)

Tzetz. *ad* Lyc. 799. An oracle of Odysseus in Aetolia.

8a

[OSch. p. 130 n. 1]

Σ *Il.* 5.843. Ochesius the son of Oeneus.

---

[1] Wilamowitz (*Hell. Dicht.* 1.35) however thought that it was a mixture of prose and verse, and ascribed it to the older Nicander. See Introd. p. 8.

COLOPHONIACA

More probably prose than verse.

9 and 10 (9)

Ath. 13.569 D, Harpocrat. s.v. πάνδημος 'Αφροδίτη. A temple of the goddess and brothels established by Solon. Athenaeus refers to Bk 3, Harpocration to Bk 6, but one figure or other is probably corrupt.

ΙΑΣΕΩΝ ΣΥΝΑΓΩΓΗ
ΠΡΟΓΝΩΣΤΙΚΑ ΔΙ' ΕΠΩΝ
ΠΕΡΙ ΧΡΗΣΤΗΡΙΩΝ ΠΑΝΤΩΝ ΒΙΒΛΙΑ ΤΡΙΑ

See Introd. p. 3. The words δι' ἐπῶν in Suidas suggest that the second (a paraphrase of Hippocrates) and perhaps also the first were in verse. Kroll (RE 17.253) supposed the third to be about utensils rather than oracles, but gave no reasons.

11

There are no certain fragments, but the statement in Cael. Aurel. de morb. chron. 1.4. p. 323 (Amsterdam, 1709) that N. in his third book was among the ancients who fell into error in his treatment of epilepsy may refer to the first work. Cf. also fr. 146.

ΠΕΡΙ ΤΩΝ ΕΚ ΚΟΛΟΦΩΝΟΣ ΠΟΙΗΤΩΝ

12 (10)

Σ Th. 3 cite from this work a statement that the poet Hermesianax was older than Nicander.

13 (21)

Nicander περὶ ποιητῶν is named in the heading to Parthenius Narr. Am. 4 as an authority for the story of Oenone, and fr. 108 has therefore been referred to it on insufficient grounds.

14 (36)

[Plut.] Vit. Hom. 2 (7. p. 337 Bern.) and Cramer An. Par. 3.98 assert that N. claimed Colophon as Homer's birthplace; and Tzetzes Exeg. in Il. 131.9 Herm. says untruly that he did so at the end of the Theriaca. The statement may have been made in a work on poets, but Tzetzes seems to base his assertion on Th. 957. It is not plain that the titles in frr. 12 and 13 refer to the same work or that they belong to a poem or poems rather than to prose.

OETAICA

15 (11)

Σ Ap. Rh. 1.1300. From Bk 1. Heracles killed the Boreadae because Boreas involved him in a storm. Cf. fr. 113.

16 (12)

On the πομπίλος see Ath. l.c., D. W. Thompson Gloss. Gk Fishes s.v.

17 (14)

Ath. 9.411 A. From Bk 2. Heracles having accidentally killed Cyathus dedicated a τέμενος to him in Proschium.

18 (13)

Ath. 7.329 A. From Bk 2. See D. W. Thompson *Gloss. Gk Fishes* s.vv. ἴωψ and the rest. Ἴωψ and σκώψ have not been certainly identified; Bussemaker gives 'σκώψ, *i.q.* γλαῦκος, *Gadi quaedam species*'.

THEBAICA

19

Megareus was king of Megara. The Pambonian hills are known only from *Th.* 214 and this passage; cf. Leake *Travels in N. Greece* 2.395 n.

20 (35)

There are no other certain fragments of the *Thebaica*, but Plut. *Mor.* 867a cites N. as saying that Anaxandrus, not Leontiadas, was in command of the Thebans at Thermopylae, and is likely to be referring to this poem.

Et. M. 27.51 cites Nicander ἐν Θηριακοῖς for Αἰγοφάγος as a cult-title of Zeus. The word does not occur in the *Theriaca*, and Meineke's Θηβαϊκοῖς is a simple though quite uncertain correction. OSch. preferred ἐν Θηρευτικοῖς: see *fr.* 99.

SICELIA

21 (15)

Zancle is the older name for Messana, and was variously explained (see *RE* 15.1215, Pfeiffer on Call. *fr.* 43.70). N. connects it with ζάγκλον (or *Al.* 180 ζάγκλη), *sickle*. See p. 204 n.

22 (16)

Text quite uncertain. For the *Cimmerii* see *fr.* 95.

23 (32)

Clem. Al. *Protrept.* 2.33 P. says that N. used καλλίγλουτος of Aphrodite in place of her Syracusan cult-title καλλίπυγος (on which see Ath. 12.554 C). He is likely to have done so in this poem.

EUROPIA

The title is uncertain, being written Εὐρώπη in 24, -πία in 25, and -πεια in 26. All three forms are recognized by Steph. Byz. for the continent, and this, rather than Europa, seems likely to have been the subject.

24 (18)

Σ Ap. Rh. 4.57. From Bk 2. Endymion and Selene. Cf. *frr.* 6, 7; also *fr.* 147.

25 (19)

Ath. 7.296F. From Bk 3. Glaucus loved by Nereus.

26 (20)

According to Σ Town. *Il.* 14.229, Eust. 980.43 the giant Athos was imprisoned by Poseidon under the mountain. This obscure and corrupt fragment provides little ground for the belief (*RE* 2.2069, Roscher 1.704) that the mountain was formed by missiles thrown by the giant. The citation is probably incomplete, for it fails, as it stands, to establish that the mountain was named from the giant. Canastrum is the extremity of the peninsula of Pallene.

Headlam's οὐδήεντος would be the equivalent of γηγενοῦς.

27, 28 (40)

Zone is a town on the coast of Thrace to which according to Ap. Rh. 1.28 the oaks from Pieria followed Orpheus. His scholia also report N. as having mentioned it. These fragments were conjecturally assigned to the *Europia* by Volkmann.

29 (41)

Steph. Byz. *s.v.* 'Ορδαία cites N. for 'Ορδαῖοι as the ethnic of this Macedonian town.

OPHIACA

The title is preserved only in the first fragment, but in Suidas *s.v.* Πάμφιλος 'Αλεξανδρεύς, where works εἰς τὰ Νικάνδρου ἀνεξήγητα καὶ τὰ καλούμενα 'Οπτικά are mentioned, Kuster wrote 'Οφιακά ('Οφικά Bernhardy, 'Οψοποιικά Wellmann).[1] If 31 and 32 are correctly assigned to the Ophiaca it would seem to have been in elegiacs, to have contained mythological and other lore connected with snakes, and not to have been didactic. The assignment of *frr.* 33–7 to the same poem is very precarious, but W. Morel (*Philol.* 83.356) suggested that some passages similar in theme to *frr.* 31 and 32 might be derived from the *Ophiaca* though N. is not named by their authors—Ael. *N.A.* 9.21, on which see *Th.* 316 n., and Plin. *N.H.* 8.229, where we are told of snakes which are harmless to natives of their country only.

30 (27)

Σ *Th.* 377. Dionysus, maddened by Hera, fell asleep and an amphisbaena bound itself round his legs. On waking Dionysus killed the snake with a vine-twig, and these are still fatal to it.

31 (28: Diehl *Anth. Lyr.* 2.239)

L. Deubner (*Philol.* 95.22) argued that these lines were an epigram, not an

---

[1] It is perhaps not out of the question that N. should have written a work on the Opici, or that the work to which Pamphilus directed his attention was part of N.'s *Sicelia*. Zancle, mentioned in *fr.* 21 of that work, had been founded by the Opici, and the Sicels had been driven into Sicily by them (Thuc. 6.2.4, 4.5).

excerpt from a poem; but an elegiac quatrain is not necessarily complete because it is self-contained.

The αὐλών is presumably the cave from which the oracular responses were given (Tac. *Ann.* 2.54, Plin. *N.H.* 2.232, Iambl. *Myst.* 3.11). It has been identified (see *B.C.H.* 39.39). For the ash as inimical to snakes see Plin. *N.H.* 16.64, and for its sap as an antidote to snake-bite also Diosc. 1.80, *Geop.* 13.8.9.

32 (29: Diehl *Anth. Lyr.* 2.239)

Aelian quotes the lines as corroborating a statement in Callias's life of Agathocles, but W. Morel (*Philol.* 83.351) suggested that Callias was N.'s source also. This does not seem very likely, and, if Aelian reports correctly, Callias mentioned the curative powers of the Psylli only in connexion with the bite of the Cerastes. For other accounts of the Psylli see Lucan 9.922ff., Plut. *Cat. Min.* 56, Dio Cass. 51.14, Strab. 13.588, Paus. 9.28.1, Plin. *N.H.* 7.14, 28.30. Cf. *Philol.* 83.347.

33

Ath. 3.99 B. The asp called ἰοχέαιρα. Cf. Eust. 1479.34.

34

Ael. *N.A.* 8.8. The skin of an amphisbaena wrapped round a stick drives off snakes and other venomous creatures. Cf. *Th.* 377 ff., n. *ad loc.*

35

Plin. *N.H.* 30.85. An amphisbaena or its skin cures *perfrictiones*, and facilitates the felling of a tree if attached to it. This snake alone emerges in winter.

The first statement comes from *Th.* 377 ff. (where see n.). It is not quite clear that what follows is derived from N., and the status of this fragment is dubious.

36

Virg. *G.* 2.214 *et tofus scaber et nigris exesa chelydris* | *creta negant alios aeque serpentibus agros* | *dulcem ferre cibum et curuas praebere latebras.* Servius: NEGANT *scilicet Solinus et Nicander qui de his rebus scripserunt.* Servius apparently connected *et...* *creta* with the preceding sentence (*glarea...uix humilis apibus casias roremque ministrat*), understanding *negant* to mean *some deny.* N.'s remarks on the subject are at least as likely to have been in the *Georgica.*

37

Σ *Th.* 781. Mentions a scorpion with two stings and calls it ἐννεάκεντρος.

HETEROEUMENA

The bulk of our information concerning this poem comes from the ms Palat. Gr. 398 which alone preserves Parthenius and Antoninus Liberalis. To the chapters in these authors there is in the majority of cases attached a statement of the author or authors who have handled the story tóld (e.g. Nic. *fr.* 39 ἱστορεῖ Νίκανδρος ἐν α΄ ῾Ετεροιουμένων). The status of these headings is obscure,[1] but though it is

---

[1] The problem is well summarised by Wendel in *Gnomon* 8.148.

unlikely that they proceed from the authors, the references to the books of N.'s poem are so precise that they can hardly be fictitious. It seems safe therefore to assume that the stories to which his name is attached were in fact handled by him. In six cases however (*frr.* 38, 40, 52, 55, 57, 61) N. is not the only author mentioned and there is no means of telling to which version Antoninus most closely conformed; nor can it be assumed that even where N.'s name stands alone the story adheres exactly to his narrative. For the purpose of this book therefore it seems sufficient to record the metamorphosis with an account of which he is credited, without transcribing the narratives of Antoninus. It is possible that some of the stories to which no authority is appended also occurred in N., and OSch. included one of them as *fr.* 67. E. Martini in the preface to his text of Antoninus (p. xlvi) claimed to detect fragments of N.'s diction in Antoninus's prose, but even if he was right they amount to very little.

Suidas (see Introd. p. 3) asserts that the work was in five books, but there are no citations expressly from a fifth, and this may be a mistake.

On the indebtedness of Ovid in the *Metamorphoses* to N.'s poem see *RE* 17.264, 18.1938.

38 (22)

Ant. Lib. 4. From Bk 1. Cragaleus turned to stone.

39

Ant. Lib. 22. From Bk 1. Cerambus turned into a beetle.

40

Ant. Lib. 23. From Bk 1. Battus turned to stone.

41

Ant. Lib. 32. From Bk 1. Dryope turned into a nymph and two girls into trees.

42

Ant. Lib. 38. From Bk 1. A wolf turned to stone.

43

Conceivably relevant is *Et. M.* 156.30 ἀσπάλαθος· εἶδος ἀκάνθης. Νίκανδρος· ἐν γὰρ ὄρει ῥάμνοι τε καὶ ἀσπάλαθοι κομέονται, but the line cited is Theocr. 4.57. Either a citation from N. has dropped out or the name is a mistake for Θεόκριτος.

44

Ant. Lib. 13. From Bk 2. The corpse of Aspalis replaced by a statue.

45

Ant. Lib. 17. From Bk 2. The daughter of Galatea (daughter of Eurytius) turned into a boy.

46

Ant. Lib. 30. From Bk 2. Byblis turned into a Nymph.

47 (23)

Ant. Lib. 31. From Bk 2. Messapian boys turned into trees.

48

Ant. Lib. 26. From Bk 2.[1] Hylas turned into an echo. Further references in Σ Theocr. 13.7, 48.

49 (24)

Ant. Lib. 1. From Bk 3. The corpse of Ctesilla replaced by a dove. See on *fr.* 50.

50

Hermochares, seeing Ctesilla at a religious festival, fell in love with her, and having inscribed on a fruit a vow by Ctesilla to Artemis that she would marry Hermochares, threw it to her in the temple of the goddess. Ctesilla having read the inscription was bound by the oath. Her father promised her to Hermochares but betrothed her to another suitor; thereafter she eloped to Athens with Hermochares. Owing to her father's perjury she died in childbirth but her corpse was replaced by a dove.

Sidus is a κώμη in Corinthian territory, Pleistus a river in Phocis, whereas Ant. Lib. 1 stages the first part of the story at Carthaea in Ceos. OSch. supposed the fruit imported for the festival. It may be doubted whether N.'s place-names are more than ornamental, but if he connected Sidus with σίδη the fruit intended is perhaps a pomegranate.

Ant. Lib. remarks on the close resemblance between this story and that of Acontius and Cydippe.

51

Ant. Lib. 2. From Bk 3. Meleager's sisters turned into guinea-fowl.

52

Ant. Lib. 12. From Bk 3. Cycnus and his mother turned into swans.

53

Ant. Lib. 8. From Bk 4. A wild beast named Lamia or Sybaris on Parnassus replaced by a well.

54

Ant. Lib. 9. From Bk 4. Nine Emathides turned into different species of birds.

55

Ant. Lib. 10. From Bk 4. Three daughters of Minyas turned into a bat and two owls.

56

Ant. Lib. 24. From Bk 4. Ascalabus turned into a gecko: cf. *Th.* 483 ff. and n.

57

Ant. Lib. 25. From Bk 4. Orion's daughters turned into comets.

[1] So Σ Ap. Rh. 1.1234. The ms of Antoninus has ἑτεροιουμένων δ΄, but Martini (p. **xlv**) accepted β΄.

58

Ant. Lib. 27. From Bk 4. Iphigenia turned into an immortal.

59

OSch. not very plausibly referred this fragment to the metamorphoses of gods attacked by Typhon which are enumerated in Ant. Lib. 28 with a reference to Bk 4 of the *Heteroeumena*. Ares there becomes a fish.

A fragment of Pancrates cited in the same context by Athenaeus gives σαῦρος, αἰολίη, and ὀρφίσκος as other names for κίχλη (a wrasse). Hence N.'s πολυώνυμον.

60

Ant. Lib. 29. From Bk 4. Galinthias turned into a marten.

61 (23)

Ant. Lib. 35. Bk not named. Herdsmen turned into frogs.

62

On the dogs of Hyrcania see *RE* 8.2546.

This and the following five fragments are assigned to the *Heteroeumena* conjecturally.

63

Plin. *N.H.* 37.31. N. cited among authorities for the metamorphosis of Phaethon's sisters into poplars.

64

Probus *ad* Virg. *G.* 1.399. N. and Theodorus said to be Ovid's authorities for the story of Alcyone. In one story Alcyone and Ceyx are turned to birds together; in the other she was transformed after being thrown into the sea by her father. Ovid narrates the first at length (*Met.* 11.410), and merely touches on the second (7.401). Probus should mean that the first story comes from N., the second from Theodorus.

65

Σ Theocr. 5.92. N. cited for the statement that the anemone sprang from the blood of Adonis. Bion (1.66) insists, perhaps in contradiction of N., that roses sprang from his blood, anemones from Aphrodite's tears.

66

Σ *Th.* 585. N. mentions the plant βούπλευρος in the work entitled Ὑάκινθος. OSch. plausibly supposed this to be a section of the *Heteroeumena*; see *fr.* 96. There were works so entitled by Euphorion and Bion, but a confusion does not seem very probable.

67

Ant. Lib. 40 narrates the disappearance of Britomartis in a chapter for which no authority is named. OSch. referred the story to N. on no very conclusive grounds. For other possible fragments of the *Heteroeumena* see *frr.* 90, 112.

FRAGMENTS

GEORGICA

Cic. *de Or.* 1.69 *constat inter doctos...de rebus rusticis hominem ab agro remotissimum Nicandrum Colophonium poetica quadam facultate, non rustica, scripsisse praeclare.* Quintilian's question (*Inst. Or.* 10.1.56) *Nicandrum frustra secuti Macer atque Vergilius?* perhaps implies no more than that Virgil, like N., wrote a didactic poem on rustic subjects. Virgil borrows from the *Theriaca* (see *Th.* 51, 359 nn.) but there is no fragment of N.'s *Georgica* which he imitates,[1] and Wilamowitz (*Hell. Dicht.* 1.85) assumed from the extant fragments that the Greek poem dealt with the vegetable and flower garden rather than agriculture. Kroll (*RE* 17.255) on the other hand thought that the colour of the fragments might be due to the fact that all which are certain come from Athenaeus, whose interests they represent. *Frr.* 68, 70–72 are kitchen recipes, 73 deals with pigeon-breeding, 69, 75, 76, 80 with trees. The last is the only subject handled in the *Georgics*, and if N.'s poem resembled Virgil's in scope the absence of any fragments relating either to agriculture or to stock-raising is surprising. On the other hand Virgil may be supposed to have known the *Georgica* and to have used it if it was to his purpose. Cf. also *fr.* 115.

68

2 H. Roehl (*Jahrb. cl. Phil.* 123.240) proposed ἠὲ κλυτοῦ ὄρνιθος from Hsch. κλυτὸς ὄρνις· ὁ ἀλεκτρυών, and Kaibel accepted the emendation. That is presumably the meaning, but ὄρνις requires no addition to convey it.

4 μιγῇ: cf. *fr.* 72.8 n., *J.H.S.* 52.151.

5f. Ath. paraphrases τὸν ἐκ τῆς τοιᾶσδε σκευῆς ἀναβρομοῦντα ζωμὸν πυκνότερον τῇ ζωμηρύσει καταμίγνυε, μηδὲν ἕτερον ἐπεγχέων ἀλλ' αὐτὸν ἀπ' αὐτοῦ ἀρυόμενος πρὸς τὸ μηδὲν ὑπερζέσαι τοῦ πιμελεστέρου. The passage seems to give the sense of words missing in the lacuna—'keep on skimming the broth and stir the skimmings into it'.

8 The verb is not secure, but ἐκδαίνυσθαι means *eat* in *Al.* 183 f. Ath. paraphrases προσφέρου, presumably in this sense.

69

Quoted in a section dealing with almonds, where its relevance is not apparent.

70

1f. According to Theophr. *C.P.* 5.6.9, Colum. 11.3.62 γογγυλίδες, *rapae*, were sown in a bed of chaff laid on the threshing-floor in order that they might make broad heads but little root. Bread was (sometimes at any rate) kneaded on round pedestal tables, or round trays on stands (see Blümner *Techn.* 1².66), and the resulting plants will resemble miniature specimens of these. Cf. *C.Q.* 45.107.

3ff. Plin. *N.H.* 20.21 *naporum duas differentias et in medicina Graeci seruant. angulosis foliorum caulibus, flore aneti* (Sillig: *floreant et* codd.), *quod bunion uocant... alterum genus buniada appellant et raphano et rapo simile.* In Diosc. 2.110ff. βουνιάς

[1] See however *fr.* 36.

comes between γογγύλη and ῥαφανίς, and βούνιον (4.123) seems to be quite a different plant; and Gal. 6.622 writes γογγυλίδων ἃς καὶ βουνιάδας ὀνομάζουσιν. Ath. 9.369 B, remarking that Theophrastus does not mention βουνιάς, suggests that it may be the male γογγυλίς, which he (*H.P.* 7.4.3) distinguishes from the female.

What follows is highly obscure to us. *Prima facie* 4 f. would seem to mean that there are two forms both of γογγυλίς and of ῥάφανος, one μακρός the other στιφρός, and that these forms should be differently prepared. It appears however from 9 that τὰς μέν in 6 means τὰς ῥαφάνους, not one of the two forms. Unless therefore there is a lacuna in the text, it appears that N. is discussing not four vegetables but two—γογγυλίς and ῥάφανος—to both of which the adjectives in 5 apply; and that the latter is not, as usual, *cabbage* but some kind of turnip or radish (cf. Ath. 2.57A). And if nothing is lost between 3 and 4, γάρ seems to establish that, as OSch. supposed, βουνιάς (whatever the meaning of 3) defines or is equivalent to ῥάφανος.

16 ff. σπέρματα...σινήπυος is cited again with *fr.* 84. We cannot interpret the remainder. C. B. Gulick in his *Athenaeus* printed the text without alteration and translated *when cream of tartar forms, and the top grows more and more bitter, then 'tis time to draw off the pickle for those who seek their dinner.* Dindorf suggested a lacuna after 17. OSch. printed ὠμοτέρη ἔτι κόρσῃ...ἀνύσαι κεχαρηόσι and translated *simul autem humectantes* τρύξ ὄξεος *et* σκίλλα *muriam tempestivam perficiant;* but for κόρση = σκίλλα his only evidence was *Al.* 253 σπειρώδεϊ κόρσῃ | σκίλλης, *Th.* 881 σκίλλης κάρη, and it would plainly be insufficient even if N. had not also written (*Al.* 527) ῥαφάνοιο...σπειρώδεα κόρσην.

71

Cited for σταφυλῖνος.

5 For ὄρνιθος γάλα see Diosc. 2.144, where ὀρνιθόγαλον is a v.l.; for the latter (identified as *starflower*) see Plin. *N.H.* 21.102, Gal. 19.739.

72

Rhein. Mus. 77.163.

The storing of gourds for eating in the winter. On σικύη see *J. Phil.* 34.297.

4 ff. ἀεργέες: or perhaps *during their idle season:* cf. *fr.* 70.7.

The remainder of this fragment is highly obscure. In 5 πανοσπρία, a concoction of various sorts of pulse, is being prepared, but attempts to connect this with what precedes are quite unconvincing (εὖθ' ἅτ' ἀμετρί OSch., ἐν δ' ἄρ' ἄμετρα Kaibel, ἐφθά τε μάκτρῃ Morel). In 6 the dried gourds are being mixed with other vegetables, and though the change from ἀλετρίς to the masc. plur. is not unlike N., the aor. βάλον is unexplained. We have suggested a lacuna on the assumption that 4 ff. said that the gourds could be added to the πανοσπρία (e.g. εὖτε δὲ μάκτρῃ...⟨gourds may be added⟩), and that the last three lines are relics of a passage recording another use for them.

8 μιγῇ καὶ εὔφρονι ῥίζῃ OSch., μιγήμεναι ἔστ' ἔαρ ἵξη Morel.

FRAGMENTS

73

1 Δρακοντιάδας: otherwise unknown, though δρακοντίς, a bird-name in *fr.* 54, is presumably the same.

2 ἄρπαι a bird of prey not certainly identified. See D. W. Thompson *Gloss. Gk Birds* s.v.

3 OSch.'s ὀστρακέοις, which is quite uncertain, should mean *eggshell* rather than, as he wished, *egg*. 'Οστρακέοις (adj.) or -ίνοις might perhaps mean the chicks in the shell. Heringa proposed οὐδέ φιν ἴρηκες. The word ὀστοκόραξ is perhaps too late to be considered.

74

2ff. ἄνθε' 'Ιαονίηθε: the two kinds of ἴον (or ἴας) here mentioned are to be identified respectively, the white (ὠχρόν) as λευκόϊον, *Matthiola incana*, stock (-gilliflower), the golden as *Cheiranthus cheiri*, wall-gilliflower. For a third see 60 n., below.

4 According to Paus. 6.22.7 (cf. Strab. 8.356) the 'Ιωνίδες were deities of a curative spring 50 stades from Olympia, and were called after Ion, son of Gargettus, who settled there. N. leaves the relation between their name and those of the man and the flower undetermined, as also the identity of Ion.

9 On the cultivation of roses in antiquity see *RE* 7.774; on the varieties of rose known to the Greeks, also Bunyard *Old Garden Roses* 10, *Antiquity* 14.250.

10 We are not sure whether the measurement refers to the length of the cuttings or to the depth of the trench.

11 On the 'gardens of Midas' in eastern Macedonia and their 100-petalled roses see Hdt. 8.138, Theophr. *H.P.* 6.6.4.

The Odones appear to be the same as the Edones, but Emathia is some way west of their district.

14ff. Nisaea is the port of Megara; Phaselis, on the borders of Lycia and Pamphylia, was reported to produce the best rose-perfume (Ath. 15.688 E); Artemis λευκοφρυηνή was worshipped at Magnesia on the Maeander, into which the Lethaeus flows close to Magnesia.

17ff. Theophrastus (*H.P.* 3.18.6–10) says that all ivy is πολύρριζος καὶ πυκνόρριζος, and he distinguishes three main kinds: (i) 'white', of which one species, with compact fruit, is sometimes called κορυμβίας, (ii) 'black', (iii) ἕλιξ. Unlike the first two this bears no fruit, and one species is by some called 'Thracian'. Plin. *N.H.* 16.144–52 gives further details. If N. wrote στέφος κορυμβήλοιο Θράσκιον he may possibly have confused (i) and (iii). By κλαδέεσσι πλανήτην he perhaps means what Theophrastus calls ἐπίγειος as opposed to εἰς ὕψος αἰρόμενος. On ivy in antiquity see *RE* 5.2826.

21 Cf. *C.Q.* 45.117. The shoots are to be twisted together, started in baskets, and then planted out with the baskets, as Theophrastus recommends for cucumbers (*C.P.* 5.6.6: cf. Arist. *Prob.* 924 b 10).

24 Cf. Theocr. 7.8 αἴγειροι πτελέαι τε... | χλωροῖσιν πετάλοισι κατηρεφέες κομόωσαι.

25 ff. Lilies were not indigenous in Greece but were cultivated for their perfume or to make garlands. The only white lily known was apparently the Madonna lily, *Lilium candidum*, but this is ruled out by vv. 29 f. as it is also in *Al.* 407 ff. On lilies in antiquity see *RE* 7.792.

28 ff. Ath. 15.681 B and Eust. 1295.26 assert on the authority of N.'s Γλῶσσαι (*fr.* 126) that ἀμβροσία is the Corinthian word for *lily*: cf. Bergk *Opusc.* 2.682. For what follows see *Al.* 407 ff., n. *ad loc.* Χάρμα will mean *source of malignant*, or *triumphant, joy*.

31 ὑακίνθῳ: it is plain that ὑ. denoted at least two different plants in antiquity. Many identifications have been proposed, but the problem remains unsettled. See Gow on Theocr. 10.28.

34 If νηλείην is right, which seems very doubtful, the reference will be to the sword-shaped leaves of the iris resembling those to which ξίφιον, *gladiolus*, or, as N. calls it below (63), φάσγανον, owes its name.

40 *C.Q.* 45.117. The text suggested in the apparatus will mean 'plant either on brinks or else on hillocks'. In the first case the thyme will reach down to the water; in the second it will catch the breeze.

43 OSch. marked a lacuna after μήκωνος since no instructions are given for cultivating the poppy as they are for the other plants mentioned. Possibly however it should rather be marked between 42 and 43.

49 After this line A incorporates a gloss on 48: θρῖα δ᾽ οὐ λέγει τὰ τῆς συκῆς ἀλλὰ τὰ τῆς μήκωνος.

52 What follows is no less corrupt and much more incoherent than what precedes. 52-54 appear to relate to plants grown in pots: 55 ff. to wild flowers gathered for garlands or posies. We mark lacunae since we do not see any means of connecting 52-54 with its context, and OSch.'s device for providing the nominatives in 55 ff. with a verb (πορσαίνουσι, by writing κήποις in 53) is unconvincing. It may be noted that Athenaeus, at the end of this long quotation, adds that the passage shows χελιδόνιον to be distinct from ἀνεμώνη; but even if 32 f. be held to contain a reference to the first plant, the distinction does not appear, and it seems likely that the full Athenaeus contained more than our abbreviated text retains.

55 For παιδέρως meaning *acanthus* cf. Diosc. 3.17, Plin. *N.H.* 22.76 acanthi... duo genera sunt...alterum leue, quod aliqui paederota uocant. The resemblance to white poplar, remarked also in Paus. 2.10.6, lies in its colour. For παιδὸς ἔρωτες = παιδέρωτες see Gow on Theocr. 15.112; cf. *fr.* 87. Πτερίς = βλῆτρον, for which see *Th.* 39 n.

59 'Flower of Zeus', i.e. carnation, *Dianthus inodorus*. Theophrastus (*H.P.* 6.6.2) and Pliny (*N.H.* 21.59) expressly state that it is scentless; hence OSch.'s proposed correction. It is however possible that Διὸς ἄνθος has here some other meaning; also that N. has made a mistake.

60 ὑάκινθον: see above 31 n. Ἰωνιὰς ὀρφνοτέρα = ἴον τὸ μέλαν, *Viola odorata*, purple violet. Cf. 2 n. above.

66 ἐλένειον: cf. *Th.* 316 n. The plant is discussed in *RE* 7.2838.

70 λείρια: if N. is speaking of flowers that grow wild perhaps λ. should be taken to mean *narcissus*, for which both κρίνον and λείριον were frequent synonyms. The lily (*Lilium candidum*, Madonna lily) was a cultivated flower;

cf. 25 n. Theophrastus (*H.P.* 6. 8. 3) mentions also the plant πόθος (*Asphodelus ramosus*) ᾧ χρῶνται περὶ τοὺς τάφους.

71 We keep ἐντραπέας and suppose it to refer to the hanging heads of the cyclamen (ἐντρέπω). OSch. printed εὐτραπέας which he wished to mean εὐτερπέας.

72 Hegesilaus is Hades (Aesch. *fr.* 406, Call. *H.* 5.130, *al.*).

75

Cf. Theophr. *C.P.* 1.17.1, Plin. *N.H.* 15.97.

76

Κάρυον is the fruit of the καρύα ἡ Εὐβοϊκή, *Castanea vesca*, the 'sweet' or 'Spanish' chestnut, which according to Theophr. *H.P.* 4.5.4 is frequent in Euboea. Cf. *Al.* 271 n., and for λόπιμον *C.Q.* 45.104.

77

Ath. 2.53 B Ποντικῶν καλουμένων καρύων, ἃ λόπιμά τινες ὀνομάζουσι, μνημονεύει Νίκανδρος. Casaubon proposed unnecessarily to unite this *fr.* with 76 by writing Εὐβοϊκῶν for Ποντικῶν.

78–9

Cf. *C.Q.* 45.109.

5 ὕδ.... νοτίζοις is cited in Eust. 906.20.

9 Cited in Eust. 1017.20 (ἐφεύσαις ἢ ἀφεύσαις ἀντὶ τοῦ φώξαις, φλογίσαις, ὀπτήσαις). *Champignons* is the name applied (in England) only to the edible *Marasmius oreades*. At the present day *Amanita* is the name of a genus which includes three deadly and two poisonous species. See J. Ramsbottom *Poisonous Fungi* (Lond. 1945).

80

2 ἐγκέφαλον: *cabbage*, also known as the *head* or *heart* of the date-palm, and defined by the *O.E.D.* as 'the tender unexpanded centre or terminal bud of palm trees, which is in most species edible'. If this is plucked, the tree withers. See Theophr. *C.P.* 1.2.3; 5.16.1, Xen. *An.* 2.3.16. Παραφυάδες are the leaves that grow immediately round the 'cabbage'.

81–2

The plant is the Indian lotus, *Nelumbium speciosum*, on which see Theophr. *H.P.* 4.8.7, Diosc. 2.106, *RE* 13.1518. The 'Egyptian bean' is its seed, up to thirty of which are contained in the seed-vessel (κιβώριον). It has a large pink flower, and an edible root (κολοκάσιον). See however *J. Phil.* 34.301.

83

For the shellfish see D. W. Thompson *Gloss. Gk Fishes* s.vv. Νηρίτης is unidentified: στρόμβος a generic term for spiral-shelled molluscs. There is a somewhat similar list in *Al.* 390ff. but it is difficult to guess why there should be one in the *Georgica*.

3 ἀλοσύδνης, if right, comes from *Od.* 4.404 φῶκαι νέποδες καλῆς ἀλοσύδνης, where it was understood to be an epithet either of the sea or of Amphitrite. At *Il.* 20.207 it is an epithet of Thetis, at Ap. Rh. 4.1599 of Nereids.

84

Ath. cites also *Th.* 921 (with a remarkable variant: see Introd. p. 11).

85

Eudemus *ap.* Ath. 9.369E distinguishes three kinds of κράμβη — ἀλμυρίς, λειόφυλλος, and σελινουσία (-οῦσσα Meineke), and Theophr. *H.P.* 7.4.4 of ῥάφανος, which is the same vegetable (Apollod. *Car. fr.* 27, Arist. *H.A.* 551 a 15) — οὐλόφυλλος, λειόφυλλος and ἀγρία. Theophrastus says also that the wild kind is πολύφυλλος and that the curly is μεγαλοφυλλοτέρα, as perhaps N. also said in 3. There is no clue in Theophrastus to the meaning of 4–7, and it is not clear whether N. is describing further sorts of cabbage or, as OSch. supposed, differently coloured varieties of the curly. We do not understand the relation of v. 5 to what precedes, nor see how to punctuate or translate the passage, which is probably corrupt. The translation is merely tentative. Κύμη was explained by Casaubon to mean Κυμαίη since Cyme is mentioned by Eudemus as a habitat of the kind he calls ἀλμυρίς. *Cyma* cited by OSch. from Plin. *N.H.* 20.90 as a kind of cabbage is there an emendation.

6 παλίμβολα: *C.Q.* 45.106.

7 Presumably its growth is an indication of what may be expected of other vegetables, though Ath. connects the name with ritual use and with the oath μὰ τὴν κράμβην.

86

Frr. 86–91, of unnamed provenance, were assigned to the *Georgica* by OSch. following, in 86, Schweighäuser.

87

Ath. on Δαμασκηνά, *damsons*, says that they are a form of κοκκύμηλα and illustrates this word. The fragment is quoted also at Eust. 917.5 for the resolution of the noun; cf. *fr.* 74.55.

88

Ath. 2.64D. N. praises the βολβοί of Megara.

89

Ath. 15.701A. N. calls τὴν τῶν καλάμων δέσμην ἑλάνην. Cf. Eust. 1571.9.

90

OSch. supposed ἐν ἑτέρῳ to mean ἐν ἄλλῳ τινὶ βιβλίῳ, but Bernhardy's ἐν Ἑτεροιουμένοις seems probable.

91

For στύφειν see also *Al.* 278.

FRAGMENTS

MELISSURGICA

This work is named only in *fr.* 92 and there are no direct quotations. It was probably in verse rather than in prose and has sometimes, not very probably, been thought to be merely a section of the *Georgica*, which Athenaeus regularly cites by that name. There is nothing to show whether Virgil used it in G. 4.

92

Ath. 2.68 B. θύμος masc., *thyme*.

93

Ael. *N.A.* 5.42. N. εὐφορεῖν τοὺς κηφῆνάς φησι. The inf. has been variously emended.

94

Colum. 9.2.4. Bees first born in Crete in the time of Saturn.

CIMMERII

95 (17)

Σ *Th.* 382 μαλκᾶν used for ναρκᾶν in a work so entitled. Cf. *frr.* 22, 143, *Th.* 382, 724, *Al.* 540.

HYACINTHUS(?)

96

Σ *Th.* 585. A work so entitled cited for βούπλευρος. See *fr.* 66.

CYNEGETICA or THEREUTICA(?)

97 (37), 98 (Diehl *Anth. Lyr.* 2.239)

Poll. 5.38 f. extracts from an unnamed work by N. statements that Indian dogs descend from Actaeon's hounds, and those of Chaonia and Molossia from a bronze dog which was made by Hephaestus for Zeus, and ultimately turned to stone together with the fox of Teumesus—ὁ μὲν ἵνα μὴ λάβῃ τὴν ἄληπτον ἀλώπεκα, ἡ δ' ἵνα μὴ φύγῃ τὸν ἄφυκτον κύνα. This is followed by matter about other breeds of dog. The metamorphosis of the dog and the fox is recorded in Ant. Lib. 41, and might come from N.'s *Heteroeumena*. The other stories however do not seem appropriate to that work. It was moreover in hexameters, and the words ψυχὴν ἐνθεὶς δῶρον ἔδωκε Διί in Pollux suggest that he is citing an elegiac poem. In *fr.* 98 the restoration of a pentameter is plausible, but there is no evidence that the two fragments belong to the same poem.

99 (26)

Et. M. 27.51 Αἰγοφάγος: see *fr.* 20.

100

The words cited do not occur in *Al.* (though JGSch. wished to introduce them into the context of 244 ff.), and are no doubt corrupt as well as untrue for the sentence in *Et. M.* is unconstruable: ἐν τῷ λέγειν Porson (for ἐν τοῖς 'A.), from a ms of d'Orville. *Et. M.* is reporting Zenobius on onomatopoeia. The same matter is reported in Cramer *An. Ox.* 1.267, where the quotation is assigned, no doubt wrongly, to Menander,[1] and the participle written, perhaps rightly, -λλ-. OSch.'s assignment of the fragment to the *Thereutica* is no more than a guess.

LITHICA(?)

A title invented by OSch. as a receptacle for the following three *frr.* assigned to unnamed works of N.

101 (34)

Plin. *N.H.* 36.127. *Magnes* called after its discoverer.

102

Plin. *N.H.* 37.102. *Sandareson* or, as N. calls it, *sandaserion*. OSch., assuming his hypothetical *Lithica* to be a verse work, took this for σανδασέρειον.

103

Serv. *ad Aen.* 4.261. N. cited for a form of *iaspis* which is *fuluus*.

HYMN TO ATTALUS

See Introd. p. 6.

104

Pelops defeated Oenomaus in the chariot race for the hand of his daughter Hippodameia, and, Oenomaus having been killed in the race, married Hippodameia, became king of Pisa, and gave his name (Peloponnese) to 'the Apian land'. Their daughter Lysidice was by some accounts mother of Alcmene, and so grandmother of Heracles. Teuthras was king of Mysia, or part of it, and is connected with Auge and with her child by Heracles, Telephus, who, according to Diod. 4.33, married his daughter and succeeded to his kingdom. His successor was thus grandson both to Teuthras and to Heracles. The genealogical pretensions of the Attalids seem otherwise unrecorded.

EPIGRAMS

Frr. 105 and 107 are ascribed in the lemmata to Nicander though *Anth. Plan.* assigns 107 to Nicarchus. *Fr.* 106 is ascribed to Nicander of Colophon, and it occurs in the ms G of the *Theriaca* and *Alexipharmaca*. If 105 and 106 are really his they show him to have been on occasion capable of a dignified simplicity sadly to seek in *Th.* and *Al.* On his interest in Spartan themes see *Rev. Et. Anc.* 3.190.

105

The town of Messene on Mt Ithome was founded by Epaminondas in 369 B.C. after the battle of Leuctra, and the name is an anachronism if, as in the next

[1] For the same mistake see E. Miller *Mélanges de Lit. Gr.* 68, 203.

epigram, the episode is taken from the early history of Sparta. Ithome was besieged by Sparta in the First Messenian War and after the Helot revolt in 464 B.C.: Messene was briefly occupied by Nabis in or about 200 B.C. (Paus. 4.29.10). If N. is commemorating history or legend (rather than fancy) one of the first two seems a more likely setting than the third.

106

A dispute between Sparta and Argos ('the Inachids') over the town of Thyrea was left to be determined by a fight between 300 of either side. The two Argives who survived went off to report their success at Argos; the one Spartan, Othryadas, collected the spoils of the dead Argives, built a trophy, and killed himself rather than survive his 299 comrades (Hdt. 1.82). The battle and the death of Othryadas, details of which are elsewhere otherwise told, provided a congenial theme for epigrammatists and rhetoricians: see *Rhein. Mus.* 29.463, 31.302.

For the form of the inscription (written, we are told elsewhere, by Othryadas in his own blood on a shield) cf. the similar story of Minucius at the Caudine Forks, where the words are Ῥωμαῖοι κατὰ Σαμνιτῶν Διὶ τροπαιούχῳ (Plut. *Mor.* 306 c).

107

The ascription to Nicarchus, by whom there are many feeble epigrams in *A.P.* xi, seems much more plausible. Cf. *RE* 17.279. The last word is a facetious improvement on ξεναπάτης.

FRAGMENTS OF UNSPECIFIED POEMS

108 (33)

Cf. *fr.* 13 n.

2 Hecker (*Philol.* 5.415) proposed ὃν τέκεν, pronouncing 3 gravely corrupt; and τέκεν, if reconcilable with what follows, would be attractive.

3 For αἴρω *rear*, cf. perhaps Hdas 9.13. This, which is JGSch.'s interpretation, seems rather more probable than *bear* preferred by OSch. Of this version of the story too little is known to determine why or in what sense Corythus should be called κακός or to make alteration plausible.

109 (39)

If the *Aetolica* was a purely prose work (see p. 201 above) this fragment cannot belong to it. Meineke's correction, which seems probable, is derived from Steph. Byz. Οἰάνθη πόλις Λοκρῶν and its ethnic Οἰανθίς. For Rhype see *Th.* 214 n. Apart from Naupactus the other places are unknown.

110

See Introd. p. 5 f.

111

Cited for the fem. gender.

112 (42)

Possibly from the *Heteroeumena* since the Cercopes according to Suidas (*s.v.* Κέρκωπες) were by one account turned to monkeys, and by another to stone.

113 (38)

Σ Ap. Rh. 1.1300. Heracles and the Boreadae. A prose phrase is apparently cited (ἐπειδὴ Ἡρακλῆς ἐμνησικάκει τῷ Βορέᾳ), which, unless the scholium is defective, precludes association with *fr.* 15.

114

Σ Arat. 161. Amalthea nurse of Zeus.

115

Macrob. 5.22. Pan and the moon in Virg. G. 3.392 derived from N. Cf. Serv. *ad loc.*

116

Σ Ov. *Ib.* 473. The story of Macelo (on whom see *J. Phil.* 35.300).

117 (43)

Tertull. *de anim.* 57. Celts sleep on the graves of brave men for the sake of dreaming of them.

118

Hsch. *s.v.* κλίσις, used or explained by N. to mean πρόθυρον.

119

Hsch. *s.v.* μέσκος, used or explained by N. to mean κῷδιον, δέρμα. The last two fragments may belong to the following work.

GLOSSAE

120–45

Citations from three books of this prose work exist, and also others from unspecified books. In the fragments set out below Γλῶσσαι is not always specified as the source of the information, but the language used makes that source probable except in the case of *frr.* 127, 129, 135. The last two may well come from N.'s poems, which teem with γλῶσσαι. Confusion with a work of the same title by Nicander of Thyatira is also possible in one or two cases though the latter seems to have confined himself to ᾽Αττικὰ ὀνόματα.

It seems unnecessary to set these notes out at length, but we give the words and in a bracket the meaning attached to them by N. **120** βρένθιν (θρίδακα)

FRAGMENTS

121 βάκχυλος (ἄρτος σποδίτης) 122 γρύλους (γόγγρους) 123 δειρήτας (στρουθούς) 124 ἀθέλγηται (ἐκπιέζηται, ἐκθλίβηται) 125 αἰσυητήρ (νομεύς) 126 ἀμβροσία (κρίνον) 127 ἀμβροσία grew from the head of a statue of Alexander in Cos. 128 ἀνδράγρια (τὰ κατ᾿ ἄνδρα λάφυρα) 129 ἄροκλον (φιάλη) 130 βάκχος (στεφάνης εἶδος) 131 βουγαίους (τοὺς ἐσθίοντας τὸ γάλα μηδὲν δὲ ἰσχύοντας) 132 γάστρας (κράμβας), ϳακελτίδας (γογγυλίδας) 133 δάμνιον (for δ᾿ ἀμνίον Od. 3.444) 134 δάρατον (τὸν ἄϳυμον ἄρτον) 135 ἐκθήλυσις (ἐκμάλθαξις) 136 θιαγόνας (ἄρτους τοὺς τοῖς θεοῖς γινομένους) 137 λάμιαν καὶ σκύλλαν (καρχαρίαν) 138 κελέβην (ποιμενικὸν ἀγγεῖον μελιτηρόν) 139 κολύβδαιναν (τὸ θαλάσσιον αἰδοῖον) 140 κύπελλα (ἐκπώματα σκύφοις ὁμοῖα) 141 κώθωνα (κωβιόν) 142 λεπαστή (κύλιξ) 143 μάλκην (ῥῖγος περὶ τοὺς πόδας καὶ χεῖρας) 144 πόθος (στέφανός τις) 145 τριτώ (κεφαλήν).

DUBIOUS AND SPURIOUS FRAGMENTS

⟨146⟩

Plin. *N.H.* 22.31 asserts that N. says nettle-seed is useful as an antidote for hemlock, fungus, and mercury poisoning. No such statement occurs in *Al.* OSch. (p. 135) asserts that it is incredible that he should have made this statement elsewhere. The ᾽Ιάσεων συναγωγή seems however a possible source.

⟨147⟩

Σ Theocr. 3.52 τὰν κεφάλαν· ὡς ἡμέραν. οὕτως Νίκανδρος—apparently a note on accentuation. Buck (followed by Wendel) transferred the last two words to the note on 49 dealing with Endymion, who, it seems, slept during the daytime and went hunting on moonlight nights. Cf. *fr.* 24 above. [OSch. p. 135.]

⟨148⟩

P. Rainer 29801, published by H. Oellacher in *Mitt. P. Nat. Bibl. Wien* n.s. 1.77, is a papyrus of the 3rd cent. A.D. preserving remains of 77 hexameters. On the recto Silenus taunts Pan with loss of his pipe: on the verso Pan robs a bees' nest for wax, makes a pipe, and plays. The order of the two scenes, which are separated by 20 lines, is not certain.

When first published the verses were ascribed to the 2nd cent. A.D.; C. Gallavotti (*Riv. Fil.* n.s. 19.233) attributed them to Bion; Oellacher, republishing them (*Stud. It.* n.s. 18.113), to Nicander, and tentatively to the *Melissurgica*. They have been printed also in Page *Gk Lit. Pap.* 1.502, Gallavotti *Bucolici Graeci* 221, and Gow *Bucolici Graeci* 168. The ascription to Nicander seems to us improbable.

⟨149⟩

A poem of 23 lines on spring which appears in *A.P.* 9.363 under the lemma Μελεάγρου was ascribed by Stadtmüller to Nicander on very trifling grounds.

⟨150⟩

P. Ox. 14 of the second century B.C. consists of 18 lines of an elegiac poem very ill-preserved but possibly dealing with the Golden Age. L. 4 is]μινύην πέλεκυν π[, and *p. Ox.* 2221, in the commentary on *Th.* 386, has

δαντον σμινύην πέλεκυν με[
..]λ' ἄρ' ἀπὸ σμινύης εκτη[
φ]ωνεῖ δὲ ἑαυτῷ ἐν τούτ[

embodying apparently a citation or citations from N. There is no trace of the second phrase in *p. Ox.* 14, but if it is from a different passage, the first phrase might, as Lobel suggested, indicate N. as the author of *p. Ox.* 14. It may be observed that the form ὁροιτύπος (6) occurs in *Th.* 5, 377 (in the second place close to the lines on which the scholiast is commenting) and that the neut. termination -ειν (7 ὀκρυόειν) is also Nicandrean (*Al.* 42 and perhaps *Th.* 748). The evidence is not strong, but since the ascription to N. has here some slight external support we append the text.

]ης ἀντὶ γεωτομίης·
Γλαύ]κῳ Λυκίῳ, ὅτε σιφλὸς ἔπειγε
ἀνθ' ἑκατομβοί]ων ἐννεάβοια λαβεῖν.
σ]μινύην πέλεκυν π[
θη]κτὴν ἀμφοτέρῳ στόμα[τι   5
]ηνος ὁροιτύπος ἐργάζη[ται
]ίης ὀκρυόειν ἔδαφος.
]ισκεν ἐνὶ σπόρον οὔτε ν[
[υἱ]ου δῶρα κυθηγενέος·
]ο σαρωνίδας οὔδας ενε[10
]ν δαῖτα παλαιοτάτην
]ν ἐς αὔλιδα[
]δ' εἰς ἔριν ἀντὶ ρ[
]..κος η καὶ π[
.   15
]δεν[
]νι[
]εεις[
].ου[20
.   .   .   .

Some notes, and references to further literature, will be found in J. U. Powell *Collectanea Alexandrina* 130.

It is quite possible that in addition to *frr.* 148–50 there may be other modern attributions to Nicander which we have overlooked.

APPENDIXES

APPENDIX I

THE BOTANICAL DRAWINGS IN Π

The drawings of plants in Π are sometimes sufficiently individualised to suggest that they might be recognisable or derive from originals which might have been so, but the artist commands also, and frequently uses, a number of facile and formalised representations of vegetables quite useless for purposes of identification. Sometimes he omits to label his plants, and even when he does so it is often hard to believe that the name and the picture have any firm connexion. On fol. 16, for instance, two plants of quite different appearance are labelled respectively ἀσφοδελός and ἀσφοδαλός: his πευκέδανον on fol. 4ʳᵒ is quite unlike the plant so named on the verso of the same leaf: his καυκαλίς on fol. 18 equally unlike that on fol. 28. The latter resembles his ὀρόβακχος on fol. 27ᵛᵒ, but ὀρόβακχος is not a plant but a fruit, and for the words πευκεδάνοιο βαρυπνόου in Th. 76, 82, οἰνηρὴν τρύγα in Al. 534, he provides pictures of plants labelled βαρύπνοον and οἰνηρή. Normally the pictures occur on the page containing the verse in which the plant depicted is named, or on one closely following it, but the leaves containing Th. 625–60 depict some plants not mentioned until 834 ff. When therefore on the leaf containing Th. 634 Παρθένιον λέπας the plant παρθένιον is represented, one may wonder whether it is borrowed from 863 or is a mistake similar to those mentioned above, and whether the plant χαμηλή on the page containing Th. 661–5 is not really an adjective derived from 841.[1]

Exclusive of the drawings mentioned above to which absurd names are attached, and of those which are without names, the ms contains 41 drawings with the following labels: ἄγχουσα*, ἄκανθος*, ἀλκίβιον, ἄννη[σον]*, ἀσφόδελος*, βλῆτρον, ἐλξίνη*, ἕρπυλλος*, εὐκνήμων, ἔχιον*, ἡλιοτρόπιον*, ἠρύγγη*, θύμβρα*, κάρδαμον*, καυκαλίς*, κόνυζα*, κόριον*, κουλυβάτιον, λύγος, μελισσόφυλλον, μελίφυλλον, μολόχη*, ὀνόγυρον*, ὀρίγανον*, παλίουρος, παρθέ-

---

[1] We cannot explain the names σεμνόν and κρίτων attached to plants on foll. 19 and 21. That labelled μόσχου on fol. 17ᵛᵒ is, we fear, a calf straying from Th. 552 two pages earlier.

νιον*, περιστερεών*, πευκέδανον*, πηγάνιον*, πολύκνημον*, ῥόδον*, σάμ[ψυχον]*, σίλφιον, σίνηπυς*, σκολοπένδριον, σκορπίου-ρος*, τριπέτηλον, τρύχνον*, φλόμος*, χαλβ[άνη], χαμαίπιτυς.[1] The great Vienna codex of Dioscorides (Vindob. Med. Gr. 1) of the sixth century[2] contains large and careful drawings of those plants to whose names we have attached an asterisk. In the case of ἄκανθος, ἔχιον, and πολύκνημον the eye of faith might discern in the drawings in Π a distant likeness to those in the Dioscorides; in the rest we can find no resemblance whatever. For this reason, and for those previously mentioned, it seems plain to us that, however interesting the drawings in Π may be to students of illuminated manuscripts, they are entirely useless to students of Nicander's botany. The drawings of snakes in the ms are plainly fanciful, and we should suppose that at least in the majority of cases those of plants are no more trustworthy.

A ms of Eutecnius's paraphrases attached to the Vienna Dioscorides (ff. 393 ff.) contains pictures of creatures, and of ten plants, seven of which are depicted also in Π. The drawings are of much finer quality than Π's and, though smaller in scale, re-semble those in the Dioscorides. Π's representations of πευκέδανον and σίλφιον might derive from the same archetype, but if the remaining five (ἀσφόδελος, μαλάχη, ὀνόγυρος, ὀρίγανον, στρύχνον) do so they have lost all resemblance to their originals. We know nothing of an illustrated Eutecnius in the Morgan library, but K. Weitzmann who mentions it (*Illustr. in Roll and Codex* 145) argues from the absence of figure-scenes in the two books that those in Π do not derive from the illustrated archetype.

[1] We retain the miniaturist's aberrant genders but disregard his careless accents and aspiration. The pictures of μολόχη, ῥόδον, and σίλφιον may be studied in the frontispiece to this book.

[2] We have used the facsimile edited by J. von Karabacek and others (Leiden, 1906). The miniatures are no doubt derived not directly from plants but from earlier miniatures. Their careful character is however some guarantee that they reproduce their exemplars faithfully.

APPENDIX II

WEIGHTS AND MEASURES

Authorities are not always in complete agreement as to the precise modern equivalents of ancient Greek measures. In the subjoined tables we have followed H. Nissen *Griechische und Römische Metrologie* (in I. von Müller's *Handbuch* 1³ 835) and Sir W. Smith *Dictionary of Greek and Roman Antiquities* 2³ 993, with which Liddell and Scott's *Greek Lexicon* (ed. 9) for the most part concurs, and we have assumed—there can be no certainty—that Nicander or his sources adopted the later Athenian standards. In stating the equivalents we have not thought it necessary to go beyond two places of decimals.

I. ATTIC LIQUID AND DRY MEASURES

	Pints (approximate)	Litres
κύαθος	$\frac{1}{12}$	0·04
ὀξύβαφον	$\frac{1}{8}$	0·06
κοτύλη	$\frac{1}{2}$	0·27

II. LIQUID MEASURE

χοῦς	6	3·2

III. DRY MEASURE

χοῖνιξ	2	1·22

IV. ATTIC MEASURES OF LENGTH

	Feet and inches		Metres
δάκτυλος	−	$\frac{3}{4}$	18 mm.
σπιθαμή	−	$8\frac{3}{4}$	22 cm.
πούς	−	$11\frac{1}{2}$	29 ,,
πυγών	1	$2\frac{1}{2}$	37 ,,
πῆχυς	1	$5\frac{1}{4}$	44 ,,
ὀργυιά	5	$9\frac{1}{2}$	1·77 m.

V. ATTIC WEIGHTS

	Grains	Grammes
ὀβολός	8·8	0·57
δραχμή	52·8	3·41

APPENDIX III

BOOKS AND PAPERS RELATING
TO NICANDER

The following list is largely indebted to Engelmann-Preuss-Kluss-mann *Bibliotheca scriptorum classicorum* (*Scriptores Graeci*), 1880, 1911, and to Bursian's *Jahresbericht ü. d. Fortschritte d. klassischen Altertums-wissenschaft.* We have attached an asterisk to papers known to us only by title.

BARWICK, K. Ovids Erzählung vom Raub der Proserpina und N.'s ΕΤΕΡΟΙΟΥΜΕΝΑ. *Philol.* 80 (1925) 454.

BENTLEY, R. N. Theriaca cum emendationibus R. Bentleii. *Museum Criticum* 1 (1814) 370, 445.

BETHE, E. Die Zeit N.'s. *Herm.* 53 (1918) 110.

—— Theon in N. Al. 11, Th. 958. *Genethliacon Gottingense* (1881) 171.

BIANCHI, H. Scholia in N. Alexipharmaca. *Stud. Ital.* 12 (1904) 321.

CESSI, C. *Spigolature alessandrine: 1. Antonino Liberale e N. *Memoria di Oddone Ravenna* (Padua, 1904).

CHANOT, E. DE Miniatures d'un MS de N. *Gaz. Arch.* 2 (1876) 87, Pll. 11, 24.

DEUBNER, L. Nic. fr. 31 Schn. *Philol.* 95 (1942) 22.

EITREM, S. De Ovidio Nicandri imitatore. *Philol.* 59 (1900) 54.

FLACELIÈRE, R. Date de la proxénie delphique conférée au poète N. de Kolophon. *Rev. Et. Gr.* 41 (1928) 83.

FOSTER, B. O. N. and Vergil. *Proc. Am. Phil. Ass.* 33 (1902) xcvi.

GOEBEL, E. Zu N. (*Al.* 214ff.). *Jb. f. class. Phil.* 141 (1890) 826.

GOW, A. S. F. Nicandrea. *C.Q.* 45[1] (1951) 95.

HERMANN, G. Nicandri versus in Schol. Eur. ad Hecubae init. *Philol.* 2 (1847) 134 (=*Opuscula* 8.313).

HERTER, H. Ovids Persephone-Erzählungen u. ihre hellenistischen Quellen. *Rhein.Mus.* 90 (1941) 236.

IMMISCH, O. Th. 76. *Glotta* 6 (1915) 193.

KELLER, O. Zu Schol. Nic. Th. 490. *Wiener Stud.* 1 (1879) 159.

KIND, F. E. Zu den Nikanderscholien. *Herm.* 44 (1909) 624.

[1] This volume, which is the first of a new series, was erroneously published as vol. 44 of the continuous series.

225

KLAUSER, H. De dicendi genere in N. …quaestiones selectae. *Diss. phil. Vindob.* 6 (1898) 1.

KNAACK, G. Arat und N. *Herm.* 23 (1888) 313.

—— *De ratione quae intercedat inter Ovidium et N. Diss. Gryphisw. 1880.

—— *Nicander (in *Conjectanea*). *Progr. d. Marienstifts-Gymn.*, Stettin, 1883.

KNOX, A. D. Atacta Alexandrina. *Proc. Camb. Phil. Soc.* 1915, 6.

KROLL, W. art. 'Nikandros' (10 and 11). Pauly-Wissowa *Real-Enc.* 17.250.

LENORMANT, F. Peintures d'un MS de N. *Gaz. Arch.* 1 (1875) 125, Pll. 18, 32.

LINGENBERG, W. Quaestiones Nicandreae. Diss. Halle, 1866.

LOBEL, E. N.'s signature. *C.Q.* 22 (1928) 114.

MOREL, W. Iologica. *Philol.* 83 (1928) 345.

OELLACHER, H. ΠΑΝ ΣΥΡΙΖωΝ (Pap. gr. Vind. 29801). *Studi Ital.* n.s. 18 (1942) 113.

PLAEHN, G. *De N. aliisque poetis graecis ab Ovidio in Metam. conscribendis adhibitis. Diss. Halle, 1882.

RITTER, F. De adjectivis et substantivis apud N. Homericis. Diss. Göttingen, 1880.

SCHMIDT, F. W. *N. Colophonius apud Ael. de N.A. xvi. 28 (in *Verisimilia*). *Progr. Gymn. Neu-Strelitz* 1886.

SCHULTZE, G. N. quid Euphorioni debeat (in *Euphorionea*). Diss. Strassburg, 1888.

SERVADIO, G. *Estratto di una 'ricostruzione della Metamorphosi' di N. Ancona, 1903.

VOLKMANN, R. De delectu vocabulorum a N. exhibito (in *Quaestiones epicae*). Leipzig, 1854.

—— *De N. vita et scriptis. Halle, 1852.

VOLLGRAFF, W. N. und Ovid. Groningen, 1909.

WENTZEL, G. Die Göttinger Scholien zu N.'s Alexipharmaca. *Abhand. d. kgl. Ges. d. Wiss. zu Gött.* 1892.

WOLFF, G. Zu griechischen Dichtern. *Rhein. Mus.* 19 (1864) 464.

ZEUNE, J. C. Animadversiones ad N. carmen utrumque. Wittenberg, 1776.

INDEXES

I. FAUNA, FLORA, ETC.

Words are entered in the form used by Nicander; where this differs from the common form given in Liddell and Scott's *Greek Lexicon*, 9th ed., the latter is added between round brackets.

Square brackets indicate that the word does not occur in the text, but is described by a periphrasis (see, e.g., βασιλίσκος) or is represented by an adjective derived therefrom (see, e.g., θρίδαξ).

The Latin equivalents of plant-names given in the notes to M. Brenning's translation and in the two articles by E. Emmanuel (see p. 25) have been added when they differ from Liddell and Scott.

An asterisk following a line-reference directs the reader to a note in the commentary.

ἁβρότονον T 66, 92, 574; A 46 wormwood, *Artemisia arborescens* [*A. maritima?* Em.]; *see also* ἀψίνθιον

ἀγαλλιάς (= ἀγαλλίς) *fr.* 74.31 dwarf iris, *Iris attica*

ἄγλις T 874 clove of garlic, *Allium sativum*

ἄγνος T 71, 530*, 946 Agnus castus, chaste-tree, *Vitex agnus-castus*

ἀγρώστης T 734* a spider

ἄγχουσα T 638, 838 alkanet, *Anchusa tinctoria* [*Alkanna tinctoria* Br.; *Echium creticum* Em.]

ἀδίαντον T 846 maiden-hair, *Adiantum capillus-Veneris* [*Asplenium trichomanes* Em.]

αἰγίλωψ T 857 haver-grass, *Aegilops ovata* [*Triticum ovatum* Br.; *Bromus rubens* Em.]

αἰγυπιός T 406 vulture or eagle

αἰετός (= ἀετός) T 449 eagle

αἱμορροΐς T [282]*, 305, 315, 318, 321 a snake

αἴξ T 672, 925 goat

ἄκανθα (i) T 329 thistle [*Cnicus syriacus* Em.]; (ii) T 107, 110, 316, 480 spine, vertebrae

ἄκανθος T 645 bearsfoot, *Acanthus mollis* or *A. spinosus*; *see also* παιδὸς ἔρως

ἀκνηστις T 52* stinging nettle [prob. *Urtica pilulifera* Br.]

ἀκόνιτον A 13, 42 aconite, leopard's bane, *Aconitum anthora* [sp. *Alliaria officin.?* Em.]; *see also* θηλυφόνον, κάμμαρος, μυοκτόνος, παρδαλιαγχές

ἀκοντίας T 491* a snake

ἀκτῆ (= ἀκτέα) T 615 elder, *Sambucus nigra*

'Αλκιβίου ἔχις T 541 Cretan bugloss, *Echium parviflorum*; 'Α. ποίη T 666* [perh. *Echium sericeum* Br.]

ἅλς T 693, 948; A 164, 518; *fr.* 70.14 salt; A 516 sea-water

ἀλώπηξ A 185 fox

ἀμανῖται *fr.* 79* 'champignons' [*Marasmius oreades*]

ἀμάρακος T [503], 575 sweet marjoram, *Origanum majorana* [*Anthemis altissima* Em.]; *see also* σάμψυχον

ἀμβροσίη *fr.* 74.28* = κρίνον, q.v.

ἀμνός A 133, 151 lamb; *see also* ἀρήν, ῥήν

[ἄμπελος] A 142, 266 vine, *Vitis vinifera*

ἀμφίσβαινα T 372*, 384 a snake

ἀνάγυρις, *see* ὀνόγυρος

ἀνάρρινον *fr.* 84 pepper-grass, *Lepidium sativum* [nose-smart L-S]

ἀνεμωνίς *fr.* 74.64 poppy anemone, *A. coronaria* [*Papaver hybridum* Em.]

ἀνθεμίς *fr.* 74.37 camomile, *Anthemis tinctoria*

ἄννησον T 650, 911 anise, *Pimpinella anisum*

ἀπαρίνη T 850, 953 cleavers, *Galium aparine*

[ἄργυρος] A 54 silver

ἀρήν *fr.* 68.1 lamb; *see also* ἀμνός

ἀριστολόχεια T 509, 937 birthwort, *Aristolochia* sp. [*A. parvifolia* or *pallida* Br.]

ἀρκευθίς T 584 berry of juniper, *Juniperus macrocarpa* [*J. phoenicea* Em.]

ἄρκτιον T 840 bearwort, *Inula candida* [*Arctium lappa?* Br.]

ἄρον *fr.* 71.4 cuckoo-pint, *Arum italicum*

ἄρπη *fr.* 73.2* a bird of prey

ἀσκάλαβος T 484* gecko

ἀσπίς T 158*, 190, 201, 359 asp, Egyptian cobra, *Naia haie*

ἀσταφίς *fr.* 70.15 raisin

ἀστέριον T 725* a spider

ἀστήρ *fr.* 74.66 blue-daisy, *Aster amellus* [*Silene* or *Lychnis* Em.]

ἄσφαλτος T 44, 525 bitumen

ἀσφόδελος T 73,534 asphodel, *Asphodelus ramosus*; see also μολόθουρος

ἀτάλυμνος A 108 plum-tree, *Prunus domestica*

ἀχράς T 512; A 354 wild pear, *Pirus amygdaliformis*

ἀψίνθιον A 298 wormwood, *Artemisia absinthium* [*A. arborescens* Br.]; see also ἀβρότονον

βάκχη T 513; A 354 common pear-tree, *Pirus communis*

βάλανος *fr.* 76.2 sweet chestnut, fruit of καρύα ἡ Εὐβοϊκή, *Castanea vesca*

βάλσαμον T 947; A 64 balsam, oil of the *Balsamodendron opobalsamum* [resin from *Commiphora opobalsamum* Br.]

βάμμα T 87*, 622; A 49, 369, 414, 531 vinegar; see also ὄξος

[βασιλίσκος] ἑρπηστῶν βασιλεύς T 397* basilisk, a snake

βάτος T 839; A 267, 332 bramble, *Rubus ulmifolius* [In *Al. Rubus fruticosus* Br.; *R. tomentosus* Em.]

βατραχίς T 416, see βάτραχος

βάτραχος T 367, 621; A 573 frog; see also βατραχίς, γέρυνος

βδέλλα T 930; A 500 leech

βέμβιξ T 806; A 183* an insect

βλήτρον (= βλήχνον) T 39* male fern, *Aspidium filix-mas* [perh. *A. aculeatum* Br.]; see also πτερίς

βοάνθεμον *fr.* 74.38 = βούφθαλμον q.v.

βολβός T 881 purse-tassels, *Muscari comosum*

βούκερας A 424* fenugreek, *Trigonella foenum-graecum*

βουνιάς *fr.* 70.3* French turnip, *Brassica napus*

βούπλευρος T 585 bishop's weed, *Ammi majus*

βούπρηστις A 335*, 346 a poisonous beetle

βούφθαλμον *fr.* 74.59 ox-eye, *Anacyclus radiatus* [*Chrysanthemum segetum* Em.]; see also βοάνθεμον

βρυώνη T 939 (= ἄμπελος μέλαινα) black bryony, *Tamus communis* [perh. *Bryonia cretica* Br.; *B. nigra* Em.]

βρυωνίς T 858 = βρυώνη q.v.

βρωμήεις A 409, 486; -ητής *fr.* 74.30; -ήτωρ T 357 ass

βύβλος A 362 paper, Egyptian papyrus, *Cyperus papyrus*

γαλέη T 689 marten

γεραὸς πώγων *fr.* 74.71 (= τραγοπώγων) salsify, goat's beard, *Tragopogon porrifolius*

γέρυνος (= γυρῖνος) T 620; A 563 tadpole

γηθυλλίς A 431 spring onion

γλεῦκος A 179, 299; *fr.* 70.13 grape-syrup, must; see also γλυκύ

γλήχων (= βλήχων) T 877; A 128, 237 pennyroyal, *Mentha pulegium*

γλυκύ A 142, 179, 205, 367, 386, (444) grape-syrup, must; see also γλεῦκος

γλυκυσίδη T 940 peony, *Paeonia officinalis* [*P. corallina* Br.]

γογγυλίς *fr.* 70.1*, 4, 9 turnip, *Brassica rapa* [*Rapa* sp. Em.]

γύψ T 406 vulture

δάκρυον T 907; A 108*, 301, 433, 484, 546 gum, resin

δάμαλις A 344 heifer

δαύκειον (= δαῦκος) T 858, 939 wild carrot, *Daucus carota* [*Rapa* sp. Em.]

δαυχμός T 94*; A 199 = δάφνη q.v.

δάφνη T 574, 943; A 198 sweet bay, *Laurus nobilis*

Διὸς ἄνθος (= διόσανθος) *fr.* 74.59* carnation, *Dianthus inodorus*

διψάς T 125, 334* a snake

δόναξ A 578, 588 reed, *Arundo donax*

δορύκνιον A 376* thorn-apple, *Datura stramonium* [*Calendula* sp. Em.]

[ἰξία] A279 pine-thistle, *Atractylis gummifera*

ἴον (i) T543 violet, *Viola odorata*; (ii) T900; *fr.* 74.2* gilliflower, *Matthiola incana*

ἴουλος T811* woodlouse

ἵππειον μάραθον (= ἱππομάραθον) T596 horse-fennel, *Prangos ferulacea* [perh. *Seseli hippomarathrum* Br.; *Oenanthe* sp. Em.]

ἵππειον σέλινον (=ἱπποσέλινον) T599 alexanders, *Smyrnium olusatrum*

ἵππειος λειχήν (=ἱππολειχήν) T945 a kind of moss

ἵππος (i) T422, 635, 669, 740, 741 horse; (ii) T566 hippopotamus

Ἶρις (i) T607, 937; A406 white iris, *I. florentina*; (ii) *fr.* 74.31 dark blue or purple iris, *I. germanica*; A203, 455 Ἰρίνεον θύος; A156, 241, Ἰρινόεν (-εον) λίπος

ἰχνεύμων T190 ichneumon, *Herpestes ichneumon*

ἰωνιάς *fr.* 74.60=ἴον (i) q.v.

ἴωψ *fr.* 18.1* a fish

καλάμινθος T60 mint, *Mentha viridis* [*Calamintha offic.* Br.; *M. gentilis?* Em.]

κάλυξ *fr.* 74.25 cupped flower (lily)

κάλχη A393 purple limpet, *Murex trunculus; see also* χάλκη

κάμμαρος A41=ἀκόνιτον q.v.

κάμπη T87; A413 caterpillar

κάμων A484*=σκαμμωνία q.v.

κανθαρίς T755*; A115 blister-beetle

κάπρος T559 boar

καρδαμίς A429, 533=κάρδαμον q.v.

κάρδαμον T41, 93; *fr.* 84 garden-cress, *Lepidium sativum*; ἀπὸ Μήδων κ. T877 Persian garden-cress [*Erucaria aleppica* Br.]; *see also* σαύρα

καρκίνος (i) T787* crab, generic term; (ii) T606*, 949 river crab [*Thelphusa fluviatilis*]

καρύη (Περσική) A108 walnut, *Juglans regia*

κάρυον (i) A99 stone, of the persea; (ii) A269, 271; *fr.* 76.1* chestnut

καστηνός A269 chestnut, *Castanea sativa*

κάστωρ T565*; A307 beaver, *Castor fiber*

καυκαλίς T843*, 892 hedge-parsley, *Torilis anthriscus* [*Pimpinella saxifraga* Em.]

[κάχρυς] T40, 850 fruit of the λιβανωτίς q.v.

κεγχρίνης (=κεγχρίας) T463* a snake

κεδρίδες T81, 597 juniper berries; *see* κέδρος (ii)

κέδρος (i) T53, 583; A488 cedar, *Juniperus excelsa*; (ii) A118 juniper, *J. communis* [*J. phoenicea* and *J. oxycedrus* Br.]

[κενταύρειον (sc. τὸ μέγα)] Χείρωνος ῥίζα T500 centaury, *Centaurea salonitana* [perh. *Chlora perfoliata*, yellow-wort Br.]; *see also* πανάκειον

κέπφος A166* perh. petrel, *Thalassidroma pelagica*

κεράστης T258*, 261, 276, 294, 318 horned viper, *Cerastes cornutus*

κηραφίς A394* a crustacean

κῆρυξ A395* a shellfish

κιβώριον *fr.* 81.3 seed-vessel of the κολοκάσιον q.v.

κίκαμα T841 unknown vegetable

κίναμον (=κιννάμωμον) T947 cassia, *Cinnamomum cassia*

κισσός *fr.*74.17* ivy; *see also* κορύμβηλος

κίχλη *fr.*59* one of the wrasses, *Labridae*

κίχορα A429 chicory, *Cichorium intybus*

κλύβατις T537=ἐλξίνη q.v.

κνίδη T880; A201, 252, 427, 550, 551 nettle, *Urtica* [*U. pilulifera* Br. Em.]

[κοκκύμηλον] μῆλον κόκκυγος *fr.* 87* plum, fruit of *Prunus domestica*

κόκκυξ T380 cuckoo

κολοκάσιον *fr.* 82* root of the κύαμος Αἰγύπτιος, *Nelumbium speciosum*

[κολοκύντη] called σικύη *fr.* 72 gourd, *Cucurbita maxima* [*Citrullus colocynthus* Em.]

[κόμμι] A110 gum, from the *Acacia arabica*

κονίλη T626 marjoram, also called Ἡράκλειον ὀρίγανον q.v.

κόνυζα T70, 83, 615, 875, 942; A331 fleabane, *Inula* sp. [perh. *I. viscosa* at T70, 615, 942; *I. graveolens* at T83, 875; A331 Br.] [*I. britannica* Em.]

I FAUNA, FLORA, ETC.

μάραθον T33, 391, 893; fr. 71.1 fennel, Foeniculum vulgare; see also ἵππειον μ.

μάσταξ T802 locust

μελάνθειον (=μελάνθιον) T43 black cummin, Nigella sativa

μελίη fr. 31.3 ash-tree, Fraxinus ornus

μελίκταινα (=μελίτταινα) T555 = πράσιον q.v.

μελίλλωτος T897 melilot, Trigonella graeca; see also λωτός

μέλισσα T555, 735, 741, 806, 810; A71, 144, 182, 374, 445, 554 bee

μελισσόφυτον (= μελισσοβότανον) T677 balm, Melissa officinalis

μελίφυλλον T554; A47 = πράσιον, q.v.

Μῆδον (=μῆλον Μηδικόν) A533 citron, Citrus medica

μήκων T946; A433; fr. 74.43 poppy, Papaver somniferum; μ. θυλακίς T851* capsuled p., Papaver rhoeas [P. hybridum Em.]; μ. ἐπιτηλίς T852 horned poppy, Glaucium flavum [G. luteum Em.]

μηκωνίς T630 wild lettuce, Lactuca scariola

μηλείη (=μηλέα) A230 wild apple, Pirus malus, var. Silvestris

μῆλον A238, 277; fr. 50.2 apple; fr. 87 μ. κόκκυγος = κοκκύμηλον plum; μ. Μηδικόν see Μῆδον

μίλος, see σμίλος

μίλτος Λημνίς T864* ruddle

μίνθα A374 mint, Mentha viridis [perh. Mentha peperita Br.]

μιννανθές T522 'brief-flower', a name of treacle-clover, Psoralea bituminosa; see also τρίφυλλον

μόλιβος (= μόλυβδος) T256; A600 lead

μολόθουρος [Qu:=ἀσφόδελος?] A147 asphodel, Asphodelus ramosus (or = ὁλόσχοινος club-rush, Scirpus holoschoenus)

μολουρίς T416 perh. = μόλουρος q.v.

μόλουρος T491* a snake

μολόχη T89=μαλάχη ἀγρία q.v.

μορέη A69; fr. 75.1 mulberry, Morus nigra

μόσχος T552; A344, 358, 446 calf

μύαγρος T490* a snake

μυγαλέη T816* shrew-mouse

μυῖα T735 fly

μύκης A525, 617; frr. 72.7, 78.5, 79 mushroom, fungus

μυοκτόνος A36 mouse-bane = ἀκόνιτον q.v.

μυρίκη T612 tamarisk, Tamarix tetrandra [T. gallica Em.]

μυρμήκειον T747* a spider

μυρτὰς ὄχνη T513 wild pear, Pirus cordata

μυρτίνη (i) A88 myrtle-olive [var. of Olea europea Br.]; (ii) A355 cordate pear, Pirus cordata

μυρτίς A355 myrtle-berry

μύρτον T892 myrtle-berry

μύρτος A275, [618] myrtle, Myrtus communis

μῦς fr. 83.2 mussel

μύωψ T417, 736* gadfly, Tabanus

νάπειον (=νᾶπυ) A430 mustard, Sinapis alba; see also σίνηπι

νάρδος (i) T604, 937; A307, 399, spikenard, Nardostachys jatamansi; (ii) A402* mountain nard, Valeriana dioscoridis

νάρθηξ T595; A272 giant fennel, Ferula communis

νεβρός T578; A67, 324 fawn

νεβροτόκος T142*=ἔλαφος q.v.

νῆρις T531* savin, Juniperus sabina

νηρίτης (=νηρείτης) fr. 83.2* a shellfish

οἰνάνθη T898 dropwort, Spiraea filipendula [Oenanthe prolifera Em.]

ὄις A139 sheep

[ὀμφάλειος] A348 navel-fig

ὀνῖτις A56 pot marjoram, Origanum onites [perh. O. vulgare Br.]

ὀνόγυρος (=ἀνάγυρος) T71 stinking bean-trefoil, Anagyris foetida [Cytisus hirsutus? Em.]

ὄνος T628=ὀνῖτις q.v.

ὄνωνις T872 rest-harrow, Ononis antiquorum

ὀξαλίς T840 sorrel, Rumex acetosa

ὄξος T539, 563, 913, 933; A320, 321, 330, 366, 375, 511, 530; fr. 70.13, 17 vinegar; see also βάμμα

233

πρόξ T578*; A324 fawn of roe (ζόρξ), Cervus capreolus

πτελέη A109 elm, Ulmus glabra [U. campestris Br.]

πτερίς fr. 74.55* male fern, Aspidium filix-mas; see also βλῆτρον

πτώξ T950 hare

πυετίη A68*, 323 curdled milk from the stomach of an animal; see also τάμισος

πύξος T516*; A579 boxwood, Buxus sempervirens

πυράκανθα (=ὀξυάκανθα) T856 fiery thorn, Cotoneaster pyracantha [Crataegus pyr. Br.]

πύρεθρον T938 pellitory, Anacyclus pyrethrum [Anthemis pyrethra Em.]

πυρῖτις T683; A531 convolvulus, bindweed, Convolvulus arvensis [=πύρεθρον L-S; perh. Anacyclus pyrethrum Br.]

ῥάμνος (i) T630* unknown shrub; (ii) T861, 883 perh. buckthorn, Rhamnus graeca (or R. cathartica?)

ῥάφανος (i) A527, fr. 70.3, 4 cabbage, Brassica cretica; (ii) A430 radish, Raphanus sativus [R. raphanistrum Em.]

ῥήν T453 lamb; see also ἀμνός

ῥητίνη A300, 554 resin

ῥοδέη A239 rose-bush

ῥόδον T900; fr. 74.9* rose, Rosa gallica; ῥόδεον T103; ῥ. λίπος A155; ῥ. θύος 452 rose-oil

ῥοιή (=ῥόα) fr. 78.2 pomegranate-tree, Punica granatum

ῥυτή T523; A306, 528, 607 rue, Ruta graveolens; see also πήγανον

ῥώξ (=ῥάξ) T716* a spider

σαλαμάνδρη [T818*]; A538 salamander, S. vulgaris

[Σαμία γῆ] A148* a kind of clay

σάμψυχον T617; fr. 74.53 = ἀμάρακος q.v.

σαύρη (i) A538; -ος T817 lizard; (ii) fr. 74.72 = κάρδαμον q.v.

σέλινον T597, 649; A604 celery, Apium graveolens; see also ἵππειον σέλινον

σέρις (κηπευτή) fr. 71.3 endive, Cichorium endivia

σηπεδών T320*, 327 a snake

σηπιάς (=σηπία) A472* cuttlefish, Sepia

σήσαμον A94 sesame, Sesamum indicum

σήψ (i) T147* a snake; (ii) T817* a lizard

σίαλος A133 fat hog

σίδη [ῑ] T72, 870; A276, 489*, 609 pomegranate, Punica granatum; see also Κυδώνια μῆλα, Προμένειος σίδη, ῥοίη, στρούθεια μῆλα

σίδη [ῑ] T887 water-lily, Nymphaea alba

σίδηρος T923; [A51] iron

σικύη fr. 72.1*, 6 gourd Cucurbita maxima

σίκυος ἀγρότερος T866 squirting cucumber, Ecballium elaterium [Momordica elaterium Em.]

σίλφιον T85*, 697, [911]; A204, 309, 329, 369 silphium; see also Λιβυκή ῥίζα, ὀπός

σίνηπι (=σίναπι) T878; σίνηπυ frr. 70.16; 84; σίνηπυς A533 mustard, Sinapis alba [Brassica alba Br.; Sinapis nigra Em.]; see also νάπειον

σισύμβριον fr. 74.57 bergamot-mint, Mentha aquatica [M. silvestris Em.]

σίσυμβρον T896 watercress, Nasturtium officinale

σκαμμώνιον A565 scammony, Convolvulus scammonia; see also κάμων

σκάρος fr. 59 parrot-wrasse, Scarus cretensis

σκίλλα T881; A254 squill, Urginea maritima [Scilla maritima Em.]

σκολόπενδρα T812* centipede

σκολοπένδρειον T684 hart's tongue, Scolopendrium officinale [S. scolopendrium Br.; Ceterach officin. Em.]

σκόλυμος T658* golden thistle, Scolymus hispanicus

σκόροδον A432 garlic, Allium sativum

σκορπίος (i) T14, 18, [654], 770, 796, 887, fr. 31.2 scorpion; (ii) T886*; A145 a plant [= σκορπιοειδές, scorpion-wort, Scorpiurus sulcata L-S; perh. Doronicum pardalianches Br.; Heliotropium europaeum Em.]

σκύρον (=ἄσκυρον) T74* hypericum, St John's wort, *Hypericum perforatum* [*Rubia tinctorum*, madder Br.]

σκυτάλη T384*, 386 a snake

σκώψ *fr.* 18.2* a fish

σμῖλος (=μῖλος, σμίλαξ) A611 yew, *Taxus baccata*

σμύραινα (=μύραινα) T823* murry, *Muraena helena*

σμύρνα T600; A601 myrrh, gum of the Arabian tree *Balsamodendron myrrha* [*Commiphora abyssinica* Br.]

σμυρνεῖον (=σμύρνιον) T848; A405; *fr.* 71.3 Cretan alexanders, *Smyrnium perfoliatum* [*S. olusatrum* Br.]

σόγκος (=σόγχος) *fr.* 71.4 sow-thistle, *Sonchus aspera* [*S. arvensis* Em.]

σταφὶς ἀγροτέρα (=σ. ἀγρία) T943 stavesacre, *Delphinium staphisagria*

σταφυλῖνος T843; *fr.* 71.2 carrot, *Daucus carota*

στρόμβος (i) A393*; *fr.* 83.2 a shellfish; (ii) T884 pine-cone

στρούθεια μῆλα A234 pear-quinces, from the *Pirus cydonia*

στρουθὸς κατοικάς A60, 535 domestic fowl

στρύχνον T74,878 perh. σ. ὑπνωτικόν sleepy (or 'deadly') nightshade, *Withania somnifera* [perh. *Solanum melongena* Br.]

συκέη A348; *fr.* 78.4 fig-tree, *Ficus carica*

συοσκύαμος (=ὑοσκύαμος) A415 henbane, *Hyoscyamus niger*

σφήκειον T738* a spider

σφήξ T739, 741, 811; A183 wasp

σφονδύλειον (=σφονδύλιον) T948 cow-parsnip, *Heracleum sphondylium*

τάμισος T577*,711,949; A373 curdled milk from the stomach of an animal; *see also* πυετίη

ταῦρος T171, 340, 741 bull; ταύρου αἷμα A312

τενθρήνη A547* a bee

[τέρμινθος] A300 terebinth, *Pistacia terebinthus*; *see also* τρέμιθος

τευθίς A471* squid, calamary, *Loligo vulgaris*

τεῦθος A471* squid, *Todarodes sagittatus*

τῆθος A396* sea-squirt, *Ascidium* (?)

τηλέφιλον T873* 'love-in-absence'

τιθύμαλλος T617 spurge, *Euphorbia peplus*

τίτανος A43 gypsum

τοξικόν A208* arrow-poison

τόρδειλον (=τόρδυλον) T841* hartwort, *Tordylium officinale*

[τραγοπώγων] *see* γεραὸς πώγων

τραγορίγανος A310 goat's marjoram, *Thymus teucrioides* [*T. graveolens?* Em.]

τρέμιθος (=τέρμινθος) T844 terebinth, *Pistacia terebinthus*; *see also* τέρμινθος

τριπέτηλον T522, 907 trefoil, =τρίσφυλλον q.v.

τρίσφυλλον (=τρίφυλλον) T520treacle-clover, *Psoralea bituminosa*; *see also* μινυανθές

τρυγών T828-9* sting-ray, *Trygon pastinaca*

τυφλώψ T492* a snake

ὑάκινθος T902; *fr.* 74.31*, 60 'hyacinth' [*Hyacinthus orientalis* Br., Em.]

ὕδρος (i) T414=δρυΐνας q.v.; (ii) T421* =χέρσυδρος q.v.

ὑπέρεικος A603* hypericum, *Hypericum crispum* [*H. coris* Br.; *H. barbatum* Em.]

ὕραξ A37 mouse

ὕσγινον T511 perh. kermes from the kermes-oak, *Quercus coccifera*

ὕσσωπος T872*; A603 hyssop, *Origanum hirtum* [*Orig. onites* Br.; *O. smyrnaeum* Em.]

φάγρος *fr.* 18.2 sea-bream, *Pagrus vulgaris*

φαλάγγιον T8, 755* spider

φάλαγξ T654, 715; *fr.* 31.1 = φαλάγγιον q.v.

φάλλαινα T760 moth

Φαρικόν A398* an unknown poison

φάσγανον *fr.* 74.63 corn-flag, *Gladiolus segetum*

φηγός T413, 418*, 439, 842; A261; *fr.* 27, 69 oak-tree, Valonia oak, *Quercus aegilops*

φιλεταιρίς T632=ῥάμνος q.v.

φλόμος T856 mullein, *Verbascum sinuatum* [*V. plicatum* Em.]

φλόξ *fr.* 74.39 wall-flower, *Cheiranthus cheiri*

φοῖνιξ A 353; *fr.* 80.1 date-palm, *Phoenix dactylifera* [*Lolium perenne* Em.]

φρύνη A 575–6*; -νός A 567* toad

φῦκος T 845; A 576 orchella-weed, *Roccella tinctoria* [*Fucus coccineus* Br.]

φυλλῖτις, *see* πεταλῖτις

χαλβάνη T 52* juice of all-heal, *Ferula galbaniflua*; χαλβανίδες ῥίζαι T 938; χαλβανόεσσα ῥίζα A 555 root of all-heal

χάλκη (= κάλχη) *fr.* 74.60 purple flower *Chrysanthemum coronarium*

χαλκός T 257* χαλκοῦ ἄνθος; A 529* χ. ἄνθη (*fem.*) verdigris or copper sulphate

[χαμαικυπάρισσος] ποίη κυπάρισσος T 910 lavender cotton, *Santolina chamaecyparissus* [perh. *Achillea* sp. Br.]

χαμαίλεος (= -λέων) T 656* pine-thistle; (i) dark, *Cardopatium corymbosum*; (ii) white *Atractylis gummifera*

χαμαίπιτυς [T 841]; A 56, 548 ground-pine, *Ajuga chamaepitys*

χαμελαίη A 48 spurge-olive, *Daphne oleoides*

χαμηλὴ πίτυς T 841 = χαμαίπιτυς q.v.

χάρμα 'Αφροδίτης *fr.* 74.28 = λείριον q.v.

Χείρωνος ῥίζα T 500, *see* κενταύρειον

χελιδόνιον T 857; *fr.* 74.32, [52*] celandine, *Chelidonium majus*

χέλυδρος T 411 = δρυΐνας q.v.

χελύνη (= χελώνη) (i) A 555 tortoise, *Testudo graeca*; (ii) T 703, A 558*; turtle, *Thalassochelys caretta*

χέλυς T 700 = χελύνη (ii) q.v.

χέρσυδρος T 359* a snake; *see also* ὕδρος

χήν A 136, 228 goose

χιμαίρη A 135 she-goat

χλούνης *fr.* 74.6 wild boar

χρυσανθές *fr.* 74.69 = ἐλίχρυσος q.v.

χρυσός A 53; *fr.* 74.3 gold

ψήν T 736* gall-insect, *Cynips psenes*

ψίλωθρον T 902* 'depilatory'

ψιμύθιον A 75 white lead

[ὤκιμον] A 280 basil, *Ocimum basilicum*

II. INDEX TO INTRODUCTION AND NOTES

A. GREEK

238

B. ENGLISH